# TIMESPLASH

Book 1 of the Timesplash series

## Graham Storrs

First published by Lyrical Press, Inc., 2010
Second edition by Pan Macmillan Australia, 2013
This Edition, Copyright © 2018, Graham Storrs

ISBN: 978-0-9945899-7-2

Published by Canta Libre
Cover design by Graham Storrs
Edited by Tara Goedjen
Interior design by Write Into Print (writeintoprint.com)

# Dedication

All the Timesplash novels are dedicated to the three brilliant and beautiful women who are at the heart of everything I am and everything I do; my mother, Audrey, my wife, Christine, and my daughter, Katherine.

# Part 1

Summer 2047

# Chapter 1

## Splashparty

The music thundered. So loud it was hard to breathe. The way the dancing crowd heaved in time to the beat made Patty feel nauseous.

Or was that just fear?

There had been lots of splashparties. Since she'd become Sniper's bitch that was all they'd done, going from one to another, right across Europe.

But she'd never seen a party from up here before. Not from inside the cage.

"Hey, honey." Sniper took hold of her jaw and turned her to face him. His gloved fingers were hard. "Relax," he told her, his smile broad and glamorous. In the maroon leather jumpgear he wore—his trademark colour—he looked like a superhero from a Hollywood vid. Tall, broad-shouldered and beautiful, in a youthful, Aryan way. He looked almost heroic … for a dangerous, psychotic killer.

He spoke unaccented English, with just a hint of a German lilt to betray his origins. "You should smile for the cameras." His grey-blue eyes flicked toward the gigantic screens behind them, some of which were showing Patty's frightened face, ten meters high, haloed in bright distortions, pulsing to the driving rhythms of the splashmusik.

"I don't think I can do this," she told him, trying to shake her head. "I shouldn't have—"

But his grip tightened, squeezing her cheeks, forcing her lips into a pout. His smile broadened. "Too late, sweetheart." To emphasize just how late it was, he grabbed the tether that ran between his harness and hers. It was as thick as a finger and as strong as modern technology could make it. His eyes bored into hers, and the anger she saw there made her forget her fear of splashing. For that moment all she feared was that Sniper might despise her, might hate her, might dump her. Desperately, she tried to force a smile onto the lips he was squeezing. With a sneer of laughter, he let her go. The cameras tracked him, sensing his movement. Turning to the dancing crowd, he raised his arms in a triumphant gesture— fists clenched and eyes blazing.

"We're gonna tear the fucking world apart!" he bellowed.

An astute teknik fed Sniper's suit mike into the mix so everyone heard his declaration. The crowd erupted in an answering roar of approval.

"We're gonna rip the fabric of the universe!" he promised them. "We're gonna shake the foundations of reality!"

The crowd went wild, raising their own arms as they screamed and yelled back at him, never once losing the beat as they rose and fell like a mat of weed on an oleaginous sea.

"Two minutes to lob," the even voice of a teknik announced. The crowd shrieked in response. A chant started up in time to the music, "Sniper! Sniper! Sniper! Sniper! Sniper!"

Patty could barely hear over the constant thunder of the sound system. Had they turned up the volume? Was that even possible? A choking panic rose up inside her. She couldn't do this. She couldn't. Two other bricks swaggered around the cage with her and Sniper. She looked at them, seeking support, but Hal and T-800 seemed excited and eager. Hal raised a gloved hand and gave her a thumbs-up, grinning wildly. They were both seasoned splashers. Big-name bricks. Not big like Sniper, of course. She looked into their faces, hoping that they would help her get out of there or stop the countdown ticking away on the big screens behind them.

"I've changed my mind. I don't want to lob," she yelled into her suit mike, looking over at the control booth, a small rectangular island in the Sargasso of dancers. "Get me out. Stop the countdown."

\* \* \* \*

Over in the relative quiet of the booth, the tekniks considered Patty's distress. "She's freaking," one of them said. "Do we pull her?"

"Too late," said Klaatu in a firm voice. Although he was the youngest, only seventeen, he was the authority. Klaatu was the uberteknik and a close personal friend of Sniper himself. In the booth, his word was law, and they all knew it. Nevertheless, it was clear the girl was panicking. She was hyperventilating and twisting about as if looking for somewhere to run.

Klaatu watched her with the fixed stare of a hungry predator. She was a beauty. Drop-dead gorgeous, as all Sniper's bitches were. This one was younger than most. Just fifteen, Sniper had said, and despite her height and her curves, Klaatu believed him. In her close-fitting jumpgear, she looked magnificent. And she'd acted it too when she first

3

went up into the cage, strutting about and showing off for the guys, but her nerve had crumbled. The wet dream supermodel she'd been playing had given way to the frightened little girl she really was. He could see how pissed off Sniper was getting, trying to ignore her, doing his thing for the crowd. Sniper knew the importance of pleasing the crowds. He knew how much a lob cost and how everything depended on the money they made from these events—tickets, dealer concessions, merchandising, all of that. It must be driving him nuts that his bitch was being such a prat. Maybe after this, the big guy would dump her and Klaatu could pick her up, make her his own bitch. It wouldn't be the first time.

"One minute to lob," Klaatu said into the PA mike. He was buggered if he was going to pull the plug for the sake of one hysterical chick—no matter how gorgeous. Once the lob was over, Sniper could sort her out at the upstream end.

\* \* \* \*

In the cage, the others were putting on their helmets. Patty watched their calm, sure movements with horror. This couldn't be happening. The countdown said fifty seconds. Just fifty seconds! She should never have agreed. It had all been bluster, the usual fuck-you bravado that had got her through so many foster homes and care centres. She wanted Sniper to think she was cool, wanted him to see her as more than just another bimbo who needed to be with him. But it was all show. She wasn't the hard-as-nails tough girl she made herself out to be. All that sassy talk and teasing the guys was someone else. Not her. Even her tag, Patty—after Patty Hearst, some badass terrorist chick from the past—was a lie.

Her real name was Sandra. Sandra Malone.

"Thirty seconds to lob," said the PA.

Someone tapped her on the shoulder. She jumped and swivelled round. It was Hal holding up her helmet, urging her to put it on. She couldn't see his face through his black visor. Hal had been looking at her all week with eyes both hungry and anxious. She knew he fancied her like hell but he didn't dare make a move while she was Sniper's girl. It was always the same with men. They all wanted her, but only the ones like Sniper were arrogant enough to think she'd want them in return. Hal would be no help.

She turned to Sniper, shouted over the noise. "I've got to get out of here!" But her voice was lost in the crashing music, his metalglass-covered features impervious to her pleading. She began pulling at her harness. She had to get it off and get out of the cage. She was past caring what Sniper thought. She just had to get free before …

"Ten! Nine! Eight!" The crowd was counting along with the big timer on the display. In a breathless panic, she heaved at her buckles. "Seven! Six! Five!" Electricity arced across the mesh of the cage—all for show, like the dry ice "smoke" falling from the cables.

Sniper grabbed her wrist, wrenching her hand away from the harness. He pushed her helmet down onto her head. "Stupid little…" he bellowed. She staggered as the helmet slammed down. Its thick padding was all that saved her face from being mashed.

"Three! Two!" the crowd screamed as she stepped back from Sniper in pain.

"Oh shit," was all she had time to say before the displacement field grabbed everyone inside the cage and flung them out of the spacetime she knew, lobbed them—in the jargon of timesplashing—out of the way of time's normal flow, threw them back, back into the past.

* * * *

Out in the crowd, some minutes earlier, Luke and his companion had just arrived.

"Yeah! Wild!" Spock shouted. He grinned maniacally, bobbing his head in time to the music. Spock was Luke's best friend but sometimes he was a complete pain in the ass. Tall, olive-skinned and long-haired, Spock lived to get wasted. Of course, Spock wasn't his friend's real name, any more than Luke was his own. It was all part of the splash scene. Spock's first act on arriving at the splashparty had been to drop two tabs of tempus. It was already beginning to show. On top of the half-bottle of vodka he'd drunk on the long drive over, it was likely he'd be totally incoherent in another ten minutes.

"We should have got here an hour ago," Luke grumbled, "instead of driving round and round the Netherlands in the dark 'cause you're too smashed to read the nav."

Splashparties were always held in obscure, out-of-the-way locations. In this case the party was in the grounds of an ancient Dutch castle—Castle Eerde—near the town of Ommen. They'd found Ommen easily enough, driving east from the Channel Tunnel depot, but Eerde had been altogether more difficult. If they hadn't ended up close enough to hear the music, they could have driven around the dark country roads all night.

Spock dismissed his friend's complaints with a wave and continued pushing his way toward the front, whooping from the sheer excitement of it. Luke had to smile despite himself. Being out with Spock was sometimes like being out with a very large puppy—and that wasn't so bad. He'd probably do a tab of tempus himself later to get in the mood, but first he wanted to take in the atmosphere for a while, scope out the chicks, and enjoy the music. The countdown was showing a few minutes to the lob. He tapped Spock on the shoulder and pointed.

"Far out!" Spock shouted back, his eyes widening into the familiar tempus-induced glaze. All through their increasingly stressful drive, Luke had been worrying that they wouldn't make it in time. If you missed the lob and the backwash, you'd missed the best part of the night. A couple of girls dancing topless in flashing, animated body paint grabbed at him as he moved past them. They were cute and stoned and very tempting. He turned to grin at them but kept moving. Plenty of time for that later. When he turned back toward the stage, he saw the cage for the first time.

He'd seen Sniper at a splashparty in Ireland last year, but even if he hadn't, he would have recognized him instantly. There wasn't a kid worth knowing on the planet who didn't hero-worship the most famous brick of them all. There wasn't a chick he knew who didn't have a Sniper poster on her bedroom wall. The lean, muscular body, the almost-white blond hair, the piercing grey eyes and cocksure grin, were part of an image as well known as any soccer player's or rock diva's. The guy was a megastar.

"Hey, it's fucking Sniper, man!" Spock yelled, slapping Luke on the chest and bouncing to the thumping music with the endless energy of the seriously wired. But Luke paid him little attention. He had just spotted the girl at Sniper's side. She was stunning. Tall and long-limbed, with long black hair and the full lips of a Spanish princess, she filled her jumpgear like it was sprayed on.

That a big-name brick had a beautiful woman with him was hardly a surprise—even when she was as beautiful as this one. Guys like Sniper had their pick of women, although Luke had never heard of a brick taking his bitch on a splash. Even more peculiar, in the big-screen closeup, despite the heavy makeup, he could see she was just a young girl. Luke was only seventeen but this girl was younger still. And he saw something else, too, something he had never seen in a brick. Ever. He saw fear in the girl's eyes.

He grabbed Spock by the shoulder and turned him to face the girl—Patty, the tag said on her jumpgear.

"Wassup, man?" Then his friend saw Patty too. "All right! Fuckin' A, man!"

Spock began shouting toward Patty as he danced, but Luke grabbed him again and shook him.

"There's something wrong, man. She's really freaked." He looked over at the control booth but could see nothing through its tinted windows.

"Looks real fine to me, mate," Spock yelled, grinning.

Frustrated, Luke let go of him and turned back to the girl. Why was nobody doing anything?

"Two minutes to lob." The announcement boomed over the music and the dancing crowd waved and yelled in response. They started to chant Sniper's name over and over. Seeing the girl looking around in what seemed to be mounting panic, Luke grabbed Spock again.

"I'm going to the booth. I don't think they've noticed." Without waiting for a response, he began to push and shove his way through the sea of bouncing people toward the mobile control centre.

For a moment he lost sight of the girl in the cage, but when he saw her again, he was shocked to see her standing with no helmet on while the others were fully suited. He didn't have much of a technical grasp of timesplashing, but he knew it was a rough ride for the brick. The lob back in time put the brick in a medium that wasn't quite spacetime and certainly had no air in it. The brick's jumpgear provided pressure and the helmet provided oxygen. People had died trying to lob without the right gear. He paused to look at the girl's beautiful, desperate face, willing her to get her helmet on.

"One minute to lob."

There was no way he could make it. The booth seemed as far away as ever and the crowd near the cage was too dense for him to make much headway. Luke looked around wildly for some other way of stopping the lob. He knew that the control cables would be running between the booth and the cage, and computing would all be in the booth. Power would come from a bunch of F2 devices in trucks parked behind the cage. The displacement field generators and the gigantic capacitor arrays would be in the platform under the cage. He knew the standard layout. He'd read the zines and wandered around at splashparties admiring the tech. But none of that helped him.

The crowd began chanting the final ten seconds of the countdown. He wouldn't be able to reach anything in time. A gasp erupted from the crowd. He looked up at the screens in time to see Sniper ramming a helmet onto Patty's head. Clearly trying to get out of there, she struggled in his grip, but at least now she wouldn't die. Whatever was going on with the girl, Sniper had saved her. The countdown hit zero, and a brilliant flash of blue light blinded them all. The bricks had been lobbed back into the timestream. The girl was gone. The cage was empty.

"Jesus," Luke said aloud, panting from the effort of trying to get to the booth, still tense from the fear he'd felt for the girl's safety. "Jesus." He kept staring at the empty cage, telling himself to calm down. He was the only still figure in that ocean of dancing, screaming people. It would be a while—an hour maybe—before the yankback happened and the bricks reappeared in the cage. A long time to wait to see if she would be all right.

He pushed his way back through the dancers to where he'd left Spock. He didn't feel like getting high now. He didn't feel like being at a party. He just wanted to be somewhere quiet where he could wait for the girl to get back. "Patty," he whispered. "Please come back safe.".

There was a commotion ahead, a knot in the crowd where people had stopped dancing and were pressed together to see something. He supposed it was someone splashdancing or maybe an impromptu sex act. There was always something going on at these parties. Some kids made quite a name for themselves by putting on shows.

He tried to push past whatever it was, but got pulled in as more people crowded in to see what was going on. The hush at the centre of the group gave him a bad feeling. Reluctantly, he let himself be pressed toward whatever it was. Soon he could hear shouting, people crying and calling for help. Everyone was so stoned they were unlikely to be of much use. Luke pushed forward roughly, hoping it wasn't anything gruesome.

When he finally broke through the crowd, he found himself in a small clearing. In front of him, Spock lay on the ground, twitching violently. People were fussing around him, shouting for a doctor. Some of them were just shouting.

Froth was coming from between Spock's clenched jaws. His eyes were wide open, staring up at the sky.

# Chapter 2

## The Lob

Lobspace was dark and cold. So dark that Patty could see nothing at all, so cold that the unsealed gap between her helmet and her jumpgear stung like a band of fire. All she could hear was her own rapid breathing and the steady hiss of air escaping from her helmet. Frantically, with clumsy, gloved fingers, she scrabbled at the seal until she had it closed around her neck. Only then did she begin to take in her situation. She was weightless, but seemed to be moving forward. Or falling forward. That thought made her heart leap into her throat, and she had to force herself to dismiss the idea. The black airless void around her gave her no sense of direction or speed. Her sense of movement, she realized, was due to a steady tug from her harness, as though someone was dragging her along by the tether. She felt for the thick cord that bound her to Sniper and found it pulled taut, disappearing into the blackness. At first she thought Sniper must somehow be reeling her in, but that didn't make any sense. She called out to him but there was no reply. Was she alone? If she was, who was pulling her along?

Minutes, they had said. It would take a couple of minutes

of "flight" before the lob was over, and they landed. Some kind of free fall, she remembered them telling her. No gravity. No stars. Like being in space, only worse. And then she realized why the tether was pulling her. She and Sniper must be rotating, orbiting one another about their common centre of gravity, held together by the tether. That's what the tether was for, of course, to stop them from being separated during the lob. But the idea that she was spinning in empty space didn't help calm her at all. It filled her with the dread that the tether might break, sending her hurtling off into the void, away from the others, helpless and alone.

They'd gone on at her about it—what to do, how to survive—but she could hardly remember a thing. At the time, she'd just let it wash over her, thinking: I'll be all right as long as Sniper's with me. But Sniper had been such a bastard in the cage. He could see how scared she was and he'd just ignored her. He'd wanted his stupid splash to go on, no matter what. She had seen it in his eyes. He thought she was a stupid, whining child and he was damned if he was going to let her spoil his fun. It made her angry to think about how much she had trusted him, and how much he had let her down. More than that, she felt humiliated when she thought of how she'd adored him, and of all the things she'd done for him.

And where did it all leave her? She was Sniper's bitch. God! She'd been proud to be called that! But without that, what was she? What was there for her now? It was almost a full year since she'd run away from that shitty care centre in Bristol and, by sheer luck, fallen in with a bunch of bricks. She'd found the head guy and become his bitch. When her group met Sniper's, she traded up. She'd thought she was doing well for herself.

The sudden light blasted away her thoughts. Light and

sound, gravity and pressure, rushed in on her. Something enormous smashed into her from the side. It crushed her shoulder, her hip, slammed into her head. If it hadn't been for the helmet …

Gasping, winded, she gaped at the great slab of green that had hit her, and her mind wheeled. It was the ground. It hadn't hit her, she had hit it. She had fallen—not very far, thank goodness!—onto a huge empty pasture. Sniper was close by, already bounding to his feet.

Patty shakily pushed herself up and looked around for the others. They were there too, about twenty meters away, also getting to their feet. Sniper took off his helmet and surveyed the area. Then with a few deft flicks of the catches, he threw off his harness and strode across the field to where Hal and T-800 were unfastening themselves.

Miserably, Patty struggled to her bruised knees and took off her helmet. Sniper hadn't even glanced her way. She might have been dead for all he cared. She began to take in her surroundings. They were in a large field. It had a rough, agricultural look about it. Could it be the same manicured and planned parkland Patty had seen earlier in the day? There were no people about, but the big house, Eerde Castle, was clearly visible, just where it ought to be. There was the sound of traffic somewhere—not the whine of normal traffic—but the growl and roar of old-fashioned petrol engines. Even in the middle of a field, she could smell exhaust.

She was back in the 1980s! For a moment the fact drove all resentment and misery from her mind. If the lob had gone as planned, they would be spatially close to where they had been lobbed from, but temporally shifted sixty-five years into the past. She tried to get a better look at the far-off mansion, but she couldn't see anything different about it.

"Are you okay?" It was Hal, standing over her, offering her his big hand and smiling. She took his hand and stood up.

"Yes, I think so." She rubbed her shoulder. "A bit bruised."

Hal grinned. "You get used to that." He stepped close to her. For a moment she thought he was going to try to kiss her, but instead he started opening her harness catches. "It's all a bit of a shock at first. You'll get your bearings in a minute."

"Is this really the past?"

"It sure is. The twelfth of July, 1982." He looked up at the sun. "About ten in the morning, at a guess."

Sniper, arriving with T-800, looked coldly at Patty but addressed himself to Hal. "Stop fussing with her. She'll be all right. We need you to get us to the house. We only get a few hours, you know."

"Right," Hal said. He and T-800 stuffed the harnesses into backpacks, and then he nodded across the field toward the castle. "The road's that way."

They picked up their helmets and set off. Patty limped a little from the pain in her hip, but everyone else seemed okay. Taking their cue from Sniper, no one spoke much, which suited Patty just fine. She watched Sniper's broad back with growing resentment and trudged along in a sulk. Her own pains and grievances gradually overwhelmed any sense of wonder she might have felt at being back in the twentieth century.

She had seen enough old vids from this era for none of it to be very surprising, yet when they left the grounds of the castle and walked into the road, little things began to catch her attention, like the number of telegraph poles, the quaint, old-fashioned cars that made such an appalling racket, and the huge, colourful signs that seemed to serve as directions for drivers. More and more, the fact that she really was in the time of her grandparents impressed itself upon her.

"Hey, watch this," Hal called to her.

They were passing an abandoned pile of builder's sand beside the road. He ran across the pile of sand, kicking it around as he went. Patty thought he was just showing off, like young men often did around her, but then she noticed what was happening to the sand in his wake. It seemed to be jumping, vibrating, squirming. She screwed shut her eyes and looked again, as if they were the source of the strange blurriness she saw. Hal stopped at the far side of the pile and looked back at it proudly. With strange shifts of colour and position, the deep prints of his feet were slowly being erased. The weird shifting of shape and colour spread briefly to the pavement around the heap, causing Patty to jump back in alarm as the effect rippled out toward her feet. In thirty dizzying seconds, the pile restored itself.

"Now do you believe we're back in time?" Hal shouted.

"Stop pissing about," Sniper shouted.

Hal gave Patty a grin and turned back to the road. Patty stared for a long time at the sand. It was a small splash, she realized. The little anomaly that Hal had caused—disturbing a pile of sand that should never have been disturbed—had righted itself. But for those few seconds before the restoration was complete, there had been a shake-up in spacetime around the sand pile. Causality had been thrown into disarray, and it had taken a while for it to settle back to how it should have been.

She set off again, hurrying to catch up with the others. She noticed for the first time that their footsteps left faint, blurry marks on the road that quickly faded behind them.

* * * *

The small town of Ommen was just five kilometres or so from where the lob had taken place. They were going to walk to it. Sniper didn't want to risk causing any paradoxes before the big one they had planned, the one that would cause the splash. Hal was still their guide and he set a fast pace, west along Hammerweg, a forest-lined road that eventually turned north. Patty was beginning to think she was doomed to trudge forever in the July heat when they began to see houses and other signs of life around them. By the time Hammerweg became Stationsweg, the street was busy and lined with buildings. The air stank of petrol fumes, and the traffic noise made it necessary for Patty to raise her voice to be heard.

"So what's so special about Ommen?" she asked Hal. Ahead she could see a bridge that would take them across the broad, flat River Vecht and into the town proper. It was a pretty place with flat fields all around, and cute old buildings visible on the far bank. There was even a windmill, beautifully preserved and picturesque, right near the town centre. Nice place for a holiday, Patty thought. If you were ninety. Definitely not the spot she would have picked for a time trip.

"It's the home of my ancestors," said Hal, looking benignly at the placid river and the quaint town beyond.

"You don't sound Dutch." In fact, he sounded American, like one of those Bible-thumping preachers she saw whenever she accidentally watched an American vid channel.

"My great-granddaddy moved the family stateside back in 1986. Took a research job with a computer company in Palo Alto and settled there. His daughter, my grandma, married a guy down in Birmingham, Alabama. That's where I grew up."

"So it's your family we're going to…"

Hal smiled. "Sure is! I'm looking forward to meeting them."

"But—"

"Don't you worry now. It all smooths over like nothing ever happened. Like the sand pile. You know how this works."

Patty nodded, feeling a bit queasy. On top of all the other things about this lob she didn't want any part of, she now added the splash itself. Until that moment, she hadn't really thought about what it actually took to make a splash. Not really. With a shake of her head, she realized what a stupid child she'd been about the whole thing. Talking to Sniper and the others, it had seemed like a big game. The ultimate extreme sport. All glamour and fun. One big rush. Now she had to face the hard reality of what was going to happen. Fear grabbed again at her stomach. The sunny fields, the placid river, and the sleepy little city made what was about to happen seem more sinister.

"Look," said Sniper, as they negotiated the narrow streets at the heart of the old market town.

"Food."

They took a table at a small street café and ordered lunch from a waiter who spoke fluent English. All around them, people stared.

"They think we're bikers." Sniper laughed, enjoying the attention.

"Bikers?" Patty asked, but Sniper just pulled a face at her ignorance.

"The town's full of foreign tourists for the Bissing tomorrow," Hal said, shrugging. "Some kind of big deal market day that kicks off a few weeks of events and stuff. A few more weirdos coming to town won't cause too much of a stir just now."

Sniper leaned across the table like a big cat, his body strong and lazily sinuous. "So Hal, we'll hang here for a while—an hour or so maybe—then we go on to your great-granddad's place, okay?"

He checked his watch. "We've only got about three more hours, but I don't want us to have too much time after the splash. We don't know how big this one will be." He grinned fiercely and his grey eyes shone with anticipation. He swivelled around to face Patty. "You're gonna love it, baby."

Patty felt her fear surge. But with Sniper deliberately trying to goad her, she was angry too. She pointedly turned away from him and spoke to Hal. "How come our time's so short? Don't these things usually last longer?"

This caused Hal to grin too. "That's 'cause we're breaking a world record, honey. This is only the longest fucking lob in the history of the world! Sixty-five years! It's never been done before. It's right there at the edge of what's theoretically possible. That Klaatu guy is a genuine, grade one, certified genius!"

Patty thought of Klaatu as a scrawny, shifty-eyed kid with personal hygiene problems and the manners of a rat, but she let it pass. "So the further back we go, the less time we have?"

"And the bigger the splash we make."

"It's like we get thrown higher," T-800 said. "You know how they talk about 'lobbing' us 'bricks' back into the timestream? Well it's a really good metaphor. The harder we get lobbed, the farther we go and the bigger the splash we make."

"Thank you, Professor Frink," Sniper said.

"That's why everything we do is causing ripples," Hal

chimed in. He moved a pepper pot on the table and let it go. A faint, jittery blurring began to engulf it. "You don't get that on a short lob." For a while the pot seemed to be in two places at once and then it was back where it started.

"Cool, ain't it? Why, I bet if I stood up, my chair would put itself right back under the table. Things we're touching get kind of tangled up with us and our timeline, but once we let them go…"

"This is too weird," Patty complained. "We shouldn't do this."

Suddenly Sniper's finger was in her face. "Just shut the fuck up. If I hear one more word from you, you'll really have something to whine about."

There was an uneasy silence around the table. The waiter, arriving with drinks, looked at them with a worried frown. Sniper sat back languorously in his chair and smiled at them all. "About time," he told the waiter.

When the drinks had been placed on the table and the waiter had gone, Sniper turned to Hal.

"They'd better be in."

"They will be. Don't worry."

"Who?" Patty asked.

"Jesus!" Sniper grabbed his drink and sat back in exasperation. Hal explained. "My great-grandma and my grandma."

"Oh."

"Great-grandma kept a diary, you see. Grandma is at home recovering from some old-time illness today. They go out to the Bissing together tomorrow."

Patty looked at the table, not wanting to look into Hal's cheerful eyes. "Did you know her?"

"Who, grandma?"

"Yes."

"Sure! The old bird's still going strong. Shit, it's only sixty-five years ago!"

"Do you like her?"

Sniper slammed his hand down on the table, leaning forward to glare at Patty. "Just shut the f—"

He stopped. The waiter, stepping up to the table, began setting plates down. There was something odd about his movements, something jittery and unnatural. Patty looked around. It was happening to other people nearby too.

Looking to see what Patty had seen, Sniper noticed it too and his scowl turned into a big, handsome smile.

"This is gonna be so good!" he shouted.

# Chapter 3

## The Splash

"Here is a new batch of your pamphlets from the printer," Nadya Krupskaya said, leading the man toward the desk in her husband's study.

On this cloudy April day in 1902, Vladimir Ilyich Lenin smiled as he watched the printer's worker set down his package and leave.

"Our friends back home say it is already being widely read," he told Nadya, who was lingering in the doorway.

"It is an excellent piece," she agreed. "If that doesn't shake up the party, nothing will. You deserve to be proud."

Lenin's birthday had been celebrated just a few days ago, right there in Holford Square in the London borough of Pentonville. The big brick terrace was yet another stop in their years of wandering about Europe. Lenin was now thirty-two years old. Nadya, a year older. She was his wife of just four years and one of his greatest admirers. They had married during their exile in Siberia. Some said that they had married for the cause, and there was some truth in that, but it was a long way from the whole truth.

She stepped forward and, taking a knife from the desktop,

cut the string and folded back the wrapping paper, revealing the pamphlet and its title, "What Is to Be Done?" in thick black ink on the cover. Both she and Lenin were confident it would be hugely influential in the Party, pushing his followers closer to Lenin's vision of the revolutionary vanguard he dreamed they could become.

"I thought I'd go over to the British Museum later on, my dear," he said, picking up a copy and turning it over in his hands to check the quality. He held it to his nose and sniffed. "I finally had a reply from that overly officious Museum Director, granting me a ticket."

Nadya smiled indulgently. The British Museum had one of the most respected library collections in the whole of Europe. Her husband had heard much about the famous Round Reading Room and was eager to visit it. She watched him leaf through the pages of his brilliant pamphlet and admired his broad brows and sensuous lips. That such a bookish, scholarly man should also be so handsome and passionate was her secret delight.

"What will you do there?" she asked, just to hear him speak.

He looked at her. "Oh, finish my comments on the program of the Northern League, but that won't take long. There is much work to do on Iskra of course, but…" He smiled impishly.

"Today I wish to spend my time coming to grips with the size and extent of this fabled collection."

He turned to look out of the window at the grey skies and the leafless trees in the gardens. "I expect to be disappointed. Nothing could be so splendid as to live up to the reports I have been hearing. But if nothing else, I shall have a good walk in the mild English spring."

Nadya gave him a wry smile. "It's not Saint Petersburg, that's certain, but don't let yourself get wet. And don't get lost. You think yourself indestructible and infallible, but you are not. And the Revolution needs you."

He turned back to her with a sigh. "There are many who would disagree with that, my dear Nadezhda Konstantinovna."

"Fools," she announced firmly, raising her chin.

Lenin smiled fondly at her, and she at him.

\* \* \* \*

They let Luke stay at the hospital, and for that he was grateful. A young policeman sat in the waiting room with him, looking barely older than Luke was. Yet the policeman carried a handgun and a stunner on his belt and had an air of responsibility and gravity that made Luke feel insubstantial and foolish.

The policeman said he had to hang around to hear the doctors' verdict on Spock. So staying with his friend wasn't all altruism. And even if he had wanted to leave, he couldn't. The reality of being held against his will by an armed man slowly sunk into the gloom that beset him.

They hadn't let Luke into the intensive care unit with Spock. A nurse had prevented him, barring his way, and then she and the policeman had led him away to answer their questions.

"What was your friend taking tonight? Does he have any allergies? Is he on any medication?"

On and on. They could have got most of it by scanning his med chip, but they asked anyway. Then it was the police officer's turn. "What's his real name? Is that his full name?

Where does he live? How do we contact his parents?"

"Why don't you just scan him?" Luke was tired and anxious.

"You kids fix up your chips," the police officer said wearily. "Damn chips lie more than the kids do."

After he'd been through it all on Spock's behalf, Luke had to explain who he was, why he was there, then give them his parents' netID and a DNA sample.

"So your name is really Jason Kennedy," the policeman said.

"Luke is just my nickname," he explained. "Like Luke Skywalker." Suddenly it seemed silly to him to call himself after someone in an old vid story. Childish. He put the whole infantile nonsense behind him in that moment. "My name's Jay," he said. The party was over. "You should call me Jay."

The policeman shook his head, his contempt for the whole splash scene summed up in that one gesture.

They had found a tab of tempus on him, two more on Spock and a small stash of assorted goodies in Spock's luggage. It hardly added much to Jay's worries. His concern was all for his friend.

"You did the right thing, bringing your friend here," the policeman said.

Jay nodded in acknowledgement. What else could he have done?

"I've heard of kids just left by the side of the road when they take some bad dope. People want to save their own necks."

"Is that what happened? It was the tempus?"

"The lab will tell us for sure, but I reckon so. We'll want to know where you got it."

Jay remembered an alley outside a club in Canterbury just

three nights ago. "It's powerful stuff, man," the dealer had told them. "Just in from Brazil." Spock had haggled for it.

"You must see some awful things," Jay said, thinking how sick he'd felt seeing Spock twitching in the back of his car as they raced down foreign roads looking for help.

The policeman shrugged. "Not so much. Ommen is a quiet place. A good town. Until you bring your splashparty and your drugs and all this." He waved a hand toward the doors through which Spock had been taken.

"Can you see if he's all right?" Jay asked. "He looked so bad."

"They said they will come when they have news." The policeman's tone was not unkind, but it was not entirely sympathetic, either. Perhaps he resented being told to hang around at the hospital. Perhaps he just didn't like stupid kids who OD'd on party drugs. Jay stared at the floor and steeled himself for a long wait.

* * * *

"Mrs. 't Hooft?" Hal said, when a woman in her thirties opened the front door to them.

"*Ja?*" she said, looking a little nervously at the four strangely dressed youngsters on her doorstep. If Hal had it right, this pleasant-looking woman was his own great-grandmother.

"Is your daughter, Lotte, at home?"

"Who are you?" Her English was heavily accented.

"I am a relative of yours from the United States," Hal explained. "These are my buddies."

She regarded the young man with a puzzled frown. "A relative?"

"Is Lotte at home, please?"

The woman was looking more ill at ease. She began to say something that was obviously going to be a brush-off, was already pushing the door closed, when a small child in a pink frock came rushing up to her mother's knees to peer at the strangers. Patty realized with a shock that this was the target. Hal's grandmother was this little six-year-old girl, her blonde hair in pigtails and scuffed, round-toed shoes on her little feet.

"No, Hal," she said, before she realized she had spoken. "Don't do it."

Hal turned to Patty, but Sniper stepped in front of him, cutting him off from her view. "Shut up, bitch, or I'll do you as well."

"What is going on?" the woman asked, frightened now. She spoke to Lotte in Dutch, urging her to get back into the house so she could close the door. "I am calling the police."

"Hal," Sniper growled. "Get on with it."

But something had given Hal pause too. Patty could see him staring down at the little girl, not moving or speaking.

The woman started to close the door again, and suddenly Sniper shoved Hal aside and rammed into the door. Woman and child were knocked back. The little girl screamed and her mother tried to grab her. Sniper stormed into the hallway, pushing the woman to the ground, drawing a pistol from the leg pocket of his suit. Patty launched herself at Sniper's back. Too late. Sniper fired before she reached him. Two huge explosions came in rapid succession, and the child twisted away from them in a spray of blood. Patty hit Sniper squarely in the back with both hands, and she and the big German fell toward the child's body. The gun went off again, blowing a hole in the plaster of the hallway wall. The child's mother began screaming.

Patty was filled with fury as Sniper and she hit the ground, sliding in the wet blood. The small limp body lay beside them. Patty wanted to tear the flesh from her former lover, pummel his face, trample him, destroy him utterly. A part of her knew he could not be so easily hurt, that he would rise up like the powerful monster he was and wreak his vengeance for what she had tried to do. But that didn't matter—she just wanted to make him suffer for what he had done. And she would, whatever it cost her.

And then the world went crazy.

Patty had heard them talk about timesplashes. Most of the bricks she knew liked to brag about them all the time. They said that causality went haywire, that spacetime became fluid, that just walking down a street was like going whitewater rafting on acid. None of what they said had ever meant much to Patty until that moment.

Sizes went all wrong. Distances varied unpredictably. The body of little Lotte kept slamming into the ground right next to her, over and over again, blood flying from the girl's chest and face. Sniper snarled and pushed Patty away from him and she took far, far too long to hit the wall. He was up and out of the house before she realized that the wall had crumbled to dust. She had rolled straight through it into another room. She heard Hal and T-800 whooping with excitement, but she couldn't get up. Gravity changed so rapidly beneath her that she no longer had any sense of balance. She crawled back into the hallway to find Lotte still falling down dead again and again while her mother was frozen in a silent scream. Hal and T-800 had disappeared. Frightened and nauseous, she kept crawling until she was through the door and out of the house.

Gravity was more normal out there, but not much else was. People and cars moved backward or forward at random. Some were shortened, some stretched—all in different directions. She clambered unsteadily to her feet. Huge, slow waves moved across the ground and through the buildings, radiating outward from where she stood.

Hal, T-800 and Sniper were in a group, looking around at the chaos and laughing like schoolkids. Staggering over to them, she found the ground spongy and unpredictable, sometimes slapping her foot hard against it, sometimes missing it and stumbling. The others saw her approaching and laughed. Everyone still had their helmets in their hands except Patty.

"You killed her, you bastard!" she yelled at Sniper, still furious.

"You left your helmet behind, stupid," he yelled back nastily. "You can wetnurse her," he told Hal. "I'm going to have some fun. Just look at this!" He slapped T-800 on the shoulder and they ran off together, shrinking to little dots after just a few paces in an unsettling distortion of perspective. Hal clearly wanted to go with them, but he waited for Patty as instructed.

"Is this it, then?" she asked angrily. "Is this all…" She stopped in mid-sentence as the sky turned black and then seemed to bend and fold.

"Whoa!" Hal breathed, both scared and excited at once. "I've never seen that before." Even as he spoke, the sun returned and the blackness was replaced by blue. The fold in the sky remained, though, and they both stared at it.

"Are we going to die?" Patty asked anxiously.

"Uh, no. I don't think so." He sounded distracted and didn't take his eyes off the sky. "We shouldn't. The local distortions don't really affect us. We're still part of a different spacetime event. You've got to watch out for falling off a cliff or whatever, though. Your body can still get hurt."

As he spoke, a nearby lamppost softened and keeled over like a strand of cooked spaghetti. The lamp smashed when it hit the road, and shards of glass vibrated in and out of the impact as if they couldn't decide which way to explode.

"That kind of thing can kill you too. Go get your helmet and we'll try and catch up with Sniper."

"He killed that little girl," she said.

Hal tried to take her by the shoulders, but he missed because of the distortions. "He had to. I should have done it myself. You have to create the paradox that makes the splash and killing your grandmother is a surefire way to do it. Holy mother!"

A truck veered and swerved out of control, heading toward them, its wheels skidding through concrete that had suddenly become liquid. As it moved, it grew enormous until it was taller than the houses around it. Hal seemed frozen to the spot so Patty grabbed him and yanked him out of its way. They would have made it to safety, but it didn't matter. The truck sank into the liquefied surface up to its windows and wallowed to a halt.

Hal seemed to think the near miss and the driver's predicament were wildly exciting.

"What's the matter with you?" Patty demanded, slapping his arm. He was shorter now than she was but even as she noticed, he grew again and she shrank. "This isn't funny. People are getting hurt."

"Not really," he said, dragging his attention back to her. "It all sorts itself out. You know the theory. All this crazy shit is just the timestream responding to the paradox. We made one hell of splash here, girl! Yee ha!"

She frowned at him "Just stay here while I get my helmet. You won't leave me, will you?" she asked.

Hal assured her he wouldn't, and she turned back to the house. One corner of the building seemed to have melted, and the lawn outside bulged as if large animals were moving beneath it. Surrounding the house was a multicoloured radiance—pastel lights moving in slow waves as though high-energy particles were sleeting down through the building's own magnetic field. None of it looked safe, but it was the thought of what she would encounter in the hallway that really held her back.

Hal's hand on her shoulder made her jump. "I'll go," he said, and set off without waiting for her to comment.

She watched him walk across the undulating lawn toward the open door. In front of the doorway there were vague, wavering shapes. Patty couldn't make them out, but the closer Hal got to them, the more substantial they became. By the time he was at the door, he was standing behind four people dressed in jumpgear. He turned to look at Patty, and she could see from his body language he was as confused and surprised as she was. The four people, even with their backs to her, were obviously herself, Sniper, Hal and T-800.

Hal stepped away from them, almost tripping as the lawn rose and fell under his feet. The farther he went, the more insubstantial the group at the door became. Patty rushed forward to meet him.

"What the hell is that?" she asked.

"It's us!" Hal was over his initial alarm and was now grinning excitedly. "This has never happened before. No one's ever seen themselves in a splash."

The group at the door, transparent but clearly

recognizable, showed no sign of being aware of Hal and Patty behind them.

"Look. The other me is at the front. He looks like he's talking to someone. It's like an echo from ten minutes ago." Hal shook his head in amazement. "This is so cool! Watch this."

With that, he ran back across the lawn to the door. Patty tried to grab him, but missed. She didn't dare run after him and she didn't want to shout in case the others heard her. But Hal seemed to have no such compunctions. He ran straight over to the echo of Patty, the whole group solidifying as he closed on them. Then he tapped her on the shoulder.

Patty watched as her double turned around, open-mouthed with surprise, looking quickly from the Hal in front of her to the Hal talking earnestly in the doorway behind her. Watching from the street, Patty felt the skin between her shoulders crawl. She could feel this other Patty's shock and confusion, could imagine every thought she must be thinking. Hal was pointing at echo-Patty's helmet. Slowly, dazedly, she raised it and handed it to him. It looked solid and weighty in his hand.

Grinning, he turned and pointed behind him to where the real Patty gaped in astonishment, but echo-Patty seemed unable to see her. Calling out his thanks, Hal left Patty's echo and returned with the helmet. The echo-Patty watched him go, slowly fading away as he left her.

"There you go," he said proudly, handing Patty the helmet. Patty wouldn't take it.

"Here."

He pushed it toward her. "It won't bite."

Reluctantly she took it from him. It was solid. It was real. She hefted it in her hands. "How …?"

"Don't ask me. But think about what a cool new anomaly this is! You got your helmet from an echo of your past self. Your past self doesn't have a helmet because the one she had just moved into the future! A splash within a splash! How cool is that?"

Patty looked again at the group by the door, but they had faded almost to nothing. Carefully, she stepped away from the house until they were completely gone. The helmet stayed solid in her hands. "Can I really wear this when we go back?"

Hal just shrugged. "Looks like it. Come on. Let's find the others. I want to tell Sniper about this."

He took her arm and led her into the road, heading in the direction of the town centre. Patty stumbled after him, remembering the look on her own face as her echo-self handed over her helmet to a duplicate Hal.

"Check it out!" Hal pointed into the air.

Patty looked up to see an old-fashioned airplane arcing down toward the Earth from a great height. Behind it smoke trailed back through the air to a ball of dark grey smoke from what must have been a huge explosion. Even as Patty watched, one of the stricken plane's wings detached itself and took a separate, steeper arc downwards.

"Oh my God!" she cried. A passenger plane would have hundreds of people on board. All of them were going to die.

"It's all right," Hal said, calmly. "It should be okay. Just keep watching."

The aircraft was falling almost vertically now. Other pieces were dropping off it. Then, with a mind-wrenching suddenness, it zipped back along its initial route, like a film being rewound. But it went back just a couple of hundred meters, and then began falling again. When it reached about the same spot as before, it shot backward, once more repeating those few seconds of descent. And then it did it again. And again.

Distressed and confused, Patty turned to Hal. "You knew that would happen?"

"Happens all the time on a splash. Not on that kind of scale, mind you." He urged her into a walk again. "They say it's because the timestream can't allow major anomalies to proliferate. There was probably someone on that plane who did something that affected a lot of people, or who will have children who did, or maybe the plane was going to hit someone who did. I dunno. Somehow these things aren't allowed to happen. If they did, the splash would just start getting bigger and bigger, increasing exponentially. And that never happens. The splash settles down. The timestream gets smoothed out and everything goes back to normal. So when things start this stuttering, looping thing, they kind of get put on hold until things are sorted out. Looks real weird, huh?"

"What about all those people?"

"They'll be fine."

"They don't know that."

Hal gave her a look of exasperation that made Patty think he'd begun to regret being kind to such a pain in the ass, even if he did fancy her.

She shook her head. "Forget it. Let's get moving. It makes me nervous just standing around like this."

A violent rush of sound and air shot past them as if an invisible truck had gone by at high speed. The backdraught was so strong it made both of them stagger sideways. Patty looked around wildly. "What the hell was that?"

Hal wasn't grinning this time. "I don't know." He looked at Patty. "We'd better get to the others."

They set off at a jog toward the town centre, but didn't

make much speed. The ground undulated unpredictably. Groaning, crashing noises from the buildings all around made them hesitant and nervous. The streets were full of people—shoppers, office workers, tourists—all of them terrified, many caught in strange loops of activity. When a three-story building fell to the ground right next to Patty and began oscillating back and forth within a cloud of its own dust and rubble, she screamed and flung herself to the ground, curling into a ball. Hal had to grab her and drag her back into motion.

"It's getting worse," she shouted over the noise of bending girders and shattering glass.

"It's the people," Hal yelled back. "The more people around, the crazier it gets. That's why we're heading for the centre. It's where Sniper and T-800 will be."

"We're going to die!"

"No, no. We'll be fine. Just keep moving."

But Patty could see the fear in Hal's eyes. This was worse than he'd seen before. Worse than anyone had ever seen.

The spatial anomalies were so bad now that it was like looking at everything through distorting lenses. The effect was dizzying. The ground heaved like the surface of the sea and in some places there were holes, or areas of strange, improbable textures.

Patty carefully watched the people around her. Some seemed unaware of the chaos, while others were caught up in the madness as walls fell on them, cars ran into buildings, and phantoms only they could see tormented them. Some people moved backward, some were frozen. Many were caught in that hideous, jerky oscillation. The entire place seemed to be on the very edge of destruction.

Patty spotted Sniper up the street. He and T-800 were

running about with shotguns—perhaps looted from a store in the town—firing into shop windows and at people they passed. Patty gaped in disbelief as the two men laughed and shouted.

"They're trying to whip up more of a splash," she said to Hal. "That's it, isn't it? This ... this ... It isn't enough for them."

Hal seemed taken aback too. "Try and get into the spirit of it," he said, uncertainly. "No one's getting hurt. Not really."

He yelled out to Sniper and then ran over to him. Patty followed slowly behind. A woman nearby screamed for help and tugged at a couple of hooked rods set into the pavement. As Patty passed the frantic woman she realized the rods were the handles of a baby stroller. The ground around the woman began to glow and slither. Then the woman started twitching and vibrating at a speed that should have shaken her to pieces. It's the timestream beginning to heal itself, Patty told herself. It's all going to go back to how it was. But her heart was hammering and her breath was coming in short gasps. When someone said into her ear, "Incredible, eh?" Patty screamed and jumped away, spinning round to find Sniper grinning maliciously at her.

"You think this is fun, do you? You sick fuck!" she shouted.

Sniper pretended to look hurt. He stepped back with a pout on his lips, but his eyes were full of the pleasure of seeing her upset. Then his face lit up. "I know what would be fun." Slowly he brought up the barrel of the big shotgun and aimed it at Patty's head. "Let's see what happens if I do this."

Patty felt a clammy coldness wash through her. She couldn't move, couldn't speak. All she could see were the two black holes in the snout of the shotgun, grown as big as dinner plates. In that moment she really believed Sniper was going to kill her, just for fun. I'm only fifteen, she thought, the words echoing in her head. Only fifteen.

# Chapter 4

## Time to Kill

"What are you reading?"

The young policeman leaned across to look at Jay's magazine.

Jay realized the guy must be as bored as he was. More so, probably, without Jay's anxiety for his friend to keep him alert. He held the magazine out for the policeman. "Here. Take it. I keep reading the same paragraph over and over and I still have no idea what it says."

The policeman sat back. "Nah. I don't read magazines much. Never anything interesting in them."

Jay looked at the man's face but decided it wasn't some kind of obscure Dutch humour.

"What do you do for fun then? Can't be much happening in a little place like this."

The policeman rolled his eyes in an exaggerated gesture of impending sarcasm. "Oh, we don't have any big, exciting splashparties, with drugs and free love, but we do all right for fun. You know, there is more to life than burning out your brain and bashing in your eardrums."

Jay stared in disbelief. Had the man really said "free love"?

Surely he was having a laugh. Jay sat back in his increasingly uncomfortable chair and tried to focus on the magazine again. The reader was a big, institution-sized, semi-rigid sheet—the kind of outdated junk you found in waiting rooms the world over. They made them like that so you couldn't easily fold them up and walk out with them in your pocket, he supposed. But who'd want to steal rubbish like that, anyway? It had a few hundred titles, mostly in Dutch, but no net connection except to a local database. He touched the compatch on his wrist, thinking yet again that he should call his parents and let them know he was in trouble. And again he decided to put it off a while longer.

\* \* \* \*

Patty woke up on the ground. Above her, people were shouting. Around her there was a cacophony of strange sounds—shearing metal, tearing brickwork, sheets of glass falling into the street. With a groan, she rolled onto her back. Sniper, Hal and T-800 stopped arguing long enough to glance down at her.

"Why would I shoot her, you arsehole? What would that get me? This is a splash, or it would be, without that whining bitch tagging along."

"Well, you brought her," T-800 complained.

"Yeah," Sniper agreed. "I thought she was cool."

The bitterness in his tone made Patty wince. She sat up, looking around. Her left elbow hurt. She must have banged it when she fainted.

"That's no reason to treat her like shit," Hal said.

"Who do you think you are, my fucking father?" Sniper squared up to Hal, chin forward, holding the shotgun with big, strong hands.

Patty stood up and picked up her helmet. She felt a little woozy—a feeling not helped by the way the buildings around her were trembling. Her concern, though, was for Hal. She'd never seen Sniper so furious before. He had always been the king of cool. But now his self-control seemed almost gone and it scared her.

"It's okay Hal. I'm okay."

Sniper turned on her in an instant, the barrels of the gun shoved hard under her chin. "Who gives a shit, bitch?"

Before she could do much more than widen her eyes in shock, Hal had grabbed the gun and pulled it so it pointed away from her. "Are you fucking crazy?" he shouted in Sniper's face. With almost contemptuous ease, Sniper jerked the gun out of Hal's grip and aimed it at him.

"What? You're going to shoot me now, you psycho?" Hal stepped forward, pressing his chest against the gun.

Patty backed away, overwhelmed by the violence and the chaos all around her. T-800 spoke up again. "Hal, for fuck's sake just shut up, will you. We're supposed to be having a good time here, not fighting over some little, whining cow."

But Hal wouldn't back down. He poked Sniper in the chest. "Go on then, sicko, shoot me. Got the balls for that, you creep? Or are you only brave when you're scaring little girls?"

With a snarl, Sniper stepped back, then swung the stock of the shotgun up in a tight arc with all the strength his anger gave him. It struck Hal on the temple. The American instantly went limp and dropped to the ground in a heap.

The three of them stood in silence, staring at Hal, motionless on the ground. After a moment, Sniper said "Shit!" through clenched teeth and turned away.

T-800 bent to feel for a pulse. He waited as tense seconds passed, then pulled back his hand as if it had been burnt. "Fucking hell," he said.

Patty took a further step backward, her hand to her mouth, her eyes wide with horror. "Oh God," she said. "You killed him."

Sniper turned to glower at her, seething with rage. She looked up, knowing she was now the focus of all his fury. Panic gripped her. Without thinking, she turned and bolted, running as fast as she could for the nearest street corner. Her only thought was to be somewhere else, somewhere away from this nightmare.

She ran, stumbling over the undulating ground, shying from falling masonry and starting at every loud noise. She heard Sniper bellowing behind her. "I'll see you soon in the cage, bitch. You know we're all going back there, yes? There's nowhere for you to run, *Liebchen*. Nowhere you can escape me."

Patty ran for her life.

But Sniper was right, she began to realize. When their time was up, they would be snatched back through time to the cage at the splashparty. Someone told her that a lob was like blowing a bubble of air into water down a long straw. When the bubble left the bottom of the straw, it shot back up to the surface. It wasn't a perfect analogy, but it captured something important about the lob. The bricks didn't belong where they landed, and pretty soon the timestream spat them out again.

No one ever talked to her about the physics of it all. They just talked in metaphors and similes. Maybe they thought she was too dumb to understand. Maybe they were right.

Soon, she found herself in a field outside the town. She must have run a couple of kilometres or more. She was so exhausted her legs were trembling. There was a low wall nearby and she made herself jog over to it, flopping down behind it before she felt safe enough to stop. She was sure Sniper wasn't chasing her any more.

This far out from the splashtarget, the effects of the splash were weaker. The ground still shifted, perspectives changed randomly, and trees and animals moved oddly, but the spontaneous self-destruction of buildings, the wild changes in gravity and light, and the horror of seeing people caught in frantic oscillations had been left behind.

She didn't know where she was and had no idea how to get back to the park with the castle. It didn't matter. In about an hour she would be pulled back there anyway. Just one hour before Sniper had her in the cage again. She'd seen him kill a man. What would he do about it? Would he kill her too?

He was armed. Even if he couldn't bring the shotgun back from 1982—and she had no idea if he could—he had a pistol with him. The one he had used to shoot the little girl. Maybe if she could find a weapon—a rock, a branch of a tree, anything—she might be able to strike him first, incapacitate him, give herself some chance to get away. Maybe she could break into one of the houses across the field and steal a knife or a gun.

But the thought of seeing Sniper again was terrifying. She knew she wouldn't have the courage to attack him. She could imagine how easily he would deflect her blows, laughing contemptuously as he struck back.

And for the first time since she met him, Patty realized how frightened she had always been of Sniper.

"Jesus!" she said aloud. "You're one sick chick!"

"*Wie is dat?*" came a tremulous, male voice from the other side of the wall. "*Wie is er?*"

Patty tried to keep still, tried not to breathe, but she could hear approaching footsteps. Not wanting to be blindsided by a stranger, she got to her feet and stepped back from the wall. On the other side, stood a man of about fifty. His weathered face and grimy clothes suggested a labourer or a farm worker.

He recoiled when he saw her, and raised the metal rod he was carrying in a defensive gesture. After an instant, the shock in his eyes gave way to amazement and she saw his gaze move down her body and back up to her face.

She held up her hands, palms outward. "It's all right. I'm just passing through."

He lowered the rod a little, relaxing. "You are English?" he asked in a broad Dutch accent.

"Yes. English." She remembered what Hal had said about a big market that would happen tomorrow. "I'm a tourist. Yes? Tourist? I've come for the market. The—er—"

*"De Bissing, ja?"*

"That's it. The Bissing. I was just…" It sounded lame but she said it anyway. "I was just taking a walk."

The man looked around, at the shimmering trees, the undulating ground, the strange lights over the town, and the aircraft still shifting back and forth along its fall to Earth. Then he looked again at Patty, tall and beautiful and outlandishly dressed. She could see his mind working toward an inevitable conclusion.

"I must go," she said, firmly. "My friends are expecting me. They'll be worried if I'm delayed." She tried to adopt an imperious attitude, the one she had often used to repel the advances of hopeful men.

The stranger didn't look sufficiently cowed for Patty's liking.

"What is happening?" he asked. "You have done

something?" A sudden anger flared in his eyes and he gripped his rod more firmly. "*Is de magie?*" he demanded, fiercely.

"What?" Patty was getting ready to run.

"*Bent u een duivel? Een heks?*"

Patty had no idea what she was being accused of, but she was pretty sure the guy had decided the splash was all her fault. He raised his rod at her, crossing himself and shouting what might have been some kind of curse or exorcism.

She turned and fled.

# Chapter 5

## Arrivals

The walk from his new house in Pentonville to the British Museum in Great Russell Street was barely a mile and a half, but Vladimir Ilyich Lenin was beginning to regret not taking an omnibus. The English spring may not have the bitter chill of Siberia, but it made up for it in dampness and greyness.

He was still learning his way around the great metropolis and finding surprises in every street name. On his left was Hatton Garden. As he turned into the blustery wind that blew straight at him along Theobold's Road, Gray's Inn Field presented itself, with the red brick of Gray's Inn just beyond, huddled grimly against the cold. He briefly considered taking a detour to further explore the city, but the miserable weather argued against it. There would be warmer days for such adventures. Pulling his scarf tight around his neck, he pressed on toward Bloomsbury and the Round Reading Room.

* * * *

Patty kept still. Crouching under a bush, in a forest, far from the craziness of Ommen, she tried not to disturb anything that might blur or twitch or jiggle its way back to how it should be. She had run as far as she could and then had walked until she found shelter among the trees. Hiding and waiting for the yankback was her only plan, and she prayed she could make it without discovery.

A good half-hour before it was due to happen, she put on her helmet, fastening the neck seal but opening the visor so as not to waste her air supply. She didn't want to face lobspace unprepared as she had done before. In fact, remembering the fear and confusion of that first trip, she didn't want to face lobspace at all.

* * * *

"Mr. Jacob Richter?" the librarian asked, peering at Lenin above his spectacles. Lenin gave a small nod of confirmation, despite the man's execrable pronunciation. Lenin had adopted the name "Richter" some time ago to throw off the Tsar's secret police. It seemed like a reasonable precaution to use it again.

The librarian riffled through a tray in which a number of documents were stacked. "Ah, here we are." He handed the printed card to Lenin. Ticket number A72453.

"It is valid for three months, and must then be renewed if you wish to continue to use the reading room. Now, if I may, there are just one or two rules our new readers need to be aware of."

The librarian began listing the library's regulations in a polite, slightly pompous tone. But Lenin was barely listening. From where he stood, the magnificent interior of the Round Reading Room wrapped itself around him in all its glory— from the highly polished reading tables, to the stuffed shelves curving beneath the splendid, domed roof. He admired it with the eye of a serious scholar, eager to explore this Aladdin's cave of intellectual riches.

The librarian was just wishing him welcome to the library when there was a commotion, coming from the door behind him. Lenin turned to see what it was.

* * * *

The door to the intensive care unit opened again and yet another nurse came hurrying through. Jay had given up jumping to his feet each time it happened. Then he'd given up even looking expectantly at them. He gave this nurse a cursory glance and his heart leapt when he saw she was coming straight toward him.

"Mr. Kennedy?"

"Yes!" He stood up and the policeman stood too.

The woman was smiling. "We've managed to stabilize your friend. It should just be a matter of time—"

The floor heaved under them and the nurse screamed and clutched at Jay. Completely disoriented, Jay didn't realize he had fallen until a chair smacked him on the head. He pushed himself up, squinting through the pain. The waiting room was in chaos. Walls rippled and bulged, lights flickered and went out. Some people crawled on the floor, some were staggering around looking for a way out. The big drinks machine near the exit seemed to sag on one side and then toppled over with a crash and a spray of sparks.

The young policeman looked wildly about. The man suddenly began to move at a frantic rate, as if he had been selectively fast-forwarded. Then, almost as soon as he started, he halted on the buckled floor, looking distressed.

"It's all right," Jay called. "It'll be over soon. It's the backwash from the lob." He raised his voice to address the whole room. "Just stay still. Don't move around. It will all be over soon."

But it wasn't. It went on and on. It was unlike any backwash he'd ever seen. There were the same changes in time and space, weird shifts in causality, but the size of the effects, their damage, and the time they persisted were all new to Jay. He had never even heard of a backwash like this one. Usually they lasted thirty seconds, or a minute at the most. Something to look forward to at a splashparty. The slight shifts in time and distance, interacting with a tempus high, gave people the kind of experience that would normally require them to take something much, much stronger. But this, Jay thought, this could be lethal. A window exploded nearby as its frame buckled, showering glass over a screaming woman in a dressing gown. Jay got to his feet and grabbed the nurse.

"Where's Spock?" he shouted. "Where's my friend?"

The nurse shouted something at him in Dutch and pulled away from him as if he were attacking her. She ran for the exit, but barely made it halfway before she fell on the undulating floor. Jay moved to help her but she seemed fine—just scared—so he turned back to the door leading to the ICU. All he could think about was getting to Spock.

The building conspired to stop him. The floors shook. It was impossible to judge distances. For an insane moment, everything around him went into high-speed fast-forward: people blurring into smears, the ground and walls vibrating like sheets in a gale. He barely had time to realize that it was he who had slowed down, not the world that had speeded up, before he was back in sync with his surroundings. And then the craziness stopped. The last chair toppled, the last bit of glass tinkled from the windows.

He looked around, hardly daring to believe it was over. The woman in the dressing gown lay on the floor against a wall, crying and covered in blood. The young policeman stood rigid, hyperventilating. Distant cries for help came from other parts of the building.

\* \* \* \*

When the yankback took her, Patty was just as surprised as the first time. One moment she was hiding in a forest, watching the time on her helmet display, the next she was in total blackness, falling through time.

In a breathless panic, she sealed her visor against the cold, hard vacuum. She breathed in short, shallow breaths until she was convinced there was air flowing and she wouldn't suffocate. Only then did she start looking around for Sniper and the others. She craned her neck side to side, down and up, trying to make her body rotate so she could see behind and above her. If she succeeded, she couldn't tell. The blackness was uniform in all directions. This time, there was no tether to tell her there was any living soul nearby. The possibility that she might be spinning out of control made her feel giddy and sick. The empty blackness began to feel like a solid weight pressing against her. Instead of floating weightless in an infinite, open space, she could just as easily be buried alive in that impenetrable black stuff.

Breathing became difficult. You're panicking, she told herself. Calm down. You'll be there soon. But it wasn't just panic, she realized, sucking in lungfuls of useless, oxygen-depleted air. She had run out of air. She was going to suffocate. In a moment of light-headedness, she began to giggle. She'd be dead before Sniper got a chance to kill her. The irony!

She smashed into the wire mesh of the cage wall and fell with a bone-jarring crash to the floor. Light and noise hit her as hard as the cage had, blinding and deafening her. She broke the seals on her helmet and tore it off, gasping for air, pummelled by the commotion around her.

Hal's body lay on the cage floor nearby. Beyond him, T-800 struggled to his feet, removing his helmet. She turned to see Sniper standing behind her, glaring down at her. Behind him, the crowd seemed strangely still and subdued. A wide path was visible in it from the outer fringes to a point about halfway in. People in dark uniforms were pushing through, making for the cage. Across the field, the unmistakable red and blue lights of police vehicles flickered.

"Now here's my problem, bitch," Sniper said, kneeling down beside her. She felt the barrel of his pistol against her ribs. "I can't shoot you with all those police around, and not when we're on the silver screen like this."

She glanced up at the screens. The gigantic images showed what could easily have been Sniper compassionately checking that she was okay after her ordeal.

"And I can't trust you to keep your story straight. So I'll make it easy for you." He dug the pistol into her ribs. "You weren't there when Hal had his terrible accident. You didn't see what happened. We got separated. You say anything other than that, and I will give you the longest, slowest, most horrible death you can possibly imagine."

He smiled as if pleased to see she was all right. "Got that, bitch?"

Not daring to speak, she nodded mutely.

The music stopped mid-beat, leaving her ears ringing. The crowd groaned in protest.

"This is the police." The cop's voice was almost drowned out by howls of feedback from the PA system. "Nobody leaves here without our permission. We believe there are prohibited drugs being sold in this area. We have a warrant to stop and search anyone we choose."

More police had reached the platform and were clambering up toward the cage.

"We also believe there has been an unauthorized time jump in contravention of the European Temporal Displacement Regulation Act of 2045. Remain where you are and we will process you as quickly as possible. Thank you."

The message began to repeat itself in Dutch.

Patty could see only half a dozen police cars on the grounds of Eerde Castle. Perhaps there were more at the gates. Even so, there were nowhere near enough police to contain a crowd this big. People started to run for the darkness beyond the lights of the party. She saw the crowd in all directions, flowing away into the night. The police had obviously acted too soon.

More police cars were arriving from the direction of the big house, called in from more distant towns, no doubt, but there weren't enough of them. The police gave chase to anyone within reach. Several kids were caught and dragged over to the waiting vans. Out of hundreds, only the three in the cage were absolutely guaranteed to be arrested.

\* \* \* \*

It took Jay several anxious minutes to locate the ICU. Throughout the hospital, people were being helped out from underneath the wreckage and treated for cuts and broken bones. Nurses and doctors had suffered along with the patients.

The young policeman caught up with him just as he entered the room where Spock was being treated. The place was a wreck. Medical equipment was strewn on the floor and a tall steel locker had toppled over and crashed through some monitoring equipment. Jay recognized the doctor standing beside Spock. Her hands were trembling. She looked up as he approached her.

"I'm afraid I have some bad news about your friend."

Even before she said it, Jay had known from the look on her face.

"Mr. Lyle passed away without regaining consciousness. He did not suffer, I think. I'm sorry." She looked around the room helplessly. "He was on life support. He should have been all right but..."

Jay's legs quivered and he sat down abruptly in a tubular-steel chair. "I should call his family," he said.

The doctor had called Spock "Mr. Lyle". Jay barely recognized his friend's real name. As if in death he had become someone else, had joined a new crowd, had lost all his personality, all his quirkiness and excitement, and was now someone more ordinary. In death, Jay thought. No longer "in life". Elsewhere, in another place, among strangers. Tears rolled down his cheeks, surprising him. The nurse touched his shoulder tenderly, having followed him and his police escort from the waiting room. Jay ignored her.

The doctor said something to the nurse in Dutch.

"I must go and see who I may help," she replied in English, for Jay's benefit.

Jay reached out a hand and laid it on Spock's, wishing the

doctor would remove all the tubes and wires from his friend's body.

The nurse took the policeman aside. They talked quickly and quietly. Making arrangements, perhaps. Working out what to do about Jay, where to send the body. Jay resented that these people should take charge of Spock's body. Spock was Jay's friend. Jay should decide what was best for him, should have the responsibility of looking after him.

But the reality of Spock lying there, cold, on a hospital bed, heavy and lifeless, made him quail. What would he do—put the body in his car and drive him home to England? He thought about going through customs at the tunnel with a dead body in his car and then saw how Spock himself would see it. Spock would think it was an enormous joke, a great caper. The thought made him smile. It would almost be worth doing as a final tribute to his crazy friend. He chortled to himself, imagining it. The nurse and policeman turned to look at him. Not long after, the policeman told Jay he was taking him to the Ommen police station.

They left the hospital in the middle of the night. There was chaos in the streets, traffic accidents, cracked roads, tumbled buildings. It looked as if an earthquake had hit the town. But they reached the station without too much trouble, and the police let him make whatever calls he wanted. His parents were angry, appalled, and concerned in equal measures. Spock's father sounded stunned and said almost nothing. They were all coming to Ommen as fast as they could get there.

He was formally charged with being in possession of banned drugs. They put him in a comfortable cell. It was a smart, new police station and had survived the backwash almost unscathed.

Jay didn't want to think about what tomorrow might be like. He curled up into a tight ball on his cot and cried himself to sleep.

# Part II

**Winter 2049-2050**

# Chapter 6

## Rumours

The storm rattled against the windows and buffeted the car. A black sedan, Paris registration, hunkered down in the quiet side street with its lights out. Jacques Bauchet sat behind the wheel, holding a cup of coffee in his large hands, and staring intently at the rain-lashed windscreen. His hawk-like profile was almost invisible in the dark. By the clock on his compatch it was already two in the morning. He looked over at Detective Sergeant Colbert sitting beside him, and then trained his eyes back on the windscreen.

A lone street lamp stood in an aura of whirling orange flecks, dimly illuminating the doorway Bauchet was studying. But sensors mounted on the car watched the alley through infrared eyes and the inside of the windscreen displayed a clear image of the wet road and the old brick buildings, superimposed perfectly on the murky scene outside.

"Maybe we got it wrong," Colbert said.

"Meaning, maybe I got it wrong, eh?" Bauchet regretted saying it immediately; he wasn't usually so touchy.

Colbert looked at his boss. "I just meant…"

"They'll be here. Don't be so impatient, Sergeant."

A bright light appeared in the main street beyond, grew and stopped just out of sight around the corner.

"Speak of the devil," said Bauchet, softly.

"It's them," said a voice through Bauchet's compatch.

There was more surveillance across the street.

"You've confirmed that?" Bauchet asked.

"Sending," said the compatch.

A moment later a still image of three men emerging from a car appeared in a viewer in the windscreen. The faces were indistinct and grainy, but the captions beside them gave their names and other personal details. The software analysis that had provided the facial recognition would be admissible as evidence in any court in the Union. Bauchet allowed himself to relax just a little.

"Give them a minute to get inside and meet up with the others," he said. Beside him, Colbert drew his stunner and flicked off the safety.

"The sweepers are pretty good, you know," Bauchet told him.

"Not against these guys."

Colbert's expression was unreadable in the dark. Bauchet looked away with a small nod of agreement.

They waited.

"Okay," Bauchet said into his compatch. "Send in the sweepers."

There was a flurry of activity out on the main road. Bauchet could just make out several grey shapes moving through the rain toward the corner building. There was noise from behind as two sweepers rushed past the car. The armored combat robots went straight to the door Bauchet had watched for so long. Without hesitating, they blew it to pieces with a small cannon and raced into the building.

"Give me telemetry," he said into his compatch. The lower half of the windscreen became a row of viewers, showing what each of the half-dozen armored robots saw. The sweepers were converging on infrared images of five men in a room two stories up. "This is Chief Inspector Bauchet," he said through the compatch to his waiting team. "Go, go, go!"

"Wish me luck." Colbert opened the door and got out, cold air and rain rushing in until he slammed it behind him.

Bauchet heard approaching footsteps and saw several armed police officers in body armour trot past him toward the shattered doorway. He kept his eyes on the view from the sweepers.

The men in the upstairs room had begun to move about. Bauchet watched their little red-and-yellow heat signatures shifting around the room. Suddenly, ten more figures appeared, then fifty. Bauchet frowned at the viewers. His quarry had deployed electronic countermeasures to confuse the sweepers' sensors. He wondered where they had acquired such good tech. The sweepers would be shooting at shadows now, with a one-in-ten chance of hitting anything. Colbert was right. This wasn't the kind of job the bots could handle. He broadcast the bad news through his compatch, then got out of the car.

Cold rain slapped his face and wind tore at his coat as he pulled it tightly around himself. A rattle of shots came from inside the building, and flashes lit the blinds of an upstairs window. A couple of shotguns, he guessed from the noise, and a machine gun. He felt a shiver of fear when he heard a buzz-gun's vicious squeal. Buzz-guns spat out thousands of tiny iron pellets at hypersonic speeds and could cut through body armour as if it were wet paper. By contrast, the sweepers' stunners were silent and non-lethal. It was impossible to tell without the telemetry whether the sweepers were returning fire or not.

He hurried to the door, pulling out his own stunner. One of his men waited there, covering the exit, looking bulky and large in his armour. Bauchet leaned his back against the wall and listened to the calm commentary from the mobile control unit on the compatch. He could see the big command-and-control van parked back down the street, out of harm's way.

"Sweeper three inactive."

"Sweeper two inactive."

The robots were going down like tenpins.

At this rate, Bauchet realized, all the sweepers would be taken out before his officers arrived.

"Sweeper four, confirmed kill."

Of course, a "kill" by the sweepers meant they had stunned one of the targets. Kills by the enemy would be the real thing.

"Unit two in position at stage one." The speaker lacked the calm detachment of the control unit. Her breathing could be heard as she climbed the staircase inside the building.

"No visual. Advancing to target."

A buzz-gun screamed again.

"Sweeper four inactive," the compatch reported.

The shooting was almost continuous. One by one, the control unit ticked off the disabled sweepers. "Unit one, report."

"Unit one, in position, ready to engage."

"Unit two?"

"Taking fire. Repeat, taking fire. Two men down. Moving to..."

The voice went silent, but the roar and screech of the gun battle continued. Bauchet clenched his teeth and glowered back at the c-and-c van, willing them to give the order.

"Unit one engage. Unit three, advance to relieve unit two. Unit one, confirm you're engaged."

"Shit!"

"Unit one…"

"Yes! We're engaged dammit!"

"Sweeper five, confirmed kill."

The armored officer at the doorway looked agitated. He was listening too and clearly wanted to get inside and help his comrades. Perhaps Bauchet's presence was all that held him back.

"Unit one, two confirmed kills. We have a runner, heading for the back stairs. In pursuit."

"All ground units converge on exit B."

Bauchet pressed himself back against the wall. The officer nearby looked at him nervously. Exit B was the doorway he was guarding. Bauchet signalled for him to step back against the wall on the other side of the door, but before he could obey, the escapee appeared in the hallway. It took the fugitive just half a second to spot the cop blocking his exit and fire with his buzz-gun. The high-pitched scream of the weapon cut through the wind and rain as a line of destruction tore through the plaster of the hallway wall, ripped the door frame to matchwood, and arced into the street where the unlucky officer was diving for cover.

Bauchet saw the pellet stream cut through the man's calf, shattering his armour. The injured officer fell to the ground and rolled out of the line of fire. But not for long. The runner burst out of the door, turning his weapon toward the fallen policeman. Bauchet took aim and brought the would-be killer down with a single shot from his stunner.

Bauchet ran toward the fugitive, motionless in the rain. He kept him covered with the stunner, its red targeting laser steady on the man's neck. Bauchet kicked away the fugitive's weapon, then kicked him hard in the ribs, just to be sure he wasn't faking. The man did not so much as twitch.

"Bauchet, here," he said into the compatch. "Confirmed kill. Get a medic over here. I have a wounded officer."

"All clear," c-and-c announced. "Roll call. Medics to the indicated locations."

The compatch chatter went on. Bauchet knelt down beside the man he'd shot and pressed a neural activity blocker to his temple. The little disc would keep the man's brain scrambled for at least an hour. Long enough for the rope-and-tie team to get him properly processed and on his way to the station.

"How are you doing?" he asked the wounded officer.

The man pulled off his helmet. He was young. No more than twenty years old.

"Okay, thank you, sir," the young man lied. Rain poured down on his head and into the neck of his armour. His face was white.

"You're lucky it's not worse," Bauchet told him. His words might have been a reprimand, but his tone was more sad than angry.

The young man looked stricken, no doubt thinking he should have had the first shot, should have done what he'd been trained to do.

"You saved my life," he said.

Bauchet turned at the sound of footsteps and waved the medic toward the young officer. Colbert was right behind him, along with several other officers to pick up Bauchet's catch.

"Tell me we didn't lose all of unit two," Bauchet said, standing up.

"We lost three officers in total, sir. Another five injured, including this one."

Bauchet looked away sharply, needing to control a sudden surge of anger. "The sweepers?"

"Scrap metal, the lot of them."

Bauchet turned and set off toward the car. "Come on. I need a hot shower and something to eat. Then we start questioning these bastards."

\* \* \* \*

The ferry terminal at Dover sprawled in the darkness. It was a dismal, decaying relic of a time long gone. In the late 2020s, toward the end of the Great Adjustment, it had already been struggling to survive. In 2034, the opening of CT2, the second Channel tunnel, put the final nail in its coffin. Since then Dover's ferry terminal had been allowed to fall victim to slowly rising sea levels and increasingly violent Channel storms.

Now Jay Kennedy sat in one of the decrepit customs sheds and peered through a night-sight at the crumbling piers and gently lapping water. It was cold as hell but Jay thanked the gods it had stopped raining.

"Trafalgar, report."

Every half hour since he started his watch at eight PM, the little voice in his ear had said the same thing. Every half hour since he started his watch, Jay had given the same reply: "Trafalgar. Nothing to report." It was now four in the morning.

"Heads up, lads and lasses." It was a new voice, the broad Yorkshire drawl of Holbrook himself. Jay sat up, his attention pricking. Holbrook was God on stilts. The highest ranking operational officer Jay knew about. The bigwig who had given the speech at Jay's graduation ceremony. The man who recruited him two years ago, after Ommen.

"New intel from our friends elsewhere," Holbrook said.

Jay knew he meant Europol. They always called them that.

"The rumours are true, it seems. The shipment will be arriving this very night. Be vigilant, everybody."

Jay felt his heartbeat quicken. This was it, then. Tonight he would discover whether he really had what it took. Tonight he would face real villains. People who would kill him if they could. He started to go over his training in his mind, then stopped just as suddenly. He wasn't cramming for an exam here. He was on an op and he needed to focus on what he was doing. He'd been on operations before, but never like this. All throughout his training they'd used him to pick up intel on the streets. He still used his old tag, Luke, and he still hung out with what was left of the splashparty crowd, picking up snippets of information about the bricks and what they were doing, working with the analysts to piece together the movements of their most-wanted splashteams. But they had never given him a gun before. They had never sent him into danger like this.

He scanned the old jetties once again. Had anything changed? Was that the same pattern of shadows he'd seen last time? He shook himself and stood up, walked a few paces and then came back to the window. Fear was sliding into him like a vapour. It tightened his lungs and scattered his thoughts. He needed to get a grip on himself or he'd miss something, get himself killed. Or worse, get someone else killed, let everyone down.

What were they thinking, letting a boy of nineteen, barely out of basic training, take on a job like this?

Jay froze. Was that a movement? Up there on the road? He fidgeted with the focus on his night-sight but could see nothing unusual. Should he call it in? What if it was nothing? Stupid rookie, panicking over a tree swaying in the breeze.

But there was no breeze tonight. Just the cold and the lapping waves.

"Agincourt to Waterloo."

The whisper of the comm almost made him fall off his chair. Shit!

So there was something up there.

"There's movement on the road," the voice continued. It was Helen. Sharp, mean-looking woman. Stationed just a hundred meters away, but higher up with a better view of the road. "Two trucks. Repeat, two trucks."

"Acknowledged, Agincourt," replied the voice of Waterloo—Barry Overman, the officer in charge of the op. "This is it, ladies and gentlemen. Hold your positions."

"They're signalling," said Helen.

Jay had seen it himself this time. Three short flashes in the infrared from up where the trucks must be parked. He turned quickly to scan the water, black as soot in his night-sight. And there it was! Three answering flashes, also infrared.

"There's a boat out in the Channel," he blurted, forgetting his comms protocol. He cursed himself silently and tried to get a grip. "Range two-hundred-and-seventy meters. Bearing one seventy degrees."

"Oh, really? And who might you be?" Overman's voice was heavy with sarcasm.

Jay screwed up his eyes in an agony of embarrassment. Of course Overman knew damned well who he was. The man just wanted to make him squirm.

"It's Trafalgar, sir. Sorry, sir."

Did he hear sniggering from other officers, or was that just his imagination adding to the torture?

"Everybody hold your positions," Overman said again.

Jay knew he would be moving people into position around

the trucks and up and down the waterline. There were motor launches on hand too, hiding among the piers.

"We'll let them come in and tie up before we make our move. If that's all right with you, Trafalgar."

Jay sighed. So this was how it was going to be. "That's fine, sir. Excellent plan."

"Kind of you to say so."

For a moment, Jay felt miserable. His first time out, and he was being picked on by the boss over an open comm line. How was he going to live this down? It seemed like the end of the world—until it occurred to him that what he thought was sniggering might just be good-natured laughter. Just a bit of fun at his expense. Everyone was tense tonight; everyone was scared. Overman was poking fun at him as a way of relaxing everybody, building up a bit of team spirit. It got them laughing even though they may be about to put their lives at risk. Maybe Overman was also subtly reminding them that they had a rookie on board, someone who might need their help. Had his boss really just done all that? Jay wanted to believe it was true.

"Hastings to Waterloo. The boat's tying up at Pier Three."

"Agincourt to Waterloo. The trucks are moving. They're heading for the pier."

"This is Waterloo. Hold your positions. And keep your eyes peeled."

Overman would be handing over control to the assault unit commander now, Jay thought. The fighting would start any second.

And it did. Several loud percussions with bright flashes came from the direction of Pier Three. Jay saw two trucks, clearly visible for a moment, with people around them in a frozen tableau. He heard shouting and running and three shots fired in rapid succession. The assault team was using live rounds, Jay remembered. Someone had probably just been killed. Out in the Channel, powerful engines whined into life as the boat made a run for it, pursued by friendlies. There was a shout. Another three shots.

After that, silence rolled back like a black tide out of the night. Seconds ticked past. Jay watched the pier through his night-sight. Soldiers moved around the trucks, but there seemed to be no other activity.

"All right, everybody. Mission accomplished. Let's go in and see what we've got."

Jay let out the breath he hadn't known he'd been holding. The assault was over, done so expertly it was almost bloodless. His relief was immense. If there had been serious trouble, his team would have been the reserves. Grabbing a torch, he ran for the pier, feeling profoundly grateful for the unit that had spared him the terrifying prospect of a gun battle.

There were several vehicles on the pier by the time he got there. Two boats with searchlights illuminated the scene. People lay on the ground, cuffed at wrists and ankles. Soldiers stood among them, looking confident and relaxed.

Jay went straight to the nearest truck and opened the back. Inside were four crates, each a cube over a meter high. Printed on the sides were a manufacturer's name, a model name and number, and the words "Made in India". Jay pulled a tag-reader from his pocket and scanned one of the crates.

"Well?" It was Overman, standing outside the truck.

Jay checked the display. "They're F2s all right, sir. State-of-the-art stuff."

"Enough for what we think they need?"

"No, sir. But two shipments like this would be about right."

"Ah, well. Our friends elsewhere ought to be glad we stopped this lot, anyway, don't you think?"

"I suppose." Jay wasn't too confident that the raid had done much to prevent the catastrophe they were all worried about.

The rumour was that a new kind of timesplash technology had emerged. Terrorist-sponsored splashteams around the world were now racing one another to make a splash so huge that whole cities would be caught in the backwash. Police and intelligence agencies everywhere were trying to stop them, but the situation looked hopeless. The best chance seemed to be in tracking F2s and other necessary technologies. F2s were focus fusion generators. A really big timesplash would need unbelievable amounts of energy. The kind of energy a large town would consume. The kind of energy that would need twenty F2s wired together.

But collecting so many F2s was not all that hard. When oil production began its rapid decline back in 2015, it plunged the world into a global depression that lasted until the end of the 2020s. The development of focus fusion dragged the world out of the Great Adjustment—the cycle of inflation, resource wars and infrastructure collapse that was threatening to destroy everything. The early focus fusion reactors were about the size of a garden shed but could produce enough electricity to power a large neighbourhood, using plentiful, cheap boron and hydrogen as fuel. By the end of the 2030s, focus fusion reactors were being mass-produced and installed by the millions. Clean, efficient and almost-free electricity transformed the world's economies, and the 2040s were a global boom time.

Currently, F2s were the size of a filing cabinet and the very latest models could produce 20 megawatts of power. The eight reactors in the two trucks Jay's team had seized would be enough to power a town of one hundred thousand homes. Each one of them was worth about half a million euros, but money seemed to be no object to the bricks they were tracking.

"Don't worry," Overman said, as if reading Jay's thoughts. "We just need to keep the technology out of their hands long enough to round them up."

Jay finished scanning the crates and then climbed down from the truck to let in the forensic team. "We can watch the new high tech stuff," he said, "but they can buy them secondhand from Russia, or China, or anywhere. How do we keep track of that?"

Overman didn't seem upset by Jay's worries. "We just do our job and we do it well. Right?" Overman clapped Jay on the shoulder. "Anyway, the boss wants to see you in that limo over there." He pointed to a long black vehicle parked at the edge of the dock.

"Sir?"

"Go on. Don't keep him waiting."

Jay wanted to ask what it was about. He suspected he was in some kind of trouble, but was unable to see what he might have done to deserve a reprimand from the boss. He walked briskly to the limo, feeling the cold again now that all the excitement was over. He pulled his hands out of his pockets as the rear door of the car opened. Inside was Holbrook, looking up at him.

"Hurry up, lad. Don't let the cold in."

Jay hadn't spoken to the old man since his friend's funeral, since the reception at Spock's parents' house in Cambridge.

Two years ago. A white-haired stranger—a man of about sixty, he guessed at the time—approached him while he stood alone in the garden. Holbrook immediately struck him as a shrewd and careful man, even though he had the round-faced, smiling appearance of a jocular old uncle. The old man had suggested that they take a walk together so that they could talk privately and Jay had agreed. He'd been happy to get away from Spock's family, who seemed to looked at him through eyes filled with open hurt and veiled recrimination.

That day, Holbrook rambled on about what a waste it was that such a young man had died. He talked about some other casualties of the Ommen splash—a woman who lost a leg in a car crash, a number of artworks destroyed in a gallery fire, some cracks that appeared in the ancient town hall and would cost a small fortune to repair. Eventually, the old man got to the point.

"So far, timesplashing has been something of a nuisance," he said. "But Ommen has taken it to new heights. There will be a concerted effort now to stamp it out." Holbrook's brow furrowed. "I imagine the whole thing will move deeper underground as it becomes more criminalized. There are some who suspect that timesplashing might stop being just a sport and turn into something altogether more serious."

They had stopped walking by this time, and stood together on a street corner in Spock's quiet, leafy suburb.

"I work for the government, Jay, in a branch of the security services. We're putting together a team to keep on top of this thing, and to provide intelligence to other services that might need it. I wonder if you might like to join us? Help us out?"

Throughout Holbrook's meandering speech, Jay had listened with only half an ear. He thought maybe he'd picked up some dotty old relative of his late friend who just wanted to talk about the Ommen disaster.

"We need young people who know what all this stuff is about, to offset the old buggers like me who aren't really into it. What do you say?"

The offer got Jay's attention. And when he looked into the old man's face, he knew he meant it.

Two years had passed since that moment. Two years of training and study—intelligence gathering in clubs and bars, and analysis work in the bowels of the HQ building. Two years from that relaxed afternoon chat to this night of tension.

"How have you been, lad?" Holbrook asked as Jay climbed into the limo.

"Er, very well, sir." Jay knew Holbrook had access to all of his training and operational reports, his psych evaluations and his officers' reports. Holbrook would know full well how he was doing.

"Nasty rumours we're hearing about this new kind of timesplash."

"Yes, sir."

Part of Jay's recent work was hanging out with local bricks and staying in touch with the splashparty scene on the UK side of the Channel. Some of the rumours Holbrook was referring to came from Jay's own reports.

"Do you think they're true?"

The service, Jay knew, had many analysts working on this very question. "After tonight, I'd definitely say so, sir."

"Really?"

"The F2s we found confirm there's at least one European splashteam trying to assemble enough generating capacity for the kind of lob people are talking about."

Holbrook nodded but said nothing. Jay wondered if he'd really sent for him just to chat about rumours.

"You did well in your training, Jay. And I've heard good things about your undercover work."

Now Jay really was confused. "Thank you, sir."

"I've got another job for you."

"Sir?"

"Ever hear of the TCU?"

# Chapter 7

## Beijing

"This is the nine o'clock news."

Sandra Malone glanced at the screen. She had been working on her physics assignment for the past hour and was keen to be distracted. Being locked away in a mental institute was punishment enough without having to catch up on a lifetime of missed school.

"Reports are just coming in from Beijing of violent disturbances in China's capital city and throughout the North China Plain. Reporters in the capital say there appear to be seismic and temporal disruptions similar to the backwash from a timesplash but on a massive scale. Chinese officials have yet to make any comment, but netlogs and biologs from the area include reports of bizarre physical phenomena and massive destruction. One netlog close to the city centre, from a financial analyst in the commercial sector of Xidan, tells of buildings collapsing and bridges melting. It even has vidstream of what looks like a marauding army of soldiers shooting civilians as they flee. To view this footage, select Xidan from the context menu."

Sandra rose to her feet, her assignment forgotten. She was

drawn toward the images on the viewer. Chaos ruled in the city of Beijing, and in the towns and countryside all around it. The ground rippled as gravity fluctuated, destroying buildings. Crowds of terrified people grew and shrank as space distorted.

"Oh my God," she whispered, clutching her head. "Oh God, not again."

She watched the panic and the fear, the cancellation of all physical normality that was tearing apart Beijing. Once more she relived the horror she'd felt two years ago. In her mind, she fled with the terrified people of Ommen. Running, hiding, trying to get away from the lethal madness all around her. Her name was Patty again and she was scared, more scared than she had ever been in her life. Sniper lurked in the shadows and Patty ran and ran, ran the way she had in her nightmares every night since that awful day.

\* \* \* \*

"It's a backwash," Detective Sergeant Colbert said, entering Bauchet's office. "The Chinese have confirmed it."

The Chief Inspector set aside the report he had been reading. "Impossible! On such a scale?"

"Official estimate is thirty thousand dead. Maybe a hundred thousand injured. The numbers keep growing. Beijing is a ruin, with total devastation in central Beijing. A hundred square kilometres flattened. Partial destruction stretching out to a thousand square kilometres."

Bauchet said nothing for a long while as he tried to take in the enormity of what had happened. "So someone's managed it," he said at last. "Now every damned brick on the planet will want to do it too."

"Maybe not. The Chinese say they found the cage and it had five dead bodies in it. As far as they can tell, no one survived. Even the tekniks died in the backwash."

Bauchet's mood grew darker. "That won't stop them. They all think they're invulnerable, better than the rest. They'll all want to be the first one to come back alive."

Colbert was flicking through the briefing. "Beijing's out of action for a while. They expect a stock market meltdown. This is going to be bad."

"Has the Prefect of Police seen this yet?"

"He should have it by now."

Bauchet's compatch chimed. He smiled grimly at Colbert.

"Yes, sir," he said into the compatch, and then listened through his earpatch. "I agree completely. Absolutely. Thank you, sir. Yes, at once."

He looked up at Colbert. "Seems Europol wants to confirm my appointment and get things moving."

"Congratulations. And money is no object, I suppose?"

"Quite right. Whatever I want, I get. No questions asked. The budget is already sanctioned under the Emergency Powers Act of 2026."

"I hope it isn't too late. We should have started on this weeks ago."

"Failure is not an option, Colbert. The Prefect just told me." He allowed himself a small smile. "Get someone in here to pack up my stuff. Yours too. We're moving to Europol Headquarters in Brussels on the first flight. Laroche will take over the team here in Paris. He knows how I want things organized at this end." He was already on his feet. "Tell Brussels we're on our way and make sure they're ready for us. I need to get over to the Palais Bourbon for a meeting. I think the president herself wants to wish me *bon voyage*."

Colbert pulled a face. "More likely it's the DCRI, DRM and every other intelligence agency in France wanting to know why they appointed a plod to head up Europol's brand new Temporal Crimes Unit and not one of their spooks."

"Especially when they hear about the funding, eh?"

"Don't let them worm their way in. They were all happy to sit on the sidelines and let you do all the work until today. They don't deserve a seat at the table."

Bauchet headed out the door. "Anyone who can really help now is welcome, Colbert. What happened to Beijing yesterday was as bad as exploding a nuclear bomb in its heart. We can't let that happen to Paris—or Rome, or Berlin, or anywhere else.

"Get that flight to Brussels organized, and I'll see you at the airport."

\* \* \* \*

Jay had been watching the news on his compatch ever since he got off the plane at Brussels Airport. The vids of refugees fleeing the ruins of Beijing played constantly on the news streams. What he saw of the great city's twisted remains brought back heart-thumping flashbacks to that night at the hospital in Ommen. A timesplash had done this. But it was something new and bigger, something people like Holbrook and Overman and everyone else in the know had been expecting for some time now.

In the cab to Europol HQ, Jay tried to contact his parents again. He hadn't been able to let them know about his reassignment, and he was supposed to be meeting them in the evening for dinner. His relationship with his parents had been strained even before Ommen, but especially over the past couple of years. It hadn't helped that he couldn't talk about his work with "Five". The official cover they'd concocted for him—that he'd joined the Metropolitan Police—had never seemed at all credible to anyone who knew him, least of all his mum and dad. The dinner that evening was one of his many bridge-building attempts. But, like so many others, it was about to fall flat on its face, doing more harm than good. With this overseas posting on secondment to Europol, it was going to look as though he was drifting even farther away from them, that he really didn't care about their relationship. And yet, since the shock of Spock's death, he wanted more than anything to feel the comfort of close family bonds. That night in Ommen had changed him in many ways.

He hefted his luggage and walked in through the big glass doors of the old Berlaymont building where the European Union's headquarters had been for so long. Much of the Berlaymont building was now sublet to commercial operators, but there were still many government departments occupying the building's massive bulk, including Europol Headquarters.

Jay looked around in dismay at the busy grand foyer. It took him a while to notice the huge wooden reception counter along the far wall. He trudged across the room to announce himself and was told to wait.

So he waited.

He'd been sitting on the bench, his bag between his feet, for at least ten minutes, when he felt a tap on his shoulder. He turned.

"*Bonjour,*" said an elegantly dressed, middle-aged woman. "You are Mr. Kennedy, yes?" she asked.

Jay jumped up and shook her hand.

"I am Marie, personal assistant to Chief Inspector Bauchet."

Jay didn't recognize the name. Before he could reply, Marie held up a small scanner and made two passes with it: one across his chest, and the other from his face to his abdomen. It looked for all the world like a benediction. But it was not. Jay had seen such devices many times since joining the service. They did a scan for ID chips, an iris scan, a facial recognition test, a sweep for concealed weapons using terahertz radar and, as a final check, a DNA analysis. Without needing to be asked, he placed his finger in the little hole in the side of the device and felt the gentle touch of the dermabrasion.

Marie considered the display for a moment, tapped the controls a couple of times and then smiled. "If you'll follow me, Mr. Kennedy." She moved off across the great expanse of marble floor with a clicking of heels.

Jay grabbed his bag and hurried after her.

"Your ID chips have been updated," she told him. "Someone will explain your security clearances later. Welcome to the Temporal Crimes Unit."

\* \* \* \*

Sandra had to get out of the ward. She couldn't stay there any more. Not with what was going on in Beijing. It could happen here next, she told herself. Her thoughts skittered on the edge of panic. It could happen everywhere. If this was the end of the world, she didn't want to be here, trapped in a psych ward studying physics, waiting for it to happen. Movement was what she needed. Escape from the Institute.

The Porringer Institute of Mental Well-Being was a big old building that used to be a country hotel long ago. Three stories high, with bars on its windows and the slightly dilapidated look of a horror-vid mansion, the Institute sat behind a high brick wall surrounded by several acres of lawns on the edge of Bodmin Moor in Cornwall. Sandra had not been outside those walls for eighteen months, since they'd first locked her up on a Custodial Rehabilitation Order.

The Institute was a low-security establishment and its patients were allowed many freedoms and comforts. Sandra had her own small room, with a bed, chest of drawers, wardrobe, and tiny en suite bathroom. It was a humane and well-run establishment but Sandra had been planning her escape ever since the day the prison officers had transferred her from the juvenile remand centre in Plymouth.

She pulled a chair over to the wardrobe and opened it. Taped to the inside at the top were the things she would need: a torch, a craft knife, two folded-up plastic bags, a length of string, a wire coat hanger bent into a hook, and an envelope stuffed with money. She pulled them all free and unfolded the plastic bags.

She didn't have many clothes, but she put on what she could—it was November and bitterly cold. The rest she stuffed into the bags. She put some of the money into her pockets and the remainder into a bag. The Institute gave all of its patients an allowance each week to buy things from the vending machines, and from the shop that sold little things like stationery, makeup, and magazines. Each week, Sandra had hidden half and spent the rest. No one had noticed, and, after eighteen months, she had accumulated a thick wad of Euros. Enough to get away, she hoped.

Next she moved her chair to the corner of the room beside the window. The curtains were drawn, so no one outside would see her stand on the chair. Her room was on the top floor and that had made the plan so much easier. She had long ago worked out where the rafters were in the ceiling by looking for the subtle indentations the nails made in the plasterboard. Now she used her craft knife to cut through the plasterboard between the rafters. The board cut easily with the sharp, thin blade. It took her barely ten minutes to make an opening almost a meter long and as wide as her shoulders.

Carefully she pushed the rectangle of plasterboard up into the roof space and slid it aside. A shower of dusty, grey granules came raining down on her, making her gasp with surprise as she accidentally breathed it in. Choking, she smothered her coughing and tried to stay calm. It was only the roof insulation. The fine, light, paper-based material was nothing to worry about. It was so lightweight it barely made a sound as it had fallen over her and onto the floor.

After she took a deep, steadying breath, she pulled herself up into the blackness above. Once inside the loft, she turned on the torch. She was in a huge, dark space. The torchlight revealed only her immediate surroundings. It was cold above the thick layer of insulation. Wooden beams arched overhead, receding into the darkness on either side of her in neat, parallel ranks. Thick cross-members braced the beams at chest height and were held by diagonal struts that secured them to the joists and rafters. On the roof above her head, there was a layer of tarred, papery stuff between the roof joists and the tiles. When she reached up and scratched at it with her fingers, it tore away to reveal the dark slates beyond. She breathed again in relief.

Sandra made her way along the inside of the loft, staying close to the edge of the roof, having to move doubled up to avoid the joists. She could barely make out where the rafters ran—since they were buried under all the insulation—but she knew she must step only where they were. If she stood on the plasterboard she would fall straight through. Several times she had to stop and push aside the paper granules, digging through them to find the wooden beam that would support her next step.

As she moved, she counted the rafters. She had carefully measured the distance between the rafters by examining the ceiling in her room. Then she had paced out the distance on the grounds outside, measuring the distance between her own window and the fire escape—the place that she needed to reach. She hadn't expected it to take her so long to get to where she was going, but then she hadn't realized how hard it would be to creep through the chilly blackness of the roof space.

When she finally made it, she looked back at the patch of light that marked the hole in the ceiling of her room. It didn't seem far away at all, so she counted the roof joists between the hole and where she stood twice more before she convinced herself she was in the right place. She took out the craft knife and cut away a big section of the tarred paper above her head. With the paper removed, she could see a series of wooden strips running horizontally between the joists, where the roof tiles had been hung. Dreading that someone might hear the noise she was making, she carefully eased one of the tiles loose. Holding it as firmly as she could with her cold fingers, she pulled the tile through the tarred paper and set it down gently beside her. The small rectangular hole revealed nothing but blackness. No stars. No moon. It's cloudy, she told herself. Yet she poked a hand up through the hole, just to make sure. Relief flooded through her. She was almost outside.

One by one, she removed more tiles until she had made a hole wide enough to get her shoulders through. The thin wooden laths were still in place, but they broke easily and she soon had them out of the way. The whole process could have taken five minutes, but Sandra figured that more than half an hour had passed as she strove to minimize the sound she was making.

Gingerly, she poked her head out of the hole and looked around. In the dark, it was hard to make out the lawns and the walls of the Institute, but the street beyond had orange street lamps, and beyond that were other streets and a handful of houses. Her hole in the roof was toward the back of the building. To the front, there were lights around the porch and all along the long gravel drive. Past the drive were the village lights and the lights of the main road. She heard the gentle sighing of the wind through the big elms that dotted the lawns, but nothing else. Nearby, a meter and a half away, the roof ended abruptly, and she could just make out the edge of a black iron gutter. She was about nine meters above the ground and a brief vertiginous awareness of all that empty space beyond the gutter made her catch her breath. Come on, girl, she told herself. Let's get this over with.

She took out the coil of string and tied one end to the handles of the plastic bags with a slipknot and the other to the wire hook. The bags slid along the roof as she fed out the string. They hung down close to the gutter. White and glistening, the bags would be obvious to anyone who happened to be outside. She suffered a moment of profound self-doubt. She should have made sure her bags were a dark colour. Or she should have used cloth bags that weren't reflective. If she could make such a stupid mistake, what other mistakes did her plan have?

But it was too late. There was no turning back now. Besides, she had to go tonight. She couldn't just sit there at the Institute while the world went to pieces. The very idea of being trapped in the psych ward spurred her into motion.

She writhed up through the hole, carefully avoiding the slates around the edges, any of which could loosen and slide away, clattering down the roof, bouncing off the gutter with a clang and sailing into the air to crash to earth like a bomb. She took a deep breath, steadying herself. Stepping out onto the roof was the most difficult part of her plan. She had spent hours in the gym working on her flexibility and strength, studying tai chi chuan until she could move like a hunting cat, with slow precision and unwavering balance. Even so—despite the icy wind—she was sweating by the time she had extracted her legs and was crouching safely on the roof.

She moved silently down to the gutter. Peering over the ledge, she gave a silent prayer of thanks when she spied the fire escape, just three meters below. Exactly where it should be.

For the first time that night, she felt a curl of excitement. She was out. Soon she would be down on the ground. There would be a nerve-racking run from the back of the building to the wall but, once there, it would be an easy climb to reach the street and freedom.

Pulling on the slipknot to release her bags, she flattened herself along the gutter and swung a leg out. Slowly, carefully, she edged her body over the side. Gripping the cold, slimy gutter with half-numb fingers, she lowered herself toward the top of the fire escape, dropping the last half meter to a near-silent landing on the metal floor.

# Chapter 8

## The TCU

Klaatu walked from the plane into a cold and miserable night. Even so, he was glad to be off the aircraft that had brought him in from London. He hated flying. The big Airbus Electroprop 320 whined and rumbled over the wet concrete as though it was keen to get back into the air, while Klaatu and his fellow passengers queued to board the coaches that would take them to the terminal building of Berlin-Brandenburg International Airport.

It had been a wasted trip. Those idiots in London hadn't a clue how to run a timesplash, especially one of the magnitude they wanted. Yes, he could have helped them, but why should he?

He had plans of his own, right here in Berlin.

London's lead brick—a tall, handsome Brit called Flash—had taken him aside when the negotiations were clearly getting nowhere.

"So why did you even bother to come over here then, man?" Flash challenged him, smiling.

"You invited me."

"Why aye, to talk about you setting us up for a big 'un. But you don't seem all that interested."

"What's that accent of yours?"

"What, have you never heard a Geordie before? And what's yours then? Czechoslovakian, I'd guess."

"I don't think your team's ready."

"Aye, and that's why we need you, man. My tekniks can't get their heads round the new gigarange formulas. They'll screw it up. But you … Well, you're the best, right? And I've told you already, money is no object. We're well connected."

Klaatu had looked the big Brit in the eye and said flatly, "None of your team is good enough. You won't make it."

At that the Geordie's smile switched off and Klaatu had gone back to Berlin. Even at ten o'clock at night, the airport was crowded, with hundreds of people swarming the check-ins and milling aimlessly in the concourse. Klaatu had only hand luggage so he marched straight past the luggage carousels and out into the main concourse. A driver he recognized took his bags without a word, and they walked out together into the cold November air. A large black limo was waiting. Klaatu quickly got into the back while the driver stowed his luggage.

"Good flight?" asked Sniper, grinning maliciously.

"Wonderful."

"Drink?" Sniper was sprawled across the back seat with a large whiskey in his hand.

Klaatu ignored the question. He didn't drink. Most of Sniper's politeness was intended to irritate, and Klaatu had long since learned to let it run off him without effect.

"The London gig's going nowhere," he told Sniper. Small talk, for whatever purpose, was not something Klaatu indulged in. "Their main guy's a dick. Their tekniks don't know their arses from their elbows."

"So you weren't tempted to stay over there?"

Klaatu eyed him carefully. "What do you think?"

Sniper's tone was breezy and light. "I like London. It's so decadent. Berlin is so prissy these days. Maybe we should go and show them how it's done?"

Klaatu fought down his irritation and stifled the angry response that sprang to his lips. Ommen had changed everything. Until then, timesplashing had been on the fringes of legality, against the law in most places but not as rigorously suppressed as it was now. Bricks were considered glamorous cult heroes then. Now they were seen as dangerous criminals. The whole splashparty scene had died out and the money from gigs and drug sales had dried up. Sniper cursed the kids that had once idolized him, calling them cowards and traitors. It had made him bitter and moody. Dangerously so. But why would kids go to a splashparty when there was a good chance they could be arrested? What would be so attractive about an event when people could be killed in the backwash?

It was that damned exponent in the displacement function, Klaatu thought. The farther back you went, the bigger the anomaly and the bigger the backwash. The past righted itself. Nothing could change that. However hard the splash hit the timestream, it would flow back and set itself right eventually. It was just the backwash—the disturbed timeflow hitting the present—that caused permanent damage. And that was where the problems from the exponential effect of going back farther came into play. Go back thirty, forty, even fifty years and you were okay. The backwash was trippy but not deadly. But go back sixty or more years—as they'd demonstrated at Ommen—and the backwash could destroy buildings and kill people.

And now there were the new gigarange formulae, brilliant

work that had extended the length of a lob indefinitely—as long as you had the huge energies required to create the displacement field. Now every brick wanted to go back a hundred years, break the record set at Ommen that night, push Sniper and Klaatu off the pedestal they'd been on for two years now. But a gigarange splash was a guaranteed nightmare when the backwash hit. Klaatu's own calculations predicted exactly what the world had witnessed in Beijing. If he and Sniper were going to pull this off in Berlin, it would require meticulous planning and a lot of money.

"Fucking Chinese!" Sniper's thoughts had obviously been similar to Klaatu's.

"No one survived," Klaatu pointed out.

Sniper's eyes narrowed. "Yeah, but that Korean bastard was the first to do it! His fucking teknik got him there, didn't she? While you're still pissing about doing your sums."

Klaatu didn't rise to the bait. He was well used to Sniper's tantrums. In the end, Sniper trusted him. In the end, they both knew they'd pull it off, while other teams rushed at it and got themselves killed.

"Kuem Dong-Min was a good brick," Klaatu said, remembering the young man's quick smile and intelligent eyes. They'd met him about a year ago in Singapore just after the gigarange formulae had first hit the net. Dong-Min's tag had been Jimmy—after James Dean. His uberteknik was a Chinese girl, Wu Yanmei, who was even younger than Klaatu, but who had a mind that had thrilled him more than her pert, young body. Klaatu had fantasized about Yanmei ever since that meeting. He had believed that she might be the only woman on Earth who would understand the loneliness that went with such an intellect as his. But she too had died in Beijing.

"I wish people would shut up about fucking Beijing," Sniper said.

Klaatu could only sympathize with that statement. Every vidlog, every netsheet, every conversation in every bar was about Beijing. It had shocked the world far, far more than Ommen had, and now every cop on the planet would be hunting any brick who stood even a remote chance of doing the same to another major capital. He and Sniper had probably been bumped up to public enemies one and two by now. Beijing had made the world a very dangerous place for both of them.

"You want to give up on Berlin?" Klaatu asked. "Go dark for a while? Let things settle down?"

Sniper frowned. Obviously the idea had occurred to him. Obviously he didn't like it. "And let some creep like Flash do London first?"

"So we're still on?"

"Of course we are. You think I'm scared of the cops?" He brightened suddenly, grinning like a shark. "They got our shipment of F2s at Dover."

Klaatu smiled too. "They must think they are such clever little policemen. And the real shipment?"

"Delivered right on time. It's in the warehouse at Neukölln-Südring. Twenty top-of-the-range reactors. Four hundred megawatts of mayhem just waiting to be unleashed!"

Klaatu's smile widened. "There, you see? It is all coming together. You are going to blow this town off the map, my friend! Be sure to say hello to Herr Hitler for me when you get to 1936."

\* \* \* \*

Jay looked again at his watch. He had had too much to drink, he was bored, and he wasn't at all sure what part of town he was in or how to get back to his new lodgings. Ben, his new best friend, was missing in action, having disappeared onto the dance floor with a beautiful young woman fifteen minutes ago. All in all, it looked like it was time to be on his way.

It wasn't as if he really knew the bloke. Ben—a young man of about Jay's age and build—had been there in the office when Jay arrived yesterday. In a manic display of extraversion, Ben had embraced Jay as though he'd found a long-lost brother. Then he'd led Jay around the building, and introduced him to people who seemed confused by the honour, and showed him where to find essential services.

Eventually, Jay had stopped him and said, "Look, I don't mean to be funny, but who are you?"

Taken aback, the young man had declared, "I am Benedicto María Alejandro García de la Peña y del Bosque. We are in the same unit. I will be your friend and guide." He winked. "You can call me Ben. It makes it easier for you, eh?"

Jay was still confused. "This is a new unit, right? They just formed it like last week, yeah?"

"Sí!" Ben seemed pleased that Jay knew so much. "I arrived yesterday from the Servicio de Información de la Guardia Civil."

Jay blinked in astonishment, not only because this seriously over-friendly nuisance was part of Spain's national intelligence service, but also because he'd let himself be so easily swept along.

"You only got here yesterday?" he had demanded, his temper rising.

"Oh, don't worry," Ben said airily. "You'll soon learn the ropes. You won't feel like the new boy forever. Not with me to help you."

And now Jay was out on the town with him. Definitely time to go. But Ben miraculously appeared out of the crowd just in time to forestall Jay's departure.

"Hey, Jay-Kay!" Ben shouted. Another annoying trait. He grinned and leaned in to speak privately. Even so, he had to raise his voice above the dance music.

"I'm sorry I was so long, man," Ben yelled. Their brief acquaintance made the apology sound less than sincere. "Some *chicas* like to play hard to get. You know? But this…" He held up a hand so Jay could see the netID written on his palm. "This will be worth the effort. Eh?"

Jay didn't doubt it. "Look, Ben, I've got to go find my digs and get some sleep. The boss is in tomorrow and I don't want to get off on the wrong foot."

Ben waved a hand. "Ah, you worry too much. I, Benedicto María Alejandro García de la Peña y del Bosque, will look after you. Are you not my friend? Shall we not stand together against the forces of evil, shoulder to shoulder, protecting the weak and needy?"

Jay sighed. He was beginning to see why the Guardia Civil had wanted Ben out of the country. Ben had also had too much to drink. But, unlike Jay, the young Spaniard seemed to be enjoying the sensation. It was time for Jay to act decisively.

"Ben, my new and enigmatic friend," he said. It irritated him that the crazy guy's speech patterns seemed to be rubbing off on him. He made an effort to sound normal. "I've gotta go, mate. Good night and good luck with the … *señorita*."

Ben protested in grandiose terms, emphasizing his arguments with a great deal of arm waving, but Jay turned toward the exit and made his way carefully through the dancing throng. Unfortunately, Ben was determined to follow Jay, and kept up a continuous stream of persuasion in his wake.

Growing annoyed, Jay turned on him to tell him to shut up and bugger off, but Ben was just one pace behind and accidentally walked straight into him, knocking Jay backward into a dancing couple. The couple, both men as it happened, went sprawling into others and, by the time they had been pushed and shoved and sworn at a few times, the larger of them rounded on Jay—who had just begun to stutter out a profuse apology—and pushed him in the chest so hard he went flying into Ben, who barely managed to keep them both on their feet.

"Hey, it was an accident," Jay complained, untangling himself and glaring at the big dancer.

The dancer squared off against Jay, shouting insults at him in a language that could have been Walloon for all Jay knew. All around them, the other dancers moved back, giving them space, Jay noticed with annoyance. What did they think was going to happen? Jay wasn't going to fight a stranger in a club. Besides, he thought, the big guy was about twice his size and looked like he might be made of rock.

He was about to make some kind of pacifying gesture and back off when Ben came to stand in front of him, putting his hands on Jay's chest as if trying to hold him back.

"Now, now, my friend," the Spaniard said. "You must not lose your temper. You must…"

And in a move so fast Jay could barely follow it, Ben spun around and whacked the big guy in the jaw with a beautiful roundhouse punch. There was a moment of stunned silence as everyone watched the guy pirouette and fall to the ground. Even as his victim toppled, Ben turned to Jay with a happy grin. Over Ben's shoulder, Jay saw the big guy's dancing partner launch himself at Ben's back.

Then everything erupted into shouting and movement—mostly directed at Ben, whose attack on the big guy was clearly not popular with the locals. Jay reached for his badge. Time to assert his authority and calm the situation. But his badge wasn't there. It was in his jacket, which he had left at the bar.

As Ben went down under the weight of several angry Belgians, Jay cursed the crazy Spaniard, and dived into the fray to save him.

\* \* \* \*

Marie Vermeulen met Acting Superintendent Jacques Bauchet in the cavernous foyer and led him up in the lift. She noticed him eyeing her discreetly as they went up. A woman of about his age, she prided herself on having a good figure and dressing well. She made a point of holding herself with a certain poise which she believed men admired. Her face was attractive, with prominent cheekbones and large dark eyes. She was fairly sure her new boss would like what he saw. When she reached out to press the button for their floor, he snuck a quick look at her left hand, no doubt looking for a wedding ring. She smiled to herself. Men were so obvious, even when they tried to be discreet.

She was less guarded in her inspection of Bauchet. She looked him over quite blatantly in the lift. A tall, angular man in his mid-forties, he was not especially handsome yet had a striking look: broad brows and a beaked nose, deep-set eyes, and thin, ascetic lips. His hands were large and bony. Despite the severity of his looks, the smile he gave her when he saw her studying him revealed something warm and gentle within. She smiled back, partly in relief.

When Marie showed him his office, she watched as he put both hands on his desk and leaned heavily on it. It was eight-thirty in the morning and he had come straight from the airport. Since the announcement of his new assignment—and temporary promotion—he'd been to over two dozen meetings. His sleep had been limited to whatever he could snatch on flights and train journeys between European capitals. She knew how tired he was because, as his new PA, she had arranged his schedule. At last he had reached his office and could get to work, yet he looked as if he might not stay awake long enough.

When Bauchet asked about his colleague, Sergeant Colbert, she told him he was attending a meeting elsewhere. Then, with her usual rapid efficiency, she brought him coffee, produced the personnel files for his senior staff, explained building security, gave him the keys to a nearby apartment and to the car waiting for him in the garage below. She also showed him how to access the unit's file system and comms and informed him that Chief Superintendent Kohl would like to see him for lunch.

"Is that all?" he asked. He sounded so weary that her heart went out to him.

"You've had enough, Superintendent?"

"My head is reeling," he said. "You'll probably have to tell me everything again, I'm afraid. But some other time."

"That won't be a problem, sir."

She felt a sudden urge to flirt with him, to say something teasing or suggestive, but she clamped down on it immediately, shocked at her impulse. Unprofessional conduct had never been one of her vices.

Marie saw Bauchet frown, as though a blind had come down over what had previously been an open and friendly expression. She puzzled over his change in demeanour. Had he read something from her own expression? She must be more careful.

"There's just one more thing that I do need to bring up, sir. A staff discipline matter."

"What? Already?" He looked down at the half-drunk coffee on his desk. She could almost hear him thinking aloud: not one cup of coffee into the first day and already there was trouble with the staff!

"The local police arrested two of the new recruits last night in a club in town. It seems there was a—"

A roar of laughter from the big open-plan area beyond the office door interrupted her report. Bauchet glanced inquiringly at her and she shrugged. A man's voice could be heard, apparently telling a story.

"Detective Inspector Moretti dealt with the Brussels police and the two young men in question have been released. DI Moretti thought you might like to have a word—" Marie started.

Another outbreak of laughter interrupted her again. This time, Bauchet rose from behind his desk and went out through the door. Marie followed close behind.

"Set up a meeting for me, would you, Marie," he said pleasantly as they crossed the room. "Everyone on my team, from Detective Sergeant upwards, in about half an hour."

A small crowd of people, mostly young, mostly male, were gathered around a good-looking olive-skinned young man who was grinning and talking animatedly.

"And then, what do you think?" the man asked his cheerful listeners with a strong Spanish accent. He had a bruised face and a bandage around his right hand. "My saviour, the great hero Jay Kennedy, finds he has left his badge in his jacket at the bar!" He threw up his hands in an exaggerated gesture of incredulity and his audience laughed. A second young man—with a cut above one eye and a swollen ear—began protesting, but this only caused more laughter.

Bauchet stepped up to the group looking stern. "What's going on here?"

Everyone stopped and stared at him with a mixture of curiosity, wariness, and then alarm as they noticed Marie standing next to him.

"Allow me to introduce myself," Bauchet said in measured tones, his hawk-like gaze moving from one person to the next in the little gathering. "I am Superintendent Jacques Bauchet, lately of the Paris Préfecture de Police, and, as of two days ago, head of the Temporal Crimes Unit of Europol."

Marie could see people edging away from the Spanish speaker and his embarrassed companion.

"Perhaps you would do me the favour of returning to your desks and continuing with whatever work you have? I will be talking to everyone quite soon."

People hurriedly removed themselves from his vicinity.

"Not you two," Bauchet said quietly, fixing his gaze upon the perplexed Ben and the white-faced Jay. "It is these two, is it not?" he asked Marie over his shoulder.

She nodded, watching the young men with disappointed eyes.

"Very well. In my office, right now."

He turned away and they followed him. Jay looked daggers at his new-found friend while Ben acted as if he were being unjustly accused.

Marie closed the outer door and went to her desk in the adjoining office. She could see them through the glass walls and clearly hear everything that was said.

"All right," Bauchet said. "Names."

They gave him their names, Ben reciting his with his usual flourish.

"Well, Constables Kennedy and de la Peña," Bauchet began, sitting down in his leather chair. Marie was impressed that he could remember even part of Ben's name after a single hearing.

"Let me tell you what the worst part of this new assignment is for me," Bauchet said, leaving the two young men standing.

"I can explain," said Jay.

"Shut up!" The anger in Bauchet's eyes silenced Jay immediately.

Marie looked across at her new boss with keen interest.

"You see, I have been pushing for the creation and funding of a team like this ever since Ommen. Two years, tracking down bricks and all the lowlifes that surround them, two years, learning every day a little more about what might happen if their activities are left unchecked. I'd hoped for a strong international force, focused on the problem. I'd hoped my team would be in place in time to stop catastrophes like Beijing. But, in the end, it took Beijing to wake people up.

"So, finally, I got my team and I got my funding and that is good. But what I also got," he growled angrily, "was every intelligence agency in Europe wanting to have one of their own people attached to my team so they could have someone on the inside. People like you, *messieurs*." He glared at Ben. "You're Spanish, yes?"

"Yes, sir."

"Servicio de Información?"

"Yes, sir."

He swivelled his aquiline nose toward Jay. "And you?"

"Five, sir."

Bauchet nodded to himself. "I don't care about what kind of stupid, juvenile scrape you two got yourselves into last night. But I'll tell you this. Beijing could have been Madrid. It could have been London. And it will be if we don't do our jobs well. People will die. Tens of thousands of people.

"You might think this is some cushy little assignment. A trip abroad with occasional reports to your home agencies about how we're doing."

Jay blushed and Marie guessed that someone had asked him to deliver just such reports. A flash of Bauchet's eyes revealed that he too had seen Jay blush.

"This is not a game!" Bauchet's voice was suddenly hard as iron. "This is not a vacation. This is the most important assignment either of you will have in your entire careers. We are fighting an enemy with the capacity to bring down our entire civilization. So you will take this assignment seriously and stop acting like stupid children, or by God you will be on the next plane back to wherever you came from with my recommendation for a dishonourable discharge on your record. Is that clear?"

Jay seemed to be struck dumb as he attempted a response. Ben's "yes, sir" was just as feeble.

"Is. That. Clear?" Bauchet almost shouted.

"Yes, sir!" they both snapped in unison, standing attention as if they were back on parade at the academy.

Bauchet regarded them steadily for several seconds. "Get out," he said at last, turning his back on them.

For a long time, Marie watched as Bauchet stared through

his window at the high-rises and motorways of Brussels. She was beginning to understand the kind of man she was now working for.

# Chapter 9

## Hide and Seek

"Good afternoon, Mr. Sniper, sir." The man in the white three-piece business suit spoke with an American accent. He was short and round and looked cold.

"It's just Sniper, okay?" Sniper was wearing a floor-length, fur-lined leather coat, fur-lined boots and a fur fedora. The morning's ice still lingered in the shadows, and the American stood out in his scant clothing. "You must be McGarry," Sniper said. "Nice suit."

They had arranged to meet in the Gendarmenmarkt, a large public square big enough to have two cathedrals and popular enough, even in late November, to be full of people. Even Europe's most wanted man could feel anonymous in a place like that, or so Sniper had thought. But he hadn't expected his guest to turn up dressed like Colonel Sanders.

"I seem to have dressed for the wrong season," the American said. "It's a little bit warmer back home in Louisiana, I gotta say."

"At least everyone will be looking at you and not at me."

McGarry smiled, weakly. "Maybe we could find a coffee house or some place out of the wind?"

Sniper regarded him with contempt. "We're not courting, McGarry. This is not our first date. I don't want to know your favourite band and what posters you have on your bedroom walls. Let's just get our business done and say goodbye."

McGarry's face lost its smile and became a blank mask. "Sure. Let's do business. I have the target details in my briefcase. In return, my associates need proof of progress."

"Just who are your mysterious associates, McGarry?"

"You know I can't tell you that. It's all part of our agreement. We supply the money. We pick the target. You get to do your timesplashing thing."

Sniper looked away, habitually scanning the crowded square for police. "Yeah, yeah. Whatever. So leave your case and fuck off, eh?"

McGarry's voice grew a little firmer. "We need that proof of progress first, Sniper."

Sniper thought briefly of taking the case anyway and telling McGarry and his bosses to get stuffed. He had a quick mental image of that bright white suit splattered with the fat man's blood. But he quickly thought better of it. He needed the money to keep flowing. And why should he care who he had to deal with to get it?

"How do I know you're not a cop?" he asked, more out of mischief than any real concern. Klaatu had vetted all their communications. Nobody slipped anything past that boy.

"I figure you're gonna have to trust me on that one, son."

Sniper's head whipped around to face McGarry. The man's accent yanked up a memory Sniper had buried long ago. For a moment he felt the heavy shotgun in his hands, felt the power of his own muscles surging, the sound of the stock hitting flesh and bone, the jarring in his wrists as he saw Hal's head snap back. Was there a connection here? Was somebody telling him they knew? Could this ridiculous little man be a warning? A threat?

"What?" the American asked, unnerved by Sniper's wide-eyed stare. "What'd I say?"

Paranoia. That's all it was, he told himself. He'd been on the run too long. Hal hadn't been from Louisiana, had he? Somewhere else. He couldn't remember now. He saw McGarry's eyes flick nervously down to his hands and he realized he had reached into his coat pocket without thinking about it. Already his fingers were curling around the stock of his Chinese-made QSZ-99, all-polymer, 9mm handgun. Deliberately, he pulled his hand out of his pocket and let it fall at his side.

"You want proof of progress?" he asked.

McGarry said nothing, just swallowed hard and licked his lips. Sniper gave him the address of the warehouse in Neukölln-Südring. "Be there at eight," Sniper told him and walked quickly away into the crowd.

\* \* \* \*

"Hey, I know you!"

The club shook to the music. It was dimly lit except where the lights pulsed and circled on the dance floor. Sandra danced in sinuous rhythm to the hard beat. An old acquaintance from her pre-Sniper days danced with her.

"You're Patty, right? You used to come in here. Long time ago."

The guy who had just interrupted her dancing by shouting in her face was someone she didn't recognize. She peered at him. He was fair-haired and gangly and smashed out of his head on something.

"Hey, dickhead," her dance partner shouted in the stoned guy's face. "Fuck off."

Taken aback and definitely not keen to argue, the guy backed away and lost himself in the crowd.

"Who was that?" Patty asked. She wasn't in the club for old times' sake—or to dance with this guy all night. She was there to renew her old contacts and gather information.

"Said he knew you."

"Yeah. Everybody knew me. Who was he?"

"A guy called Cooke. Stephen Cooke."

"What was his tag?"

Her partner lowered his voice. "People don't use their tags any more. The cops are always sniffing around now. You never know who to trust."

"Yeah, but what was it?"

"I dunno, Zorro or something. Zaphod, that was it."

"So you're right out of that scene now."

"Damn right! It's a mug's lark. Anyway, what's the point now? The bricks are more like terrorists these days. Not my idea of fun. Back then they used to be cool, you know?"

"Yeah, I know. Look, I'm going to go and sit down for a while."

"Yeah, I could do with a break myself."

She put a hand on his chest to stop him from following her. "I'll be all right. I'll see you later, okay?"

He watched her go with a puzzled frown.

As soon as she was out of sight, Sandra changed direction and headed for where she'd seen Zaphod go. After several minutes, she finally located the gangly youth sitting beside a girl and shouting sweet nothings in her tattooed ear.

"There you are, Stevie," she gushed, rushing up to him and kissing him on the cheek. He turned a blurry expression of surprise her way that quickly reverted to his sloppy grin when he realized who it was. But Sandra had already turned her attention to the equally surprised girl next to him. "And who are you?" she demanded, hands on hips.

The girl gave them both a look then got up and stalked off without a backward glance.

"Let's go somewhere where we can talk," Sandra said. She had to tug at him quite hard to get him to his feet, but he eventually got the message.

She led him out of the club and into the quiet streets. He kept up a constant stream of chatter to which she contributed the occasional nod until they were well clear of anyone who might see or hear them.

"Don't you miss the old days?" she asked as they settled into a deeply shadowed doorway. He was fumbling at her clothes and trying to kiss her in a clumsy, ineffectual way. She pulled him close, partly to make him feel he was getting somewhere, partly because she was freezing cold in her skimpy dance gear. "Are you still in touch with any of the old gang?"

"Oh yeah," he mumbled. "See 'em all the time."

"You mean, like, Buzz and Snoopy?" Buzz was the nearest thing to a hard-core brick she had known back then, and Snoopy had been his best friend.

"Snoopy's around. Dunno about Buzz. God, you're so beautiful. I always liked you, you know?"

"I always liked you too, Zaphod. Where does Snoopy hang out these days?"

He was slobbering on her neck and had a hand inside her short skirt. If he didn't give her something useful in a minute, she told herself, she'd have to do something to cool him off.

"Remember the old Night Creatures Club?"

"Yes! Is that where he is?"

"Nah," he said, taking a firm hold of her left breast. "Pulled it down. You know, I feel like we really connect. Y'know what I mean?"

She felt like thumping the spaced-out moron, but instead she nibbled his earlobe. "So where's Snoopy then, if they pulled down the club?"

"Oh, that's nice," he breathed.

"Wonderful," she agreed through gritted teeth. "What about Snoopy though?"

"Built a new club in the same place. Snobby sort of place. That's where he goes now."

She wriggled free of him and pushed him back against the door. "Sweetie, I've just got to go for a pee. Okay? I'll be right back."

He looked at her as if she were speaking Icelandic, the combination of strong drugs and lust having left him more than usually out of it.

"You wait here for me, all right? I'll be back in a few minutes. Don't go away now."

He managed a grin. "No worries. I'll be right here."

"Sorry about this," she said and ran off. She picked up her coat and bag from the club where she'd stashed them and rushed straight out to the main road to hail a cab. One more step up the food chain, she told herself. One step closer. Being out here, among people who knew her, was scary and dangerous, not because the cops might find her—she wasn't too worried about that—but because Sniper might. Every night her old boyfriend hunted her in her nightmares. Every night the ground sucked her down, buildings fell and rose again, oscillating on the edge of destruction, and Sniper, his cold grey eyes fixed upon her, struck people down as he made his way toward her. She had no doubt he was hunting her outside of her dreams, too. Now that he could make a backwash that could level a city, she would never be safe from him. He would find her and turn her world into a bedlam of chaos. She would be caught again in the madness of causal anomalies and temporal switchbacks and this time it would destroy her.

She couldn't face it. She couldn't live with the knowledge that Sniper was out there, plotting to rain destruction down on her—down on everyone. So there was only one thing she could do. Only one way to save herself from this gnawing, terrible fear. She had to find Sniper and kill him.

* * * *

"Next," said Jay, wearily.

The display flicked up yet another rap sheet. Some minor teknik who had been arrested for shoplifting in Norway. All morning Jay had been working through intelligence files, setting his filters broader and broader so that by now they were displaying just about anything from anywhere in Europe that was even remotely connected with timesplashing. In the absence of anything real to do, this was the best he could think of.

"Next." Another news item flashed up. This one was about a researcher at CERN who thought he might have a way of detecting a lob by triangulating its effects on nearby comm nodes.

"Next."

"Busy?" Ben appeared at his elbow.

"What do you want?" Jay asked, annoyed. Ben was not his favourite person at the moment.

"I just thought I'd say hello. I see you're keeping yourself occupied by checking out the babes online."

Jay turned back to see what Ben was going on about and did a double take. On the display, there was a headshot of an incredibly beautiful girl. He stared hard, not just because she was gorgeous but because he had a feeling he knew her. His first thought was maybe she was a vid star and he'd seen her in something. He scanned the text. Apparently he was looking at a wanted poster for someone called Sandra Malone, an escapee from a mental institution in the UK.

"You stand a chance with her, my friend," Ben said, grinning. "She is nuts, after all."

Jay rounded on him. "Did you come here just to annoy me or are you warming up for a bear baiting?"

Ben obviously didn't get the reference but was happy to let it pass. "I came to invite you to join me and some of the others for a drink after work tonight."

Jay shook his head in disbelief. "You think I'd go anywhere with you after what happened last time?"

"You make no sense, my friend. You were in trouble and I rescued you. How can you blame me for that?"

"Look, I don't want to talk to you about it. In fact, I don't want to talk to you about anything. So, can I get back to my work?"

Ben shrugged, clearly irritated. "Sure. Be like that." He took a last look at the picture of Sandra Malone and walked off to join a couple of others, calling out to them as he went, "It's no good, he is still sulking."

Gritting his teeth, Jay returned to his display. It struck him again how beautiful the girl was, but this time he saw something more in her face. There was a tension there, a hint of pleading. Her eyes had a haunted look and her slightly parted lips suggested fear. He scanned the report again, more carefully, looking for some clue as to why the filters had selected this item. Could it have been a random false positive?

He was about to request more information when a call came through on his compatch.

"That you, Jay?" the voice at the other end asked. He recognized Holbrook immediately. The "secure channel" indicator was on, Jay noticed.

"Yes, sir." He unconsciously sat up a little straighter in his chair.

"Keeping you busy, are they?"

"Well…"

After all the officers had been closeted with Bauchet for a couple of hours yesterday, the work had started picking up. Yet there still didn't seem to be enough to go around. The team was still growing, with new people arriving every morning, and there was a general feeling of preparation and getting organized. The real work hadn't begun yet.

"Thought so," Holbrook said. It was his way of saying the chitchat was over and they should get down to business. "We've been following up on those trucks we found the other day. We drove them on to their destination, you know. There was nobody there to receive them except a very confused shoe factory owner who thought he was getting a shipment of leather hides. Seems the whole thing was a distraction."

"But…"

"Aye, they were real F2s all right. Worth millions. These people have obviously got more money than God.

"So we traced them back along their route, then lost them in a cloud of obfuscation and misinformation along the way. Fact is, we have only one good lead. A chap in Poland—currently helping the local police with their enquiries—who may have been one of the early middlemen. Not much of a lead I'm afraid, but I thought you might like to follow it up from your end. I'm sending the files across as we speak."

"Thank you, sir." Jay checked his display as it tracked the receipt of the data. "Got it."

"Good. Nice to talk to you again, Jay."

"You too, sir, but can I just ask…"

"Yes?"

"Why are you passing this to me, sir? Why not have your own people do it, or go through channels?"

"No mystery there, lad. I thought it might be a good idea to make sure you're front and centre in your new team and that you don't get overlooked. We'd all like it best if you were in the thick of things, if you know what I mean. In with the in crowd, so to speak."

"Yes, sir. I see." And he did. All too well. "I'll try not to waste the opportunity, sir."

"Best not. Cheerio. And let me know how you go with this Polish thing."

They hung up and Jay stared into space for a long while, mulling over the conversation. With a sigh, he turned back to his display. "Whoever you are," he told the troubled girl on the screen, "I can't stay to chat." He saved her details and pulled up the new files that Holbrook had sent.

Jay read through the Polish Internal Security Agency reports and the transcripts of several interviews they had put their detainee through. The last was time-stamped just a few hours ago. The interviews, however, seemed to contain very little hard information. The man they had caught was a small-time crook called Janusz. Janusz claimed that he'd been contacted by a man who spoke Polish and who asked him to deliver some hardware, no questions asked. The two men agreed on how the shipment would be handled and on a sum, and that was about it. Janusz didn't actually handle the shipment himself, but used a subcontractor. He did not know his customer except by the name Kapitan Kloss—the name of a Polish comic-book hero, Jay discovered.

Janusz had met Kapitan Kloss just once, at Warsaw's Frederic Chopin Airport, Terminal 2, since Janusz had insisted on being paid in cash. Kloss handed over the money at a bar in the airport. Kloss was already there when Janusz arrived. Janusz described him as "ordinary" and "a bit weedy". The men exchanged very few words during their meeting. Janusz showed Kloss the travel documents for the shipment, took the bag with the money, and left. He never saw or heard from the Kapitan again.

Jay ran the Polish documents through a second translator, to check the accuracy of the unit's default software, but the result came up almost identical to the first. For a while, he stared at the Polish Ministry of Internal Affairs and Administration logo on the coversheet, his mind blank. There didn't seem to be any useful information in the interviews or from the police investigation that could take the trail any farther.

A curl of anxiety turned in his stomach. After just a few days in his new job, he had already let down his new boss and now he was about to let down his old boss too. He got up and walked about, too agitated to sit still. He was surprised to see that the rest of his shift had left the building already and that the night shift had moved in. He supposed his shift would all be at the bar by now, with Ben acting as the life and soul of the party as usual. Maybe they were all talking about the English kid with the attitude problem and having a good laugh.

Jay was angry with himself for caring so much what people might think of him. In frustration, he kicked a nearby chair. Heads popped up and turned to look at him all over the big office. He lifted his hands in a gesture of apology and went back to pacing about the room. At one end, near the senior officers' glass-walled offices, was a floor-to-ceiling display with a network of mug shots all over it. The wall featured all the major European bricks who were still at large, their known associates and their tekniks. Photos of a number of key players from other parts of the world were also included—alive or dead. Each mug shot was the centre of a radiating set of labelled links to other mug shots. A software algorithm adjusted the lengths of the links to show the closeness of the association between each person. What emerged were tight clusters, mostly centred on the bricks. By pointing at the faces, it was possible to drag them around the display with their network of linked faces trailing after them. Other gestures enlarged the pictures or added textual detail.

Jay stopped pacing to study the display. There were mug shots of the bricks he knew from his work with Five: Flash, Sting, The Doctor, Daneel and the rest. There was a lot of detail on the French bricks, brought over with Bauchet's team: Asterix, Tin Tin, a dozen others. There were quite a few Asians—including Jimmy and his team, all dead now.

He was about to move on when the photo of Sniper caught his eye. Immediately the memories came back. Once again, he was looking at his friend's dead body among the wreckage of the Ommen intensive care unit.

He dragged Sniper's image close and expanded it. This was what he needed, a reminder of why he was here, a fresh dose of motivation. It was still an open wound. It galled him all the more that Bauchet thought he was a dilettante, had accused him of not being serious about the team. He should go and tell the Superintendent, make it clear to the man that—

Jay froze as an image leapt out from the rest. He expanded the picture of Klaatu, Sniper's uberteknik. The details he had just read in the transcript from Poland could have been written to describe Klaatu's mug shot. "A bit weedy." He studied the thin face, the mousy hair. "About one-point-seven meters," Janusz had said when pressed. "Greasy hair."

He dredged up Klaatu's data file. Not much was known, but Klaatu's physical description matched. And there! Real name: Gomółka, Dobry. Date of birth: 2039. Country of origin: Poland. Jay gasped as the realization hit him. He'd made the connection! It was Klaatu. It had to be. Which meant Sniper was the one sending false shipments of F2s all over Europe. Sniper! One of the biggest names in the game two years ago and now considered to be one of the bricks most likely to attempt a gigarange timesplash.

He wanted to rush to Bauchet's office and shout out his discovery, but Bauchet was not in the building. Anyway, he knew better than that. He needed to get everything down in a report, marshal his facts, make the connection as solid as he could. Then the proper thing to do would be to take his report to Detective Inspector Ostenstad, his immediate boss. Let him pass it up the line to Bauchet. He needed to show some professionalism here or his reputation would be completely trashed. He walked around for a moment then went back to his desk. He was so excited by what he'd found that he could hardly bring himself to sit down and start putting a report together. When at last he did, he almost jumped out of his seat again. They were both Poles, so why meet at the airport? Did it mean that Klaatu flew in from somewhere to meet Janusz? If it did, then knowing the time of the meeting might tell him what flight Klaatu had been on. Supposedly, Klaatu had already been there when Janusz arrived and was still there when he left. If Klaatu had suggested the meeting time, did he choose it to be just after his flight arrived or just before his flight departed?

Jay was pretty sure it would be the latter. Less chance of a cock-up. More chance for Klaatu to check out the venue before the meeting. Less time after the meeting to spend hanging around, in case he needed to get away for the return flight. Jay paused to reconsider but then shook his head. Klaatu definitely would have been on a round trip. His point of origin and destination would be wherever Sniper was. And Sniper was not the sort to hide out in a place like Poland with the rest of the world to choose from.

Jay burrowed into the documents again. The meeting was at ten in the morning, but it didn't say who picked the time. He looked up the netID and placed a call to the Internal Security Agency office in Warsaw. It took him half an hour, but he eventually spoke to someone there who could put the question to Janusz. It was another half an hour before the answer came back. Klaatu had picked the meeting place and the time.

During his long wait on hold, Jay had pulled up the scheduled flights into and out of Warsaw Airport on the morning in question, looking for an arrival and departure destination that would put someone in Warsaw well before ten, but leave not long after. Then he'd checked the passenger manifests for all the possible flights, looking for someone who had flown in and out at the right times. And he'd found him. And now he knew where he was.

Berlin.

* * * *

Sandra looked up groggily. For a moment panic clutched at her. Where was she? What was going on? Then she remembered. She was on a train.

The people around her were on their feet, filing down the aisle, hefting bags, struggling into coats and scarves and gloves. The train had stopped. They'd arrived. Outside, more people moved past her window. The antique bricks and steel of Waterloo Station were visible above the crowds. She'd slept all the way to London.

Still feeling dopey, she got to her feet, grabbed her stuff from the overhead luggage rack and joined the crowd on the platform. The outside of the train was wet. Looking back along its length to where the platform ended, she could see grey sheets of rain billowing across the snaking rails. She pulled her coat around her and tried to ignore the cold. Reaching the broad concourse, she headed for the underground. A taxi would have been easier but she needed to conserve her money. She took the Bakerloo line to Oxford Circus and emerged—flinching from the driving, icy rain— into a pandemonium of shoppers and traffic. Oxford Street ran straight and gaudy into the rain ahead of her and she set off along it. She needed clothes for tonight. Snoopy had been a pushover last night, though the bouncers had almost not let her into the club when they saw how she was dressed. In the end, their standing orders to admit beautiful girls—and her insistence that they tell Snoopy his old friend Patty was being made to wait outside in the cold—had persuaded them to wave her in.

Snoopy had seemed pleased to see her and didn't try to

paw her and get her into bed as she had imagined he would. His status in the neighbourhood had risen considerably since he'd got out from under Buzz's shadow, and he was now something of a minor gang boss, putting the organizational and destructive skills he'd acquired as a brick to good use. He had treated Sandra with courtesy and respect—which, she gathered, was part of his new image—and was happy to tell her everything he knew about the highly criminalized, post-Ommen underworld of timesplashing.

It was Snoopy's recommendation that she go to London to see a brick calling himself Flash.

"He's the biggest there is, these days," he had said with a trace of nostalgia. "If you're looking to hook up with the top dog, Flash is your man." She hadn't told him why she was so interested in big-name bricks but he could think whatever he liked, as long as he helped her. Besides, the last time he'd seen her, that's exactly the kind of girl she'd been.

Sandra bought the best cocktail dress she could afford and a pair of slingback heels to go with it. She still had enough money for a cheap room and a hairdo, she hoped. But that was it. After today she was broke and had no idea what to do about it. All she knew was that she would walk, swim or crawl if she had to. She would do anything to get to Sniper and kill the evil bastard.

# Chapter 10

## Berlin

It was a tense meeting. The conference room seated ten and it was filled to capacity. At the head of the table sat Bauchet. His right-hand man, Colbert, sat beside him, as did his PA, Marie. There were also two Chief Inspectors, four Detective Inspectors and Acting Detective Constable Jay Kennedy.

Jay was the only one standing. He had just given the room a run-down of his evidence connecting a spurious shipment of F2 generators in Dover with the infamous brick, Sniper, and his uberteknik, Klaatu. He had concluded his briefing with his reasons for believing that the two of them were now based in Berlin.

Bauchet thanked him and then took the floor.

"It is a tenuous thread, is it not, mesdames et messieurs? But I would like to give it a tug and see what is on the other end. It may be nothing at all. It may be that there really is something serious going on, but that the connection to Berlin is an illusion. Or it may be that one of our most important capital cities is about to be destroyed the same way Beijing was.

"I confess, I don't find the evidence as convincing as Detective Kennedy seems to, but I find it convincing enough to think we should look a little closer. Any comments? Any questions?"

The room immediately became a hubbub of both comments and questions—most of them directed at Jay. Playing the role of chairman skilfully, Bauchet controlled the flow of the debate for the next thirty minutes or so, by which time the members were in unanimous agreement with his assessment.

"Very well," he said at last, calling the meeting to order. "I want a team to fly out to Berlin today. Chief Inspector Kappelhoff, I'd like you to put a team together. Have a list of names on my desk in one hour for approval, please. Make sure Detective Kennedy's name is on the list. Liaise directly with the Berlin police and any other authorities you need to. Any issues about jurisdiction, bring them to me. Remember, although Europol's role has traditionally been coordination and liaison, the TCU is different. We may act directly whenever we so choose, and local police and intelligence agencies have been instructed to give us whatever cooperation and support we need."

He looked straight at Jay for the first time since he'd started speaking. "Let's hope you haven't sent us on a wild goose chase, eh?"

\* \* \* \*

"So what's going on?"

Jay looked up to find Ben in the act of perching himself on Jay's desk.

"I haven't got time for a chat," Jay said. He was uploading

data from the main grid into his personal net. "I'm on an assignment and I need to get home and pack right now."

"Assignment, eh? Is that what the big meeting was about earlier on? Where are you going? What's all the excitement about?"

Jay gave up the struggle and stopped trying to ignore the young Spaniard. He turned to face him. "There's a team being put together. We're going to Berlin. It's possible that Sniper and his crew are there plotting a gigarange timesplash."

"Sniper, eh? And you're on this team, then?"

Jay couldn't help doing a bit of bragging. "I was the one who worked it out—while you were at the pub last night." *Having a laugh at my expense*, he thought. "Now, I'm sorry but I really must be—"

"Better get a move on, Kennedy," said Colbert, passing by the desk. "Chief Inspector Kappelhoff is holding a briefing at fifteen hundred. You need to be packed and ready to go by then. You too, Ben."

"Yes, Sarge," they said in unison as the Frenchman walked away. Jay looked at Ben with his mouth open.

Ben gave a little shrug. "I'm packed already. What's taking you so long?"

"You bastard! You knew. And you wangled your way onto the team somehow."

"I don't know this word 'wangled', but if it means my value to the operation was recognized, then I suppose that's what happened."

Jay closed his mouth and set his jaw. What was the matter with this guy? Why was he plaguing him like this? He was about to say something about how Ben had better keep out of his way when Ben cut him short by laughing at him.

"Oh, come on, Jay-Kay. Don't be such an uptight English

prick. It'll be great, you and me on the town in Berlin! We'll have a ball! Where's your sense of adventure? Where's your sense of fun?"

"Fun?" It was all Jay could say. He was practically speechless. "Fun?"

Ben nodded, grinning. "*Sí*. Fun. You know fun? It's what you used to have before they fitted that broom up your arse."

Jay stood up to confront his tormentor. Ben stood up too, backing away a step in mock alarm.

"There's a gang of screwed-up killers in Berlin," Jay said, grinding out his words. "They think it's fun to kill and destroy. They think it's clever. They think the more damage and suffering they cause, the more they'll be admired." He glared at Ben, glad to see the guy's grin was faltering.

"I'm going there to hunt them down and stop them. I'll arrest them if I can and I'll kill them if I have to. I'm not going to Berlin for 'fun'. I'm not going there to pick up chicks and get drunk and brawl in bars. I'm going there to do my job, to put my life on the line, to stop those maniacs before they wreck the whole fucking world. That's why I'm going. I've got something serious to do and I don't want to play with you. So get off my back and find someone else to annoy."

By now, everyone nearby was staring at them. Jay continued to glower at Ben, who was looking angry and confused. To Jay's amazement, he saw hurt in Ben's eyes too. The young Spaniard looked around at the expectant faces staring at him, waiting for his reaction, and then Jay saw him take control of himself. The smile came back to Ben's face, just as big and bright as ever.

"Okay. Be like that, Jay-Kay. It's your loss if you can't enjoy yourself a little now and then."

He turned away with a big "what can you do?" gesture to the room at large. Furiously, Jay grabbed his bag from under the desk and stomped off home to pack.

\* \* \* \*

Sandra waited in the shadows. She had been there watching the club entrance for three hours. She was bitterly cold, so cold she thought she would have to give up soon or she'd be too numb to move or speak. Yet another limo pulled up in front of the club. The driver got out and walked around to the curbside rear door. She watched with desperate hope as one leggy blonde girl and then another slid elegantly from the car's dark interior. She sized them up automatically. Both were beautiful, but neither too beautiful.

A man in a stylish suit came out next and the blondes attached themselves to his arms. He was a tall good-looking man with a vid-star smile and long, wavy hair. He was about the right age—early twenties. That and his arrogant, self-confident bearing revealed to her at once that he was the man she was looking for.

Sandra stepped out of the shadows and began walking toward him. A heavily built bodyguard had emerged from the car. Now he took up a position in front of Flash and his blondes as they walked the short distance to the club entrance. Sandra hurried a little. No one had noticed her yet. By the time the bodyguard's eyes flicked her way, she was too close for him to do anything about it. She stepped directly into Flash's path and everyone had to stop. She looked into Flash's eyes and smiled. He looked back at her with startled blue eyes that showed fear for a moment before switching to irritation mixed with curiosity.

"Hello, Flash," she said. Her dress fitted her beautifully, and she felt a surge of confidence as she saw his eyes slide quickly down her body and back up to her smile. "I'm Patty."

There was only curiosity in his expression now as he recovered his equilibrium. "I don't think I know you," he said cautiously.

She smiled invitingly. "You could if you like."

Now it was his turn to smile. He turned to the blondes. "Why don't you two go on in with Ravi? I'll be along in a moment."

The girls were not happy. One of them scowled openly at Sandra, but they did as they were told and followed the bodyguard in through the doors. Flash and Sandra were alone in the street. The club bouncers watched from the doorway.

"What did you say your name was, love?"

"Patty."

"I'm not short of women, Patty. So what's the deal?"

Sandra had hoped for a rather warmer welcome than this. She could see he liked the look of her, but it wasn't enough. The way bricks were being hunted now had made them all so damned cautious. She needed to find something more alluring than just the promise of sex.

"I'm a friend of Sniper's," she said. "I used to be his bitch."

That got his attention. He studied her more closely. She could almost hear the wheels turning in his pretty blond head.

"You were there on the Ommen splash," he said, slowly. "I remember you from the vidlogs. Did he send you?"

She smiled again. "I'm not his bitch any more."

"Then why…"

She stepped close to him. She was a tall woman but even in her high heels she had to look up into Flash's face. "You know, I'm freezing out here." She opened her coat wide so he could look down past her cleavage to the dress, which was lightly caressing her curves. "I don't have a lot on." In fact, all her muscles were tensed as she struggled to stop shivering.

"Then let's go inside where it's warmer," he said and led her in, the bouncers politely opening the doors for them.

The staff greeted Flash like an old friend, leading him to his own table in a raised area of the floor that seemed to be less crowded and better attended by the smartly uniformed staff. Her coat was discreetly whisked away, and some functionary or other murmured his welcomes and wishes for the enjoyment of her stay as she and Flash crossed the room. Sandra had expected nothing less. She had been used to this kind of treatment when she was with Sniper. She was more interested in the warmth of the room and the relief that flooded her as her shivering slowly subsided. Flash put an arm around her shoulder as they reached the table and she moved against him, her body remembering the role.

"Everybody," Flash said to the two blondes. The bodyguard was at the table too but sat discreetly separate from the women. "This is my special guest, Patty," Flash said. "I want everyone to be especially nice to her."

Sandra smiled graciously and took a seat beside Flash. The blondes looked confused, but their consternation was clearly their own problem and no concern of Flash's. When Flash asked, Sandra ordered champagne and settled in for a long night.

Three other men joined them later—another brick and two tekniks—along with a couple more women. The club played late twentieth century music and Flash was talkative and entertaining. Having eaten nothing all day, the champagne went straight to Sandra's head and she enjoyed the lovely woozy feeling of being half-drunk in a crowd of people who were just having fun. Flash held Sandra close to him, and she remembered how good it felt to be held by a strong, confident man. After all the fear and stress of the past few days, she was happy to relax into the comfort of this stranger's arms. In fact, she began to wish she could stay there with him. Flash seemed okay. He'd been nice to her and he was very good-looking. Maybe she could stick around with him and be his girl? She was pretty sure he'd want to take her to bed that night. It was something she had been prepared to do for the sake of getting to Sniper. Now she began to think it might be nice.

When someone took out a little silver pillbox full of tempus and passed it around the table, she gladly took a couple herself, popping one in her mouth and washing it down with champagne, putting the other in her handbag for later—a habit she'd got into when she'd been living on the streets and making her first entrance into the splashparty scene.

When the first rush of euphoria hit her, she ran her hand up Flash's thigh and whispered in his ear, "Take me home and make me your bitch."

He smiled back at her, his eyes bright after having dropped a couple of tabs himself. A thrill went through Sandra, knowing she'd be his.

"Soon," he promised her, his large hand stroking the curve of her hip. "The night is still young."

One of the blondes leaned across—the other one had disappeared somewhere—and said, "Why don't we make it a threesome?" She put a hand lightly on Sandra's thigh and pushed up the hem of her dress.

Sandra looked into the woman's lovely, smiling face and

thought, Why not? It might be fun. But then her head filled with the anticipation of how Flash would take her, ravage her body, how she would surrender to his strength and be his bitch.

She ran a hand over his chest. "Just me tonight," she told him. "We can play about later, but tonight I want to give you something special."

Flash turned to the blonde with a look of mock regret and shrugged helplessly. "I've a feeling Patty here is all I'll be able to handle tonight, love. Sorry."

The blonde pouted but didn't argue.

"You won't regret it," Sandra murmured into his ear.

Her head was reeling; her body felt like it was floating. At some point in the evening, she got up to dance. She had always danced well, and the tai chi training she had done lately had made her even more supple and sinuous. A group of strange men gathered around and danced with her, but she kept her eyes on Flash and Flash kept his eyes on her.

When Flash took her home to his luxurious apartment in Chelsea, she was dizzy with happiness. She had drunk more and taken more tempus from the little silver box and she was as high as she could ever remember being. But, most of all, she was full of the joy of having found this strong, powerful man who would keep her safe and give her a home and adore her and make love to her with ferocious need.

They fell into bed, tearing off their clothes, and Sandra yielded her eager body to his, adrift in a sea of whirling, surging pleasure.

\* \* \* \*

Jay woke early, wishing he could go back to sleep.

Yesterday, by the time the team had been assembled and they'd got themselves to the airport, Marie had needed to shift their reservations to a much later flight. So, they arrived in Berlin too late to do anything except go to their hotel, check in, disperse to their rooms, and reassemble in the bar for a bout of desultory and joyless drinking that even Ben's extravert bonhomie could not enliven. Like Jay, most of the team returned to their rooms late, watched vids, and read the novels they'd packed until exhaustion overcame them in the small hours.

They breakfasted as a group and then went to the impressive Federal Police Headquarters, newly relocated from Potsdam and now commanding an imposing position on Bulgarische Strasse, overlooking Treptower Park and the broad River Spree. The building was a gorgeous post-Adjustment extravaganza—with whole stories on madly cantilevered projections—looking like it had grown from an alien seedpod obeying a physics very different from the one with which most Earthlings were familiar.

The team disembarked from their three taxis and stared in amazement at the astonishing, gravity-defying structure with open mouths until Kappelhoff chivvied them back into action and got them inside.

They were greeted by a senior officer in the Bundespolizei who very quickly handed them over to Chief Inspector Kaplan from GSG 9, the Federal Police's elite antiterrorism group. Kaplan was to be their main liaison for the operation.

He took them on a ride in one of the building's many transport pods, moving horizontally and vertically in a complex route that eventually led to a disappointingly ordinary open-plan office where they were to be based.

Within half an hour, a briefing was underway to bring a

roomful of the local police up to speed with Jay's findings. Then their team was briefed in return on a wide range of matters which may or may not be related to the existence of a plot by timesplashers to destroy Berlin. By lunchtime, Jay was exhausted, confused and wishing he'd had a few more hours' sleep. There was an awful lot of liaising going on, most of it at levels well above that of a young Detective Constable. As the local intelligence was sifted and assessed, correlated with international intel and fed into the operational planning process, Jay found himself sitting in an empty office with Ben, trying to think of something useful to do.

"We should be out on the streets," Ben said, breaking a silence that had lasted an uncomfortably long time. "That's why they have people like us, right? Young people. So we can go out there and get into the scene and put our ears to the ground, right?"

Jay had to agree. That's why even the Europol team was full of young men and women. But he wasn't going to concede anything. Not to Ben.

The young Spaniard looked at his British colleague with exasperation. "You know, I had you all wrong. I thought you were okay. It is very rare I misjudge a person but I will admit, I made a mistake in your case. You, my friend, are a backroom boy. You are a delver into databases, a wizard on the compatch, a reader of reports, whereas I, Benedicto Maria Alejandro Garcia de la Peña y del Bosque, am a man of action." As if to demonstrate, Ben jumped to his feet. "I am going out there to find out what is going on in this city. You, my clerical friend, can stay here and think up elegant net queries." And with that, he turned and walked out of the room.

Jay stared after him in disbelief. The guy was stark staring mad in Jay's opinion—and definitely in line for disciplinary action.

Still, Ben had a point. Sitting around in a BPOL office wasn't going to help anybody, whereas making contact with the local bricks and asking a few questions might just make some difference. All the same, he wasn't about to go AWOL like Ben and risk being sent home on the next flight. Instead, he settled in front of an as-yet-untouched workstation and pulled up a display. He needed to know more before he went out into the streets, and a review of the local lowlifes might be a good place to start. Then maybe he could check up on places where twenty or more F2 generators could be delivered and stored. After that, he'd look at movements of heavy-duty electrical equipment in and around the city. It might even be worth checking hotels for guests with Polish accents ...

It occurred to him that thinking up "elegant net queries" was exactly what he was doing. But that just made him angrier, that Ben should think something so sensible was some kind of character flaw. We'll see who gets to Sniper first, he told himself. We'll see.

\* \* \* \*

When Sandra woke the next morning she wished she were dead. It wasn't just the pain in her head, the nausea and the deep weariness in all her limbs, it was the memory of how she had behaved, what she had said and done, and, worst of all, what she had felt.

It was mid-morning according to her compatch. Flash was still sprawled across the huge bed beside her, satin sheets tangled about his naked body. Carefully, quietly, she got out of bed. She felt so sick standing up that she only managed a few paces before she had to sit down again in the first chair she passed. She was naked too. "Oh God," she whispered to herself. "You fucking idiot!"

She had thought herself so clever, so determined and bold. Yet, at the first opportunity, she had reverted to the stupid, craven child she had always been, desperately giving herself to the first man she found who had the swagger and strength to make her feel safe.

And what was she now? Was she still the huntress she had been yesterday, a stalking Nemesis, doing whatever it took to set herself free from fear? Or was she Flash's bitch, another in a series of pathetic creatures whose life was to pander and please him in return for his protection and his reflected status? She could be, she thought, and felt the thought tempt her. She could stay here and be this man's pet.

Full of self-loathing, she dragged herself to her feet and left the room. Her muscles trembled and her throat closed against the nausea, but her physical distress was nothing compared to the feelings of shame and self-disgust that filled her. She saw her dress on the floor as she passed through the bedroom door. It was torn, useless. She remembered Flash ripping it off her and thinking in a wild ecstasy that it didn't matter, that he would get her new ones, better ones. All that had mattered was that he wanted her so much—and that he would soon have her.

Despair hit her like a fist to the chest and she leaned on the kitchen counter to save herself from falling down. She'd had her chance to find Sniper and had blown it, choosing instead to gratify her childish longing for security and love. That's how Dr. Mason at the Institute had put it. He had explained how her early years of neglect and rejection had damaged her psyche, how her self-esteem was dangerously low, how she sought the validation of powerful men, how she would barter her body—the only thing she believed anyone valued—in a doomed attempt to gain their love. He had told her how vulnerable she was to people like Sniper, and wasn't he just right! So much of what the doctor had said came back to her now as she leaned against the counter, naked and trembling, with tears running down her face. In response to all his insights and his concern, what had she done? She had flirted with him. In fact, she had tried so hard to seduce Dr. Mason that he had taken himself off her case and that old witch Dr. Brannigan had taken over. At the time, she had seen it as a victory, as proof that he couldn't resist her.

With a little jolt, she realized how long she had been standing there in Flash's kitchen. This was crazy. She had to get out of there before he woke up. She also realized that her mind was made up. She must go. Otherwise she would lose herself utterly and stay lost forever. She would find another way of tracking Sniper. She'd have to.

Yet, before she could leave, she needed clothes and she needed money. And that meant going back to the bedroom.

Trying to control her breathing, and stepping with absolutely silent tread, she re-entered the room. Flash lay just as she had last seen him—face down on the bed, arms and legs spread. She paused to be sure he wasn't stirring, then made her way across the room to his discarded trousers on the floor. She found his wallet in the back pocket and removed it gently before going on to the dressing room. She grabbed a pair of jeans and put them on, rolling the legs up until they fit, tying them tight at the waist with a cord from a dressing gown. She put the wallet in her pocket and pulled on a t-shirt and then a thick jumper. In the mirror, a startled creature stared furtively at her, buried in oversized clothes, eyes and cheeks streaked with spoiled mascara, hair wild and unkempt. She looked a mess and she was still barefoot, but at least she wouldn't freeze. It would do to get her back to her hotel room. She could put her high-heeled sandals on once she was well clear of the apartment.

"Not a good look on you."

She whirled around to find Flash leaning against the door frame. Her heart raced as she judged her chances of getting past him and away.

"So what's going on, Patty?"

"I just want to go," she said.

He pushed his lip up as if he were considering her request, but then shook his head. "No, I don't think so. Not after all we've come to mean to one another."

Sandra's fear was turning to anger. "Piss off. You can't keep me here. I'll send your clothes back when I get to my room."

Flash stood upright, filling the doorway, his muscular arms hanging ready at his sides. "First you're going to explain to me what last night was all about, love."

Sandra stepped away from the wall to give herself room to move. "It wasn't about anything. I ... I just..."

"You just wanted a shag, is that it?"

She nodded dumbly.

"And the fact that you're an old friend of Sniper's is just pure coincidence, like?" He took a step toward her and she took a step back.

"What's Sniper got to do with it?"

"You tell me, love. First I have his snotty little teknik over here giving me a load of crap, then I'm ambushed by his fucking bitch." He took another step toward her. "Not that I minded getting lucky, but now it's time for you to tell me why, pet."

He took another quick step and lashed out at her with his fist. Moving even faster than he did, Sandra stepped aside and deflected the blow, smoothly shifting her balance into a defensive tai chi posture. She swallowed hard. The blow had almost struck her. Deflecting it had been pure luck. The strength behind it had been terrifying.

Nevertheless, Flash stepped back. Her defence and the fact that she now stood poised and ready for another attack had left him puzzled at least. He stood there watching her for a few moments. Then a grin slowly spread across his face. "Well, well," he said. "Little Patty's a fucking ninja."

The idea seemed to please him rather than deter him. She wished she had spent the last two years studying karate instead of tai chi. Tai chi was as "soft" a martial art as they came. Flash began moving around her, watching carefully as she adjusted her balance and shifted her stance.

"So why did Sniper send his little kung fu queen to get into my bed, eh? What sort of game is he playing, Patty?"

"This has got nothing to do with Sn—"

He struck at her again. Again she parried the blow, but this time he struck over and over. Sandra kept up a desperate defence, backing away into racks of suits until she hit a wall and had nowhere else to go. Flash was huge and relentless. As he pressed his attack Sandra knew she couldn't hold him off any longer. The first blow that struck her would knock her to the floor, break her jaw, finish her off.

With a scream, she brought her arms up around her head and pulled herself down into a fetal position, cowering on the floor at Flash's feet, waiting for the blows to fall. But they didn't come. She waited and waited before she dared to look up. Flash stood over her with triumph blazing in his eyes.

A flicker of contempt rekindled her defiance. That's where Sniper has you beaten, she thought. Sniper never would have stopped until I was utterly broken.

Gently but insistently, Flash reached a hand under her chin and raised her to her feet. "Now you are going to tell me everything you planned to do for Sniper. Do you hear me?"

She shook her head. "I'm not working for Sniper."

Anger flashed in his eyes and he drew back a hand to hit her.

"I'm trying to find Sniper!" she shouted, to forestall the blow. "I thought I could get you to tell me where he is."

"Tell you where he is?" The idea seemed to open dark avenues of thought in Flash's mind.

"What are you, a cop? If you're a cop, I'll—"

"I'm going to kill him."

"What?" Flash seemed genuinely incredulous. He even gave a brief snort of laughter. "You?"

His reaction stabbed at Sandra's heart. Was it that hopeless? Was she that ridiculous? She gathered her anger and her fear and focused it into a defiant glare. "Yes, me! Stupid, silly little girl, me. I'm going to find that vicious bastard and I'm going to kill him. Me! Me! Me!"

Suddenly Flash was smiling again. He stepped back from her and let her go. "Well, why didn't you say so in the first place?" He walked calmly across to a shelf and grabbed some underwear. "I think we should discuss this over breakfast. I'm sure there's lots of ways I could help."

# Chapter 11

### Hunters and Prey

"Look, you little Yankee faggot, get out of my face or you can do the fucking lob yourself!"

Sniper was raging, pacing up and down inside an enormous warehouse, yelling into his compatch.

"Do you hear me, McGarry? I'm this close to telling you and your chickenshit friends to take their money and stuff it."

The little image of McGarry looked mortified. "I, sir, am no Yankee."

"I don't care if you're a fucking Martian! If I see your face again before the lob it's all off. *Comprendes?*" He cut the call before the American had a chance to respond.

"What do they want from me?" he shouted into the echoing spaces of the warehouse. "I don't need a bloody nanny!"

Klaatu stood up, wiping his hands on his overalls. Wiring up the power circuits for a forty-megawatt supply was serious engineering and tricky enough without Sniper doing his *prima donna* routine.

"What's the problem?" he asked.

"It's these money people you found us, they want to have their noses in everything all the time."

"It's a lot of money." Klaatu's tone said: "stop being such a baby".

Sniper looked sharply at his teknik. They'd had a long and successful association, and yet they weren't friends, however much Sniper liked to say they were. They were oil and water. They didn't mix; one of them was always going to be on top. Yet there was a powerful, mutual need.

"Who are these people?" Sniper demanded, his tone quieter but by no means conversational. "What are they getting out of this?"

He walked up to Klaatu and stood so close that the young teknik had to look up at him. "What have you got us involved in?"

"I've told you. It's a consortium of American fundamentalist churches. They want God's wrath to fall on the decadent fleshpots of Europe, starting with Berlin, Satan's home away from home. What do you care?"

Around them Klaatu's team of tekniks carried on working, but the clatter of tools and the whine of forklifts faded out of Klaatu's awareness as Sniper's cold eyes bored into him.

"I don't like anyone thinking they have any control over me," Sniper said in a level voice.

"If these religious freaks think I'm their bitch, they're wrong."

Klaatu nodded without speaking.

Sniper seemed to feel he'd made his point and turned away. But then he turned back. "And who paid for the Beijing lob?" he asked.

Klaatu shrugged. Jimmy, the Korean, had been connected to nationalist elements in his own country, people who resented China's annexation of the Korean Peninsula in '26. Klaatu had always assumed it was the nationalists who had put up the money.

"And what about Flash? From what you said, he's living like a king. Where's his money coming from?"

"He didn't say, but one of his guys told me there are gangsters in Hong Kong who have a problem with the black market diamond trade going through London. They'd like it disrupted."

Sniper ran a hand through his hair in a gesture of frustration. He walked away and then walked back again. "So we're hired guns now? Terrorists for rent? Any crook or crank with an agenda can throw a few million our way and we'll take out whatever city they want? Is that who we are now?"

Klaatu didn't know how to respond. Surely Sniper knew all this? Surely Sniper hadn't been kidding himself that it was still like the old days? Yet, looking into the big man's tortured eyes, Klaatu could easily believe that was exactly what he had been thinking.

"We still get the fancy cars, the penthouse suites, the girls…" But he could see that wasn't enough to appease Sniper. Klaatu tried something else. "And you still get to do the splash. That's the big thing, eh? You still get to do the lob and you still get to be the best."

Human psychology wasn't exactly Klaatu's greatest strength, but he could see from Sniper's expression that he had hit on something at last that might mollify him. "Every brick on the planet knows you're the best. No one's beaten Ommen in more than two years—except those jerks in Beijing and they got themselves killed. Once you pull this off, no one will be able to touch you for years to come. You'll be a legend."

Sniper wasn't frowning so much now. He seemed to be relaxing.

"Who gives a toss where the money comes from or what other people want? This is what you want. This is your legend we're building here. Not theirs," Klaatu said.

He thought he saw something like relief in Sniper's expression.

"You're right. Fuck 'em!" Sniper said. "This is my show, my triumph. Everything else is just noise, just gnats buzzing in my ears." He smiled and slapped Klaatu on the shoulder.

"Come on, let's go out and have a drink. You spend too much time cooped up in here. Let's get some girls and have a party!"

Klaatu shrugged. "The work is going well. A few hours off won't hurt too much." Besides, Klaatu knew it was best not to say no to such invitations. "I'll get changed," he said. "But I must talk to you about some equipment we still need. Some switches."

"Switches?" Sniper laughed. He was in a good mood now. "Send someone down to the hardware store."

"I don't think they'd stock the kind of thing I have in mind."

\* \* \* \*

Superintendent Jacques Bauchet faced a prestigious and attentive audience. The auditorium in the Berlaymont Building had a capacity of two hundred and was about halfway full. As he looked around, he saw Euro MPs, cabinet ministers from various European governments, heads of intelligence agencies and police forces, as well as senior civil servants from many different countries. It was his first high-level briefing as head of the Temporal Crimes Unit. The size and quality of his audience gave him the grim satisfaction of knowing how rattled everyone was. The Chair of the European Parliament's Standing Committee on Civil Liberties, Justice and Home Affairs, no less, made the opening remarks and introduced Bauchet. Now the Frenchman had the job of focusing all these powerful people on the job that needed to be done.

"Travelling in time has been one of the most unusual technological developments ever." He gazed out at the audience from the podium. "For most of its history it has not been part of mainstream science or technology." He remotely controlled the room's huge 3-D display as he spoke. "The original scientific work was done in the early part of this century but was ridiculed by the scientific establishment at the time. The so-called Kentucky formula, which clearly showed how it could be done, was rejected as pseudoscience and ignored by almost every respectable research lab. Of course, when the oil ran out, a few years later, mainstream physics and the more obscure scientific backwaters alike were swept aside by the global depression that we now call the Great Adjustment. Basic science came to be seen as an unnecessary luxury. Any country that could still afford science at all set its best people onto finding alternative energy sources.

"It was during this period of economic collapse and resource wars that two former PhD students in the north of England used the Kentucky formula to build the first time machine. They were unemployed and disaffected. So were most young people at the time. They used this remarkable invention recreationally, as a kind of sport.

"Pretty soon, they had developed a following. Others started building time machines. A party culture developed around the weird effects, with its own music, its own heroes, and its own jargon based on the metaphor of lobbing bricks back into the timestream."

Bauchet's eyes swept the room. His audience was growing restless. No doubt most of them knew this much already.

"For many years, it was a minor phenomenon and well below the radar of law enforcement agencies. Travelling back in time requires a lot of energy and, fortunately, when you try to go farther, the energy requirement goes up exponentially. These early timesplashers went back just a few years—ten if they were lucky. The fun involved for the participants and the partygoers is in creating an anomaly. The biggest anomaly of all is a temporal paradox. If you kill your past self, or stop yourself from being born, for example, you create a logical impossibility which the universe must reject. This creates what they call the "timesplash"—an area of disruption in spacetime where causality is damaged. The damage is self-healing and localized so there is never any possibility of changing the past, but there is always a certain amount of disruption that flows to the present. There, where the edge of the timesplash meets the present—" He paused, gave a self-deprecating smile. "There, for reasons any physicists in the audience might like to explain to me afterwards, the disruptions to causality are not repaired and may cause permanent damage.

"As I said, the early bricks could not travel far and the anomalies they created were not large. What is more, the strength of the effect diminishes rapidly as it flows upstream to the present. It was enough for the bricks to have some excitement and for the kids at the splashparties to enjoy a little weirdness. Nothing dangerous.

"Until the focus fusion generator was perfected in 2035.

Timesplashers quickly realized the potential of these small, powerful generators. While we were building F2s as fast as we could and dragging ourselves out of the depression, the splashparty craze was sweeping the whole world. Kids everywhere were organizing bigger and bigger parties and the bricks and their technicians were pushing their lobs farther and farther into the past.

"Incredibly, it was only then, when splashparties had become a huge global phenomenon and the most daring bricks had their faces on our children's bedroom walls, that the world's scientists woke up to the fact that time travel had been invented and had actually been practised regularly for more than a decade!"

He shook his head in amazement and looked around the large room once more. "Of course, splashparties themselves became big enough to attract the interest of law enforcers. The use of recreational drugs, particularly tempus, at these events had prompted some authorities to ban such parties. However, the sheer scale of the phenomenon meant that most law enforcement agencies focused on containing the noise and disruption from the events—happy to force them out into remote country areas—and used their resources to crack down on the drug suppliers. Most people still considered the theatre of the timesplash—the brick, the cage, the backwash—just a harmless show. Very few in authority actually believed that kids were going back in time to shoot their own mothers!

"It was not until Ommen that the real dangers became apparent." The display behind him showed vidlog footage of damaged buildings and people being rescued from under fallen masonry.

"A young man died that day, one woman lost a leg, and

twelve more were injured. The insurance bill for the damage to buildings and infrastructure ran to millions of Euros."

He began a series of still shots from other disaster scenes. "Ommen was a lob of sixty-five years—the absolute maximum that the technology was capable of at the time. We also believe the anomaly created was from one of the bricks shooting his own grandmother. Other bricks have tried to emulate Ommen, but have been unable to go so far back—it takes a lot of technical expertise." Wanted posters for Sniper and Klaatu appeared behind him. "After Ommen, new laws came into force throughout Europe and vastly increased the penalties for unauthorized time travel. The bricks and their tekniks have now all gone underground. The great majority have given up timesplashing but there is still a hard core who continue to timesplash. Finding out where they are getting the money to do this and stopping it, is one of our top priorities.

"For the past ten years, mainstream physics has been running to catch up with what these youngsters can do. Unfortunately, this resulted in a far deeper understanding of the theory behind time travel. I say 'unfortunately' because this new understanding led to a new, generalized time travel formula. About a year ago, scientists at CERN developed the 'gigarange formula', as it has become known, and immediately let it leak onto the net.

"With the gigarange formula, timesplashers can hugely increase the length of their journeys back in time. All that limits them now is the energy required for the lob. Like most things connected with this technology, the energy requirements for a lob increase exponentially with its length. However, it is now believed that a lob of one hundred and fifty years or thereabouts is quite feasible.

"What happened in Beijing was, without doubt, the first application of this new formula. Preliminary reports from a group at Cambridge University tasked with analysing the event, suggest that the temporal distance travelled in Beijing was approximately one hundred and forty years.

"Given this and the obvious size of the anomaly they created, our best guess is that they took the opportunity to assassinate the then twenty-five-year-old Mao Tse-dung when he travelled to Beijing to attend a student rally on the fourth of May, 1919."

A murmur went around the room.

"Going after targets such as the future Chairman of the People's Republic of China, a man believed to be among the most influential people of the twentieth century, is the kind of attack we now face. This new range would easily include major figures in World Wars I and II—think Hitler, Churchill, Archduke Franz Ferdinand, Emperor Shōwa, Woodrow Wilson—and many others whose influence on history have been profound. Gandhi, Albert Einstein, John Logie Baird, Henry Ford..."

He threw up his hands to signify the enormity of what he was saying. "We have suddenly become extremely vulnerable. The assassination of any of these people—or their parents, or of others they relied on—before they became the globally influential people we know, would have the same kind of effect as the assassination of the young Mao in Beijing. Bricks are making plans right now to devastate major cities using precisely these tactics. I don't have to remind you of how far stock markets have plummeted since Beijing. A few more attacks like this and we will be plunged into another depression—one that will make the Adjustment look like a minor hiccup."

He leaned on his podium, scouring the audience with his deep, dark eyes. On the screen behind him, injured people crawled through the rubble of Beijing, crying for help.

"I do not exaggerate. For a price that many terrorist groups, organized crime gangs, rogue governments, and even wealthy individuals can afford, you can now devastate a major city as effectively as if you'd set off a nuclear bomb. How many cities would need to be nuked before a country could no longer recover? How many would it take to bring down our whole civilization?

"This, ladies and gentlemen, is the threat we face."

\* \* \* \*

The truck came to a halt with a massive screech as it dumped energy to its flywheels, followed by an explosive hiss from its air-brakes. For a moment it juddered and settled on its shock absorbers, and then was silent except for the hum of its big electric motors. It was standing in a long, broad lay-by—a big pull-off beside the Autobahn. To the left, separating the lay-by from the main road, was a row of tall shrubs. To the right were open fields. Ahead of the truck, blocking its exit, was a green and white police car and a silver Mercedes beyond. Beside the truck, the motorcycle policeman who had flagged it down dismounted.

Sniper, looking smart in a fake Berliner Polizei uniform, stepped up to the cab and called for the driver to get out.

Instead of complying, the man leaned out of his window and shouted to Sniper in German,

"What's the problem, officer? I wasn't speeding."

Frowning at the man from under his peaked crash helmet, Sniper summoned him with a peremptory wave of the hand.

"I'd like you to step down from your vehicle please, sir," he said in a tone that would permit no discussion.

Reluctantly, the driver threw open his door and climbed down to the ground. Without another word, Sniper drew his QSZ-99 handgun and shot the man through the temple, making sure the blood spattered away from the truck. Klaatu and another teknik ran out from the police car toward the back of the truck.

Sniper could hear them opening the big door and clambering in. It was a quiet stretch of road and the lay-by was sheltered by the shrubbery, but there were still too many cars and trucks going by to leave a dead man lying there for long. Moving quickly, Sniper opened the pannier on his police bike and took out a folded cloth. He flicked it open and threw it over the body. The cloth, a smart fabric, took light striking it from the sides and carried it laterally, releasing the light from the opposite side. The effect was a kind of camouflage. When you looked at the cloth, you didn't see the cloth but a blurred image of what was beside it. Sniper squinted at the strange, disturbing effect, stepping away from it toward the road. Instead of a dead body, he saw a curious distortion, a bump in the tarmac, perhaps, or an odd reflection from the truck's paintwork. Good enough, he decided, and went to join the others.

"This is fine," Klaatu told him as he peered into the gloomy interior. Klaatu and the other teknik had flashlights and tag-readers. "It's everything we need." Despite this, Klaatu's expression was dark and surly. Robbing a truck in broad daylight—he had told Sniper earlier—and stealing components that any cop with half a brain would know were for a displacement field rig, was incredibly stupid. Sniper had shouted him down and shut him up.

"Good," Sniper said. "Get the police car shifted, then take the Merc and get lost. I'll join you at the warehouse. I'll be at least an hour driving this thing." He grinned into Klaatu's face. He knew just how much his teknik resented his plan. "Cheer up, my gloomy friend. By the time the cops work it out, we'll have done what we came to do."

Klaatu said nothing. He pulled another device out of his jacket and went to the truck's cab to reprogram the vehicle's ID responder. When it passed the toll points and police checks, it would feed them a false ID, identifying its load as farm produce. He gave a quick check that the license plate displays at the front and back had changed to reflect the truck's new designation and then went back to join Sniper.

"You sure that's going to be okay?" Klaatu asked, glancing at the logo on the side of the truck.

"Don't worry. There are thousands of these things on the streets." Sniper looked across at the main road. "Half a dozen must have gone past while you've were dicking about with the registration."

Klaatu nodded and set off for the Mercedes. Sniper took one last look at the equipment they had just stolen before he closed the back of the truck. It would be soon now. Very soon.

\* \* \* \*

No one noticed Ben was missing until the next day. Jay was the first to mention it, worried that something might have happened to him.

"What do you mean, he might have gone out to ask a few questions?" Kappelhoff demanded. Jay struggled with his concern for the young Spaniard's safety and his unwillingness to get a fellow officer into trouble. "It's just that, the last time I saw him, he sort of mentioned he might just, you know, pop into a club or two to, well, get a feel for the local scene."

The Chief Inspector eyed him with a dangerous calm. "And just when did he just mention all this?"

"Yesterday afternoon, sir."

Kappelhoff looked at his compatch. "And it is now ten fifteen in the morning. And you say you checked with the hotel and he didn't use his room last night?"

"Yes, sir."

"And you can't raise him on his compatch?"

"No, sir."

"So one of my officers has been missing for about eighteen hours and you only just thought you'd come and mention it?"

Jay bridled. "I don't think that's fair, sir."

Kappelhoff lifted the lid on his anger just a fraction. "Oh, really. You let a member of my team—" He paused, staring past Jay. "What the…"

Jay turned too, and saw Ben sauntering across the room to his desk.

"What the hell is that boy's name?" Kappelhoff growled, transferring his anger to Ben.

Jay grimaced. "I haven't quite got it yet, sir. He says it a lot but it's a bit long."

Kappelhoff scowled at Ben. "You!" he bellowed. Every head in the room turned, so that when Kappelhoff pointed at him and yelled, "Yes, you! In my office right now!" there was no mistaking whom he meant. As the Chief Inspector set off after Ben, he added, "You too, DC Kennedy."

"Where have you been?" Kappelhoff asked Ben as soon as he walked through the door.

Ben cast an accusatory frown at Jay. "I have been talking to some local people, sir, trying to get the lie of the land."

"You report to Detective Inspector Moretti, do you not?"

"Yes, sir."

"Did Moretti order you to go out talking to people?"

"I wasn't doing anything else, sir. I thought it would be useful if I—"

Kappelhoff raised his voice. "Did Moretti order you to go out talking to people?"

Ben stopped trying to justify himself. "No, sir."

Kappelhoff simmered down in turn. "No, sir. And you." He turned to Jay. "You knew he had gone off without explicit orders but you said nothing to anyone?"

"No, sir. I mean, yes, that's right, sir."

Kappelhoff regarded them sternly. "This is the second time in as many days that you two have been in trouble for a breach of discipline. If it wouldn't be such a waste of taxpayers' money, I'd ship you both back to Brussels right now. So, since I'm stuck with you, I'll have to put you to use somehow. But I don't like officers who don't understand basic discipline. Consider yourself warned. Do you understand me?"

They both "yessirred" in unison and were dismissed.

After they had gone, Moretti wandered into the Chief's office. "What do you think?" Moretti asked. "A couple of bad ones?"

Kappelhoff shrugged. "I don't think so. The Spanish boy is a bit too full of himself but his heart's in the right place. You can't blame him for being frustrated with all the bureaucracy we're having to go through. I want to get on with some real police work myself. As for the other one ... I don't know ... His only real crime so far seems to be a willingness to get dragged into his friend's stupid antics.

"Nevertheless, don't let them think they've got away with anything. Pile a lot of grunt work on them for a while. Make them feel they're being crapped on."

Moretti smiled. "I was going to do that anyway. The Bundespolizei have done a dump of everything they know about every timesplasher in the whole country. It'll take a lot of sifting to find any patterns in it."

\* \* \* \*

"So you went and told them about me." Ben sounded grimly satisfied, as if pleased to have his opinion of Jay validated.

Jay looked up from the stack of reports on his display. "I was worried about you. I assumed, understandably, that you'd done something stupid and you were in trouble. I know now I should have just left you in whatever mess you might have been in."

"Ha!"

"What do you mean, 'Ha!'?"

"I mean, ha! That's what I mean."

"God, you're a pain in the arse!"

There was a short silence while both of them fumed over their private thoughts. Ben, of course, was the one to break it.

"I suppose you are wondering what success I had last night."

Jay snorted. "If you'd had any success, you'd have been crowing it round the office."

Ben rolled his chair over to Jay's desk and leaned in to him confidentially. "I met a guy who said there was someone recruiting electrical engineers—electrical power engineers, not electronics engineers. You know the difference, yes?"

"Of course."

"Good. Then you can tell me. I did not want to ask, you understand."

Jay sighed. "Power engineers are the guys who rig the overhead cables, substations, power stations, all that. Electronics is all the small stuff."

Ben nodded. "Excellent!"

"Why is that ... Oh, I see." Jay felt very stupid. He should have seen it straight away, and would have if he hadn't been so irritated with Ben. "You think there is a brick out there recruiting tekniks with power engineering skills because they're wiring together a bloody big power supply?"

"Exactly! I would have offered my services, only my electrical skills are a little nonexistent. They'd spot me immediately."

Jay shook his head in amazement. "It's a good job you didn't! Kappelhoff would have carved out your liver and fed it to the crows. Didn't they train you at all in the Guardia Civil?"

Ben just grinned. "They tried, my friend. They tried."

It was no use trying to understand him, Jay thought. The man would always be a mystery.

"So why haven't you passed this on to Moretti, or Kappelhoff? Don't you think they might like to know?"

Ben's expression said he wasn't so sure about that. "I thought I would tell you first," he said.

"Me? Why tell me? I don't want to be involved in any more of your nonsense. Just leave me right out—"

An alert from his desk unit interrupted him. Both young men turned to look. On the display was a message from one of the many search agents he had set loose on the Bundespolizei databases and local news channels. The software had found an item of interest, using the many complex parameters he had provided.

An armed robbery and murder had just been reported. A truck belonging to RWE.ON, one of Europe's biggest power companies, had been hijacked and its entire cargo of heavy-duty electrical switches and capacitors had been stolen.

As Ben read the display, a big smile spread across his face. "There, you see, my backroom boy! That is why I brought this to you. And there you are, already gathering the evidence I need to confirm my suspicions."

Jay glared at him.

"Now we can go and tell Kappelhoff what we know," Ben said, grinning.

# Chapter 12

## Closing In

In Brussels, Jacques Bauchet and several others were being briefed by a CIA agent. They were in a windowless room at the heart of the Berlaymont Building and the American woman was talking in a slow, nasal voice that was both soporific and grating. Surveillance vids of various degrees of quality and interest flickered on the big display at the end of the room as she described the movements and probable activities of the blurry people in the images.

Bauchet had Colbert with him and a couple of his senior officers. There were also four Belgian intelligence officers, two police officers from Interpol, and an Assistant Director from Britain's MI6 who just happened to be in the neighbourhood, she said, with a couple of hours to kill.

"And this is Carmody Delacroix," the nasal American said as the image of a portly man in a white suit and a big white hat strolled across the screen. "A.k.a. Stephen Winston, a.k.a. Stephen McGarry, a.k.a. Mansfield Sinclair, a.k.a. Jonathan Douglas…" The litany of aliases droned on and Bauchet looked at his compatch.

"Delacroix works for a banned fundamentalist group called the Measurers of the Temple," the CIA agent said at last. "He does little jobs for them. We believe he left for Europe two weeks ago but his whereabouts are unknown."

"Why does Delacroix matter?" one of the Belgians asked.

The American blinked at him for a moment. "We know the Measurers have been looking at timesplash technology lately and we know they are cashed up and considering projects. If they've sent someone over here, it's possible he's scouting for bricks to do a job."

"Why over here?" the Belgian asked. "Plenty of targets back home, aren't there?"

The woman looked at him with calm eyes. "Many Americans feel that Europe represents something of a haven for the ungodly, a place where atheists and Satanists are allowed to congregate and prosper. It is a natural target for those who would like to cleanse the planet. Spiritually, I mean."

A stillness fell over the room. Bauchet studied the woman, noting the high-buttoned collar and long plain skirt, the little gold crucifix, and the complete absence of other jewellery or makeup. Of course, the CIA had strict "moral criteria" for admission these days. That is, you needed to prove your Christian credentials. It wasn't quite the FBI, which had become a much-feared arm of the USA's Department of Religious Affairs, but the CIA had steadily changed its role since the Adjustment from serving American political policy abroad to serving American religious policy. In fact, religion and politics had become indistinguishable in post-Adjustment America thanks to the twenty-ninth amendment to their constitution, which repealed the first amendment and instituted Christianity as the official State Religion.

"I imagine there would be lots of support for such views in the American government," the woman from MI6 said casually.

"I couldn't comment on that, ma'am."

"Well, in the CIA then?"

The American gave a taut smile but said nothing.

One of the Interpol officers spoke up. "So how many fundamentalist religious groups are your people tracking who might be interested in blowing up this little nest of vipers we call home?"

"I couldn't say, sir. Quite a few."

"Quite a few," the Interpol man echoed. "Is that ten? Twenty? More?"

"Definitely more, sir. Possibly a couple of hundred all up, but most of them don't have the resources to pull off something like this."

"But the Measurers of the Temple have the resources?" Bauchet asked.

"Yes, sir. They most certainly do."

The briefing lasted another thirty minutes, after which the CIA agent left the room and the meeting broke up.

"It's a pity the CIA isn't a bit more proactive with its intel," said the Interpol man who'd been asking the questions when only he, Colbert and Bauchet were left standing together outside the room.

"You didn't find the briefing helpful?" Bauchet asked.

"Too little, too late, if you ask me. All those people she listed as having possible ties to timesplashing, I don't suppose one in ten of them is of any real interest."

Bauchet smiled. "And it would have been nice to have been told when one of them gets on a plane for Europe, yes?"

"Right. Instead of hearing about it two weeks later."

"Your people have access to security camera records for the period when our visitors might have arrived?" Bauchet asked.

The Interpol man nodded. "It will be hard to spot one face when we don't have dates and times."

"And we don't know which of a hundred airports he might have arrived at."

Bauchet smiled. "But it is the software that will do all the hard work, fortunately."

"Yeah." The man still looked glum, but he gave Bauchet what he wanted. "I'll let you know if we find any matches."

"You will keep looking beyond the point of entry?" Bauchet asked. "It would be nice to know where everybody is right now, would it not?"

"It would," the Interpol man agreed.

They shook hands and he left. Colbert took the opportunity to ride his favourite hobbyhorse as they headed for the lifts.

"Damned Americans give me the creeps."

Bauchet shrugged. "You can't judge a nation by the people who govern it, thank heavens!"

"They voted them in."

"The Germans voted for the Nazis too. It was the Depression in the 1930s that helped Hitler to power, just as it was the Adjustment in the 2020s that got the religious right into power in the U.S. You've got to remember how badly hit the U.S. was when the petrol dried up. They were lucky to hang on to any kind of government at all for a while there."

Colbert grunted as they stepped into the lift. "They might have been better off."

It was a popular view. The inquisitions and mass

executions that had taken place under the Lord's True Path Party when it seized power were horrifying. Many said the atrocities were still going on, but it was more likely that all effective opposition had long since been crushed and the LTP—established by the twenty-eighth amendment as the only legal political party in America—no longer needed to be as ruthless as it had once been.

"The important thing for us now," Bauchet said, ignoring Colbert's comment, "is to decide to what extent organizations inside the USA are directly involved in exporting terrorism to our patch."

"I don't think I trust that CIA woman," said Colbert. "She could have been feeding us pure Texas bullshit. Even before the LTP, the CIA was never especially shy about screwing around with foreign governments to protect American interests."

Bauchet sighed. He liked Colbert—he was a good police officer—but this sniping at the Americans was getting them nowhere.

"It is possible she was leading us astray, but I don't think so." The lift doors opened and they stepped out into the corridor. "The CIA may not care too much what happens to us atheists and Satanists, but I can't see any advantage to them in deliberately destabilizing European governments. We provide more aid to the USA than anyone else—than all the rest put together! It would jeopardize their own government if they lost our support. They have almost no science base now, very little high tech, no software industry. All their great universities were turned into theological seminaries. They need us. Why would they try to harm us?"

They had reached Bauchet's office. Marie was clearly hovering, waiting for them to finish talking before handing

Bauchet a sheaf of messages.

"You assume that they're thinking rationally," Colbert said. "The LTP are first and foremost religious zealots. Only second are they politicians."

He went off to his desk. Bauchet watched him go with a heavy frown. Like most people, Bauchet believed America was a fundamentally democratic nation. If it could just get back on its feet, its people's natural tolerance and common sense would be reasserted. Then the LTP would be booted out and become a footnote in history.

Nevertheless, the prospect that other countries were behind the funding of splashteams in Europe could not be ignored, even though it was almost too frightening to contemplate. It elevated what was so far criminal activity and terrorism, to outright acts of war. Bauchet could not bring himself to suspect the U.S., but just days ago the Chinese had made a very dangerous speech in the UN Assembly. They said they believed "foreign agents" were behind the Beijing disaster. And then there was Russia, still just a squabbling gang of warlords from the Urals to the China Sea. Yet some of those warlords had nuclear warheads under their control. Since the Adjustment, the world had become a far more dangerous place.

\* \* \* \*

As night fell, Jay found himself in the back of a German police van. His team was laughing and joking, the usual pre-raid tension making it sound a little strained. Jay hadn't done more than say hello to most of them and now he was about to risk his life with them on a full-scale armed raid. He looked at the men and women around him. He hoped they'd all be coming back together.

Ben, of course, held centre stage, as loud and cheerful as ever. He seemed to have picked a good-looking female officer as the focus of this evening's charm offensive. She was too old for him, Jay thought, but that didn't stop her from lapping it up. Watching the young Spaniard perform, Jay couldn't help smiling. There was just something infectious about Ben's good humour., however big a jerk he was.

Jay hadn't been smiling a few hours earlier when Ben had dragged him into Kappelhoff's office and told the Chief Inspector how he had solved the case. It looked for a while as if the Chief would kick them both out and keep kicking till they reached Brussels, but he took them seriously, despite Ben's demeanour. Pretty soon the whole staff was in an uproar—everyone glued to their compatches and terminals, chasing down information—and the Chief firing off orders faster than anyone could write them down.

Jay got the job of liaising with the Stadtspolizei as they searched security vid and toll event databases to spot the stolen truck. They had a major piece of luck when someone found a European Space Agency satellite that had been taking pictures of the region as part of a biodiversity survey. The data included two clear shots of the truck, one in the lay-by and the other as it turned off the motorway. With an idea of the direction the truck was heading, the search was narrowed down enormously. Once they had correlated the satellite images with ground-based cameras, they even turned up a shot of the white-haired driver.

"Sniper!" Jay shouted when he saw the picture.

"Jesus, we've got him!"

People grinned as they turned back to their own work. Jay wasn't smiling though. He stared at the angular features of the man he had admired so much just a couple of years ago. Another world, he realized. A simple, innocent world. A place where you felt free and safe, no matter what damned fool thing you were doing. A place where Spock was still alive, still young, grinning fit to split his head in half over some idiotic joke, or just because it felt good.

The image on the viewer swam and Jay's Adam's apple seemed about to burst in his throat. Sniper was the one who had killed Spock. Sniper was the one who had changed Jay's life, who had yanked him out of that simple, easy world and dropped him into a darker, more dangerous place. It was long ago and so much had happened since then, yet the sight of Sniper's face brought the old pain back to stab at his heart.

The positive ID from Jay, verified a few minutes later by the computer, earned them a warrant for the raid. The Bundespolizei ran the show, with the Stadtspolizei in support, and Europol offering intel and tactical support. The fact that a vanload of Europol officers was present on the raid was a courtesy the Bundespolizei had grudgingly extended. A grim-faced officer with "BPOL" stencilled on his body armour had made it very clear that they were to keep out of his way and not even to think of drawing their weapons unless expressly ordered to do so by him personally. Jay hoped and prayed he'd get the order.

The truck had been traced to Neukölln-Südring, an old industrial district close to the city centre. It looked half-derelict, with close-packed industrial units and decaying warehouses lining the broken roads. Berlin, like all the world's big cities, had plenty of spots like this left over from the Adjustment, places where industries had died and no one had bothered to carry away the corpses.

The vans pulled into a particularly dismal area and

disgorged their human and robotic cargoes. Jay saw two squads of sweepers being herded into the shadows by their handlers while human spotters and snipers were deployed to the target site. BPOL and SPOL troopers set off on the double to take up their positions. They looked dark and mean. Jay wished he were with them, and not sitting in safety beside the command and control truck.

* * * *

"I'm off for a sausage," Klaatu said, wiping grimy hands on his grimy overalls. The work was going well but the hours were long and Sniper was pushing him hard. He was tired and unhappy. The big German grew more restless and unstable every day, and Klaatu worried more about what Sniper might do than whether the police might find them. That stunt with the RWE.ON truck was madness. They could have got the parts from other, more discreet sources. Stealing the truck and killing the driver was just Sniper being impatient, needing some excitement. Like a big kid.

This was going to be Klaatu's last timesplash.

"I'll come with you," Sniper said from where he sat watching animated interactives. He stretched his long limbs and rose to his feet in a fluid catlike movement. With a slow sweep of his eyes, he looked around the big warehouse—the bank of generators, the cage, the switches, the computers and electronics, all strung together in a rat's nest of scaffolding and wires. Klaatu's tekniks were dotted among the gear, with their heads buried inside equipment racks, bodies crouched over lathes and welding arcs. Around them were Sniper's people, hired muscle watching the entrances, patrolling the boundaries, making sure the work wasn't interrupted.

Klaatu and Sniper strolled over to a side entrance and Sniper nodded to the guard at the door. The man spoke into his compatch, alerting the guards outside so they wouldn't be shot.

"We don't need all this security," Klaatu grumbled as they walked through an echoing alley between huge metal sheds.

Sniper paid him little attention. Klaatu's growing discontent did not seem to bother him. "Indulge me," was all he said.

Klaatu heard the warning in his voice and said no more.

They were heading for an all-night sausage stall a few blocks away that served the remaining businesses on the industrial estate. It sold weak coffee and thick, oily bratwursts with hunks of bread and mustard. As the work intensified and the hours grew longer and harder, both of them had become used to eating most of their meals there.

They were halfway to the stall when Sniper stopped suddenly, listening. He grabbed a handful of Klaatu's overalls and dragged him effortlessly into the shadows. The young teknik's eyes, already wide with alarm, widened farther when he saw the gun in Sniper's hand. Sniper held him still for a long moment, staring back the way they had come. Klaatu peered past him, trying to hear what Sniper had heard. He saw a pair of dark shapes emerge from a corner and enter the alley, moving at speed, heading toward the warehouse.

"What the hell..." Klaatu whispered.

"Sweepers!" Sniper hissed.

Klaatu looked up at Sniper's face, unreadable in the darkness. They both knew what it meant. The warehouse was about to be raided. The sweepers would be the tip of an iceberg of heavily armed law enforcement officers. The place must be thick with them. They would be lucky to escape with their lives. Yet Klaatu could feel Sniper being drawn toward the warehouse, his body taut and yearning for a fight.

"You'll be killed if you go back," Klaatu whispered. "You wouldn't stand a chance."

Still Sniper remained silent, straining toward the impending gunfight like a dog on a leash.

"You can't save the lob now. It's gone. You'll just get yourself killed."

Sniper snapped round to face him. His lips were drawn into a snarl and his eyes smouldered with rage. It was clear that he badly wanted to kill somebody and Klaatu didn't like being the only one around. Then anger welled in Klaatu's chest. It was obvious that the only way the cops could have found them was by tracking the stolen truck. And that was all down to Sniper's stupidity.

His anger gave him the courage to face Sniper's rage one more time. Slowly and firmly he said, "We have got to go. Right now. Or die here."

At last, the words seemed to penetrate. Sniper, hissing like a wild animal, released Klaatu from his gaze and looked about for a way of escape.

\* \* \* \*

The sound of gunfire froze the small Europol contingent.

It had begun. In Jay's compatch, the voice of the Bundespolizei commander droned in German as he moved his people around.

"This is not right!" Ben declared, standing beside Jay. "We should be up there, helping." The young Spaniard was agitated and tight-lipped.

Jay couldn't have agreed more. It would have been better

to have stayed at the office than to be so close and feel so useless.

"We did all the work," Ben complained, inaccurately. "Now they're going to grab all the glory for themselves."

"That's not what's going on," Jay started to explain, but gave up immediately. Ben had a way of looking at the world that Jay couldn't begin to understand. He'd be wasting his breath.

"Well, I'm not waiting," said Ben, looking intently at Jay. "Are you coming?"

"What?" As Jay gaped at his friend in astonishment, Ben flashed him a wild grin and ran off into the shadows. "Ben!" he called after him, his voice low. He looked around to see who else had seen Ben leave.

But no one had been watching. The others were all peering into the van to see the status displays or staring toward the sounds of the rattling gunfire and screaming buzz-guns. Without stopping to consider his own career prospects, Jay set off after Ben, his only thought being to stop him and bring him safely back.

He followed the path Ben had taken around the back of a low, unlit building and turned toward the warehouse, knowing that was the way Ben would have gone. He found himself in a narrow alley and could see Ben ahead, keeping low and running fast. There was another building between them and the warehouse and Ben turned across the front of it, disappearing from view. Jay ran faster. A couple more blocks and they would be in the middle of the fighting. He had to stop Ben. He took the same turn, just in time to see Ben duck into another alley to the left. Jay was gaining on him and started thinking about what he would do when he finally caught up with him. He took the left turn at top speed into a broad street with dim lighting, and almost stumbled when he saw what was ahead.

Jay's adrenaline levels shot through the roof at the sight. There was Ben, weapon drawn, skidding to a halt and trying to bring his gun to bear on two men who were standing stock-still ahead of him. One of the men was short and slight, wearing workman's overalls. The other was tall and broad shouldered. Even in the uncertain light, Jay recognized Sniper and Klaatu immediately.

Sniper's long leather coat flicked back as his hand reached across to a shoulder holster beneath it. Ben shouted, "Stop! Armed police!" but Sniper was already pulling out his weapon. Jay reached for his own gun, fumbling with the catch on the unfamiliar, police-issued holster and saw Ben fire three times, all three shots going wide as he fought to get his balance. Sniper's face was handsome, cool. A small smile formed as he steadied his own weapon.

Jay kept running, closing the distance, shouting, "No!"—a desperate plea to the gods as much as it was an attempt to stop the inevitable. Sniper's eyes flicked across to Jay in the same instant his gun went off. Out of the corner of his eye, Jay saw Ben jerk sideways as Sniper's bullet hit him. Ahead, Sniper was already swinging round to fire at Jay, but Jay kept running and smashed into the tall German with all the speed he could muster.

The impact lifted Sniper off his feet. They both hit the ground with a crash that sent them rolling apart, knocking the wind out of Jay. He heard Sniper's gun clatter across the concrete pavement, but had no time to appreciate his luck as Sniper lurched to his feet. Jay scrabbled to get upright, pulling his gun free just in time to have Klaatu whack him in the upper arm with a heavy wrench. Pain shot through him as the gun fell from his hand. Even so, he managed to swing the elbow of his uninjured arm back into Klaatu's face, sending the teknik staggering away, stunned.

Then lights exploded in his head. He twisted and fell to the ground. Sniper stood over him, the fist that had just smashed Jay's face pulling back for another blow. Jay looked up into Sniper's eyes. He waited, dizzy and mesmerized, for the blow to fall.

But it never did. A shot rang out, zipping through the air close to Jay's head. Another smashed concrete near Sniper's feet. Klaatu shouted something in German. Jay couldn't see who was shooting and neither could Sniper. Another shot snapped through the tail of the big man's leather coat. And then Sniper and Klaatu were both running down the street, away from Jay. Two more shots followed them. Both misses.

"Who's there?" Jay had seen the muzzle flashes, but could not make out who had fired the gun. He peered into the darkness, still a little groggy, the pain in his arm and face making the world outside his head seem distant and disconnected.

"Help me," he managed. "My friend was shot."

Out of the darkness, a figure stepped into the dim street light. Jay blinked and screwed up his eyes. A woman, tall, long legged, in tight jeans and a thick furry jacket stood in front of him. The gun was still in her hand and she kept looking anxiously toward where Sniper had disappeared.

"It's you!" Jay gasped as she went down on one knee beside him. It occurred to him that he might be delirious or dreaming. "You're the girl from the splashparty." He remembered something else. Something he'd forgotten he'd seen in the press of events. "You're the one who ran away from that mental hospital."

"Can you stand?" she asked, speaking with an English accent. "I think your friend is only wounded. I can see him breathing."

She touched his arm gently and he winced. "I think that's broken," she said.

"He's all right?" Jay could hardly believe it. "Look, there's more of us not far away. You've got to—"

She looked up quickly. "More cops?"

"It's Patty, isn't it? Your name. It's Patty."

She looked at him with a frown. "How do you know?"

He tried to sit up but the world whirled around him. The girl caught him before he hit the ground. After a moment, the dizziness passed and he looked at her again.

"I saw you in Ommen," he said, his voice slurring. "The most beautiful girl I've ever seen."

Then his eyes closed and he felt himself slump heavily in her grip, all his strength gone. It felt like a dream as she lowered him gently, cursing under her breath. He felt her touch his compatch as pain shot through his arm. She seemed to be dialling a number but, in his semi-conscious state, he could not understand why.

He barely registered the sound of her running away, back into the shadows.

# Part III

## Summer 2050

# Chapter 13

## An Invitation

An English summer. Jay looked around his parents' garden and smiled to himself. Neat borders of alternating alyssum and lobelia interspersed with bright salvias surrounded a lush green lawn. A row of stepping stones meandered through the lawn to a small wooden shed where bumblebees hummed over nodding roses. Beyond, peas and tomatoes stood tall over rows of lettuce and carrot. The sun was warm overhead as Jay sat back in a cane chair sipping home-made lemonade. His mother appeared from the kitchen, carrying yet more cake and drinks, smiling when she saw him watching her. He smiled back. Apart from the dull thud of pop music coming from a neighbour's house, it was a perfect idyll.

"I don't know why you can't just stay here with us, Jason," his mother said, setting down the tray. "We'd love to have you."

Jay groaned inwardly, but kept his smile more or less in place. "I don't think Dad would be too happy."

"Oh, rubbish. You saw how pleased he was to see you last night."

It wasn't quite how Jay remembered it. The geniality had

lasted about ten minutes before his father had started on about why Jay should give up all this "police nonsense" and go to university.

"You're still a young lad, Jason. You shouldn't be wasting your life chasing criminals around Europe. You should be studying for a degree. A man needs an education behind him these days. You're a bright lad. You could do so much more with your life."

Jay had begun to explain that he was doing something worthwhile, that he was making an important contribution to the world, but his father hadn't listened.

"You're barely out of short trousers, Jason. You can't expect to have a mature perspective on these things. I'm sure your life is very exciting, playing cops and robbers in exotic places—"

"You've obviously never seen Brussels."

"—but having a good time isn't everything, you know. You'll be wanting to settle down one day, have a family. You'll be glad then of a good professional salary instead of whatever pittance the police pay you."

At which point, Jay stopped listening too.

"I don't think Dad understands how committed I am to what I do," he told his mother. Ice cubes clinked in his lemonade glass. It was mid-morning and his father was at work. Jay's six-month Europol assignment had ended and he had returned to the UK to resume work at MI5. Of course, to his parents, all he could say was that he was back working for the Metropolitan Police.

"You'll have to give him time, love. He just worries about you. That's all. We both do."

Jay shook his head. After more than two years of working for Five, he had hoped his father would start to accept it.

"Anyway," he said, "that's the sort of reason I can't move in here. Besides, I'm used to living on my own now. I'd probably be a terrible house guest these days."

"Teenagers are always terrible house guests," his mother said. "Especially when they're your own."

"But I'll be able to visit more often now that I'm back in London. I'm thinking of getting a car. Not that I really need one but it might be a bit of a laugh. I could take you and Dad for a run out to the beach at the weekend or something."

His mother laughed as if he were still five years old and telling her his plans to build a moon rocket. She handed him another piece of cake. He eyed it queasily and thanked her.

"So did you meet any nice girls over in Europe?" she asked.

He laughed. "Only policewomen and femmes fatales. You wouldn't like the policewomen because they're all tougher than me and can drink me under the table. The femmes fatales are great but they're mostly over thirty and not one of them knows how to make angel cake like you, Mum."

His mother pulled a face and slapped his arm in mock annoyance. "I'm only interested in how you're getting on. I know you, you'll turn up on the doorstep one day with some postpunk girl with a bolt through her neck saying, 'Mum, meet Eviscerator, she's your new daughter-in-law.'"

"Well, if that's how you feel about body piercing, I don't think I'll mention the biker chick I've been shacked up with for the past six months."

They chatted on for a long, languorous time, neither of them caring much what they talked about. The mention of girls had brought back the memory of Sandra Malone. The thought of her ran in the back of Jay's mind as the conversation meandered about. After that night in Berlin when she had saved Jay's life—and Ben's—he had tried everything he could to find her. He still thought of her as "Patty", even though he had soon discovered her real name. He could still remember her appearing like a guardian angel out of the cold November night, reaching out to hold him as he spiralled down into darkness. But she was gone. The bullets from her gun had been tied by forensics to a shooting in London more than ten years ago. Too long ago to have anything to do with her. How she was carrying a weapon with that kind of history he could only guess. What had she been doing there, in that street, on that night? Jay knew it had something to do with Sniper, but knew little else. Had she gone back to Sniper after she'd escaped from the Institution? If so, why had she fired at him? Had she really tried to kill her old lover, or had she deliberately missed, scaring him off to save Jay?

Jay had spoken to the police who arrested her in Ommen and the psychiatrist who treated her in Cornwall, but still had no clear understanding of her. Beautiful, intelligent, severely traumatized and probably paranoid, the psychiatrist had told him, living in constant fear for her life, dreading the power and evil intent of a man she imagined as a demigod of vengeance and destruction. Not such a bad description of Sniper, Jay had thought.

The Mexico City disaster two months ago had put so much pressure on the TCU that Jay had dropped his search for the mysterious Sandra Malone to focus on more pressing investigations. But he still kept looking, quietly in the background, determined to find her.

His reminiscences were stopped by the sound of the front doorbell. Jay's mother got up with a "who can that be?" expression and disappeared into the house. She was gone so long that Jay began once more to relax. The past few months—the past two and a half years!—had been so full-on that he'd hardly ever had a chance to just sit around and do nothing. Yet, even now, with the gentle English sun warming him and the quiet hum of the bees lulling him, he couldn't help wondering about the work he'd left behind in Brussels and the assignment that was ahead of him here in London. After that night in Berlin, there had been no sign of Sniper or his teknik. It was impossible to believe that a man like that would have just given up. No, he was still out there, somewhere in the world, planning another big splash. Jay had done all he could to track him down, Europol had done all it could too, but, in the end, the trail had gone cold. Sniper had vanished into the ether. Other bricks had been found and other splashes had been thwarted but not the one that mattered, not the one that Sniper was planning.

And now Jay was back in the UK and someone else was on secondment to Europol. When Jay had asked to stay with the Temporal Crimes Unit, Holbrook had said what a good job Jay had done and how his talents were needed "on the home front". Jay tried to argue that he was of more use staying in Brussels, but it didn't get him anywhere. So, here he was, home again.

He heard voices approaching through the house; a man was talking to his mother, a deep-voiced man who must be flattering her atrociously judging from the way she was giggling. Then his mother and the guest emerged into the garden and Jay jumped to his feet immediately.

"Superintendent!"

Bauchet turned his aquiline face to Jay and smiled. "Your charming mother has been telling me all about what a good boy you used to be when you were little."

Jay goggled in alarm at his mother.

"I assured her that she can still be just as proud of you."

Embarrassment grabbed Jay by the throat and left him speechless. If the sky could have fallen on him right that minute, he would have considered it a blessing. His mother didn't help matters by standing there beaming at him as if he was her chubby little baby once more.

"Now, if I may, Mrs. Kennedy," said Bauchet. "I need to have a few words in private with your son. It is important police business, you understand."

Jay's mother all but simpered as she assured him it would be all right and bustled away to leave them alone in the garden. Bauchet thanked her profusely and went over to sit opposite Jay. He folded his long body into the wicker chair as if it were something he had never done before and regarded Jay with his usual sombre expression, all smiles gone. Jay felt much more comfortable to see those deep-set eyes without a twinkle in them. Cautiously, he sat down too.

"Can I get you a drink, sir? Or something?"

"Your mother and I have just had that conversation—at length."

"Ah. Then…"

"I am sorry for coming here, to your parents' home, but I needed to talk to you somewhere private, where there would be no bugs. You understand?"

"Bugs? No, I'm afraid…"

"It is important to stop the bricks from launching more attacks," Bauchet said. "It is the most important matter facing humankind at the moment. Do you not agree?"

Jay tried to weigh it against curing cancer or stopping poverty, ending the Sino-Indian war or beating the latest flu pandemic, but quickly gave up. It was well up there with the rest, wherever its exact place in the running order was. So he said, "I suppose."

"In the last six months, two major cities have been reduced to rubble. Tens of thousands are dead." He waited while Jay nodded. "So it is a rather odd time to be taking experienced staff—like you—away from the TCU, is it not?"

"Well, yes. But I was told…"

Bauchet raised a hand. "Yes, yes. It is possible, I suppose, that national governments are becoming scared and want their people back home, protecting their more narrow interests. But you and I know that this is wrong-headed. This kind of terrorism has worldwide networks of financing and support. The bricks are mobile and flexible. They choose their targets from all over the world and they go where the work is. National intelligence agencies cannot hope to mount adequate defences without strong, effective international coordination and collaboration."

He paused, meaningfully. "So why am I losing my people, Jay? Why are my new secondees stupid third-rate people who couldn't find their arses with both hands?"

For some reason, Bauchet's French accent seemed exaggerated and exotic in the context of Jay's parents' garden.

"I still don't…"

"Jay, you know I have had a small team reporting directly to me. A team that has been chasing the money."

Jay nodded. The Super's right-hand man, Colbert, had been running it.

"The trail goes round and round in circles and never ends anywhere! We are not looking at criminal gangs and religious nutcases." He waved his hand as if to dismiss such naïve notions. "Only the most sophisticated of organizations could have set up such clever and elaborate paper trails."

Jay blinked, suddenly realizing where this was going. "Governments? You think there are rogue governments behind all this?"

"What they used to call state-sponsored terrorism."

Jay's mind was racing. During the Adjustment, many governments collapsed. There were coups and revolutions, sometimes long periods of anarchy. When looking for rogues, there was a long list to choose from.

"America?" he asked, shocking himself as the possibility dawned on him.

He knew they had traced the money behind Sniper's team to a number of religious groups—some of them quite legal or at least tolerated in the USA. Were they just a front for an American government agency, the CIA, perhaps?

"I don't think so," Bauchet said. Then he shrugged. "Who knows? We have no evidence, and I doubt that we will ever have any either way. But we must keep an open mind and not jump to obvious conclusions. Such a hasty revelation might start a war. It is not something to speculate about idly."

Jay sat back in his chair, letting the implications go round in his head. Bauchet sat back too, allowing him a moment to think.

When the Frenchman spoke again, it was in a much lighter tone. "You know, when TCU first started up, all you young whelps from all over Europe were the last thing I wanted. Your governments forced me to accept representatives of their intelligence agencies, so that you could all report back on our progress and give them first-hand intelligence, as it were. It used to drive me crazy, I'll tell you. But it hasn't been so bad. There has even been a little competition among the people who sent you that has been to our benefit." Jay wondered if Bauchet knew about the tip-off Five had given him about Klaatu's visit to Poland. There was no sign of it in Bauchet's face, but then how do you read the expression of an eagle?

"Now, I wonder if we might be able to get the same process working in reverse."

He looked hard at Jay as though he'd said something very significant, but Jay was struggling to see where the conversation was going.

"There are all of you ex-TCU people out there in your national agencies, gathering intelligence, sifting and analysing, hearing this and that. Perhaps now and then you would call your old friends at the Unit and let us know how things are going. It would help everybody in the long run, don't you think?"

Jay was shocked all over again. This was turning out to be quite a conversation.

"You want me to spy on my own department?"

Bauchet held his gaze steadily and said nothing.

Jay shook his head. "I can't do that. I'm not a traitor—or a mole, or whatever that would make me." He stood up, too agitated to stay still. "Anyway, what would be the point? Europol gets whatever we find. There are regular channels, standing protocols. Surely you're not saying Five is withholding intelligence? What would be the point? Everyone would be losers. It doesn't make any sense."

He turned away from Bauchet's silent gaze—feeling pinned by it—and began to pace the garden. The only advantage Jay's intel could give Bauchet would be to cross-check it against what was coming down the official channel. Though the only reason Bauchet would have for doing that was if he suspected the official channel was being manipulated. But what reason might the government have to hide anything?

"Oh my God," Jay said, turning back to Bauchet. "You think the Brits are funding splashteams. You think my government is behind this." It was outrageous. Impossible.

Bauchet shook his head. "No, that is not what I think. I do not even have any reason to suspect it. But I would like to know who I can trust. As I told you, the money trail suggests a level of skill and organization well beyond the reach of the groups we have heard about so far. If there is a government—or several governments—behind this, we need to know which ones."

It all sounded so sane and reasonable when Bauchet said it, but Jay's heart was pounding. Something inside his skull was shouting at him to get the hell out of there and run for cover.

"I can't," he said, shaking his head again. "I'm sorry. I can't."

Bauchet sighed and rose to his feet. "I'm sorry to ask you, Jay. It is only because I trust you that I offer you this burden." He took a card out of his pocket and laid it on the table beside the cakes and lemonade. "This is a secure netID. Think about it and call me when you are ready. I'll be in London for the next couple of days and then I go back to Bruxelles. I would not ask you if this were not so important."

He left, passing through the house. Jay heard him saying goodbye to his mother. Slowly, Jay reached out and picked up the card. He stared at it for a long time before putting it away in his pocket.

# Chapter 14

## Another Invitation

Jay touched the lock on the run-down Canary Wharf apartment block where he lived. His compatch negotiated with the building security system to let him in. The lock chimed and the door clicked open. The mechanism said, "Welcome home, Mr. Kennedy. You have had—no—visitors. No—messages are waiting for you. Have a pleasant evening." Jay barely heard the machine's chirpy voice. Lost in thought, he shook the rain from his coat and got into the lift. Bauchet's visit had left him edgy and confused. A long walk had seemed like a good idea, but instead of clearing his head and helping him think, it had just left him cold and wet. The clear skies of the morning had slowly given way to thick cloud and a chill northerly wind. Now his only thought was to get into his flat, turn the heating up full and fall into a hot bath with a six-pack of beer. If he could find something mindless to watch on the vid later, he'd watch it.

When he touched the lock to his own door, it opened immediately. It had, after all, been expecting him. Inside, the flat remained in darkness although the lights should have come on. Normally, he would have dismissed this as yet another fault in the building's ageing systems, but not tonight. His talk with Bauchet had him wound up tight and he was in a mood to distrust anything and everything.

Drawing his gun and flipping off the safety, he ducked low and moved away from the doorway, where the light from the entrance hall made him a perfect target. He was in a short hallway that opened into bedrooms to his right and left and a large sitting room with a kitchenette at the end. His heart was racing, but he made himself wait while his eyes got used to the dark. If there was somebody in there, he didn't want them to have all the advantages. Steadying his breathing, he moved slowly up the hallway toward the sitting room. From a crouch, he peered around the corner into the room.

"Lights," a woman's voice said, and he was momentarily blinded as all the lights came on at once.

"Don't move," the voice said again. "I have a gun."

Jay froze, then slowly turned his head toward the voice. Sitting in his armchair was Sandra Malone, pointing a large 9mm Enfield at him. Apart from astonishment, his main emotion was relief.

"Drop the gun," she told him.

He rose slowly to a standing position, careful to keep his own gun pointing downwards. "Or what?" he asked. "You'll shoot me?"

The girl's face set. "If I have to."

Jay smiled. "I've seen the way you shoot, Sandra. I don't think I have anything to worry about."

"Very funny. For your information, I've been taking lessons. Lots of them. Next time I use this, I won't miss. So just put the gun down. I want to talk to you."

Jay relaxed a little more. "Okay. If you want to talk, put your gun down first. I only talk to people who aren't trying to kill me. It's one of those rules I try to live by."

Sandra scowled at him. "You'd probably live longer if you had different rules." Her gun did not waver.

Jay felt a surge of irritation. Being ambushed by beautiful young women was all well and good, but he'd had a difficult day and there wasn't a lot of fun left to be squeezed out of this situation. Enough was enough.

"Look," he said, turning his back on her and walking to the kitchenette. "I'm bloody freezing and I'm going to get myself a hot drink. You might have turned the heating on when you came in."

He put his gun down on the kitchen worktop and picked up the kettle. As he filled it, he looked at her again. "Do you want something? Tea? Coffee?"

She stood up, looking cross. "I don't know what you think you're—"

"Sandra," he interrupted her. "I'm making a cup of tea." The kettle sorted, he crossed the room to turn on the heating. "My mum warned me about teenage house guests just this afternoon."

He took off his coat and threw it over a chair, then went back to preparing the tea. Sandra glared at him for a moment longer, plainly feeling like a complete idiot and not liking it one bit. Reluctantly, she lowered her gun and put it away in a bulky underarm holster. Jay shook his head. "You know, that gun is way too big for you. You'd be better off with a nice little Walther PPK or a Heckler-Koch HK45C. You can still get them both."

Sandra went back to the armchair and sat down. "It was a present from a friend."

"Nice friends you have."

"He's dead now. How's your friend? The guy Sniper shot."

"His name is Ben. The bullet missed his heart by two centimetres, but took out his left lung. He's got a desk job back in Barcelona now while they grow him a new one." Jay had been to see Ben once since the shooting. He'd been recuperating at home at the time, trying to pretend he'd soon be back on active duty in the field.

Sandra interrupted his reverie. "You saved his life."

"What?"

"If you hadn't charged at Sniper like a madman, he'd have hit your friend bang on target. You were very brave."

Jay was unexpectedly embarrassed. "Yeah? Tell my boss." He busied himself with pouring the tea, thinking he'd rather tackle Sniper again any day than face another bollocking like the ones he got from Kappelhoff, Bauchet, and the Bundespolizei once he got out of hospital.

He brought two drinks over in mugs and gave one to Sandra. "I put sugar in it," he said, taking a seat opposite her. She put her hands around the cup to warm them and he noticed how pinched and cold she looked. "The heating'll kick in in a few minutes," he said. "You didn't have to sit here in the cold."

She shook her head. "All the electrical systems are tied to your netID. They only work when you're around."

"Ah. Right. Do you mind telling me how you got in?"

She took a sip of tea, steam curling into the air around her eyes. "Bedroom window. I had to break it." He must have looked as confused as he felt because she added, "I came down on a rope from the roof."

"Jesus!"

She smiled for the first time since he came in. "I couldn't exactly call for an appointment, could I?"

"No, not really." She was wanted by every police force in

Europe, and Interpol was looking for her worldwide. He suddenly remembered Bauchet saying, "I needed to talk to you somewhere private, where there would be no bugs. You understand?"

Jay jumped out of his chair, holding a finger to his lips. If his apartment were bugged, he could expect his colleagues to kick down his door any minute now. Sandra set down her drink, got up and followed him as he ran to the bedroom and dragged a small electronic device out of a box in the wardrobe. He ran from room to room, waving the device around, watching its display. It was a full five minutes later before he stopped and relaxed. The scan revealed no bugs—none that were transmitting anyway. There might still be ones passively recording, and there were other ways to eavesdrop—a laser targeted at one of his windows, for instance, sensitive to the tiny vibrations that voices would make in the glass—but his moment of paranoia was over and he settled back into his chair with a sheepish grin.

"You never know," he said.

Sandra remained standing, blinking at him. It had obviously just dawned on her what he had been doing. "Shit," she said.

He smiled up at her. "Not this time."

"I should've been more careful."

"So, am I ever going to find out why you've risked your freedom and my career?"

She sat down again and picked up her drink. "I need your help," she said.

He nodded. It made sense that she would want to turn herself in. All those months on the run must have been hell. It was good that she had come to him. It was better she went straight to Five than wander into a local police station.

"Okay," he said. "You should stay here tonight. In the morning we'll go to my office together and I'll take you to the right people."

"What?"

"The SIS Building. It's where I work. It's best we go there first."

"I mean, what the hell are you talking about? I'm not handing myself in to the spooks. Are you a total moron?"

Jay was completely at a loss. "Well, what then? What are you doing here? I mean—shit!—what am I supposed to think?"

Sandra got up and paced across the room. She stood with her back to him. "Maybe this was all a mistake. I didn't know you were a spook. I thought you were just, you know, a cop." She turned to look at him, concern all over her lovely face. "It's because you're young too. I thought…"

He walked toward her. "You thought I'd understand?"

She nodded.

"Understand what, Sandra?"

She looked up to the heavens, looking for the words, then back at Jay. "Me, I suppose."

He took a step closer. Suddenly, she looked like she might cry at any moment. Her eyes glistened, her lips pressed together and her nostrils narrowed. He could have reached out and touched her troubled face if he dared, if he didn't dread her flying away like a startled bird.

"Look, I'll try," he said. "Don't worry. I won't tell anyone you're here unless you want me to." His own words frightened him. They took him over a line he shouldn't have crossed, putting him where his heart had already gone.

With a sob of relief she closed the distance between them, wrapping her arms around him and burying her head in his shoulder. "Oh God," she gasped. "Oh God, thank you!"

\* \* \* \*

Jay woke early, easing himself into a sitting position on the sofa so as not to aggravate the crick in his neck.

"Oh good, you're awake."

Sandra's voice behind him sounded cheerful and bright, nothing like last night. He grabbed a blanket and wrapped it round himself before turning to say good morning. She was in the kitchenette, looking through cupboards and throwing packets on the worktop.

"You don't seem to have much actual food in the house," she said.

"No. Not really. I'm not quite organized yet. I only moved in a few days ago."

"I know," she said, smiling. "I've been following you."

"I meant to ask how you knew where to find me."

"I was lucky. I started with the Berlin police and tracked you to Europol in Brussels. The day I decided to talk to you, I called your office and someone told me I'd just missed you. You were catching a train home that very day. So I checked the times and went to the Eurostar terminal at St. Pancras and—eventually—there you were."

"So you've been trailing me ever since I got off the train?"

She grinned. "That's right, spy boy." She looked at a packet she had in one hand and a tin she had in the other. "I could do you cream crackers and sardines for breakfast. How does that sound?"

"It sounds disgusting. Give me five minutes to get showered and we'll go somewhere to eat."

Nothing much was open early so they ended up in a small

café near the river which was doing a brisk trade in heavy breakfasts for heavy-eyed workmen. They ordered bacon, eggs, sausages, mushrooms and mugs of tea and took them to a corner table where they could talk with some privacy. The morning was bright and clear and the traffic outside had already started to clog the roads. They both ate as though they were starving and all conversation stopped until they were well into the meal.

"So what's it all about?" Jay asked. "You've had a bed for the night, the pleasure of my company, and a free meal so far. Now you can tell me what you're really after."

Sandra set down her knife and fork but kept looking at her plate for some time. When she looked up into Jay's eyes, her own were troubled and dark again. The light mood of the morning had disappeared completely.

"I want you to help me take down Sniper and his team."

Jay almost burst out laughing. "To help you? What do you think Europol's been doing since last year? What do you think we've all been doing since Ommen? There are hundreds of people out there looking for Sniper! Hundreds!" He saw the anger building in her expression and changed his tone. "Look, if you have any information that might help us find Sniper, I'll be happy to listen—and I'll pass it on as an anonymous tipoff if that's what you want."

She regarded him with her lips pursed. "Are they all such pompous little pricks where you work?" she asked.

Now that he was over his surprise, Jay studied his strange companion and tried to understand what she was so angry about. She talked as if she had appointed herself Sniper's personal nemesis. The thought flashed through his mind that she was an escapee from a mental institution, but he tried to ignore it. It also occurred to him that she had once been

Sniper's girlfriend. He put that aside too.

"I tried to help you, you know," he said. "Back in Ommen, at the splashparty. I arrived late and I saw you all in the cage. At first all I could see was how incredibly hot you looked in that catsuit." She scowled at him and he hurried on. "But then I realized you were upset. You were trying to get free. I tried to reach you but I was too far back and the crowd was too dense. I was nowhere near when the countdown reached zero." Sandra watched him with wide eyes, her expression blank. "By the time you were all back, I'd had to leave. My friend…"

Suddenly Sandra was on her feet and walking fast out of the café. Jay caught up with her in the street. He had to hurry to keep up with her.

"What's the matter?"

"I don't want to talk about Ommen."

"I was just saying…"

"I don't want to talk about it! All right?"

"I didn't mean to…"

She stopped and glared at him, eyes full of fury. "Just shut the fuck up about it!" She was shouting now and people turned to look at them.

Angry at this rough treatment, Jay nevertheless managed to stay calm. He could see how close Sandra was to completely losing it and he didn't want her running off. If she got away from him, he might never see her again.

"All right," he said. "Not another word. Okay?" She kept her eyes on him but he could see she was starting to calm down. "Let's go for a walk," he suggested. "Work off some of that lard we just ate." He ventured a small smile. "And you can tell me how the police forces of twenty-nine countries can help the great Sherlock Malone capture the world's most wanted man."

Her lips twitched a reluctant smile in return. "God, you're a prat," she said, but then she linked her arm into his and set off with him toward the river.

\* \* \* \*

"Holy shit!" Jay could hardly believe what he was hearing. "You know where he is?"

"Yes."

They were walking in the sunshine beside the Thames, heading almost due south into the fast-climbing sun and bright glare from the river. Jay had persuaded Sandra onto a Jubilee Line tube at Canary Wharf and, with a change at Cannon Street to the Circle Line, had brought them back up into the light at Westminster. From there they had walked through Victoria Tower Gardens to Millbank while Sandra filled Jay in on the past six months.

"But this is ... That's..."

Sandra looked at him sideways. "A big surprise, obviously."

"Big? It's mega! My God, we've been looking for him everywhere. And he's here? In London?"

Sandra nodded.

For a moment Jay was just overwhelmed by the news. He had to tell Holbrook. He'd tell Bauchet too, of course. Bugger protocol. Then the implication of what she'd said hit him.

"Jesus!" He stopped walking. He looked at Sandra, stupefied with shock. "He's gonna do London. Oh my God, he's gonna do London. That's why he's here. It's the only reason he'd be here." He studied Sandra's eyes for confirmation.

"When's it going to happen? Do you know?"

She shook her head. "That's why I need your help. I've been tracking him but I can't get close. I had a … a guy who was helping me, but he's dead."

"The friend who gave you the gun."

"I think 'friend' was a bit of an exaggeration. His name was Flash. You probably knew him."

Jay goggled. "Flash? You mean the number one brick in the UK? That Flash? He's your friend?"

"Was. Sniper shot him about two weeks ago."

Jay's head was reeling. There was a bench nearby and he sat down on it, pressing his palm against his forehead. All of this was news to him—and therefore to the British and European intelligence agencies and police forces. "Flash is dead? And Sniper killed him? And you've been trailing Sniper for months? And you know where he is but you don't know what he's up to?"

Sandra sat down beside him. "Yep."

Across the river, beside Vauxhall Bridge, was the Secret Intelligence Services Building where Jay worked. Originally built in the 1990s to house MI6, Five had moved in just twenty years later when Six lost the argument that Europe was foreign, not domestic, territory. Six was downsized and shunted off to a smaller building in Wapping and Five rode triumphant into the vacated space. Jay had planned to tell Sandra all this and show off his eccentric-looking workplace. Now his mind was full of her incredible revelations, and the time for casual chatter had gone.

"And Flash was helping you trail Sniper? But, now he's dead, you can't?"

"Yep."

"And that's why you need my help, to get you close to Sniper?"

Sandra didn't reply. She looked out at the river as if she were waiting for him to catch up.

"But why the hell have you been trailing Sniper all this time anyway?"

"Because I'm going to kill him."

Jay looked at her calm, beautiful face. He remembered last night when she said, "I've been taking lessons. Lots of them."

"Jesus," he said, unable to think of anything more appropriate.

\* \* \* \*

Klaatu could hear the screams as he walked down the corridor. He was still straightening his clothes from the excessively thorough searching the security guards at the door had given him. There was another armed man at the door to the gym and he made Klaatu wait while he spoke on his compatch. Inside the gym, the screaming stopped and a few seconds later the door was thrown open.

"Klaatu! Old friend! Come on in!"

Sniper wore tight trunks, a silk robe hanging open, a feral grin, and nothing else. His sculpted body looked hard and tough. The well-crafted bones of his handsome face were more prominent than ever, giving him a hungry, energetic look. His grey eyes fixed Klaatu with a fevered excitement that made the young teknik glance across the room to see what the crazy bastard had been up to. He wished he hadn't.

A naked woman hung from a square frame, arms and legs pulled taut, head lolling, like a big pink X. Her long blonde hair covered most of her torso but her skin that showed had cuts and gouges visible, some of them dripping blood. He watched her in shocked fascination. She lifted her head and looked back at him. Her face was puffy and bruised and blood ran from her mouth and nose. To his horror, he saw her lips stretch into a smile.

He turned quickly back to Sniper, but whatever he had come there to say had gone completely from his mind.

"How do you like my little pet?" Sniper asked, his eyes sliding round to look briefly at the naked woman. "Camilla found her for me."

"She's…" Whatever she was, Klaatu couldn't find the words to describe it. This was sick, even for Sniper.

"You can have her when I'm finished, if you like. Camilla can get me another one."

Klaatu looked again at the smiling, bleeding woman. She might once have been beautiful. There was a time when Sniper's cast-offs had been worth having. Not any more.

"I've got to get back to work," he lied. "We're still decrypting Flash's files." He remembered why he had made the trip out to Sniper's little Surrey hideaway. "But we know the target now."

Sniper's eyes flashed but he didn't comment.

"We're getting the whole thing," Klaatu said. "It won't be long. We should start assembling the rig. I'll be able to spec the lob properly in just a day or two, I think."

Sniper's grin broadened. "Tell Camilla. She's organizing things."

"What? Since when?"

The grin disappeared in an instant but the eyes stayed the same. Sniper's hand shot out and grabbed Klaatu around the neck before the teknik had even realized it was coming.

"Tell Camilla," Sniper repeated in a soft, reasonable tone, as he pushed Klaatu up against the door frame with irresistible force. "She's organizing things."

Across the room, the naked woman giggled. Unable to speak with Sniper's hand crushing his throat, Klaatu nodded as best he could. Sniper held him there several seconds more, studying his face as Klaatu's alarm mounted toward panic. Then he released him.

Klaatu fell back against the door frame, gasping for air. Relief and the urge to run mingled with the cold fury inside him. He kept his head down so Sniper wouldn't see it.

"Was that all?" Sniper asked. "I'm rather busy."

Klaatu nodded and staggered out into the corridor. Sniper turned back to the naked woman who was watching him with wide, eager eyes. The guard closed the door without a word and stood like a statue, watching Klaatu.

It took Klaatu a while to recover his voice. When he did, he said, "I need to see Camilla. Is she here?"

"Yes, Mr. Gomółka." From his respectful tone and expression, you would never guess the guard had been a witness to the scene in the gym. He spoke into his compatch again, then said, "Ms. Vergara is in the conservatory. Would you like an escort?"

Klaatu scowled at him. "I know the way."

\* \* \* \*

Camilla Vergara was an attractive woman in her middle thirties, a little over average height, well over average curvaceousness, and she favoured tight pencil skirts and severely cut jackets. She had a lot of cleavage and liked to show it. Her lips and nails were always scarlet. Her eyebrows and lashes always black. A "MILF" as Klaatu liked to think of her.

Camilla was working at a computer when he walked in. Upon seeing him, she made a final couple of gestures, and then took her hands out of the sensor field. She rose from her seat with a practised elegance and stepped toward him, her heels clicking on the tiled floor, hand outstretched in greeting. Her red lips formed a professional smile.

"Klaatu. How nice to see you." Her tone had something matronly about it, as if Klaatu were a little boy in her care whom she was humouring in his pretence of being grown up.

Klaatu eyed her sullenly. "Sniper says I should tell you we've located the target."

"Excellent!" She showed him a chair and went to take one herself. He watched her hips and ass in the tight skirt. To his annoyance, she caught him watching her. "Would you like something to drink? I'll have one of the boys bring something." She tapped her compatch and ordered coffee, not waiting for Klaatu's reply. She brought her dark brown eyes to rest on him.

"We should have a chat. In all the rushing about we haven't really made time to get to know one another."

Klaatu ignored her. He let his eyes roam around the conservatory. It was now, quite clearly, Camilla's office. "I see you've made yourself at home," he said.

She smiled. "I like to make myself useful and that means being here twenty-four-seven. This is such a lovely room, don't you think?"

He shrugged. The conservatory was very large, built onto the south side of a very large house. Its glass walls commanded a multi-million-euro view across extensive lawns to the rolling hills beyond.

If his rudeness annoyed her, Camilla didn't let it show. "The investors have been reviewing the new management situation," she said. The "new management situation" was Camilla-speak for Sniper having killed Flash and taken over his splashteam. The "investors" were a bunch of Chinese gangsters who were putting up the money for the splash.

"As you know, the investors were not happy with the progress being made by the previous management. They feel they should give Sniper an opportunity to prove himself."

"You mean they don't have much choice. They either let Sniper do it or their investment so far is down the drain."

Her pleasant expression didn't falter. "Sniper would not have been our first choice. After what happened in Berlin, his reputation is not what it once was."

"That's why you're here, huh? To stop him fucking up again? Well, good luck with that."

Her smile broadened. "Ah, the boy genius. So sharp. What an asset to the team." The coffee arrived and nothing was said during the time it took for the tray to be set on a table and for the armed guard delivering it to leave again.

"Shall I be mum?" Camilla asked, reaching over to pour from a silver coffee jug, thighs straining at her skirt, breasts almost falling out of her blouse. Klaatu forced himself to look away.

"The thing is," Camilla went on, "we're all a bit worried about Sniper's state of mind. He doesn't seem to trust anybody any more. He keeps all the lights on all the time, you know, because he says someone might hide in the shadows and try to kill him. And the money he spends on security! Well, you've seen it." She handed him his coffee in a fine bone china cup and saucer. He took hold of it, but for a moment she held on. "He doesn't seem to trust you, either,

Klaatu. He seems to think you want to leave the project."

Anger bubbled up in him. "Fuck you," he snarled.

He turned to go, disconcerted by the fact that she was still smiling, that she had clearly expected his reaction and was not bothered by it.

"Just to be absolutely clear," Camilla said to his retreating back. "The investors don't want anybody leaving the project until it is successfully completed. You know what that means, don't you?"

He stopped by the door and turned to look at her. She leaned back in her chair, smug and relaxed, absolutely confident that she was in control.

His thin lips twisted into a sneer. "I know what it means, all right. It means you need me, you stupid cow. More importantly, it means Sniper needs me. And as long as Sniper needs me, you can't touch me, bitch."

He took a step toward her. For the first time her smile wavered. "You don't know what he is, do you? You think he's just another thug in the pay of your ridiculous 'investors'. Well, let me tell you this. Every fucking cop in the world is out looking for me and every intelligence agency. The people we worked for in Berlin have a contract out on me. Daft bastards. And now you're threatening me with some jerk-off diamond smugglers who have no more clue than to employ a dumb little tart like you as their mouthpiece."

He took another step toward her and was pleased to see her hand move toward her compatch, ready to call security.

"There are so many people who would like to see me dead, I've lost count. And you know what? The only person in the world I'm actually scared of is that fucking headcase in the gym. And you know what else? I'm going to ask him to call me the day he has you strung up on that scaffold of his, and I'll be there to watch him cut little pieces out of your tasty little hide, and to fuck what's left of you when he's had his fun."

He glared into her eyes for a moment, letting her see his contempt. Her smile was completely gone now, her face pale beneath the makeup.

"I'm so glad we had this chat," he said. "We must do it again."

# Chapter 15

## Targets

"She's a what?" Denzil Porterhouse shouted. He was a big man, square-jawed and broad chested. He looked more like a boxer than an MI5 section leader and Jay swallowed hard before replying.

"An escaped mental patient, sir."

"And this is what you've brought us?" Porterhouse's eyes narrowed under heavy brows. "A teenage mental patient, trying to palm her fantasies off on us?"

Barry Overman lifted a hand, and Porterhouse subsided into his seat, glowering at Jay. The young agent hoped that Overman wouldn't be leaving the room any time soon. "You can see how this looks, Jay," Overman said reasonably. "I don't see how we could trust anything she said."

"I trust her, sir. I'd—"

Overman's compatch beeped and he listened for a moment. "We've got the file," he said. He reached out and turned on the viewscreen. An image of Sandra Malone's head and shoulders appeared in the room, slowly rotating.

"I think I understand everything now," said Porterhouse.

Jay winced at the pointed tone. It was the shot the hospital had used on her wanted poster and, even though it was an institutional shot and Sandra was looking glum, the picture still looked like it was copied from *VogueOnline*.

"Certainly an attractive young lady," Overman murmured.

Jay rallied to his own defence. "Look, it doesn't matter what she looks like. Her information is solid gold. She's been keeping tabs on Sniper's operation for months. She can lead us right to him. I don't see what the problem is."

"I agree that's all useful intel—" Overman began, but Porterhouse cut in.

"It's a load of bollocks. That's what it is. This little cutie has got you wrapped around her little finger and she's using you to get herself off the hook with the police. It's a scam, that's what it is." His angry glare intensified. "I suppose you're sleeping with her."

Jay was on his feet in an instant. "No, I'm bloody well not. Not that it's any of your damned business." He turned to Overman. "What the hell is going on here? Good boss, bad boss? I'm offering you prime intel and you're playing silly buggers!"

Porterhouse was on his feet too. "Sit down! Right now."

Jay switched his anger back to the big man, not in the least bit inclined to go back to the interrogation he'd been enduring.

"Please do as he says, Jay," said Overman in such a calm and relaxed way that it caught Jay quite off guard. It made him feel just a little bit silly standing there red-faced and scowling. He sat down.

Overman switched off the viewer and stood up. "I think that's all, don't you?" he said to Porterhouse.

The other man nodded his agreement and headed for the door.

"If you'd just stay here for a little while longer," Overman said to Jay, "someone will be along in a minute."

Jay watched them leave the room and stared at the closed door in confusion. It opened again thirty seconds later and Holbrook walked in.

"No, no. Don't get up," the Director said. He took the seat Overman had been using and chuckled. "Quite a performance those two gave, don't you think?"

"You were watching?"

"Oh, aye."

Jay began to protest but Holbrook talked over him. "It's not a small thing you're asking us to do, lad. To get Ms. Malone's conviction dropped will require me to persuade the Minister. She will in turn need to persuade the Home Secretary. He's the only power in the land capable of quashing it, you understand. And of revoking the Custodial Rehabilitation Order. Your pretty friend is asking a high price for her information, if I may say so."

He looked closely at Jay for a few seconds, long enough that Jay began to wonder if some kind of a reply were needed.

"Nevertheless," he went on, "I agree that this is a deal we have to do. I've scheduled a meeting with the Minister for this afternoon and I expect the whole thing to be sorted out before tomorrow lunchtime." He gave Jay a thin smile. "You can tell your friend she's a free woman again."

"Thank you, sir, I will. There's a couple more things though."

Holbrook said nothing but raised a very eloquent eyebrow. Jay pushed himself on. He had expected to be dealing with Overman, not the Director himself. But it couldn't be helped.

"I'll have to be her handler, sir. She won't accept anybody else."

Holbrook regarded him steadily, his face giving nothing away. "Jay, you're a good lad, and I predict that you'll go far in the service, but you're—what?—nineteen? Twenty? Handling an informant is a delicate business. It calls for experience. You're barely out of the academy. You've been with us just a couple of years. And this is intelligence that all our lives might depend on."

He leaned forward and clasped his hands together. "Listen, lad, on the strength of what you've said already, I've put emergency plans into effect that will move the King and the Parliament out of London within the next couple of days. After Beijing and Mexico City, no one is taking any chances. Certainly not me. How can I leave the fate of the nation's capital in the hands of a boy who's only just started shaving regularly?"

Jay shifted uncomfortably. The trouble was, Jay couldn't agree more with what Holbrook had just said. He was too young for all this to be on his head. And inexperienced. Yet . . .

"You said yourself how delicate this is," Jay pressed. "Sandra is living right on the edge. If we give her the slightest reason not to trust us, she'll bolt, and I doubt that we'd find her again. I don't want to be in this position any more than you want me to be, but I'm the only one she'll talk to. It has to be me, sir. I'm sorry."

Holbrook didn't look happy. He spent a long time looking into Jay's eyes—a scrutiny Jay managed to sustain without backing down.

"Okay, lad, you're the handler. Report directly to Overman. Tell him everything. Absolutely everything. He'll supervise. Listen to what he tells you and don't do anything too stupid."

He stood up and made for the door. Jay stood too. "Thank you, sir."

Holbrook stopped and looked back. He shook his head sadly. "God help us all, eh lad?"

"Amen, sir."

* * * *

"I want you to replace him. He's unstable and unreliable."

Camilla paced the sumptuous sitting room in Sniper's Surrey mansion. Sniper was sprawled on a white leather sofa, watching her. As she spoke she glanced at him to gauge his reaction. Her expression grew a fraction more sour at the sight.

"You'd be safer without him," she said, changing tack. "I don't think you can trust him any more."

Sniper looked away, bored.

"What's so special about him anyway?" she wanted to know. "The world must be full of tekniks just as good. Ones that aren't planning to stab you in the back. Let me talk to the investors. I'm sure we can find you an excellent replacement."

"Klaatu stays."

Camilla tried to hide her anger. "I know you've been together a long time. You're used to him and how he works. He's like a … comfort blanket or something. I'll be happy to tell him if you don't want to."

She looked at him, imploring him to be reasonable, but when his eyes turned to meet hers, she saw only implacable determination.

"Klaatu stays," he said again, more firmly this time.

Her temper snapped and she gave up the effort of trying to appear calm and professional.

"For God's sake, why? You know the little creep wants to back out. He's a danger to this project and I want him off the team."

Sniper smiled, happy now that she was thoroughly riled. "What did he do, make a pass at you?"

She pursed her lips at the insult to her professionalism. "I can't work with that jumped-up little rodent. Who the hell does he think he is? I insist that you get rid of him!"

Sniper shook his head, smiling sadly. "For you? You're the office temp, remember? One call to your precious investors and I'll have your replacement on the next plane from Hong Kong."

He got up and walked across the big room, restlessly prowling near the big windows that opened onto the gardens. "You need to grow up, Camilla, my sweet. Klaatu will stay until I let him go. He knows I'd kill him if he tries to leave before I want him to. More importantly, I know he will do the best job he can on this splash because he wants it as much as I do.

"You're right that we go back a long way. And I'll tell you the secret of our success. We both want the same thing and we both need each other to get it. You, on the other hand, I don't know at all. You've got no interest in what we're doing here. For you, it's just another job. You should keep in mind that you're here to make my life easier, to smooth things out, to pander to my needs. And, of course, to spy on me for the investors. It's a convenience I can easily live without."

He was looking directly at her now, challenging her to contradict him. Her nostrils flared and her eyes narrowed but she kept her mouth shut and forced herself to keep control.

"Very well," she said, her eyes slipping away from his in a rare moment of humiliation. "Klaatu stays."

She took a breath, pulled herself up, and brought her expression back to neutral. "Did you see the files he sent on the target?"

Sniper sauntered back to the sofa and sprawled into it again. "I can't believe you guys let Flash keep all that stuff secret from you."

"That's why I'm here spying on you, I suppose," Camilla said, her anger turning to bitterness. "So it doesn't happen again. The investors feel that Flash had far too much freedom."

"Good choice of target, though." Sniper had read the decrypted files like a gourmet savouring an excellent meal. "It's perfect," he said. "The target details, the analysis of the repercussions, the calculations of the size of the splash … It's beautiful. Just think what an impact on the timestream this is going to have. And the date! 1902! Almost a full one hundred and fifty years. Flash was a stupid tosser with ambitions well beyond his capabilities, but the choice of Vladimir Ilyich Lenin is inspired." He closed his eyes, perhaps imagining meeting the man.

"You should get on to Klaatu and hurry him up," he said, as if Camilla's earlier complaint had not been voiced. "Keep the little prick focused. He'll spend weeks working out the lob parameters to the twentieth decimal place if you let him. I want his tekniks putting the equipment together now, not waiting around for him to find the perfect solution."

Camilla was thinking about the next time she would speak to her bosses. There was going to be a big bonus in this for her or these assholes could find themselves another punching bag. "The equipment's no problem," she said distractedly.

"Flash's people had already acquired most of it. Lots of it is already assembled. It just needs finishing."

"Take it apart," Sniper told her. "Strip it right down and start again. I don't trust anybody but Klaatu to build my rigs." He waved a dismissive hand. "*Ach*, don't worry about it. Klaatu wouldn't trust anyone else's tekniks either. He'll rebuild it anyway. Just keep the pressure on him. He's too much of a perfectionist. He'll take forever if you let him."

"You want him to rebuild..." God, they were such *prima donnas*! Never mind. Some messages would be passed to Klaatu. Some would not.

"We've got more important matters to worry about than schedules," Sniper said, moving to stand by the window. "The girl is still out there."

Now what? Camilla sat down, feeling cross and agitated. This man's mind was like a child's. It leapt from topic to topic, never resolving anything.

"You mean your bitch?" His latest neurotic obsession.

"My ex-bitch. Patty. She's still out there." He gazed across the fields as if he might see her lurking among the shrubbery.

"So what? She's a child. A girl. What can she do?"

He whirled to face her. "She nearly killed me in Berlin. She's followed me here. She's stalking me, asking questions. People have seen her. She's always looking for me, hunting me."

Camilla eyed him with distaste. "This is the one you told me about, yes? The escaped lunatic?"

Sniper nodded.

"You don't have any reason to believe it was her in Berlin. How could it have been? She's on the run from the police. She was only seventeen at the time you say she shot at you. You're getting worked up over nothing." Camilla shook her head impatiently. Nursemaiding paranoiacs was not part of her job description. "You need to get out more. You sit in here week in week out, surrounded by armed guards. It would drive anybody nuts."

Sniper snarled at her, but behind his eyes there was the need for reassurance.

"I know Patty. She's beautiful, clever, cunning. I don't want her sneaking around trying to kill me. I want her dead!"

Outside were the sun and the lawns, the trees and the little white clouds, all the bright apparatus of a lovely summer's day, but none of it could dispel the darkness which hung about Sniper like a shroud.

Camilla sighed. Oh yes, it would so much better if the girl were dead.

\* \* \* \*

Jay got home late but it was still light outside. Unlike the previous evening, it was warm and pleasant. He looked forward to seeing Sandra. She would be there at his flat as they had agreed. He planned to take her out for a meal, then maybe to a club. They could dance. It had been a long, long time since he'd danced, and even longer since he'd been on a date. Not that he should really think of it as a date. He was her handler now. She was his informant. They had a professional relationship. Besides, he hardly knew her. He'd seen her a few times, spoken to her for a few hours. Hardly the basis for anything, really.

Yet as he stood outside his flat, he couldn't help feeling buoyed up and excited. The feeling lasted until he swung the door open.

Cupboards were open, their contents strewn on the floor.

The doors to the bedrooms were open. Beyond the entrance hall, he could see upturned furniture in the sitting room. In an instant, without even thinking about it, he had his department-standard Glock 18 in a two-handed grip, muzzle down, safety off, just as he had been trained. He moved swiftly and quietly down the hallway, checking each room as he passed until he reached the sitting room. A quick left-right glance showed it was empty. He stepped lightly across to the kitchen counter and checked behind it. Nothing. No one.

Yet someone had been in his apartment, ransacked it, and left. Had Sandra been here when it happened? There was no blood anywhere, which was good news. Had someone got her? Taken her?

"Jesus, what a mess."

He whirled around, gun up, to find Sandra standing in the doorway, looking at the devastation of his belongings with serious eyes. He struggled to control his breathing, his heart hammering in his chest. "Christ! I nearly shot you!"

"What, again? Maybe you should keep it in your holster."

Jay took a couple of deep, calming breaths and put his gun away. Whoever had been here was long gone. "Is it going to be like this every night when I come home now? 'Cause if it is, I don't think my nerves can stand it."

Sandra straightened a chair and sat down in it. "Put the kettle on, would you?"

Automatically, Jay did as he was asked. In his mind the possible reasons for what had happened were already chasing each other round and round. "Lucky you weren't in when this happened."

"I was in," she said. "The lucky thing is I was taking a nap in the bedroom."

Jay put down the cups he was holding and stared at her.

"I heard them in the hallway while they were working on the lock. I barely got out in time."

"But how could you get out? There's only one door."

She grinned at him. "The same way I got in yesterday, of course. Through the bedroom window. The rope was still there. Neither of us had removed it. And the window is still broken. I just climbed out and up the rope to the roof. Then I pulled the rope up after me."

"But it must be twenty meters to the roof from here!"

"Nah, not that much. It wasn't so hard—except for the last bit. That was tricky."

"Jesus."

"Anyway, I stayed on the roof until they'd left and then watched them go back to their car. Two men, late twenties, early thirties, short hair, casual clothes, nice car. They came at about three o'clock."

"And you've been on the roof ever since then?"

"Yup. What do you think they were after?"

A man's voice said, "You, love."

They both looked toward the door where a short-haired man in his early thirties, wearing casual clothes, stood with a Russian PP2030 submachine gun pointed at Sandra. Behind him, in the hallway, was another man, similarly armed. Jay reached for his own gun, but the muzzle of the PP2030 swung his way before his hand was halfway there.

"Don't be stupid," the gunman said. "We just want the girl."

Then all hell broke loose.

With the gun aimed at Jay, Sandra shot out of the chair, delivering a flying kick that took the gun right out of the man's hands. Before Jay had even had time to gasp in surprise, she had whirled around to slam the man in the stomach with a straight-arm punch that sent him staggering back into his companion. The other man pushed his partner roughly aside and brought his gun to bear on Sandra. Like a cat, she crouched low and dived to the side as flame and noise erupted into the room. Even though the weapon was silenced, it made an ear-splitting clatter as it spat bullets into the apartment at ten rounds a second. Furniture, floor and walls exploded into fragments as the stream of bullets ripped across the room.

Sandra disappeared behind a cloud of smoke and dust, scrambling for nonexistent cover. The destruction followed her until a rapid series of explosions from Jay's handgun stopped it dead. The gunman, two bullets in his torso and one in his head, fell to the ground in a bloody heap. By the time Jay had turned to take aim at the other man, he was already running down the corridor. Jay let him go.

As the dust and smoke cleared, he saw Sandra sitting on the floor against the far wall. She was panting heavily and there was blood all over her left calf. He holstered his gun and ran to her, jumping over the fallen man.

"Did he hit you? Are you okay?"

Sandra pulled up the leg of her jeans and studied her wounds. She shook her head without looking up. "It's just splinters—bits of concrete from the floor, I think." She gingerly pulled a small grey shard from her ankle, setting off another trickle of blood. "Hurts like hell though."

Jay inspected the cuts. None of them looked too deep. "God, you were lucky. I'll get some water to clean you up. Stay here." He went back to the kitchenette, stepped over the body again, grabbed some disinfectant and put some warm water in a bowl.

"You'll have to do something about him," Sandra said,

nodding at the dead body.

Sandra looked pale but otherwise seemed to be all right. Jay's hands had a slight tremor as he cleaned Sandra's many small cuts. He had often wondered if he would have the nerve to kill a man. It hadn't been the moral dilemma he had expected, just a simple matter of necessity. In fact, he had wanted the man dead very much in that moment and had felt nothing but satisfaction when he saw him fall. He still only felt gratitude that the stranger was dead and not Sandra.

Jay got up and fetched some Band-Aids from the bathroom. As he was sticking them on, he felt Sandra's hand on his cheek. He looked up at her for the first time since the shooting. There was an intense tenderness in her eyes that made him catch his breath.

"Thank you," she said. "Thank you." And then she leaned forward and gently, slowly, kissed his lips.

For a moment, he was happy just to let her kiss him, but then a wave of passion surged in him and he grabbed her shoulders and pulled her to him, crushing her mouth with his, letting loose the desire that had been building in him. In response, she held his head and opened up to him. When the kiss was over, they drew apart. Jay stared into her eyes, openmouthed, the feel of her lips still on his, his breath shallow and his heart pounding. "I—" he said, feeling he ought to say something, but all he could think of saying was how much he loved her. But then the horrible reality of the situation flooded back into the moment. He blinked, remembering the shooting, the gunmen, the dead body behind him.

"We need to get out of here, right now," he said, jumping to his feet. "Can you walk? It won't be long before they're back. And the police will probably show up soon too. We've got to be gone before they get here."

They left the flat, pausing only to pick up the two submachine guns and to check the dead man's pockets. There was no ID on him, but they found two ammo clips in a back pocket.

Leaving the building through an emergency exit at the back, they kept moving for several blocks. Sandra was limping a little, but her leg seemed okay and the bleeding had stopped by the time they got into a taxi on Westferry Road. They headed for the West End, for want of anywhere specific to go, and got out of the cab when Jay spotted an electronics shop that was open. He grabbed a dozen prepaid compads— the "poor man's compatch"—from a bin, and bought the lot using cash.

"What are you doing?" Sandra demanded when they were outside again.

"I need to make a call and I've had to disable my compatch."

She looked down at his wrist. "What?"

"They can trace an active compatch. So if we need to make a call, we use these." He gave her a handful and she put them in her jacket pocket. They started walking up the street, still heading west.

"Who can trace a compatch? The police?"

"No. Well, yes, they could, but it's not the police I'm worried about. Look, who do you think sent those guys after you?"

She shrugged. "Sniper. Who else?"

"I don't think so. How did Sniper know where you were?"

"I don't know. Someone must have told him they'd seen me. Then he had me followed…"

Jay shook his head. "The only people who knew exactly where you'd be are the people in my office."

"But you work for…"

"Yes, I do. And that's how they can trace my compatch. And that's why I'm going to call them using one of these." He held up a compad. "One call on each and then we throw it away. Got it?"

"Call them? Are you mad? Didn't you just imply they tried to kill me?"

"I don't know if that was the plan. They came to get you, but, if you hadn't started kicking the crap out of them, maybe that's all they'd have done."

"They seemed pretty trigger-happy to me."

Jay had to admit she was right. Whoever sent them to collect her clearly hadn't cared if they delivered her in one piece. "I need to call Five. They can take possession of the body, keep the police off my back. Otherwise I'll be on the run too and I need to be on the inside or we'll never find out who's doing what—and we'll never stop Sniper."

She stepped away from him and stopped walking. "So you're just going to hand me in? Just like that?"

"No, of course not." He moved toward her but she stepped back. "I'm going to find you somewhere safe to stay. Then I'll tell them you ran off and I lost you."

"I've got somewhere safe to stay."

"No, you haven't. Five has your address. I spent most of the day briefing them about you. They know everything I know."

"Well, that's not much." She was being petulant and sulky, but at least she had stopped being hostile. She closed her eyes and lifted her face to the sky. "Why did I ever trust you in the first place?"

"I've got kind eyes."

"What?" She looked at him to see if he was joking.

"My mum told me. I have kind eyes."

Despite herself, she started to smile. "Do you know somewhere safe?" she asked.

"Not really, but I know a man who does. Come on."

They set off walking again.

"We need to get on a tube as soon as we can," Jay said.

"Why's that? No one's following us."

"You looked up at the sky. If they just happen to have a spy satellite over the area, your face will be lighting up every alarm in GCHQ right now."

Sandra grinned at him and pointed up at the gathering cloud. "I think we're safe on that score."

* * * *

A sudden summer storm pelted fat raindrops at the French windows. The evening sky had darkened prematurely. Sniper sat in an overstuffed armchair facing the dreary weather. His head hung down and his breathing was slow and steady. Little flecks of blood spattered his bare chest.

He muttered and swore to himself in German, sometimes clenching his big fists, sometimes shaking his head angrily. "It's all coming apart!" he wailed to the empty room. Everything was screwed up. Everything was wrong.

The girl in the gym was dead. He'd taken it too far in the end. Long after she had stopped enjoying it, long after he had, she had spat out a final litany of invective against him and died. Just like that.

It had shaken him. Not because the silly cow had died, but because, after the first hour or so, he had taken so little pleasure in it. Her degradation and torture had been almost automatic, a compulsion he endured because he needed to do it. Needed to, like some pathetic addict jacking up just so he could get through the day, all pleasure gone, all meaning lost. He'd given Camilla the job of organizing the disposal of the body. She had told him just what she thought of his recklessness and stupidity. She'd also been very specific about what she thought about his mental health. She had described in detail what would happen to him if his inability to keep himself under control brought the police to their door. And he'd let her rant and curse at him. As long as she got that mess cleaned up, he didn't care what she said.

"Just like Berlin," he said aloud. The rush of insight made him gasp with surprise. It was just like Berlin. They were within days of the lob. Everything had gone so smoothly, but then he'd pulled that stunt with the stolen switches. Had he been deliberately trying to sabotage the timesplash? It hadn't seemed so at the time. He just needed to do something exciting to make himself feel alive, something his damned Yank paymasters wouldn't like. It had driven Klaatu away. Maybe the kid had seen something Sniper hadn't?

Was that what he'd just done with the girl, set out to wreck the lob again? Could he really be trying to fail? Was he such a coward? The biggest damned splash of all time was waiting for him. Wasn't that what he wanted? Wasn't that his destiny?

"You're my big brave boy. Such a big strong boy."

At the sound of his mother's voice, he spun around looking for her. She wasn't in the room.

Outside, thunder crashed. A wind had sprung up and was bending the trees, slapping rain against the windows. Sniper opened the French doors and walked out into the storm. Cold, wet air gusted against his naked torso. He felt his mother's hands on his skin, her fingers caressing his nipples.

"*Mutti*!" he shouted. But he couldn't see her anywhere.

Her lips moved down his chest. Her hand slid along his thigh.

He was thirteen. Confused. Frightened by what was happening. His erection ached and yearned for her touch. It disgusted him, enraged him. "No!" he cried, slapping her hands away. His fingers found a heavy ornament, curled around it. "No! No! No!"

Thunder cracked the sky, above him like the voice of God. He gaped at his empty hand, fingers clawed, trembling with fury. A wall of rain smacked against his bare skin, clean and invigorating. Cold as ice, it sluiced the blood from his face and chest, waking him up, clearing his thoughts.

He would tear it all down, wipe it all out. He would rip the rotten fabric of the universe. "I can do it!" he bellowed into the storm. "I will do it!" He would make a splash like no one ever could or would make again. He would shred reality, smash it to a pulp. It would be his *magnum opus*, his *meisterwerk*.

Lightning snaked across the clouds and he looked up at it, his face a snarl of determination. He would tear the world down brick by brick with his bare hands if that's what it took. Somehow, he had forgotten who he was. Somewhere along the way, he had become a pawn in the game, not a player. Well that was over now. It was time to remember himself. Time to take back control of his life.

He bellowed at the downpour, at the crashing thunder. He filled his lungs, threw back his head and roared.

# Chapter 16

### Time Enough

Jay's mother left Sandra in the spare bedroom and went to find her son. He was in the kitchen, making a couple of sandwiches. Waving him aside, she took over the job.

"It's just for one night, Mum. I'll find somewhere else in the morning."

"And your place is a wreck because the ceiling fell in?" She sounded sceptical.

"The guy upstairs let his bath overflow."

"So, if that hadn't happened, Sandra would have been staying in your flat tonight?"

Jay finally realized where this was going. "It's not like that, Mum. Honest. I'm just helping her out."

"Just helping her out. And that's because her flat is being redecorated. Isn't that what you said?" Jay wasn't quite sure what he'd said, but he bluffed it out with a noncommittal smile. His mother changed tack. "She's a very pretty girl."

"I—I suppose."

"I daresay you hadn't noticed. Boys don't notice things like that, do they?"

"All right, she's gorgeous. What's that got to do with anything?"

"Pretty girls like that can get men to do all kinds of things for them—especially young men who don't look past the big helpless eyes and the long sexy legs."

"Mu-um!"

"I'm just saying you have to be careful. Obviously there's more to this than you're telling me and I don't want you getting into any kind of trouble."

Touched by this admission of concern, Jay put an arm round his mother's shoulders and gave her a squeeze. "I'll be all right, Mum. There's nothing to worry about."

Except the killers hunting for us, and the crazies trying to blow up London, he thought, but it was probably best not to mention that kind of thing to his mother.

"I do worry about you, Jay," his mother said.

"Oh, er, sorry." Sandra, having just walked into the kitchen, started backing out again.

"Oh, hello, Sandra. Come on in."

"Mum's just made us some sandwiches," Jay said. "Pull up a chair. I'll put the kettle on."

"My goodness but you look lovely," Jay's mother exclaimed.

Sandra had showered and changed and was looking fresh and relaxed in a light summer dress and sandals.

"Jay's dad and I often wondered what kind of girl he would bring home one day." Jay gaped at his mother, hardly believing his ears. "We never expected anyone as pretty as you, dear."

"Mu-um!" Wailing pathetically was all Jay could do in the face of such an excruciating gaffe. Sandra giggled and beamed at Jay, enjoying both the compliment and Jay's embarrassment.

"So I'm the first one?" she asked, twisting the knife.

"He's never really been much of a one for the girls," Jay's mother confided, and Jay closed his eyes and prayed for death.

"I'll leave you two alone then," his mother said brightly and hurried out of the room.

"I didn't say anything that would have made her think … you know … that we were…"

"Oh, shut up," Sandra said, laughing, and sat down to eat her sandwich. "Your mum's sweet. And she certainly knows how to press your buttons." She bit into the thick bread. "Ummm, I'm starving."

"You mean she was saying all that on purpose?"

Sandra regarded him, head cocked. "Do they make you pass an idiot test or something before they let you into the secret service?"

Sulking a little, Jay sat down too.

"Did you call your friend?" she asked.

"It's all fixed up. Or it will be by tomorrow." He had taken a walk out to the main road and used the number Bauchet had left with him. The superintendent had been surprised, but had agreed to sort out something by the morning. Then Jay had got onto a bus, dropped his compad under the seat, got off at the next stop and walked home.

"I wish we could stay here," Sandra said. "I'd like to get to know your mum and dad."

Jay looked into her big eyes and wondered why she would want such a thing. "You're an orphan, right?" A little frown crossed her face. Jay rattled off what he'd read in her file. "Born 2032. Both parents dead. Raised in orphanages and foster homes. Ran away from a foster family aged thirteen. Arrested in Ommen, Holland, aged fifteen. Sentenced to six months imprisonment under the Temporal Displacement Regulation Act, plus three years for reckless endangerment. Both of which you would have served by now—given good behaviour—if they hadn't extradited you to the UK where they promptly detained you under Section Eight of the Mental Health Act of 2022."

Sandra chewed her sandwich, looking at the table. She said nothing.

"How come they did that? Sectioned you, I mean." Jay had a horrible feeling he should keep his mouth shut, but he couldn't help asking. The whole subject was troubling him more and more all the time. "You don't seem all that crazy to me."

She looked up at him at last. "Didn't you pull my medical records too?"

He nodded. "They didn't really make much sense. Obsession, paranoia, post-traumatic shock, that kind of thing." He couldn't read her expression but he went on, anyway. "Sounds to me like you had a bad experience that really shook you up and, well, people overreacted a bit."

Her eyes fell again. "I needed taking care of," she said flatly. "After what happened at Ommen ... and then the police and the trial ... I was glad when they put me in the Institute. If they'd kept me in prison..."

On an impulse, he reached across the table and took her hand. She didn't pull away. "But you're all right now?"

She shook her head. "Maybe." She didn't seem too certain.

It struck him that he might have done the wrong thing, getting the Section 8 revoked, that maybe she would be better off where they could help her. A gritty wind pushed against the kitchen window. Jay hadn't noticed that it was raining.

"Why did you run away?"

"From the Institute? I had to. I wasn't safe there. Nobody's safe any more."

He thought he understood. He hoped he did. "When this is over—" he began, but she lifted her eyes and looked straight into his. He stopped, surprised by the powerful need he saw there. He took a breath. "When this is over, and we're all safe again, will you stay here in London, so I can still see you?"

With a slow smile, she reached out her other hand and laid it over his. She nodded, eyes bright.

\* \* \* \*

Two black armored Mercedes pulled into the parking lot. The mid-morning sun was high over the shiny offices of Bailey and Sons Light Industrial Ltd. of Deptford, London. The storms of last night had washed everything clean.

Four armed men emerged from one of the cars and took up positions around the building's entrance. A moment later, four more men got out of the other car. Two of these went into the building while the other two flanked the car. They exchanged a few words on a closed compatch channel. Then one of the men beside the second Merc opened the door, letting Sniper step out. Without looking at him, the armed men scanned the quiet streets for signs of trouble.

Sniper moved quickly into the building. One of the guards who had preceded him said, "All clear, sir," and the group relaxed just a fraction.

Inside, a young receptionist who had been murmuring into the comm looked up with a smile and said, "Ms. Vergara will be along shortly, sir."

"Ah, there you are." Camilla managed to sound more accusatory than welcoming. Sniper was, after all, two hours late and she wasn't going to let him get away scot-free. She bustled into the small foyer and took charge, leading him toward the double doors beyond the reception desk.

"This way. We've all been waiting."

Sniper shrugged her hand off his arm and stopped dead. "What do you think you're doing?"

Camilla stopped too, as if remembering herself. She took a breath. "You're right. I'm being rude. I get so used to people being on time for meetings, I forget that the great Sniper doesn't live by ordinary rules. I should have asked first, of course, whether you can be bothered to come inside and do what you're being paid to do, or whether you'd rather I pimped a couple more whores for you to go home and play with."

Sniper hit her across the face so fast she didn't have time to flinch. It was an open-handed slap that sent her sprawling to the ground, momentarily stunned. The receptionist cried out and immediately clasped her hands to her mouth.

Sniper looked down at Camilla who was too dazed to get up. "*Arschloch*," he said, spitting out the word with utter contempt. Without a backward glance, he strode off through the double doors.

\* \* \* \*

"Klaatu!" Sniper shouted as he entered the workshop.

Bailey and Sons was a light engineering company that Flash had bought and used as the front for his operations. Apart from the few offices and reception, the main body of the building was a large open workshop with a delivery yard and storage at the rear.

At the moment, there was little activity. The F2 generators had been disconnected and were standing on palettes in one corner, and the cage itself was under a tarpaulin at the centre of the room. A forklift truck stood idle, as did the drills, lathes and other machinery.

A door opened from a small office at the back and Klaatu stepped out. Behind him was a bank of glowing displays. Sniper strode toward his teknik and they met halfway across the stained concrete floor. They stood in silence looking at one another. Beside them, the bulk of the cage loomed.

"I have been a crazy man," Sniper said, a little stiffly. "You are right to want to leave me. I would have brought us both down."

Klaatu watched him warily, saying nothing.

"I promise you, there will be no more shit like that, no more stupid risks, no more childishness. From today, I am focused on what must be done. From today, I am completely dedicated to making this splash work."

Klaatu studied the big man's eyes. "Good," he said, not bothering to hide his anger. "And afterwards?"

Sniper nodded, acknowledging Klaatu's right to ask. "Afterwards, it is over. For me anyway. The splash is all I care about. All this other shit…" He vaguely waved a hand but Klaatu knew what it indicated. "It spoils the fun, don't you think?" He gave a wan smile. "This is my show now. Mine and yours. Like it used to be. Camilla and the rest can go fuck themselves."

Slowly, Klaatu nodded, hardly daring to believe the change that had come. "And the target?"

Sniper shrugged. "It's a good target. We'll still use it."

"And the money?"

Sniper's smile became wolfish. "That's one of the big mistakes I've been making. Relying on other people makes you weak. I don't like being weak. It makes me cranky."

For the first time, Klaatu smiled too. "So I should probably start building the rig, then?"

Sniper inclined his head in agreement. "Do your thing, man. And I'll do mine."

He held out his hand and Klaatu shook it without hesitation. To the young teknik it felt as if the sun had come out from behind a cloud.

"I need to take care of some business," Sniper said. "It won't take long. Then I'll be back to go through the plans, okay?"

\* \* \* \*

Sniper went back out to the reception area. Camilla, blood smeared across her face, was shouting into her compatch. When she saw Sniper, she stopped immediately and backed away from him.

"Hang up," he said, quietly. After a little hesitation, she complied.

"Take her back to the house," he told one of the armed guards, not taking his eyes off Camilla.

"If she resists, break her legs, but keep her alive. I need information from her—names, netIDs, account numbers."

Her eyes flashed defiance. She turned to the guard. "Don't you dare touch me. Who the hell do you think pays your wages?"

The guard took a look at Sniper and quickly made his mind up about where his best interests lay. He stepped forward and took her by the arm. She stiffened and for a moment it looked like she might argue with him. But the moment passed and she let herself be led outside. Sniper watched her go. Man, it felt good to be back in control!

\* \* \* \*

Bauchet paced the small sitting room deep in thought. His head was down and he walked with a slight stoop, making him look like a vulture pondering its latest carcass. Jay sat on the edge of an old and uncomfortable sofa and watched him pass back and forth.

"This is not what I expected when I gave you my number, my young friend."

"I didn't know who else to ask for help. If I can't trust Five…"

They were in a Metropolitan Police safe house in the London suburb of Barnes, south of the river and well to the west of the city centre.

"I can't keep her with me," Jay went on, "and I don't want to let her fend for herself. She isn't safe."

Bauchet shook his head in a brisk dismissal. "Of course, you did the right thing. My contact at Scotland Yard is very discreet. He told everyone he has a small-time drug dealer here 'ratting out' his friends, as he put it. The young lady will be safe. We can debrief her here and no one will find her."

Sandra was in the kitchen with a plain-clothes policewoman at Bauchet's request. The superintendent's insistence on a few minutes alone with Jay was not unexpected, but it still had Jay nervously watching him as he paced.

"Tell me again everything that was said when you

introduced this girl to your superiors."

Jay did so.

"And you told no one else about her? And you are sure she spoke to no one else about you?"

Jay gave his affirmatives and Bauchet shook his head.

"This gives us a difficult problem, you agree?"

Jay couldn't guess from among the many problems he could see which one Bauchet had in mind.

"I don't think MI5 is going to blow up London. Do you, Jay?"

"I suppose not."

"So it is not MI5 that sent those killers after Ms. Malone, n' est-ce pas?"

"I ... Well, yes, but who else could it have been? Only Five knew she was with me."

Bauchet made an impatient gesture. "Your security services are not a single organism. MI5 is just a group of people. We need to ask ourselves who in the service knew about Ms. Malone. Then we have our list of suspects."

"You mean there's a traitor in my office?"

"Precisely. A mole, as they say."

"Working for who?"

Bauchet gave a Gallic shrug. "When we find him, we must ask him."

They both fell silent.

"Only Holbrook, Overman and Porterhouse were at the briefing." Jay was unhappy to think it could be any of them. "I don't know if they told anyone else. It's Holbrook's baby, really—and Overman's. Porterhouse was just there to act scary. Which he does very well, by the way."

"I will look into it," Bauchet said, ending the conversation. "It may not be easy. Meanwhile, you must take Ms. Malone to the office and she must tell them what she knows. Tell them she ran away last night but returned in the morning. She should have a story too. She has decided Sniper is trying to kill her and she will be safer with your people. Something like that. Remember, you must not tell your superiors what you suspect. Tell them you believe the girl. It is better they think you are an idiot than that they try to kill you. Do not call ahead. Do not give them warning. Just walk into the building and announce yourself. That way no one can intercept you. You understand?"

Jay understood all right.

\* \* \* \*

"This isn't why I came to you, Jay."

Sandra sat in the back of the taxi, showing no signs of getting out. The SIS Building gleamed in the bright sunshine, right next to them. The taxi driver, isolated in his attack-proof cage, glanced over his shoulder and then turned the meter back on.

"I just wanted you to help me get past Sniper's guards. Something like that. I didn't expect … all this. It's all got out of control."

"Yeah. I suppose it has, but what else can we do? There are people hunting for you out there. You'll be safe with Bauchet's people. And the deal we've done with Five means you're free again. That's got to be worth changing your plans for."

She smiled weakly. "Tell me that your people can stop Sniper."

"If they can't, I don't know who can."

Sandra clearly didn't like the answer. Jay could see how she must feel. She couldn't stop Sniper on her own. The brick was so surrounded by security now that she couldn't get near him. She had to rely on Jay. But even he realized that trusting MI5 might be a dangerous mistake. And then he had asked her to trust Bauchet and the London police too. So many people and any one of them could give her away.

"Nothing can happen to you in there," he said, nodding toward the building. "I won't let anyone hurt you."

Unexpectedly, she laughed. "I can take care of myself," she said. Just as quickly, the laugh was gone. "Sniper can't get away." Her eyes willed him to understand. "He has to die. Promise me that. Tell me he'll die. That's what I want to hear."

Jay swallowed. He looked around as if he might find help in the taxi's dingy interior, in the ads flickering across its seat backs and doors. Finding nothing, he said, "I can't promise you that, Sandra. I can't promise to kill someone. It's just … I'll do my best to stop him though, and bring him to justice."

She looked away from him, at the slow-moving traffic and the river beyond. In the end, she said, "Okay. Let's do it."

Jay wanted to say more, but decided he should leave it at that. Sandra's fragile acceptance of the situation was probably all he could hope for at the moment.

They went into the building and he called Holbrook from the front desk. Within minutes, building security officers were leading them up to the top floor, where Overman greeted them with an uncertain frown.

"I thought we'd lost you, young lady," the section head said, leading them into a comfortably appointed meeting room.

Sandra turned to Jay, looking cross. "If he's going to talk to me like a patronizing jerk, I'm leaving now."

Instantly, Overman's manner changed. He stepped up to Sandra and glowered into her face. He was only a little taller than her, yet his physical presence was completely dominating. "All right, so you're a hot streetwise little bitch. We all get it. Now sit down and stop trying to impress me."

For an instant, shock, then anger, flicked across Sandra's features, then something else—curiosity, mingled with recognition. She smiled sweetly and took a seat. "Anything you like," she simpered, keeping her eyes on Overman's, crossing her long legs deliberately. Overman did not seem even slightly mollified by her sudden compliance. He took a seat opposite her and tapped the desk. A virtual keyboard and display appeared and he busied himself setting up the recording equipment.

"Thank you, Jay," Overman said to him. "Close the door on your way out."

"Ah, yeah. Okay." He turned to Sandra. "I'll see you later."

She looked at him with distant eyes and gave him a vague acknowledgement., then turned back to Overman.

Jay stumbled into the corridor and leaned against the wall. His stomach clenched and he felt hollow inside. Whatever had just happened between Overman and Sandra, he could not begin to understand except on a visceral level. All he knew was that he hated it. This sophisticated and flirtatious woman was nothing like the Sandra he thought he knew. She was playing a game with Overman in which Jay had no part. Some kind of offer was being made, a relationship established. It was an aspect of Sandra that Jay had never seen, that he felt excluded from. That look she had exchanged with Overman was one he knew instinctively would never be turned on him. For all the feelings for her he thought he had, he was shockingly reminded that he didn't know her at all. He wanted to get out into the air. He needed to be alone to nurse his pain.

* * * *

Sniper was at the airport again, in a hired limo. This time, Klaatu was in the back with him. The driver was armed, and so was the man riding shotgun. The limo was armored. More paranoia, Klaatu thought. A third security guard arrived with two other men in tow. They waited outside the car until Sniper had scrutinized them through the tinted windows.

"That's the correct package," Sniper said into his compatch and the guard opened the door to let the two men enter, closing it after them and moving away to put their luggage in the boot.

Inside the car, there was the sound of reunion.

T-800, as dark and saturnine as ever, cracked a smile Klaatu had rarely seen. "Man, I'm glad to see you again!" he told Sniper, gripping the German's hand with both of his. "I am so looking forward to this!"

"Me too, mate," said the man beside him. His Australian accent was obvious. He grabbed Sniper's hand as soon as T-800 released it. "Glad to see you again, you crazy bastard."

Sniper turned back to T-800 and grinned. "I take it you've met Edna. We go back a long way."

The Aussie answered for him. "We met on the plane. Had a good old chin-wag."

Sniper laughed. "Yeah, right. And this is my uberteknik, Klaatu."

T-800 nodded in Klaatu's direction. Klaatu nodded back.

Edna looked from one to the other. "Jeez, you two make more noise than a two dollar radio!"

226

He laughed at his own observation. Then he put out his hand. "I've heard a lot about you, mate."

Klaatu shook it briefly.

"Of course, most of it was from this lying bastard, so I don't believe a word of it."

Klaatu tried not to let his smile waver too much. These were the bricks Sniper had recruited for the splash. They didn't need to be intelligent, he told himself, just physically robust, and crazy enough to cause as much mayhem as possible at the other end. The Aussie certainly looked tough. The fact that the Aussie had a girl's name puzzled him, but bricks weren't like normal people. Maybe he picked the name just to get into fights.

"Okay, Sniper," T-800 said, cutting through the geniality of the moment. "Let's hear about the target. What's your plan?"

Sniper waved his question away. "Tomorrow. We'll talk plans tomorrow. In fact, I'll take you both to the target site. It's still here. But, tonight, we party!" His compatch chimed and he glanced at it in annoyance. "Get that will you, Klaatu?"

Klaatu gave the commands to route the call while Sniper described the venue and the entertainment he'd arranged for his friends. Klaatu listened silently for a while, then said, "It's the investors."

"Tell them to fuck off."

"I think you need to hear this."

Sniper gave him a look that said he'd better be sure, but Klaatu remained impassive. Eventually, Sniper took the call. He snapped at the voice on the other end, saying he didn't want to know, but, after a short while, he shut up and listened. When he hung up, he glanced around at the others.

His face was rigid with anger. He hit the limo's intercom. "Forget the house," he said.

"Take us to the engineering works. And make it fast."

# Chapter 17

## Plots and Plans

"The plan has three parts," said Overman. He was in the same meeting room in which he had interviewed Sandra that morning, but Sandra was long gone. Now Holbrook, Porterhouse, Jay, and three other MI5 officers were his audience. There was also a well-built stranger with a visitor's pass to whom Jay had not been introduced.

"The first is to infiltrate Sniper's operation with a teknik from our staff. If they're in the building phase, they will be recruiting. There's a good chance we can get someone inside. We have several undercover operatives already in the field attempting to make contact. The successful agent's main priorities will be to identify the target for the splash and to sabotage the work where possible. They will also provide intel on the movements of the principals so that the second part of the plan can be put into operation."

Jay eyed the man discreetly. Overman had been locked away with Sandra most of the day. Was it possible he had done more than just interview her? After all, the way she had looked at him ...

"Currently, we have a home address for Sniper and the

address of an engineering works in Deptford." The information appeared on their desk viewers. "If we are unsuccessful with the first part of the plan, we will raid both these locations. I have invited Colonel Davidson here from The Regiment to undertake the raids." Jay knew that meant 22 Regiment, Special Air Service. Overman nodded at the SAS colonel as if they were old acquaintances. "However, I'm hoping we can get an officer inside and gather as much intel as possible before we need to take this step."

Jay glanced at his compatch. It was already early evening. He imagined the undercover agents already out there, cruising the bars and clubs, trying to let it be known they were splash tekniks looking for work, hoping to connect with Sniper's recruiters, possibly even Klaatu himself. He wondered what Sandra was doing. Had she gone back to the safe house in Barnes? Should he go there too after the meeting? If he did, what would he say to her?

"Finally," Overman said, "the third part of the plan is a fallback in case the raids go pear-shaped." He glanced at Holbrook and received a discreet nod. "I'd like you all to follow me, please. There's something I'd like to show you."

He led them out of the meeting and down the corridor to the lifts. He ushered them inside and took them down to the ground floor. They went down another corridor and then another until they reached a steel door.

"From now on," he said, "you each have access to this area." He put his finger into the DNA sampler. When he got a green light, he pushed the door open and led them inside. There was another short corridor and then double doors that opened onto a large room that was mostly empty.

Jay looked around. There were steel cabinets lining the walls and a long bench of workstations with banks of displays facing the handful of people working there. Fat cables crossed the floor from several places and ended at a three-meter-square platform at the centre of the room. The platform had a handrail and black and yellow tape marking its edges, but was otherwise unremarkable.

A woman at one of the workstations stood up and crossed the room to greet them. She looked young, not much older than Jay. She wore jeans and a red blouse and seemed unreasonably casual beside the suited men and women who had just entered her domain.

"This is Nahrees," Overman told them, "and she runs this facility."

Jay did a double take. Wasn't that a minor character from an old Marvel comic book? In which case, "Nahrees" was a tag. In which case … He looked around the room again, more carefully this time.

"What we have here—" Overman went on, but was interrupted by Jay.

"It's a lobsite!" Jay couldn't contain himself. "You plan to go back and intercept Sniper at the splash target before he can cause an anomaly!"

"Give the man a coconut," said Nahrees, amused at his excitement. "We haven't met, have we?"

Jay looked at her, not really taking in what she said. He was shocked at the audacity of the plan. His head was whirling, thinking through the consequences. "Oh, this is a really bad idea," he said. "You're going to lob the SAS back to fight Sniper and his guys on the streets of old London. That's just…"

As Jay searched for a word that expressed the full extent of the stupidity of the idea, Overman spoke up. "As I said, this is the third part of the plan. The fallback. If all else fails,

Colonel Davidson's team will jump back to the splash target and neutralize Sniper and his crew."

Holbrook was looking at Jay with a curious expression. "Why is that such a bad idea, Jay?"

Overman pursed his lips, clamping down on an angry retort. Jay saw it and it gave him an unexpected moment of satisfaction.

"A timesplash works when you create a paradox in the past," Jay said. "You kill your own mother, or you stop Einstein inventing special relativity or whatever. The anomaly sends spacetime wild but the timestream flows back into place. I don't know the physics of how that works…"

"Metatemporal pseudodimensionality," Nahrees said.

Jay shook his head as if there was a gnat in his ear. "Whatever. The backwash from all this eventually hits the present and that's what brings down the cities."

"Is this going somewhere?" Overman asked.

Jay took a breath. "The thing is, if you go back to, say, the early 1900s, in central London, and start a shoot-out with armed maniacs, you don't know who might get hurt. Just think of the people who were around at that time and place!" He closed his eyes. "I can't think of anybody offhand, but there's bound to be loads of scientists, philosophers, writers, politicians, inventors, industrialists, philanthropists … If any one of them is killed, it could be just as bad as whatever Sniper is planning."

"My men are trained to avoid collateral damage," the SAS colonel said.

"But that's all that Sniper lives for. Once you get him cornered, he'll take out as many random passers-by as he can. Would you risk the lives of maybe two million people on the chance that you'll get all Sniper's people before they have a chance to spray the streets with machine gun bullets?"

"As I said," Overman repeated through clenched teeth, "this is our fallback. We know the risks. It's better than letting Sniper just go ahead and do what he wants."

Nahrees spoke to Jay. "He's right. We've run the simulations. The chances of our guys shooting someone really important are thousands to one." Jay turned to her feeling vaguely betrayed, as if she should have been supporting him.

"Look at it this way," she went on. "If we leave Sniper alone, the probability that he'll kill someone important is one. Certainty."

Overman had his irritation under control again. "It's good that you're raising these issues, Jay, but you have to trust that we're not going into this blindly." He spoke as much for Holbrook's benefit as for Jay's. "We've done our sums. The very fact of a shoot-out in central London with modern weapons—even if no one but Sniper's team and our own people get killed—will create an anomaly big enough to cause some pretty serious damage. But, if all else fails, this is a calculated risk we have to take."

Jay backed down, unwilling to argue any more. He still thought it was a crazy, dangerous plan. In fact, just the kind of plan that an MI5 mole would come up with to make sure that the timesplash succeeded—one way or another. He eyed Overman with the growing conviction that he was the traitor.

# Chapter 18

## Night Time

Sandra didn't go back to the safe house when she left the SIS Building. Instead, she went to Waterloo Station and caught the first train she could get to Godalming in Surrey. It was a slow train and she had to change at Woking, but by the early evening she was in a taxi heading south east into the gentle hills and open farmland of the Surrey countryside. She paid off the taxi and walked the last couple of kilometres. She had done this before many times over the past two months. At a point under a low ridge, she left the road and crossed a field, climbing to a spot at the other side where she could follow the line of a hedge into the trees at the back of Sniper's house.

The light was beginning to fail, but the evening was warm. The big house looked peaceful. She did a circuit of it, keeping well away. One of Sniper's Mercedes was missing. So was the big black all-terrain vehicle his guards liked to travel in. That was good. There might only be a couple of guards in the house. Sniper liked lots of them with him when he travelled.

She had bought herself a sandwich, a chocolate bar and some bottled water from a kiosk in Waterloo and settled now to her evening meal as she waited for night to fall. Once it was dark, she could approach the house. Until then, she would wait and watch. The interview with Overman had been a strange experience. Almost from his first words, he had treated her with an intense, almost hostile, disdain. Her retaliation was automatic. She flirted with him—and not just a little, but the full-on, no-holds-barred, seduction routine. She told herself he deserved it. She told herself she'd teach him a lesson. Yet, even at the time, she had felt a powerful thrill, an excitement that made her skin tingle, and her heart race. Sitting in the cool evening air, watching the darkness gather around Sniper's house, she ran over what had happened, letting her mind drift back to the interview that morning.

"Okay. How long have you been following Sniper?" Overman had asked.

She ignored the question. "What's your name? I can't keep calling you Mr. Overman."

"Yes, you can. How long were you following Sniper?"

She shrugged. "Since I escaped from the Institution. The day Beijing was destroyed, whenever that was."

"Why?"

She looked at him sweetly. "Why what, Mr. Overman?"

"Will you stop pissing about? It was your idea to come in here, so let's just get on with it, shall we?"

"You don't seem very friendly. I don't see why we can't be friends."

"Why are you following Sniper?"

She looked him in the eyes. "He's a good-looking guy. Strong. I like strong men."

He slammed his hand down on the desk so hard she jumped. "If you really want to fuck me, we can do it later. No problem. All right? Until then, you're going to stop this little game and you're going to tell me what I want to know."

A smart-aleck response sprang to her lips, but she suppressed it. The excitement she'd been feeling flipped over into anger. She wanted to tell him she wouldn't fuck him if he were the last man left on Earth. But she bit that down too.

"If that doesn't suit you," he said, his eyes boring into hers, "we can use other means to get information out of you. They won't be much fun."

As Sandra pondered her memories of the interview, a light came on in one of the downstairs rooms of Sniper's mansion and Sandra realized how dark it had grown. Her sandwich was gone so she started on the chocolate.

Overman had known exactly how to handle her, she realized. He hadn't let her get away with any nonsense. He'd even played her at her own game and won. And that was despite the fact that he did want her. She could see it. He even admitted it. But it wasn't important to him. He could take it or leave it. She'd only ever seen that once before, when Dr. Mason at the Institute had removed himself from her case. But even then, she'd won, got what she wanted, beaten him. He'd had to run away, confess his weakness to the others. How humiliating it must have been for him! Odd that. She'd never considered before that she had humiliated him. Not Overman, though. He was hard as nails. He'd have made a good brick. She wondered where Jay was. She wondered what he must be thinking. She should probably call him, try to explain, but what could she say?

Another light came on in an upstairs window. It would soon be time to take a closer look. She checked her compatch. Any minute now a guard would come out and do a circuit of the house. There! A man with a submachine gun in his right hand and a flashlight in his left stepped through the door and stood on the back veranda, looking around. Letting his eyes adjust to the light, Sandra thought. Then the man set off, walking slowly.

Time to go.

Crouching low, she moved quickly and quietly toward the house, keeping close to the hedge, staying behind the guard. She let him round the corner of the house before she went to the windows. It was a big rambling place with several wings in a haphazard arrangement—the main house, an extension at each end coming off at right angles, and a huge set of stables-turned-garage off one of the extensions. The guard would take several minutes before he was back again.

She went to the door he had come out of, turned the handle and pushed. It was unlocked. Once she was inside, she pulled her gun and looked about her. She was in a utility room as big as her last bedsit had been. There was a big sink in one corner and a bench with wooden slats. Coats hung on the opposite wall and Wellington boots were lined up beneath them. She moved on through a wooden door and into a carpeted corridor. She knew the layout of the ground floor. She had observed it often enough and long enough to be thoroughly familiar with it. Sniper spent most of his time in the big sitting room or in the home theatre. There was a woman who drove a bright red sports car—also missing, she realized—who had an office in the conservatory. She seemed to do all Sniper's admin. If what she was looking for was anywhere, it would be in that office.

It was easy to move silently on the carpet and listen to the sounds from the conservatory as she drew closer. A man's voice spoke in harsh, clipped phrases. A woman answered him in monosyllables, her voice low and half-sobbing. As

Sandra reached the door, the man raised his voice in anger. She heard two quick footsteps on the conservatory's stone tiles and a slap. The woman cried out—a gasp of pain and shock.

Not waiting to think about it, Sandra burst through the door, gun high. A burly, overweight man was standing over a woman. The woman was tied to an office chair with tape. Her blouse was ripped open and her hair was awry. Blood ran from a cut in her lower lip. They both looked at Sandra in surprise, but neither spoke.

"Untie her," Sandra said, taking aim at the man's big chest.

"Who the fuck are you?" he asked, sounding more irritated than scared. His eyes flicked to the big desk nearby. A submachine gun was lying there, almost within his reach.

"Don't be stupid," Sandra warned him.

He reached slowly into his trouser pocket and pulled out a penknife. Sandra watched him carefully as he unfolded the blade. He reached down to the woman's feet and cut her ankles free.

"If you're lookin' for Sniper, he ain't here, love." He had a strong London accent. He moved to the side of the chair and cut loose one of the ties around the woman's arms. Then, in a movement unexpectedly fluid and swift, he grabbed the chair and hurled it along with the woman toward Sandra.

Unable to get a clear shot and seeing the man's meaty hands reaching for the gun, Sandra launched herself at him, grabbing the chair as she went past to give herself more speed, and sending it rolling even farther. The woman cried out in alarm but by then, Sandra was barrelling into the big man.

He was knocked sideways as Sandra fell into him. The gun was in his hand but he had it by the barrel and couldn't use it—except as a club. She rolled off him and sprang to her feet. He stayed where he was. A grim smile crossed his face as he swung the muzzle round.

Sandra's first kick took him in the throat and the second mashed his fingers and sent the gun clattering across the tiles. She dropped to one knee beside him and three rapid punches to the face had him dazed and groaning. He choked as blood filled his nose and mouth. She stood up, watching him in case she needed to hit him again.

"You must be Patty." The woman in the chair had freed her other arm but remained seated, looking more relaxed and composed than she had a few moments ago. Sandra regarded her from under drawn brows. "Who are you?"

"I'm Camilla. You seem to have saved my life."

"You work here. How come Sniper's muscle was roughing you up?" She found she had her gun in her left hand and pushed it back into its holster.

"I can see why he's so scared of you."

"There's another guard outside," Sandra said. "You should get out of here."

"No one's going anywhere." They turned to find a tall, lean man filling the doorway, his gun pointed at them. He noticed his colleague, still flailing feebly on the ground. "Jesus, Wayne, you big pussy."

Sandra measured the distance between them. Too far to try to jump him, too close for him to miss if she went for her gun.

"Get back against the wall," he told her, stepping into the room. He must have thought that Camilla was still tied up because he reached for the back of the chair to push it toward Sandra. As he did, Camilla lunged at him.

At first Sandra thought that the woman had punched him

in the stomach and was amazed that such a feeble blow could double him over the way it did. The guard screeched in pain and clutched at his stomach, dropping the gun in his agony, grabbing at the woman's hand. Camilla sprang from her chair and away from him. When she pulled her hand from his belly, it was dark and wet. In her grasp, the other guard's penknife dripped blood onto the stone floor. Slowly, the wounded man sank to his knees.

Camilla was panting and shaken. She let the knife fall. She kept her eyes on the guard as he slumped to the floor. "Now we're even, I think," she said.

Sandra wasn't sure whether Camilla was addressing her or the dying man. "You'd better get out of here," Sandra said again.

Camilla dragged her eyes away from her victim and turned to Sandra. "I've got nowhere to go. My employers are going to want me dead when they hear what's happened. Sniper ... Well, you've seen how our working relationship has deteriorated of late. What the hell are you doing here?"

"I came for some information. I want the lob target. Date and place."

"I thought you came to kill Sniper."

"Are you his new bitch, or what?"

Camilla snorted. It might have been a laugh. "Whatever you need. I know everything about this operation. Have you got any money?" Sandra shook her head. Camilla shrugged. "Never mind. This one's on me. My enemy's enemy is my friend, as they say."

"You'll tell me the target?" Sandra eyed the woman suspiciously.

"Anything you want to know."

"Okay then, friend. Let's go."

"Just a minute." Camilla bent down and picked up the guard's submachine gun. She examined it for a second, then set the weapon to single-shot, slid the bolt to chamber a round, and fired twice into each of the two guards. Sandra drew her own gun again, levelling it at Camilla just in case, but the woman seemed happy with what she'd done. With a satisfied smile, she turned and walked away.

\* \* \* \*

Sniper's mood was grim. Someone had betrayed him. Again! It must have been that bitch Camilla. Or the investors, talking carelessly, bragging about what they were going to do. Or maybe one of the security guys. Camilla had picked them. He should have done that himself. He saw that now.

God! Where had his head been these past few weeks?

The engineering works was a mess. The minute they got back, Klaatu had organized his guys to pack everything up. Luckily, they'd already disassembled it all. Three trucks were on their way from a local haulage company, hired and standing by week after week for just this contingency. Sniper hadn't really believed he would need them but, after what happened in Berlin, fallback plans were in place for everything.

"I'm not cool with this, mate," the Aussie brick, Edna, said. He had left T-800 in one of the front offices and had come to find Sniper to make his displeasure known.

"You think I'm happy?" One of the many things Sniper was unhappy about that night was looking foolish in front of his friends. "You think I like being betrayed?"

"Didn't it go down like this in Berlin? I heard you got dobbed in to the cops there too."

Sniper turned on him with a snarl, but he caught himself and forced himself to calm down.

"That's why I've got plans in place this time. The fucking cops are getting too good, but they're still not good enough." He put an arm around Edna's shoulders. The young man stiffened nervously, but knew better than to pull away.

"You see, it works like this," Sniper said. "I've got someone on the inside. They heard the cops are about to discover this location. So they let me know. But what they don't know—what nobody knows except me and Klaatu—is that we have a second location, not far away, and we can have all this stuff in trucks and over there in a couple of hours. No worries, as you say. Is that right?"

Edna still looked unhappy. "Yeah, right. No worries. I knew you'd have a plan. I don't like the cops being this close, though."

"Come on. This is for me to deal with." He led his friend back to the front offices. "You should sit down with a beer and relax. Listen! That's the trucks arriving. Everything is okay, my friend. Just chill out and I'll call you when it's time to go. Okay?"

Edna regarded him doubtfully. "Anyone else, mate, and I'd be out of here and heading for the airport. You know what I'm saying? Anyone else."

Sniper knew all right. "Don't worry. This is all going to work out fine."

Edna nodded slowly and let himself be ushered out of the way. As soon as he was out of sight, Sniper strode quickly across to Klaatu. "We're moving the schedule up," he said. "I want you to start putting this lot together as soon as you get to the warehouse."

Sniper saw comprehension in his teknik's eyes. If the

police had found this place, it might not be long before they found the other. They needed to get the timesplash underway before that happened. After that, the cops would be in no state to find anyone.

"How soon are we talking?" Klaatu asked.

"Tomorrow."

"Impossible! A week, minimum."

"A week is too long. Two days." Klaatu seemed about to protest. "Forty-eight hours or I pull the plug and we walk away. Forty-eight hours or we find a new town, a new target, and start all over again."

Klaatu shook his head. "We can't start again, man. Neither of us can do that."

"Forty-eight hours then."

"I can try…"

"No." Sniper wanted his commitment. If Klaatu said he would do it, it would be done. Angrily, Klaatu looked away. "I'll need workers. Lots of them. You and the others too. No one sleeps. No one gets breaks. No one does anything but build this damned rig for the next forty-eight hours. Okay?"

Sniper grinned, excited by the drama of it. "Whatever you need. Get this lot loaded and on the road, then go out and recruit your workers. Get as many as you like. Promise them whatever it takes. I don't plan to pay any of them." He slapped Klaatu on the shoulder. "Forty-eight hours, man, and then we make history!"

Klaatu gave a grim smile in return. "I'm not thinking about history. I'm thinking about all the work that has to be done."

\* \* \* \*

Jay left the lift and trudged across to the door of his flat. It was almost two in the morning and he was tired and miserable. He prayed that the glazier had turned up as arranged to fix his windows. The flat would still look like someone had blasted it to pieces with a submachine gun— which they had—but at least he could sleep there without the wind howling through the place. He raised his hand to the lock and froze. Someone was inside. The log on the lock showed someone had entered at eleven PM. And had not yet left. Not again! he thought as he drew his gun and flattened himself against the wall. He really didn't need this kind of hassle every time he came home. And especially not tonight. Anger welled up inside him. Whoever the hell this was, they'd picked the wrong night to piss him off.

He keyed the lock and burst through the door at top speed. The lights were off inside but with the curtains missing, enough light came in through the windows to see by. But there was no one to be seen. Not slowing, he rushed down the hall and dived into the sitting room, rolled once and sprang up facing into the room with his gun sweeping left and right. Still no one. He heard the handle turn on the bedroom door and he dropped to one knee, taking aim. Even as he did so, he noticed that someone had tidied up much of the mess.

The bedroom door opened and Sandra walked out into the hallway, wearing only a t-shirt and panties. She squinted across at him grumpily and said, "What the hell are you doing? Do you know what time it is?"

Still crouching with his gun pointed at her, he opened his mouth to protest but couldn't find words to begin to express what he would like to say. Sandra stood and watched his armed guppy impersonation for a few seconds, then padded across to the kitchenette.

"Do you want a coffee?" she asked and picked up the kettle.

"Coffee?" he demanded, jumping to his feet. "Coffee?"

She regarded him blearily for a while, clearly waiting for him to add something more. When he didn't, she filled the kettle anyway.

"And where have you been till…" She checked her compatch. "Jesus."

"Where have I been?" he spluttered. "Where have I been?" He took a small step forward and then one backward as if undecided, in his agitation, how close to stand in relation to her. She shook her head, and carried on making the drinks.

"I'll tell you where I've been," he said. "I've been sitting in a police safe house playing poker with two policewomen, waiting for you to show up. That's where I've been." He took a couple of steps toward her, forgetting his earlier indecision. "But I don't have to guess where you've been, do I?" She looked up at him sharply. "Out with bloody Overman, that's where. What was it? A quiet little restaurant and then round to his place for a quickie?"

A frown crossed her face. "God, you're a stupid boy."

"Oh, I'm a boy now, am I? Now that you've found yourself a real man!"

Sandra set down the cups with a bang. "What the hell are you talking about? You sound like some kind of jealous jerk!"

"Jealous? Me? Jealous?" Which, he realized, is exactly what he sounded like. In confusion, he shut his mouth and stared at the kitchen counter, unable, suddenly, to meet Sandra's eyes.

"What do you see in him, anyway?" he grumbled. He was acutely aware of Sandra's glare on him. It made him feel like shrivelling up and hiding in a corner. Yesterday, at his mother's house, they had talked. They'd been close. He felt she really liked him. Hell, the last time they'd been in this flat, she'd kissed him! Hadn't he the right to think ... But whatever he had thought her feelings were, after this little tantrum he'd be lucky if she ever spoke to him again. He closed his eyes. The pain of wanting her to want him in the face of her indifference was a torment he had never known before. He turned to go. She could have the flat for all he cared. He just wanted to be out of there as quickly as he could.

"No, don't go," she said, and something in the tone of her voice stopped him dead. "I'm sorry."

He turned back to her, more confused than ever. She looked unhappy, not angry.

"You're right," Jay said. "I'm a jerk. It's none of my business who you sleep with. I should just keep my mouth shut."

She regarded him with a serious face and he still couldn't hold her gaze. He felt embarrassed now, ashamed of himself. Still, she kept watching him.

"You are a jerk," she said, but there was a softness, a fondness in her voice that made him look at her again. "And it isn't any of your business who I sleep with, but I'm going to tell you this anyway. I haven't been with Overman. We had our interview. It lasted about four hours. Then I left and went somewhere else. What you saw when you were there was just ... well, I don't really know what it was. Hard, heartless bastards like that bring it out in me. It's..."

Jay saw tears suddenly well up in her eyes and roll down her cheeks. He moved toward her, but she shook her head and stiffened. She brushed the tears aside with her arm in a quick, angry motion. "God, I'm screwed up," she said. "There's something really wrong with me. When this is over, when we've stopped Sniper, I'm going back to the Institute. I don't care that you got my sentence quashed. There's someone there I need to apologize to. And to listen to."

For only the second time since he'd met her, she looked young and frightened. Her armour of bravado had fallen away and she was vulnerable and weak.- That first day, in Ommen, he'd seen it as she struggled to free herself from the cage. Strange emotions surged in Jay's chest. He didn't know what to do or how to help her. He thought he might cry himself.

"I love you," he said, offering to suffer with her. Wanting to suffer for her if he could.

She frowned at him, and looked perplexed, as if he had spoken in a language she didn't understand. He couldn't stand it that the counter was between them. He moved quickly to her and stood there, close but not touching, not daring to touch. For a moment she went on looking at him in pain, then she grabbed for him and buried her face in his shoulder, crying, wailing as though all the hurt in all her life had found her right there and then. He hung on to her while a storm of misery wracked her body, while she howled into his shoulder, wetting him, scaring him, sagging against him. He bore the onslaught of a suffering that blasted through him, shredding his own emotions, until, at last, the crying subsided, the howling faded to sobbing and then to exhausted, ragged breathing.

He led her to the sofa and they sat down. She kept her head in his chest and climbed onto his lap, curling against him like a wounded animal.

It was hours later, in the middle of the night, that she said, "I know the target."

"Wha…" He was half asleep, not sure what he'd heard.

She looked up at him, eyes red and cheeks blotched, and smiled. "I know the splash target. Exactly where, exactly who, and exactly when."

# Chapter 19

## At the Marina

Everyone was tired. T-800 and Edna went out and brought back some folding beds and sleeping bags so that Klaatu's workers could take short naps when they needed to. People grumbled about the arrangements but, for the money they had been promised, they were willing to rough it. Klaatu worked miracles. By the time the trucks had reached the new warehouse and the equipment was unloaded, he had arrived with a vanload of new recruits. He took Sniper aside and spoke to him in a hushed voice.

"I don't know all these people," he said. "Some of them are recommended by people I know. One or two of them found me because they heard I was recruiting."

"You're saying you don't trust them."

"I used the Bedford to bring them here." It was a van they had used often to move equipment, with covered windows so nosy people could not stare into the back. Equally, anyone inside was unable to see out. "I took the E.M. suppressor so no one could use their compatches and so any bugs would be neutralized. I've got it running now in the warehouse. We shouldn't let any of them go outside. Just in case."

Sniper nodded and put a hand on his teknik's shoulder. "Trust me. No one leaves here before the lob except in a body bag."

A young man came up to them. They fell silent and turned to look at him. He glanced nervously at Sniper, then addressed Klaatu. "We need you to come and help with the displacement field coil alignment. None of us really knows how to do it."

Klaatu gave Sniper a last glance and went off with the young man. "You shouldn't be doing that yet, not till the cage assembly's complete…"

Sniper watched them go. He looked around the warehouse. The rig was already taking shape. The F2s were being cabled to each other, to the big switches, and to the capacitor arrays. People crawled over them and between them. The cage was being carried across the floor by six people—including the other two bricks—to where it would be bolted onto the platform above the field coils. The control console was still a pile of computer junk, reels of optic cable, and a comms rack, but Sniper wasn't worried. Progress looked good; they were close to completion.

\* \* \* \*

"No, we can't tell them."

Jay and Sandra were in a café near his flat, empty breakfast plates between them. The place was stuffed with early-morning commuters, and loud with clattering dishes and people talking over the noise of the cappuccino machines. Canary Wharf tube station was just out of sight along the busy road. Sandra was growing annoyed.

"You don't know what I went through to get that

information," she said.

"Maybe not, but it doesn't make any difference. If we give them the spacetime coordinates for the splash, what do you think they'll do with them?"

"They'll go back and stop Sniper. You said yourself, they've got an SAS team on standby for this very thing. Why on Earth should we not tell them?"

Jay could hardly believe she was being so thick. "You just said it. If we tell them, they'll send a squad of trained killers storming through central London armed to the teeth and looking like the Devil himself to the people back then. They might as well just go back and shoot Lenin themselves and have done with it. In fact, shooting Lenin in the crossfire as they try to take out Sniper is the most likely scenario to my mind. And do you know who else was around in London in 1902?" Sandra made a face, but Jay went on. "Well, I do. I spent ten minutes on the net this morning and came up with a few names—names of people who might just be in Bloomsbury that day, might even be visiting the British Museum or the Round Reading Room for all we know. I'm talking about people like Winston Churchill, Alexander Fleming, Lord Kitchener, Asquith, Marie Stopes, E. M. Forster, Bertrand Russell ... Shoot any one of them and you'd have a major splash on your hands!"

Sandra frowned at him. "I don't even know who half those people are."

Jay sat back with a sigh. "Well, neither did I until this morning, but I tell you, back in 1902 London was packed to the rafters with brilliant people just starting on world-changing careers. If we send a bunch of soldiers back there and they start a shootout, who knows how bad the splash could be?"

"Not as bad as shooting Lenin, I bet."

"I suppose. But how bad is acceptable? If they shoot Lenin—before he founds the Bolshevik Party and leads the Communist Revolution, before he elevates Stalin to a position of power—it changes the lives of hundreds of millions of people in Russia alone. Hell, it probably changes everybody's life. What if the revolution had never happened? What if it had but they didn't have the mass exiles and executions? What if there never was a Cold War?"

"You really have been doing your research, haven't you?" Sandra looked as if she was fed up with being lectured to.

Jay kept on, anyway. "A splash like that could wipe out all of central London. But what if it had been Chamberlain who was walking along by the Round Reading Room that day?"

"Who?"

"He was the Prime Minister when World War Two started. He had a policy of appeasement of Adolf Hitler and the Nazis. 'Peace in our time'? You know?"

Sandra just stared at him looking mildly irritated.

"If someone else had been Prime Minister, maybe it would have changed the way the war went. Maybe it wouldn't have happened at all. Not like it did, anyway. The point is, that would be a bloody big splash too. A whopper. Not as big as Lenin, probably, but big enough.

"Even the smaller fry, Marie Stopes, how many lives has she affected over the past hundred and fifty years? How big a splash would that be? Hundreds dead? Thousands alive? Who knows? And what about…"

"All right! All right!" Sandra held up her hands in surrender. "So doing our own lob isn't a great idea. I don't think it's as dangerous as you say, but I agree, there's a risk. But so what? If we don't stop Sniper before he lobs, what else can we do?"

Jay opened his mouth to give his answer, and realized he didn't have one. "We just have to stop him. That's all."

"No. It's not good enough. What if we can't? Whatever the risk is, they'd have to send someone back. It's got to be better to take a chance than the absolute bloody certainty that London is wiped off the map. Christ, Jay, it's six months since this happened to Beijing and they're still clearing away the rubble. When Mexico City went down it started a civil war!"

They sat in silence for a moment, Jay staring at the table, Sandra glowering at Jay. With a big sigh, Jay raised his head. "Okay. We give it to them. You're right."

Sandra smiled at him. A warm, admiring smile that made his heart skip and confused him utterly.

"What?" he asked. "What's that for?"

She kept on smiling. "'Cause you're really, really nice. That's all. 'Cause you looked after me last night and because you want to look after all of London today."

He wasn't absolutely sure she wasn't joking but he started to smile back all the same. Then her smile was gone in a flash and his with it.

"Don't look round," she whispered quickly, staring past him toward the entrance. He twitched, almost unable to stop himself. "Two men just came in. One of them's the guy we fought off at your place." She snapped her eyes away and ducked her head toward the table. "They're looking this way. They must have seen me by now."

Jay looked around at whatever he could see without turning his head. There were no other exits, except maybe behind the counter, and the only access was near the till beside the entrance. He glanced at the street through the big plate-glass window. If he could smash that … But the chairs and tables were all bolted to the floor.

Sandra risked a glance up at the two men. "One's coming toward us. The other's by the door." She reached for her gun.

Jay's eyes widened in alarm. He shook his head emphatically and she reluctantly put her hand back on the table. Not knowing what else to do, Jay got up and stood in the aisle between the tables, facing the man. The last thing he wanted was for people to start shooting in such a crowded place. The man was about Jay's height, in his mid-thirties and solidly built. He looked intelligent and serious. His pale eyes flicked across Jay's body in a quick appraisal. When he was within arm's reach he stopped and said, "Don't give me any trouble. I want you and the girl to come with me right now. No fuss." His voice was low but people around them noticed the confrontation and began to look around uneasily.

Jay stood his ground. "Who are you? Five? Private? Who wants us?"

"Shut the fuck up and start walking. No one said I had to bring you back alive."

Jay wondered what Sandra was doing. There was no way she'd just sit still and let herself be taken. This could soon turn into a bloodbath. If only he had something to throw through the damned window.

And then the man reached out and grabbed Jay by the lapel and solved his problem. Moving with all the speed he could muster, Jay swung around under the man's extended arm, pulling him forward, bending low to get the man's body above him. The man toppled forward onto Jay's back. Jay pushed up under him, putting all his strength into it, flipping the man over his back as if they'd been practising their tumbling routine all week. Someone screamed just as the man flew across the table and into the window.

With a bang like a gigantic barrel being hit with a sledge hammer, the window took the impact. The people inside the café collectively gasped as the glass wobbled on the edge of destruction but did not break. For a long moment there was silence. The man sprawled against the window opened one eye to take a tentative look, his face screwed up against the shattering impact that hadn't happened. Jay glanced back at the second gunman and saw him, gun drawn, struggling to get past a large man intent on leaving the café.

"Look out! She's got a gun!" The shout and the shots were simultaneous. Jay saw Sandra at the edge of his vision as she fired two rounds. There was screaming and shouting and a general panic as the window exploded into a million fragments and the man on the table rolled through it into the street, glass cascading down onto him.

Even though it only lasted mere seconds, it seemed to take an age for the storm of glass to smash down onto the pavement and the cringing, bellowing man. The instant it did, Jay and Sandra jumped through the empty window almost in unison, skidding on the shattered glass. Jay noticed two men down the street reach for their guns and head toward them.

"Bandits at nine o'clock!" he shouted to Sandra, but she'd already grabbed his arm and was pulling him the other way. Shots rang out behind them, coming from inside the café. The second gunman was fighting his way through the panicking breakfasters. Sandra and Jay were down the street and round the first corner before the pair in the street had managed to get in a good shot at them.

The streets were relatively empty once they were off the main road. Any passer-by jumped aside in alarm at the sight of two terrified people running—one of them with a gun in her hand.

"Where are we going?" Sandra asked as they turned another corner.

"I don't know. Away from here."

"Come on," she said, in between gasps of breath. "You live round here. Where do we go?"

Jay found it hard to think that far ahead. Picking the next side street to hide in was as much as he could manage. He looked around, forcing himself to be strategic. He and Sandra had already reached unfamiliar territory. His local knowledge extended to the route to the tube station and the shops and no farther. But a glimpse of open space at the end of a long street to his right gave him his bearings.

"The river's that way," he said, pointing.

"Right," said Sandra, mistaking his intent, and shot off in that direction. Almost falling over, he managed to make the turn at full speed and follow her.

"What then?" she called over her shoulder.

Jay was about to ask for suggestions when he heard booted feet clattering on the pavement behind him. He turned quickly and saw three men pounding along the street. At least one of them had a machine gun in his hands.

"They're on our six," he said.

"Will you stop talking like that?" Sandra shouted back. "You sound really stupid."

He scowled back at her. "Just run faster. Okay?"

The street emptied onto a busy road. Huge glass office blocks loomed over them as they dodged the slow-moving traffic and then crossed over a canal, following the curve of a road that arced around a semicircular block. Then they struck out east again, toward the river. They found themselves running along a broad avenue, which left them exposed and vulnerable. Up ahead was an open space and beyond it some low, red-roofed buildings.

"Keep going. The river must be right in front of us, past those buildings." As soon as he'd said it, Jay wondered what the hell he was talking about. It was Sandra's idea to head for the river, not his. He started looking about for somewhere else to go.

"Isn't that the Fusimax Building?" Sandra pointed to a large, multi-turreted, post-Adjustment monstrosity visible dead ahead of them.

"Right. That means the Blackwall Tunnel's to our left." If they could get to the tunnel they could cross the river. What good that would do, Jay had no idea, but it was a plan of sorts.

They were both panting from running fast for so long, yet the river and tunnel were still far away. A bullet ricocheted off the road five meters ahead of them, and suddenly all thoughts of exhaustion were gone. Sandra looked over her shoulder and said "Shit!" which told Jay all he needed to know. Together, they leapt a safety barrier onto a huge, busy roundabout and cut across its grassy centre, heading for an exit to the left, vaguely following Jay's notion of getting to the tunnel and across the river. From the honking of horns and squealing of brakes that followed just fifteen seconds later, Jay could easily tell how far behind their pursuers were. They reached the far side of the roundabout and plunged into the traffic. At the same time they heard cracking noises from behind them, like distant fireworks. A car window shattered as Jay dodged past it. Two holes appeared in the bodywork of a BMW ahead of him. With reckless determination, the two of them sprinted around the slow-moving cars and leapt the barrier at the other side. Jay hoped that their pursuers stopping to shoot at them would slow them enough for him and Sandra to get off the long streets and out of the line of fire for a while.

But the road they had run onto was elevated, and stretched out in a long curve.

"Look!" Sandra pointed to their right. The system of canals that characterized the area opened into a large body of water—a marina. Roughly oval, it had a long curving jetty at one side following the shoreline with what looked like twenty or so houseboats moored along it, all pointing the same way, with their noses to the jetty. In the morning sunlight, the colourful boats and the sparkling water were pretty and, to Jay's eyes, jarringly peaceful. But he could not see why Sandra had pointed it out.

"Come on," Sandra said and swerved across to the rail at the edge of the overpass. She ran alongside it, peering downwards, and Jay had the horrible feeling she was planning to jump into the water. But they had passed the point where the canal entered the little marina under the overpass and there was only concrete below them now. So, when Sandra suddenly climbed the fence and jumped, Jay's heart almost stopped.

He peered down frantically, in time to see Sandra climbing down from the roof of a parked car. She looked up at him expectantly. It was a long way down. Best not to think about that, he told himself, and climbed the fence. If he didn't hit that car roof squarely and dead centre ...

He jumped, falling for a surprisingly short time before he slammed into the car below. The vehicle sagged under him and the roof, already dented by Sandra, buckled farther. The side windows burst and sprayed glass over Sandra, who squealed and jumped back. It took him a second or two to realize he was all right.

"This way," Sandra called and set off toward the jetty. Jay bounced off the roof onto the ground, racing to catch up with her.

The jetty had a single entrance that was protected by a wrought iron gate and a high fence. Jay clung to it and stared at the biometric lock, not knowing what to do with it. If he had the right equipment with him, this would be child's play. Without it …

Sandra pulled him back and fired two shots into the lock at close range, smashing it to pieces. After that, it was easy to get in. Jay guessed that the blokes following them must be up on the flyover by now and easily able to see them. It was too late now to hide on one of the houseboats. But Sandra burst through the gate and sprinted along the jetty toward the far end. A rattle of gunfire behind them was matched by a row of splashes in the water to Jay's left.

He looked back to see the three men up on the flyover. Two seemed to be arguing—probably about whether to risk their necks jumping down—but the third was kneeling with his machine gun spitting fire. The row of splashes tracked toward Jay, then bullets started smashing up the jetty around his feet. He tried to run faster, straining for breath. Ahead, he saw the end of the jetty approaching. There was no way back to shore except back the way they had come. And that would be suicide.

"What the hell are we doing?" he shouted.

"Come on!" was all the reply he got.

The bullets stopped chewing up the planking around him and he chanced another look back. The argument seemed to be finished and the three guys were lowering themselves down the side of the flyover. When he looked ahead, Sandra had jumped onto one of the houseboats—the last one on the jetty. She was peering through the boat's windows. He was with her in a second.

"Cast off," she shouted at him.

"What?"

"Untie the sodding boat!"

"You're joking!"

"Just do it!"

He looked around. Extensions of the jetty came out from the main run at right angles and each boat was moored snugly against these spurs. The boat they were on was tied front and back with thick ropes that were lashed to metal capstans. Jay jumped off the boat and went to the capstan at the back. After a bit of tugging the rope came free. He was about to run to the other end when a shot zipped past him. Another hit the side of the boat and he threw himself aboard and flattened himself to the deck behind the low gunwale. Their pursuers were on the jetty and all three were firing at him. It would take them just seconds to get to the boat unless he did something.

He took a peek over the edge. The men weren't shooting now, just running hard. He drew his gun and took careful aim. His first shot went wide and so did his second. The constant movement of both boat and jetty wasn't something he'd noticed until now. The running men scurried off the main jetty, finding cover among the boats. Jay gave a gasp of relief. It would be several seconds now before they could start shooting back and edging their way closer. He took the time to consider his position.

If anyone had seen or heard the shooting, they must surely have called the police. That meant help was probably already on its way. Yet it was the height of the morning rush hour, and it would take forever for the police to get there.

Meanwhile, he and Sandra were pinned down on the last boat at the end of a long jetty with three armed men not twenty meters away. The only sensible way he could see of getting out of this was to swim for it—and that didn't seem like much of an option. Maybe if they could jump from the other side of the boat …

Then the boat's engine spluttered into life.

From the back of the boat where he was hiding, Jay heard the churning of water as the propeller thrashed it into a foam. He felt the deep throbbing of the engine under his hands and knees, and wondered what the hell Sandra thought she was doing. Jay saw two of the pursuers emerge to see what was going on. He took a shot at one of them and they ducked back out of sight. Sandra's head appeared from over a rail above him. She whooped a victory cry. "I'll take her out onto the river through that canal over there."

Jay couldn't see a thing from where he was cowering behind the gunwale. "Can you drive one of these things?" he yelled.

"How hard can it be? Bugger. Hang on."

She ducked back inside for a moment then reappeared. "Something's wrong. I can't steer it."

A shot splintered the wood near her head and she bobbed back inside. Jay popped up and let off a couple of shots. While they'd been talking, one of the men had moved forward by two whole boats. He also saw the problem with the boat. The back of it was swinging out from the jetty, leaving an increasing gap between him and the gunmen, but the front of the narrow boat was still tied to its capstan. There was no way now that he could get onto the jetty to untie it. He'd have to work his way along the deck and hope that he didn't get shot.

"The boat's still tied up!" Sandra yelled from above.

"I know!"

"I told you to cast off. What are you messing about at?"

He glowered up at where her voice was coming from. "I'm just trying to stop the bad guys killing us both, dear. Is that all right? Or shall I just let them come aboard?"

"Stop being such a prat and get us untied!"

"Yes, dear," he snapped, crawling forward. "Anything you say, dear."

"And stop calling me 'dear' like that. It's creepy."

A burst of machine gun fire spattered across the cabins just above Jay's back and he threw himself flat again. "Well how about a bit of covering fire then?"

The boat had swung out into the open water and was almost pointing directly toward the three gunmen, who were steadily advancing toward them. Realizing that the gunwale wasn't going to hide him much longer, Jay got up on one knee, fired several shots in the general direction of their attackers and sprinted forward to the bow. The rope that tied the boat to the capstan was taut and straining as the boat pushed against it. He tried pulling at it but it wouldn't budge a millimetre.

"Turn off the bloody engine!" he bellowed. He could see Sandra's face through the window of what must have been a small bridge. She put a hand to her ear indicating she couldn't hear him. He gestured angrily at the rope, slapping it to show how taut it was. She leaned forward, peering at him.

Bullets shattered the glass and splintered wood all around her. Horrified, Jay spun back toward the jetty and fired several more rounds at the machine gunner where the man crouched behind the very next boat, just one boat-length away now. And if the machine gunner was there, what was to prevent someone else running along behind the next boat on the pier and shooting from it?

As soon as he looked, he saw a man turning to shoot, less than six meters away. Jay's gun came round and up as he sighted the man along its barrel. He could see his opponent sighting him in return. It was just like a scene from his weapons training. A wooden figure would flip up out of nowhere with a painted gun, a stubbly, square jaw, and a painted scowl on its face. Bang, bang, bang! And the figure would flip down again.

This gunman didn't have an exaggerated scowl. He had a calm, neutral expression. His eyes were a pale blue under light brown hair, his face narrow-jawed and clean shaven. Bang, bang, bang!

Three shots to the man's head all but tore it apart. For a moment, bile rose in Jay's throat and he thought he was going to throw up. The dead man toppled backward into the water.

In the nick of time, Jay ducked under cover as the machine gunner sought him out. It gave him a chance to look back up at the bridge, desperate for a sign that Sandra was okay. What he saw was a bloody face behind a gun, taking careful aim. His relief was overwhelming. When Sandra fired, he didn't notice for a few seconds that the machine gun had stopped strafing him.

He peered over the gunwale and saw the machine gun lying on the jetty. The man beside it was wounded but alive, groaning and clutching at his stomach. Sandra fired again, and then again, but not at the wounded man. Jay saw the third gunman running for his life along the jetty, heading for the shore and safety.

The boat's engine roared, then died. The silence was blissful. Jay rushed back to the bridge and met Sandra coming down a steep flight of steps. She had a couple of small cuts on her forehead that were bleeding, but she seemed otherwise intact. Without thinking, he grabbed her and hugged her to him.

When he finally let her go, she stood and looked at him with a sloppy grin on her face.

"What?" he asked. But he was smiling too, well aware of the way her eyes were shining. Slowly, they let the moment drift past.

"I'd better make a call," he said, pulling one of the compads out of his pocket. "The police will be here soon and we're going to need Bauchet's help explaining all this."

# Chapter 20

## Ready to Go

Samana Karim was wishing she'd never volunteered. That guy Sniper and his mates were psycho, and she wasn't too sure about Klaatu either. It gave her the creeps the way he kept staring at her. But she wanted to get into field work and this was her big break. The section head, Overman, had been so keen to get volunteers who were experienced tekniks he'd have taken anybody. And he did. He took her. Straight out of Aldermaston and into the heart of this operation with barely a moment to reprogram her compatch with her call signs and encryption keys.

They'd tagged her too, with a Galileo global positioning chip injected into her abdominal cavity. It had seemed exciting at the time. She'd gone to the bar they told her about. She'd seen the guy they'd showed her pictures of. Had started a conversation with him. Had said, "Yeah, okay," as casually as she could when he asked if she was looking for a job, 'cause he knew a guy with a big project on and he could make a few calls for her if she liked. She'd gone to the ladies' while he made the call, and she'd made a call of her own, telling the MI5 operator that her aunt Najmah was feeling better and she'd be home soon. It wasn't until she saw the lashed-up field dampener in Klaatu's van that she realized the operation had stopped going according to plan. There was another one at the warehouse they took her to. So no calls, and no tracking. And now they wouldn't let anybody out—not for anything—until the job was over. How the hell was she going to tell Overman where she was? For that matter, where the hell was she?

"Nice work," Klaatu said, leaning over her as she adjusted wave envelopes, tuning the wave guides to the exact specifications the young Pole had given her. She'd heard of Klaatu—who in her line of business had not? In some ways, it was a real buzz to work with him. But she never expected him to look like such a creep, or to keep touching her and "accidentally" brushing against her the way he did.

"It's going to be a big lob," she said, "judging by these power figures. I hope we're a long way from the splashtarget." She tried to make her voice sound light but, even to her, it sounded strained and nervous.

He put a hand on her shoulder. "Don't worry, we're well away from any danger here."

She tried not to flinch. "We'd have to be at least five kilometres away, maybe ten. Where's the target?"

He looked at her but said nothing. It made her jittery and flustered.

"I'm only saying … I mean, it's like, we don't want to get caught in the backwash, right?"

He stared at her for a few more seconds and said, "You'd better hurry up with that. We'll be putting the field assembly together in an hour or so."

She nodded and tried to force a smile. "Yeah. No problem."

He walked away, leaving her feeling wrung out and frightened. God! What an idiot she was, asking him like that. He had to suspect her now. Didn't he? The way he'd looked at her. She glanced about the warehouse, not really taking in the high, dirty walls and the piles of equipment. Sniper and his brick friends were out, fetching some stuff they needed. If they'd been there, maybe Klaatu would be talking to them by now. Maybe the big German would be walking over to her with that horrible smirk.

She tried to calm herself down. She needed to think. She needed to stop her hands shaking and slow down her racing heart and think. When Sniper got back, she was as good as dead. She was so sure of it, all of her muscles tensed. Klaatu had sussed her. He'd have to be an idiot not to. And, whatever he was, he wasn't that. Which meant she had to get out of there fast.

Once the bricks got back, she wouldn't stand a chance. But right now, there was only Klaatu. He carried a gun. She'd seen it, tucked into the belt of his trousers. And the other tekniks, of course. They weren't like her. They were here for the money and the kicks. They'd be on Klaatu's side if she tried anything. But they weren't armed. They weren't psycho creeps like Klaatu, either. It was him she had to worry about.

Without thinking about it, she put down the test equipment she was carrying and stood up. There were three doors in the warehouse: the big sliding doors by the loading bay, a small metal door in the side, and a wooden door at the far end that led to a little office and probably out onto the street. She walked toward the office door. The bathrooms were next to it and she hoped it would just look like she was taking a toilet break.

She tried not to look left or right as she neared the office but, at the last minute, as she turned toward its door, she glanced over her shoulder to where she'd last seen Klaatu. The young teknik was standing with his hands on his hips, watching her. A grim smile was on his face. Yet he hadn't reached for his gun and he wasn't running to catch her. She grabbed the handle of the door almost overwhelmed with panic. What did it mean? Why wasn't he doing anything?

It could only be that there was no way out through the office. Stifling a cry of anguish, she let go of the handle and ran flat out for the little side door. It bounced in her vision as she raced toward it. Her feet slapped against the concrete floor, making a god-awful racket. Everyone must be looking. Klaatu must be chasing her by now. Why couldn't she hear his footsteps? Why wasn't he shouting? She daren't look. She didn't want to see his face. She had to reach the door first. She was so close. The only way he could stop her now was to shoot her. The idea made her skin crawl as she anticipated the noise, the hot metal slamming into her body. She hit the door with an explosive crash, shoving at the bar-push release, frantically grabbing it and pulling, pushing, yanking at it. But the door didn't open. The door was locked. The bastards had locked the doors! Of course they'd locked the doors! Only an idiot wouldn't have expected that. Fear and defeat clamped down on her. It really felt like they were crushing her from the inside. She sagged against the stubborn metal. Her legs were weak and couldn't hold her any more. Tears flowed down her cheeks as she slumped to the oily concrete floor. Now she could hear Klaatu's footsteps. He approached her slowly, with all the time in the world.

\* \* \* \*

Overman played the recording for Holbrook and Porterhouse in Holbrook's office. It was a closeup of Sniper's grinning head, with only a brick wall behind him. The timestamp was just thirty minutes old.

"So you see, Mr. Overman, you're going to have to do better than that if you want to catch me. Or is your real name Bond, James Bond? Little Samana told me all about you and your sad little spy games before she died. You really shouldn't have sent out such an inexperienced young thing to do your dirty work. Maybe you'll have bad dreams tonight thinking about what you've done."

The face in the recording grinned maliciously. "But if you have any more hot little chicks like her, don't you hesitate to send them right along. Let me tell you about some of the sexy fun we had together before she died—"

Overman cut the playback. Sniper's face remained frozen on the display, cocky and malevolent.

"Fucking bastard," Porterhouse growled, looking like he'd tear Sniper's throat out with his teeth given the chance.

"Bond was Six, wasn't he?" Holbrook said, absently.

"You think it has any significance?" Overman asked.

"Probably not. Just ignorance, or a careless attitude to the truth."

Overman looked at his boss, trying to weigh up his response, but gave up. He said, "They found her body twenty minutes ago in Vauxhall Park, just two minutes away from where we are now."

"He thinks it's all a fucking game!" Porterhouse snarled.

"We didn't manage to insert any other agents, did we?" Holbrook said. Overman shook his head. "No. She was the only one."

"You'll have that analysed, of course." Holbrook glanced

toward the display.

"We won't find anything."

"No. Quite."

There was a short silence while Holbrook seemed to consider all the options he no longer had.

"Where's that bloody girl? That's what I want to know." Porterhouse glared at Overman as if the section head was deliberately hiding her. "And the little pansy who's supposed to be minding her."

Holbrook grimaced. He seemed wounded, a little lost, not at all his usual self. He turned his gaze on Porterhouse. "You're right to remind us of our failings, of course, but I think a more positive attitude is what we need right now." He lifted his head and straightened his back, as if taking his own advice.

"Overman, get your SAS friends over here and suited up. Put them on round-the-clock readiness. You never know, we might get some good news. Meanwhile, your top priority is to locate Sandra Malone—and Jay, if you think it will help." He touched a paper report on his desk. "I see you raided the house in Surrey this morning, Porterhouse, but all you found were two dead bodies."

"That's right. Both hired guns. Local muscle. Also plenty of forensics to suggest that one other person was injured there, probably tortured. DNA matches a local prostitute. Specializes in sadomasochism. Went missing three days ago. And they found Sandra Malone's DNA all over one of the dead men, so she's in the frame for at least one of the killings. There was other stuff too. Another woman. Several other men. The labs are still going over it."

"Nothing actually useful then?"

Porterhouse glared at Holbrook. "No folder marked 'Top

secret plan to kill Winston Churchill's mother', if that's what you mean?"

"That's exactly what I mean." He shook his head and turned to Overman. "The analysts are considering Winnie's mother, I suppose?"

Overman knew that half the service was working on identifying the most probable splashtargets. Assuming it was going to happen within Greater London any time between 1880 and 1920, they'd narrowed it down to just fifteen hundred possibilities. "I'll ask them," he said, dryly.

Holbrook ignored the hint of insubordination. "The girl was at the house. I think that means we need to have a word with her, don't you?"

"Oh yes."

"On your way, then."

Holbrook let the two men leave, then swivelled his chair to face the big window and its panoramic view across the Thames and south London. He could see Vauxhall Park quite clearly from where he sat. He could even see the police cars and the crowd of onlookers at the spot where the body must have been found. He needed to make some calls. The Royals were safely away. So were the politicians. A more general evacuation was now essential.

But no one was going to like that idea.

\* \* \* \*

Bauchet finished his call and turned his sharp, hooded eyes on Jay and Sandra. "That was Five," he said. "Their agent inside Sniper's team has been executed."

Jay knew immediately what this meant. So did Sandra.

"We should go," she said.

"I will go with you," said Bauchet. "There is still the mole to think about." He spoke to Sandra. "If you reveal your information too soon, it will be worthless. Sniper will find out that we know about his plans and he will call off the lob. Then he will simply disappear and try again somewhere else." He paused as if checking his own reasoning. "No, no. We must be there at the moment Sniper makes his move. It is our only hope now to send people back in time to stop him. I suspect you will need help in keeping your knowledge from Jay's friends at Five until the last moment. And there, I think I can be of service."

He excused himself and made some more calls. Sandra took Jay aside.

"What's he talking about? They still can't go back in time and stop Sniper unless they know just when he's going to make his lob. And that's not something Camilla knew. Only Sniper decides when to do the lob."

"I know. Even if she had known, Sniper's changed his plans by now, brought the lob forward."

"So how does us knowing the splashtarget help? If we jump back now and Sniper hasn't gone already, the timestream will be smooth. He won't be there. If we jump even a few hours after he's been and gone, the timestream will have smoothed out again. It will be just like he'd never been back. A timesplash doesn't change history, you know. It just messes it up for a short while. Bricks are still anchored in the present. That's why they get yanked back, why the splash doesn't affect them much while they're there. If it wasn't for the backwash, you'd never know a splash had happened."

"You have a good grasp of metatemporal physics, *Mademoiselle* Malone." Bauchet joined them, his calls done.

"I don't know metatemporal physics from a hole in the

ground," she snapped back. "But I talk to a lot of bricks."

Bauchet smiled. "You should talk to a few more tekniks then, because they would tell you we can now detect a temporal displacement field when it is activated."

Jay and Sandra looked at him in astonishment. Bauchet shrugged. "It is only a prototype, and it runs only at CERN, but a field as big as the one Sniper hopes to create can be detected from anywhere in the world. Or so I am told." He held up his compatch. "As soon as the lob starts, I will know about it."

"And can you pinpoint it?" Jay asked.

"Sadly, no. They're still working on that. But we have Mlle. Malone's intel, do we not? So we know just where Sniper will be—and when—at the other end of the lob."

Sandra grinned.

A police officer put her head around the door and told them their car was ready.

Jay shook his head as they started to leave. "God, this is so risky," he grumbled.

Sandra thwacked him across the shoulder. "Oh, shut up, you big wuss."

Jay frowned back at her. With all their lives at risk, and millions more, she seemed in unusually high spirits. She thinks they're going to kill Sniper, he realized. This is the day she's been waiting for.

* * * *

"We're going now!" Sniper was shouting, banging his fist on the workbench, glowering at the implacable Klaatu.

"It isn't ready yet."

"It's ready. I can see it's ready."

"A lob this big needs a lot of control. The gear needs very fine adjustment. It's delicate work."

With a roar of frustration, Sniper turned and paced across the floor. "When then?" he demanded, whirling back to face Klaatu. "When? When? When?"

Edna stood nearby, grinning at Sniper's tantrum. T-800 was sitting in a plastic chair, reading a newspaper. All three bricks wore their splashgear, the close-fitting pressure suits that would protect them during the lob. They looked like a group of fighter pilots from a sci-fi vid. Their helmets and weapons were on a table nearby, along with the costumes they'd been out to collect that morning.

"Soon," Klaatu reassured him. He lifted his hands in a gesture of surrender. "An hour. Maybe two. You want to survive this, don't you?" The way Sniper's eyes narrowed made him try a more conciliatory tone. "Look, get changed into your fancy dress outfits and we'll be finished as soon as we can be."

Sniper glared for a moment more then turned away. "They're close, Klaatu. We've got to get this done now, or they'll find us. Just fucking hurry it up, all right?"

He walked away to brood and Klaatu turned back to his work. The "fancy dress outfits" Klaatu had mentioned were Edwardian costumes the bricks would wear over their splashgear. Everything they did in 1902 was going to be anomalous to an extent none of them had experienced before: every pebble out of place, every person who saw them, every horse that shied. The clothes would be needed so that they could walk through the streets of old London without starting a minor splash by shocking everybody they passed.

Sniper stalked over to the table where the costumes were.

He eyed them with distaste.

"Goes against the grain, right?" Edna said, standing next to him. "We should be kicking up as big a shit-storm as we can, not creeping about on our tiptoes."

Sniper looked at him. "Without these, we'd never make it to the splash." He spoke in a subdued voice, though it pained him to accept the constraints of the situation. "We're five kilometres away. We should be at least ten, but we've only got fifty-six minutes when we get there. If things start going crazy, it will delay us too much."

"Yeah, but … mate!" The Aussie shook his head sadly.

T-800 appeared behind them and put a hand on each of their shoulders. He was grinning broadly—something rarely seen. "Yes, but when we finally get there and take that crap off … Man! We're going to be like killer demons from the fucking apocalypse!"

Sniper barked out a laugh and slapped him on the chest. "Fucking A, man!"

Edna whooped and jumped up on T-800's back. In a moment, they were wrestling and shouting and tumbling about like a cageful of monkeys. From the control console, Klaatu watched them in silence.

# Chapter 21

## False Start

People in the SIS Building foyer looked nervous. Six heavily armed Metropolitan Police officers stood like robots in full body armour, weapons at the ready. They formed a perimeter around Bauchet, Colbert, Jay and Sandra. No one in the group spoke. Everybody waited. Around them, people averted their gaze and spoke in hushed voices, trying not to attract the attention of the hard-eyed police officers.

At last, Director Holbrook walked in with Overman and Porterhouse flanking him. Bauchet stepped forward to greet him.

"Jonathan, how good to see you again."

Holbrook took the Europol Superintendent's hand and shook it. "It's always a pleasure, Jacques." He let his eyes wander over the armed guard. "I see you brought a few friends."

"Just a precaution. I have with me the most important person in all London—possibly in all the world. I couldn't risk her being mugged in the street now, could I?"

Holbrook looked past one of the bulky police officers. "Hello, Sandra. And Jay, how nice of you to drop by."

"Don't be too hard on the boy, Jonathan. I assure you he has been working hard to protect the interests of your nation. If not for him, I would not be able to bring you the information you need to save the city."

Holbrook's expression was suddenly very serious. "If you have the target coordinates, I want them right now. I also want these clowns out of my building."

Bauchet's smile vanished too, leaving him looking hawk-like and dangerous. "First, I want a complete block on communications in and out of this building—except for a single netID I will give you shortly. We have the splashtarget and I don't want your mole letting Sniper's team know about it."

"My mole?" Holbrook seemed about to argue the point but didn't. He spoke into his compatch for a moment then looked at Bauchet. "The netID?"

Bauchet gave him his own compatch address. Holbrook passed it on.

"There. It's done."

Overman could not contain himself any longer. "Director, whatever our internal security issues are, we can't just let another agency march in here and—"

"Be quiet, Overman. You know as well as I do we're leaking like a sieve. I hoped we'd have time to find out who it was, but we don't. Superintendent Bauchet is quite right. This agency is a danger to the safety of London. My directorate! Whatever it takes, we will stop these damned maniacs, and your pride is not going to be an obstacle."

Overman was clearly unhappy but he backed down with a surly "Yes, sir."

Porterhouse looked like his close-cropped head might explode from sheer fury but he said nothing.

Holbrook turned back to Bauchet. There was no more cordiality in his manner. "The netID was so that you can be contacted by the CERN detector team, I take it?"

Bauchet nodded.

"Then let's get to the lobsite. And I meant it about getting your storm troopers out of my lobby."

Bauchet gave a nod to the sergeant in command of the squad and he marched the officers out to the street. Meanwhile, Holbrook looked over to the reception desk.

"Would one of you kindly arrange some refreshments to be brought to room G-twenty-seven, please?" he called out. "We might be a while in there. Oh yes, and I'm invoking Operation Scorched Earth. Deputy Director Anderson will know what to do about it. But don't forget the refreshments, will you?"

He led them through the corridors toward the lobsite.

"Scorched Earth?" Bauchet asked.

"Evacuate the city, get everyone out of harm's way, that kind of thing. There'll be a general announcement on all the news channels telling people to evacuate central London. The Mayor's office will be coordinating. The Army's been standing by to help out. Your friends in the Met are in on it too, along with London Transport and all the other players we need to empty a hundred square kilometres packed with people in fourteen hours."

"Fourteen hours?"

"Absolute best-case scenario, Jacques. More likely the whole thing will be a bloody shambles, of course, but it's the best we can do."

He sounded defeated and Jay, walking along in silence, realized that giving such an order could easily be the last act of Holbrook's career. Succeed or fail, splash or no splash, no one would be happy about evacuating the city. Someone's head would have to roll. And, of course, this was probably the last act of Jay's career too. After the way he'd hidden Sandra away, after he'd gone to Europol for protection, after he'd helped Bauchet force Holbrook's compliance, he couldn't imagine having much of a career in Five. Besides all the other trouble he'd caused, he was also part of the team that had failed to stop Sniper pulling off a timesplash, right here in the nation's capital. That kind of stain didn't wash out.

As they entered the MI5 lobsite, the teknik Nahrees was there to greet them. The room was humming and Jay guessed that the big capacitors were being kept fully charged. Colonel Davidson, the SAS team leader, was there too, already wearing splashgear.

"You have the coordinates?" the Colonel asked. He looked grim. As well he might, thought Jay.

"All in good time, Colonel," Holbrook said. He introduced Bauchet. "We're waiting for a message from CERN to say the balloon's gone up."

"CERN, sir?"

"They have a detector at their facility near Geneva. They can tell us when Sniper makes his move."

Nahrees seemed agitated. "If you could give me the coordinates now, sir, we could get them programmed into the system."

"It makes sense, sir," said Porterhouse. "We shouldn't be wasting time. The Colonel's men will have a hard enough time of it without all this bullshit." Although he was speaking to Holbrook, he was glaring at Bauchet. Bauchet returned the stare calmly.

Holbrook snapped at Porterhouse. "You have my orders." Then, to the Colonel: "Where are your men, Davidson?"

"In the back there, playing cards."

"Very well. I suggest we all make ourselves comfortable. It could be a long wait."

# Chapter 22

## Timesplash

Klaatu threw the switch with a flourish and the F2 generator array hummed into life. They all stood around his displays as the readouts rapidly flicked across to full power. He nodded to one of the tekniks, who pulled down a row of levers, one by one, feeding power into the little grid they'd built and firing up the heavy capacitors.

"Two minutes and you're ready to go," Klaatu told Sniper.

"You're a fucking genius," Sniper said. His voice contained genuine admiration. "No one else could have put this together so fast."

In his Edwardian morning coat, high-buttoned collar, and elaborate necktie, Sniper looked handsome and elegant. His almost-white hair gave him an air of distinction, and his slender, athletic physique was enhanced by the long lines of the frock coat. He held a carpetbag in one hand with his weapons and a top hat inside, and in the other he held his helmet.

"I miss the countdowns," he said softly to Klaatu.

Sniper looked wistful and Klaatu had a sudden flashback to the days when he'd watch Sniper out in the cage: strutting and yelling, the music thundering, the girls screaming, his arrogant face beaming from a wall of gigantic displays. "Yeah," said the teknik with a small smile. "Me too." An indicator switched to green. "Okay. Time to go."

"Hey, look at that." Edna was pointing at the one of the displays that was running a news channel. "They're evacuating London."

"Too late," said T-800, darkly.

The display showed roads clogged with vehicles and tube stations jammed solid with people.

"Some will make it," Edna said. "They've got an hour."

Sniper flashed a feral grin. "The whole world's going to remember this one." Laughing with excitement, he led his two companions over to the cage. He grabbed the door and pulled, but nothing happened. Confused, he turned to his teknik.

"Push it," Klaatu called. "Someone put the door on the wrong way round. It's no big deal. I just didn't have time to make them do it again."

Sniper pushed and the door swung inwards. He walked into the cage, looking unsettled. The other two followed him in and closed the door behind them.

"Anything else you put together backward?" Sniper asked.

Klaatu grinned. "Don't worry. I checked everything myself. This rig will get you there in one piece. The rest is up to you."

For a moment, Sniper looked uncertain. T-800 and Edna looked at him, waiting for him to make the call.

"You fucking Polish bastard!" he shouted, but the excitement was back in his eyes. "You did that on purpose to freak me out."

Klaatu said nothing.

"Just push the button, you damned punk." Sniper said.

He pushed on his headgear and raised a gloved thumb. He looked like an Edwardian gentleman in a space helmet.

Klaatu watched them, straight-faced. "See you in fifty-six minutes."

He hit the button and Sniper and his crew were gone. The tekniks and security guards gave a ripple of applause.

"Okay, everyone," Klaatu shouted. "Wrap up and get out of here." A phony rendezvous had been arranged where the tekniks expected to be paid. "If I know Sniper, you'll want to be at least ten more kilometres farther out before the backwash hits."

Klaatu would wait alone for Sniper. His last act as uberteknik would be to drive the splashteam clear of the destruction that would follow them back.

* * * *

Bauchet took the call with every eye in the room on him. It lasted all of five seconds. Then he turned to Holbrook. "They've lobbed. Two minutes ago."

Holbrook turned his eyes to Sandra. Sandra nodded and went over to Nahrees. "It's the Round Reading Room at the British Museum, April twenty-nine, 1902, ten-thirty in the morning. The target is Vladimir Ilyich Lenin."

The teknik and her team began work immediately, setting up the lob parameters. Sandra watched over her shoulder for a moment, then went back to stand with Jay. Porterhouse took her place, scowling at the displays as if they were his personal enemy. Colonel Davidson went into the next room to fetch his team.

"Lenin is not a bad choice, eh?" Bauchet said to

Holbrook. "Especially in 1902. He had not yet even formed the Bolshevik Party. He had not yet met Stalin. Without Lenin's patronage, it is likely young Stalin would never have risen to power. Without Lenin, a Russian revolution might still have happened, but it would have been a very different beast. Without him to organize it and to crush all opposition, who knows what it would have achieved. Certainly not the communism we all know from our history books."

Holbrook looked at him blankly. "I suppose these times will turn us all into historians."

"They say Stalin had twenty million of his own people executed by the secret police,"

Bauchet went on. "If this timesplash affects only those twenty million, it will be at least as big as Beijing. But there is Russia's involvement in World War Two to consider, and the Cold War, the oppression of Eastern Europe..." He stopped talking, lost in dark contemplation.

"When can we go?" Davidson asked. He had re-entered with half a dozen men, all suited up and armed.

"I need a couple more minutes," Nahrees said, not taking her eyes from the displays. Holbrook spoke to Davidson, and the Colonel assembled his men on the platform at the centre of the room.

"You should all get back behind the yellow line," Nahrees called, and people shuffled away from the platform, leaving the SAS troops isolated.

Jay stepped forward. "Colonel, you know how careful you have to be, don't you?"

The colonel frowned at him. "We've been briefed."

"You know you have to cross London, that you won't have much time."

"What's your point, Mr. ... er..."

Sandra spoke up. "His point is that you look like a biker gang from another galaxy—or you will to the people you see back there. Just walking down the street you'll create a panic—and that means a splash will start happening all around you. And that means just walking down the street will become almost impossible. Trust me, I've seen it."

Davidson smiled, grimly. "Don't worry, love, we'll get through."

Sandra turned to Jay, her eyes firing sparks. "Shit, I think you were right. This is going to be a complete—"

"We're ready," Nahrees called out. "Everybody stand back. Colonel?" She put her finger on the button.

"Ready when you are." He pulled on his helmet.

"Okay. Good luck."

Then Nahrees cried out and fell back from the console.

Porterhouse shouted, "Oh my God, what has she done?" He reached into the control space and flicked his hands through the controls.

"What the—" Holbrook asked.

And then Porterhouse stabbed down at the lob button. The lights dimmed and the SAS squad flicked out of the timestream. There was silence in the room. No one quite knew what had happened. The teknik was on the ground, holding her head. Porterhouse stepped back from the controls. Everyone looked from Nahrees to Porterhouse in astonishment. Then Porterhouse raised his gun and it all became perfectly clear.

"Everybody get back against the wall over there," he told them. "No one here has to die."

\* \* \* \*

Sniper lay on the ground, winded, trying to reorient himself. Above him, a low grey sky threatened rain. When he pulled off his helmet, he felt a thin, cold wind on his face. He checked the readouts. The lob had lasted a little over four minutes. He would have plenty of air to get back. Klaatu was the man! In the last couple of minutes he had felt the chill of the extratemporal medium seeping through his splashgear and had been glad of the heavy Edwardian clothes he was wearing on top. They had made all the difference.

He stood up and looked around. T-800 was already on his feet about twenty meters to Sniper's right. Edna was nowhere to be seen.

Sniper was standing on a broad paved area, a yard in some grimy, industrial landscape, nothing like the yuppified, neatly trimmed Deptford they had just left. Around him were wooden sheds and, beyond them, gantries and cranes. He tried to get his bearings, but it was difficult.

"Christ, what's that smell?" T-800 said. He had his helmet off too, and was striding over to Sniper through the puddled yard. The thick, cloying stink of dead meat and live cattle mixed with the sharp, sulphurous stench of burning coal.

"Welcome to 1902, my friend. Now where's that fucking creek? And where's Edna?"

"Hey!"

They turned to see the Australian emerging from one of the wooden sheds. He was holding his left arm as if he'd hurt it, and his morning coat was covered in dust and cobwebs. He was wearing his top hat; his helmet bulged inside the carpet bag he carried.

"I don't think it's broken," Edna told them when he was close enough. "She'll be right. I landed on a bloody staircase, would you believe? Fell arse over apex all the way down."

But Sniper and T-800 weren't listening. "It's there." T-800 pointed to where a mass of cranes huddled over Deptford Creek. He turned to face away from it. "Creekside's over that way."

"Gear up," Sniper told him, and they spent a few seconds stashing their helmets and putting on their toppers. They each took a stunner from their bags and slipped it into a shoulder holster under their frock coats.

When they were ready, they picked up their bags and headed for the road. So far they had seen no one and had not been challenged.

"Fifty minutes to go," said Sniper.

They reached the road by kicking down a wooden fence and then walked quickly down Creekside, turning west at the crossroads toward the train station. Behind them, the broken pieces of the fence jerked back and forth, caught in their own small time loop.

A road called ran under the railway line, and they broke into a jog when they reached it. The road had its own odour of engine oil and coal. The smell was strong but nothing could overcome the stench of death that came from the town's massive gutting sheds.

They reached the station entrance in the High Street and bounded up the steps to the viaduct. By the time they were on the platform at Deptford Station, they had just forty-three minutes left. They were the only people on the westbound platform, and for that they were grateful.

"It should be here by now," Edna grumbled. The big station clock showed 10:03. The train was a minute late. "I never thought I'd see the day when I had to catch a train to a splash." Then something caught his attention. "Heads up everyone."

* * * *

The stationmaster, a small rotund man in a peaked hat, hurried toward them across the platform. His round face was almost buried beneath a huge moustache and bristling sideburns. He studied them as he approached, giving most attention to T-800. His eyes widened as he saw the disreputable state of Edna's suit. For a moment he was too flustered to speak.

"The train is late," Sniper said.

"Er, yes," the little man said, dragging his eyes off Edna's suit to meet Sniper's frosty glare. "Yes, it is. My apologies, er, gentlemen. It may be another minute or two."

The strangeness of the group was beginning to impress itself upon the man. Although they dressed like gentlemen, there were many odd things about them, he thought. None had a moustache or beard, for example, and they had all shaved their sideburns right off! Their hairstyles were uniformly wild beneath their rather old-fashioned hats and there was not a trace of brilliantine between them. All three of them wore boots that were more like rubber galoshes than proper gentlemen's footwear. They were all quite young— university men, he guessed—and, on reflection, that probably explained everything.

"Perhaps I could assist you in some way?" he asked uncertainly. "Would you care to purchase tickets for your journey?"

"My servant procured our tickets some days ago," said Edna, with considerable hauteur. "You may go now."

The stationmaster bristled. Impudent puppy! He drew a deep breath, preparing to demand that they produce their tickets, when a racket from behind him announced the arrival of the delayed 10:02 to London, Cannon Street.

* * * *

Sniper took his hand off the grip of his stunner and relaxed. The steam locomotive that pulled into the station with its train of bright red carriages looked like an overgrown toy. The engine was painted green, with a red undercarriage and a gleaming gold dome on top of the boiler. The letters "S. E. & C. R." were painted prominently on the tender. It hissed and belched steam and smoke, brakes screeching like banshees as it slowed and stopped.

Sniper and his crew piled into the first class carriage and found an empty compartment with red plush seats. They immediately pulled down all the blinds as planned. The fewer people who saw them, the better.

Edna lifted the blind a little and they all peered out the window. The stationmaster was talking agitatedly to the guard. When the man turned and pointed at the first class carriage, Edna dropped the blind again.

"Trouble," he said, not looking too unhappy about it. They sat in tense silence until the train lurched into motion again. They had been moving for only a couple of minutes when the guard opened the door to their compartment. He took in the drawn blinds and the three hatless men with scruffy hair and frowned.

"Tickets, please, gentlemen," he said, clearly looking for a confrontation. The door frame around him was twisting and warping but he didn't seem to notice.

Sniper could only see the splash getting worse if they got into an argument with the guard. So he drew his stunner and shot him, hoping it would be the lesser of two evils.

The guard immediately went into paroxysms of falling and bouncing back up, while all around him the railway carriage buckled and twisted. The glass in the door shattered and the wooden panelling began to break and splinter. The reaction was more extreme and violent than Sniper had expected.

"Shit!" Edna shouted.

The three bricks jumped up and pressed themselves against the outer wall of the carriage, away from the spatial distortions. The chaos around the stunned guard was rapidly spreading. The seats on one side of their compartment began to melt into the floor.

"We've got to get out of here." T-800's voice was unruffled, but it was clear from his face that he too was shocked by the way the carriage was dissolving. Without a word, Sniper grabbed his bag and plunged into the chaos, pushing the guard aside and staggering across the quaking floor and into the corridor beyond. The others followed behind him. They managed to get clear of the most dangerous area just as the floor erupted in a shower of planking that hung in the air, oscillating. Below the cloud of broken wood, they could see the tracks streaming past.

They edged away from the hole toward the front of the train but had hardly gone a couple of meters when the guard's body fell through the gap and onto the line. There was a howling scream from the exposed metal chassis beneath them.

"Run!" Sniper shouted, and they turned their back on the destruction and raced to the door at the end of the corridor. Sniper shot the lock with his QSZ-99 and they scrambled through into the open air. They emerged behind the bucking, rocking coal tender and one by one jumped from the carriage across to it, landing on a narrow metal rim. They held onto the oily black edge of the steel railway truck and began making their way to the side, where they could edge forward toward the engine.

They heard an explosive crash, but they couldn't see past the end of the carriage behind them. As the engine lurched to a higher speed, Sniper realized that the first class carriage had probably broken in half and, most likely, derailed the whole train behind it.

"Hope there was no one important back there," Sniper shouted over the din of the engine. Something like this could cause a major splash and he didn't want to be yanked back into a dangerous backwash. "Remember when we get back that we need to leave Deptford fast."

T-800 poked him with his bag. "We need to get off." He was looking at the carriage they had just jumped from. It was rocking from side to side, unstable and ready to topple over. If it did, it might easily drag them with it.

Sniper had barely time to utter an expletive when he was slammed against the back of the tender. The engine's wheels were locked and screaming. The engine driver, realizing the danger they were in, had pulled the brake.

Clinging to the tender as the engine shuddered to a halt, Sniper ground his teeth in fury. This was not the way it was meant to go down!

He leaned toward T-800 so he didn't need to shout too much and pointed at the damaged carriage.

"When we stop, uncouple that bastard, then get up to the engine. Edna and I are going to have a little chat with the driver."

Sniper jumped down from the tender and looked back. Several hundred meters away, the disconnected carriages had piled into a writhing, shimmering mass. In the fields around the wreck, he could see fractures twisting out, distorting the fields, folding trees and houses. A hole opened in the sky and began to draw up the air into itself.

"Better hurry up, boys!" he shouted.

# Chapter 23

## Another Chance

"You're thicker than you look if you think you'll get away with this." Overman's baleful eyes had not left Porterhouse for a moment since the gun had appeared.

"Shut up!" Porterhouse yelled. Holding a roomful of people at gunpoint was not improving the big man's temper.

"I should shoot the lot of you!"

"Your gun's a standard issue Glock," Overman said. "Fifteen rounds. There are nine of us in the room, maybe six of us armed. I know you're a good shot, but you'd have to be bloody Annie Oakley to hit all nine of us before someone jumped you or shot you."

Porterhouse had already done the calculation and come to a similar conclusion. As things stood, he was safe. If the shooting started, he was a dead man. But his plan was simple. Get to the door, lock it behind him, then get to the fast boat he had moored on the river. As for pursuit, that wouldn't amount to much with a full-scale evacuation underway. Everything had gone to shit and he'd been forced to take a big risk, but he could still make it, if he kept his head and no silly bugger decided to be a hero.

"Everyone over there," Porterhouse said, waving his gun. He kept his eyes on them. In his view, Overman and Colbert were the most dangerous. Then maybe Bauchet and Holbrook—although he doubted that Holbrook was armed. That left the kid, Jay, and the girl. Jay would be armed but he didn't rate him much. The girl was a nutter, and unpredictable, but a steady eye and a cool head were what counted in a stand-off. None of the three tekniks mattered.

He didn't dare make them take their guns out and throw them down. He'd never be able to keep them all covered and someone was bound to try something. He could make them disarm one at a time, though. That might work. If he could just move them all away from the door and get himself over there before someone did something heroic.

"Get moving," he shouted.

They started shuffling along the wall. They knew what he was up to, so they were all moving slowly and looking for their chance.

"Hurry it up! I can easily start shortening the odds by picking one or two of you off." It might not be a bad idea at that.

"Tell me it wasn't just for money," Holbrook said, his voice dripping with contempt.

Porterhouse almost shot him for that. Of course it was for the money—but it didn't help that his wife and kids were being held as collateral. "Just for insurance," that bitch Camilla had said. Until an hour ago, it hadn't seemed like a big problem.

He almost spat as he addressed Holbrook. "What else is there but money any more? This world is going to shit, and we can't stop it. A few more big splashes and governments will start to fall. Then it'll be every man for himself. While you losers are sitting around hoping the mob in charge will honour your civil service pensions, I'll be laughing at you from a good, safe distance. If any of us make it past today, that is."

They had all moved clear of the door now. To escape, all Porterhouse had to do was cross the room, step outside, lock the door and smash the electronic lock after him.

"Who's behind it?" Bauchet asked. "Who's paying you?"

"Why should I care?"

"If you don't care, then tell me."

Porterhouse sneered at him and continued edging toward the door. There was a bigger picture here. It was a matter of survival. Yet they still wanted to play spy games while the world went down in flames around them. Damn them all to hell! Especially that bloody girl! What did she have to stick her nose in for? He glanced at her, wondering if he could risk a shot. If it hadn't been for her, the SAS could never have attempted a lob, and he wouldn't have had to give himself away to stop them.

He noticed that the girl had tensed up, eyes watching his eyes like a fighter, ready to jump him if she could see an opening. The very idea that she thought she could take him on infuriated him. He wanted to tell the stupid brat to bring it on. It would feel unbelievably good to beat the crap out of her. What the hell? A hostage wouldn't hurt. "You. Nutjob. You with the tits." He kept his eyes mostly on Overman and Colbert, but everyone knew who he meant. "Put your weapon on the floor and get over here."

"Go to hell, creep."

He pointed his gun straight at her. "Nobody move or she dies!" He let everyone think about that for a moment. "Now, you put down your gun and get over here, darling. I won't tell you again."

Carefully, Sandra reached for her gun and drew it out. She held it with two fingers and slowly bent down to place it on the floor. From a crouching position, she looked up at Jay. "Now don't do anything stupid," she said.

Jay gave her a look of pure astonishment and quickly turned to Porterhouse. "I'm not doing anything," he said, holding up his hands.

Overman and Colbert both took their chances while this little scene was being played out. Almost simultaneously, they leapt from the wall, drawing their weapons and diving for cover.

As soon as he saw them move, Porterhouse knew he was dead. He fired three shots, hitting both of them. He swung his weapon back, desperate to take out as many of the rest of them as he could before they got him, but Sandra already had a proper grip on her gun and fired back. As her shot smacked into Porterhouse's chest, Bauchet and Jay fired too—a fusillade of rapid shots knocking Porterhouse off his feet. The room seemed to spin away from him as the blackness closed in.

* * * *

Before Porterhouse's body hit the ground, Nahrees ran straight past Overman and Colbert to her consoles.

The rest hurried to help the fallen men. Overman was dead, with two bullets in him. Colbert was still alive, bleeding profusely from a wound in his thigh. One of the tekniks ran for a medical kit, while Bauchet used his compatch to call for an ambulance.

"Holy crap," Nahrees said.

Everyone fell silent, listening for the verdict.

"He messed with the targeting controls. They went back over three hundred years." Nahrees did a quick calculation in her head. "It's a nine minute lob. They only have enough air for six minutes each way—the four minutes we expected it to take, plus a fifty percent contingency. Nearly two-thirds of it will have gone before they even reach the target. At that distance in time, they'll have just a few minutes at the other end and then…" She stopped, staring bleakly at the platform. "Partway through the yankback, their air will run out."

Holbrook checked his compatch. "They've only been gone a few minutes so far. If you could stop them, bring them back…"

Nahrees shook her head. "I'm sorry. It doesn't work like that. It's like throwing a rock. Once you let go, that's it."

Bauchet paced angrily across the room. Seven men dead. Plus Overman, the MI5 agent. And Colbert wounded, perhaps fatally. "We have to call in a second SAS team," he said.

"It's too late." Holbrook sounded defeated. He stared at Porterhouse's body.

"No, no." Bauchet wasn't going to give up yet. "Sniper's team set off—" He glanced at his compatch. "Fourteen minutes ago. We still have forty-two minutes."

It was Holbrook's turn to shake his head. "The Regiment is based at Aldershot these days. It's only fifty kilometres away, but even if they scrambled a helicopter, it would take them—what?—a total of forty minutes to reach us? They could suit up and be briefed on the way, but that still gives us just two minutes after they get here. The trip from now to 1902 takes four minutes. And then they still have to cross

London to get to the British Museum. It's impossible."

"Then I will call in some police officers. We can get them ready in ten minutes. We cannot give up now, Jonathan! We are London's last chance!"

"It still won't work, sir." Jay had been helping with Colbert's wound. Now he stood up and faced Bauchet. "If we send untrained police officers back there, we'll just create the same kind of disaster we're trying to avoid. I've been trying to tell everyone this for days now. They'll get themselves killed just trying to get to the target, and they'll create a splash that ... well, it won't be on the Beijing scale, but it might still kill hundreds or thousands of people."

Bauchet snarled in disgust, talking past Jay to Holbrook. "So you want to give up? You want to let the city be destroyed without even putting up a fight?"

"No, sir," said Jay, stepping into Bauchet's line of sight. "There is a way to do this."

"You can send me."

Everyone, including Jay, looked round in surprise.

"After all," said Sandra, "I'm the only one who's done this before."

"That's not what I meant!" cried Jay. "I meant that I should go." He turned to Holbrook.

"She's ... she's just a civilian, sir."

"She shoots pretty well for a civilian," said Bauchet.

Sandra exchanged a small smile with him as something kindled in Holbrook's eyes.

"Jesus Christ almighty," Holbrook whispered, as much in prayer as in amazement. "Okay. You're both going. Get suited up."

Jay looked like he was about to argue.

"On the double, Kennedy!" Holbrook turned to Nahrees.

"Fire up that infernal machine of yours, young woman. We're tossing two more Christians to the lions. God help us."

Sandra ran for the changing room. She grabbed Jay's arm on the way, dragging him with her.

* * * *

The steam engine rattled along at a hair-raising speed. Sniper leaned out the side of the cab, his blond hair streaming in the wind. For the hundredth time, he blew the whistle and laughed like a maniac.

Edna and T-800 were stoking and driving the engine by guesswork and inspiration. They'd had to leave the engineer and fireman behind because the two astonished men were creating too much of a splash around them. The bricks' madcap dash across the English countryside was not without ill effects. As they pushed the engine farther from its abandoned train and off its original spacetime coordinates, it began leaving a trail of temporal anomalies behind it. At first, the disturbance was minor, but it grew as they travelled. Now, as they approached Cannon Street railway bridge, they could see a shimmering, rippling wake of acausal mayhem spreading out behind them.

"You'd better slow this thing," Sniper shouted.

"What?"

"Stop the fucking train!"

They were sweeping along a wide curve of track toward the bridge. Immediately beyond that were two brick towers flanking the huge glass arch of the station. Sniper had researched the route in 2050, riding the same line into the same station. But now it looked different: a massive glass arch where Sniper had seen decaying office blocks, thick brown grime over everything.

Edna and T-800 had already worked out the main controls, so applying the brakes was no problem.

"Slow us down more!" Sniper yelled.

The bridge was not far away now and it was clear that they weren't going to stop in time.

Edna applied the brakes with a vengeance. They were all pushed forward into the nest of valves and gauges that filled the front of the cab.

"That better?" he asked.

Sniper stuck his head out again. They were on the bridge, crossing the Thames, and still going too fast. Sparks were flying from the wheels as they ground along the rails.

"Put it in reverse," he shouted. He considered jumping out while they were still over the river and taking his chances in the water. He didn't want to die uselessly in a train wreck. Yet the idea of surviving without being able to reach the target on time was unacceptable. He must live, but he must complete the splash, too.

T-800 managed to dump some of the pressure from the boiler, steam billowing from the engine in massive white clouds. But it had no effect on their speed at all. When they reached the station they all looked out, clinging to whatever they could as the engine swerved wildly through a branching spaghetti maze of tracks. Some of the platforms already had trains in them. If they hit the back of one, they were done for.

With a final, gut-wrenching swerve, they switched away from a full platform onto an empty one. They were still slowing, but not enough. Even the extra train-length they had won would not give them time to slow to a stop. They crowded into the front of the cab bracing themselves against the wall of controls clutching their carpetbags and eyeing the massive coal-filled tender behind them.

Even though the steam engine was hardly moving, it smashed through the buffers at the end of the platform as though they were made of balsa. The engine ploughed into the concourse, burying its undercarriage in concrete and earth, sending people running as debris exploded into the air and steam burst from every broken pipe. The tender slammed forward into the back of the cab, crushing its couplings, as engine and tender jack-knifed into the air, lifting Sniper and his crew before the slow-motion crash came to a stop.

Then it unwound again. The back of the engine and front of the tender dropped to the ground. The coupling unbuckled, concrete and earth gathered out of the air and reformed the concourse, and the engine reversed out of it.

But then it started all over again—the engine crashing into the concourse, tender and engine mounting into the air.

Sniper grabbed T-800 as soon as the second bone-jarring impact was over and everything started un-crashing again. As soon as the wheels hit the ground again, he dragged him to the edge of the cab and they both jumped clear.

Behind them, Edna didn't quite make the jump before the crash started again. This time, it threw him against the front of the cab, his face smashing into the valves and gauges. Then the oncoming tender pushed the engine up once more and they lost sight of him. Sniper tried to get to Edna when the back of the engine came down once more, but the ground around him was heaving and shifting so much he couldn't even stand. Then they saw Edna's limp body slam against the boiler yet again with the same sickening force.

They turned and half-crawled, half-staggered away from the wreck that was smashing their friend's body again and again. They said nothing, but kept going doggedly across the madly bucking concourse. People all around them were screaming. Some were trapped in an oscillating motion, others were sinking into the floor. Above them, the great glass arch shattered and tons of broken glass fell in sheets of deadly rain.

Sniper and T-800 made it to the relative safety of the main entrance before the glass hit the concourse. They sprinted out through the frightened crowds while people behind them looked up at a million soot-covered blades dancing in the air above them.

"This way!" They'd both lost their top hats, but they still had their carpet bags. Sniper led them at a run down Cannon Street, dashed recklessly across the busy road, and turned into St. Swithin's Lane. They stopped in the archway of the first courtyard they came to and caught their breath, out of sight to all but a very few. They were dirty and dishevelled., bruised and hatless, smeared with oil and soot, but they were alive.

Sniper started laughing.

T-800 looked at him and gave a wry smile. He shook his head. "Edna just died, you know?"

"Yeah, but we didn't."

They tidied themselves up as much as they could and set off again. At the bottom of the road they turned left into King William Street. They were still attracting wary looks from the people they passed. All around them was a shimmer—a slight blurring of outlines, a movement of road and wall, even of the air itself. Everything threatened to explode into madness at any moment. They crossed the street, dodging past horse-drawn carriages and coaches, and even a chugging, rattling motor car.

At the end of the street was Bank underground station.

They hurried inside and down the stairs, ignoring the ticket booths and going unchallenged. The westbound platform was busy but not crowded. They quickly found a quiet spot at the end of the platform where they could wait without too many people staring at them.

"There's only twenty minutes left," Sniper growled.

"Maybe we'd be better off on the surface?"

"No way. Look." He nodded toward a young couple, a few meters away. The couple was watching them. The woman's hand was twitching back and forth and the platform around them was undulating in small ripples that spread from her feet. "Just the sight of us standing here seems to be enough to trigger a splash. If we go up there and sprint through central London, think how many people we'd shock, bump into, knock over. We'd get about twenty meters before we had a full-scale splash on our hands."

"I thought that's what we wanted."

Sniper turned on him angrily. "This isn't some amateur-night outing, man. We're not here for a few cheap laughs and a bit of excitement. This is the biggest lob of all time and we're going to make the biggest splash ever recorded. We're going to shoot fucking Lenin, man! Nothing else is good enough. You understand?"

T-800 met Sniper's stare for several long seconds before he gave a small nod of agreement. A breath of dusty air along the platform announced the imminent arrival of the tube train.

"About fucking time," Sniper growled.

\* \* \* \*

"What the hell do you think you're doing?" Jay demanded. He

was wearing a one-piece pressure suit in pale blue and feeling gangly and self-conscious. The suits were there for the lobsite staff and were mostly unused and spotless because none of the equipment had been tested yet. Jay tried not to dwell on that.

Sandra was still in one of the changing cubicles, getting into Nahrees' splashgear. "I'm doing what I have to," she shouted.

Jay was worried. "I know what you went through at Ommen. I've read your file, remember. I saw you. This could be much, much worse. You don't have to do this. Bauchet can get some police in. I can do it on my own. For God's sake, I—"

His jaw dropped as Sandra walked out of the cubicle. He had a vague memory of how great she'd looked in the cage at Ommen, and he knew she was beautiful, but the way she filled that figure-hugging, pale blue catsuit was quite literally breathtaking.

Seeing him standing there with his mouth hanging open, Sandra put her hands on her hips and regarded him through narrowed eyes. "You were saying?"

He blinked, having forgotten whatever he'd been about to say. Instead, he managed a feeble, "You look … nice."

Sandra shook her head, sighing in exasperation. She grabbed her helmet and stomped past him. Jay picked up his own and followed her into the other room, where all conversation immediately stopped. Everyone was staring at Sandra, even the two medics attending to Colbert, even Holbrook as he organized the disposal of Porterhouse's body, even Nahrees, who said, "Wow, it didn't look that good when I tried it on."

Holbrook was the first to regain his composure. "There's

bad news," he said, addressing Jay.

"You can't lob until the SAS team returns."

"What? Why not?"

Nahrees jumped in. "We don't know if it's safe. No one has ever tried to send someone back from a lobsite that was already in use. No one can calculate extratemporal trajectories yet. There are theories, of course. Lee Chin Wu just published a paper on supertemporal coordinate systems that looks promising, but it's all speculation, really. However, there has to be a finite probability that—"

"What she's saying," said Holbrook, loudly enough to stop her saying it, "is that the SAS team will be yanked back. Right here." He nodded toward the lobsite.

"If we send you from here and they're being drawn back to the very same spot, there might be a chance you'll bump into the SAS team on their way back. We don't know what that would mean, and we can't take that risk, so we're going to wait until they arrive."

"Wait!" Sandra was outraged at the suggestion. "Do you know what the time is? Do you know how long we've got?"

"It's not as bad as it seems," Nahrees said, flinching as Sandra turned to glare at her.

"We don't need to sync with Sniper's timeline, we just need to overlap with it. I can send you back to a slightly earlier time so that you can still make it across town and arrive at the museum in time to meet Sniper."

Sandra tried to puzzle out the various timelines—the one they were in, the one Sniper was in, and the one they would need to be in to get the job done.

"How much earlier?" Jay asked.

"Well, if we assume Sniper will arrive at the museum with a few minutes to spare, we can send you back to anything up to fifty-six minutes before that time and you'd still see him. Of course, it would be better if you arrived well before he did in case he gets there early. So we should give you enough time to have, say, twenty minutes at the museum."

Sandra gave a sharp laugh. "We can't just hang around outside the British Museum for twenty minutes! Look at us. Can you imagine the splash we'd cause? And if anything is going to give us away to Sniper, it's a splash happening before he even gets there. Besides, Lenin will be there and we'd put him in danger if we start a splash nearby. We might end up doing Sniper's job for him!"

Holbrook shot an angry glance at Bauchet. "If we'd known in advance what the target was, we could have had maps and plans here, and found you a safe place to hide, instead of all this seat-of-the-pants stuff."

Bauchet scowled back at him. "It is because of your mole that my hands were tied, my friend."

Holbrook shook his head and backed down with a groan. "You're right, Jacques, it was our mess."

The medics lifted Colbert and carried him out to a police helicopter that was waiting. Porterhouse's body still lay bagged on a gurney, attended by officers. Getting an ambulance to Vauxhall in the middle of a general evacuation had proven impossible. In the end, Bauchet had pulled strings and got the Met to send in a chopper. More would be arriving soon to take away the rest of them once the lob was over.

Holbrook turned to Nahrees. "Find them a schedule that gets them to the museum ten minutes before Sniper gets there."

Nahrees nodded. "I'll aim for forty minutes into Sniper's lob. Is that okay?"

He nodded, his mind already elsewhere. "Jacques, could

you make sure we have enough police officers on hand to deal with the SAS team when it returns?"

"It's taken care of. They're standing by. And medics too, just in case." He shrugged, acknowledging what a negligible chance there was that any of them would still be alive when they returned.

They all turned to look at the lobsite, empty now, but soon to be piled with the bodies of seven unfortunate time travellers.

\* \* \* \*

"It should be about … now," Nahrees said and a moment later, the whole SAS team materialized on the platform. It was more like they'd been tossed into the room by the hand of God. The seven men went sprawling and rolling across the platform, most of them ending up tumbling onto the floor. By a miracle, two of them were still alive, but barely. Police and medics rushed to their aid. One of the men pushed away any attempts to help him, determined to report.

Holbrook glanced at Nahrees. "Get those two on their way," he said, meaning Jay and Sandra, then went to the stubborn soldier.

"Clear the platform," Nahrees was shouting. "Everybody behind the yellow line."

"Sir," the SAS man said to Holbrook. His voice was faint and his lips were blue with cold. Jay and Sandra jumped onto the platform, watching the man as he struggled to speak. "Something went wrong."

"We know, lad. Let the medics take care of you."

"We went back too far. It was so cold. The colonel realized there wouldn't be enough air to get us all back alive. We drew straws, sir." Tears ran down his anguished face. "The losers got to keep their helmets and … and another man's helmet for when his own air ran out. The rest…"

"Lob in ten seconds," Nahrees said.

Holbrook looked around at the fallen soldiers. Only three had been wearing helmets, he now realized. Yet even one of those had succumbed to the cold. He looked up at Jay and Sandra, tethered together on the platform. They were looking back at him with horror in their eyes.

"Helmets on," Nahrees said. "Five. Four. Three. Two. One."

And they were both gone.

# Chapter 24

## 1902

Jay hit the ground hard. He thanked the gods that someone in MI5 had had the sense to put their lobsite on the ground floor of the SIS Building. Almost as soon as he hit the ground, he was wrenched sideways by the tether. He slid across a rough, cobbled surface. Anxiously, he looked around for Sandra but couldn't see her. The tether that was dragging him along disappeared into the ground just a meter or so ahead of him. No, he realized, not into the ground but over an edge. Sandra was dangling over some kind of precipice and pulling him toward it.

He jerked his body round so his feet were ahead of him and managed to dig his heels in hard enough to stop himself sliding forward. Frantically, he looked around for something to hold onto but there was nothing, just the round, smooth cobbles.

They'd landed in some kind of scruffy dockyard—a series of small inlets along the edge of the Thames. Sandra must have materialized in mid-air and fallen toward the dirty, oily water, while he had landed on the wharf.

No one was around, no ships nearby. An empty berth, then. There was a crane about ten meters away, a black tower of criss-crossed wooden beams, sitting on a bogey with steel wheels. He wondered about shouting for help, but he thought that bringing people to him would only make matters worse. If that crane would only roll his way ... Then it hit him that the crane was on rails, steel rails set into the cobbles. The rails ran right past him, just a little way behind him. If he could somehow reach them without letting himself get dragged over the edge ...

The tether began tugging and pulling. He almost lost his tenuous grip on the cobbles. It didn't help that his fingers were almost numb with cold from the lob.

"Hey!" Sandra had obviously managed to get her helmet off. "Hey! I could use a bit of help here!"

He shouted back but he doubted she could hear him through his own helmet. He tried crawling backward but he couldn't budge; he just risked slipping on the cobbles. He had to reach the rail. It was his only hope.

He launched himself backward with all his strength, twisting and diving for the rail. He caught it with one hand and quickly got his other hand onto it. With a firm grip now, he heaved himself forward, crawling on his belly, dragging Sandra's dead weight inch by inch up the sheer wall of the wharf. When he could, he stretched out a hand to the next rail and slowly dragged himself farther.

Once he could get his toes against the first rail, he was home and dry. Holding her weight with his feet, he turned, carefully, onto his back, putting his heels against the rail. Now, supported by the rail with his hands free, he could grab the tether and haul her up.

When Sandra's arm appeared over the edge of the wharf

and she took some of her own weight, he almost sobbed with relief. Within seconds she was over the edge and safely on dry land. They both lay on the ground gasping for a while before Sandra got up and walked over to him. Looking him over, she took off her backpack and her harness. She gave him an impatient look. "Come on. We haven't got all day."

"You're welcome," he said bitterly and struggled to his feet.

They packed the harnesses, tether and helmets into their backpacks and, orienting themselves by the river, set off east toward Albert Embankment and Lambeth Bridge. Behind them, the corroded and half-demolished Vauxhall Bridge looked bleak in the dreary greyness. of the cold April morning. Jay looked at the grimy, ramshackle wharves and warehouses they were passing and decided he didn't much like 1902.

They walked quickly for several minutes, glad of the exercise. Four minutes in the bitter cold of the extratemporal medium had chilled them both to the bone. They reached the southern end of the Albert Embankment without anyone noticing them, but the pedestrian traffic increased near the fashionable northern end, as did the number of carriages on the road. Ahead of them was Lambeth Bridge—not the neat bridge Jay knew with its painted arches—but a rickety decaying suspension bridge that he did not look forward to crossing.

They hurried along, Jay increasingly conscious that they must look almost naked in their splashgear compared to the men and women they passed. Everyone wore three-piece suits and floor-length dresses. They were all muffled in coats and scarves and hats. Most of the men had beards and large sideburns, and the women had their hair piled up on their heads. Jay and Sandra stood out in almost every conceivable way.

"We need to get off the street," Sandra said.

She pointed to a man in a top hat who was staring at them. He seemed to shrink as he spoke to a companion, then returned to his original size.

"There!" said Jay.

Up ahead, a row of four hansom cabs were parked by the curb. He had thought they would need to cross the river to Millbank before they'd find a cab rank, but was happy to have luck on his side.

The hansoms were two-seaters, with one big wheel on each side of the cab, a single horse at the front, and a high seat at the back for the cabbie. The cabs had little half-doors just behind the horse for the passengers.

"Just like in a Sherlock Holmes vid!" Sandra exclaimed as they drew close. Jay looked at her sideways, worried by how cheerful she seemed about all this.

The cabbies were standing together, chatting, when the two time travellers. arrived. The four men looked a rough lot. They wore a variety of coats and hats and two had huge bushy beards.

"Lumme!" said one of them, softly.

They all gaped at Sandra. One of them even took his hat off, he was so amazed.

"I, er, we need a ride to—" Jay began, awkwardly, stopping as a couple of the men turned and looked him up and down. Their shocked expressions made him painfully aware of how odd he must look.

Sandra stepped forward, speaking smoothly and with a sweetness of tone Jay had not heard her use before. "My brother and I are circus performers," she told them. "Only we seem to have become separated from our troupe." A couple of the men nodded, as if this explained everything.

"Trapeze artists," said Jay, and grabbed an imaginary bar, miming a swinging motion. Sandra scowled at him. "I hope you'll forgive our appearance. We were in a parade, you see. And now we're lost, I'm afraid." She put on a face to match their supposed plight and Jay marvelled at the sympathetic expressions of the hard-faced cabbies.

"Would any of you be kind enough to help us? We need to get to the British Museum as quickly as possible. One of the owners is there. If we can reach him before he leaves, everything will be all right. If not, I don't know what we'll do."

There was a sudden rush of volunteers. The cabbies almost fell to squabbling among themselves for the privilege of helping this beautiful young damsel in distress.

"Oi!" one of them protested, pushing himself forward. "It's my cab is at the front." The others subsided, acknowledging this incontestable right. The cabbie straightened up, preened himself, and said, "Now then, miss, if you'd care to step this way. You too, sir. And don't you worry about catching this 'ere owner chap you're after. 'Arry Endsleigh's known the length and breadth of all Lunnun for being the fastest cab on two wheels." He nodded proudly, chest out.

He led them to his hansom and helped Sandra inside, averting his face—but not his eyes, Jay noticed—as she climbed in. He closed the doors on them and walked forward to take the nosebag off his horse. On his way back, he stopped and patted the horse's rump. "Ol' Bucephalus here might look a bit rickety," he told Sandra, "but he's a strong 'un, he is. Mark my words. He'll get you there." The man seemed to have grown mesmerized by the sight of Sandra's legs and simply stopped speaking.

Jay leaned forward, irritably. "If we could get going. We're in a bit of a hurry."

The cabbie snapped out of it. "Ah. Um," he said and dragged himself off to the back of the cab. Shortly, they felt the hansom rock on its springs as the cabbie climbed up to his seat. The reins, which ran from the horse over their heads and across the roof, flicked once and the cab jolted into motion.

Sandra turned to Jay with an impish grin. "I think he likes me," she said.

Jake snorted. "I think the Pope would like you in that outfit."

"Why do you think we're getting a ride with no splash starting up?"

"I don't know. Maybe this guy just wasn't doing anything that would change the timeline this morning. Maybe his life was just totally inconsequential."

Sandra grinned at him. "You're just saying that 'cause you're jealous."

Jay realized he was—stupidly and needlessly jealous. Deep in thought, he sank back into the cab's seat while Sandra peered at the people in the street. Being in love with Sandra was always going to be a problem for him, he realized. A woman so spectacularly beautiful would have guys hitting on her all the time—and not just bristly, old cabbies either. One day someone really cool would come along, and then …

If only she loved him too, loved him so much he'd never have to worry about some other bloke catching her eye. Yet for that to happen, he'd have to be someone else entirely, someone far more glamorous and interesting than Jay

Kennedy, soon-to-be-unemployed secret agent. It was a deeply depressing thought.

"Shit!" Sandra threw herself into the back of the cab. "Someone out there was watching me. I saw him start that vibrating thing."

Jay snapped out of his dismal reverie. He looked around. There were blinds on the side windows and leather curtains across the open front of the cab, above the folding doors. He reached over and drew them all. It was gloomy inside but at least they were private.

A hatch on the roof opened, and, as if to dispel any sense of security they might be feeling, the cabbie peered in at them. "You all right in there? Only I heard the curtains closin' and bein' as there ain't no rain nor nuffin', I thought I'd best ask, like."

Sandra managed to force a smile. "You're very kind, Mr. Endsleigh. We just thought it would be better not to be seen in public dressed as we are. We wouldn't want to offend anyone, you understand."

"Very considerate of you, miss." He coughed uncomfortably. "I daresay how there's plenty of narrow-minded types abaht as might take offence at the sight of a pretty girl in, er, in her professional costume, as it were, but not 'Arry Endsleigh! Live an' let live. That's what I says. Live an' let live."

Jay reached up and took hold of the hatch. "Very broad-minded of you," he said. "Thank you." He firmly closed the hatch.

He looked at Sandra through narrowed eyes. "You're too damned good at this lying. It makes me nervous."

She put a hand on his leg. "I'd never lie to you, Jay."

She looked sincere, and the hand on his leg was a

convincing argument, but she had looked just as sincere telling the cabbie she was a circus performer.

"And why did you tell them we were brother and sister?" he demanded.

She regarded him with her head cocked. "Because I might have needed to flirt with one of them. I couldn't easily do that if you were supposed to be my husband or whatever, could I? And anyway, it was probably not done for a young lady and her beau to be gadding about town in a hansom. This way you're my chaperone." She grinned. "And it explains your grumpy, overprotective attitude."

Jay sat back again, cross and confused.

"And, by the way," she went on. "Do you really think it's appropriate to be sulking about your wounded feelings when the lives of millions of people are at risk?"

Jay opened his mouth to defend himself but found he couldn't. She was absolutely right. He just couldn't understand why he was behaving like this.

"How long have we got?" she asked.

He checked his compatch. "Thirty-one minutes."

Sandra opened the hatch above them. "Mr. Endsleigh?"

The weather-beaten face smiled down at her, revealing teeth she would rather not have known about. "You can call me 'Arry, my dear. Everyone calls me 'Arry."

"Thank you, Harry. Look, we really need to be at the museum within the next twenty minutes. Do you think we'll make it in time?"

The cabbie went into a kind of ecstasy, rolling his eyes and his head. "Lord bless you, miss! Twenty minutes? To get from 'ere to Great Russell Street? At this time of day? In 'Arry Endsleigh's cab? Well known to be the best 'ansom for a quick trip in the 'ole of Lunnun? Ha!"

He was silent then, apparently believing he had answered the question. He beamed down at Sandra's legs, happily.

"So we'll get there in time, then?" Jay asked.

The cabbie turned a frown on him. "I just said so, didn't I?"

"Of course he did, silly," Sandra said, shooting a quick scowl at Jay. "Thank you very much, Harry. You've been very helpful." She reached up to close the hatch again but Harry interrupted her.

"If you'll pardon me asking, Miss, but is that a trace of a foreign accent I 'ears in your voice?"

Without skipping a beat, Sandra laughed gaily. "That's very perceptive of you, Harry. You have a very good ear. My brother and I are from Canada. Our accents may be strange, but we're still loyal subjects. God save the Queen!"

Harry pulled back in surprise.

"She means King," said Jay. "We only got the news in Canada quite recently. We're still not quite used to it." He reached up quickly and shut the hatch.

"King Henry the Seventh," he told Sandra. "Victoria died last year. Didn't they teach you anything in school?"

Looking chastened, Sandra sat back in her seat. "I didn't go to school much. I changed foster homes a lot so it was easy to play truant. It always took them ages to cotton on. A couple of times I got expelled for making trouble." She turned to him, mustering a little defiance.

"You read my file. I ran off at thirteen and that was the end of it until they put me in the Institute."

She turned away again with a shrug and flopped back in the seat. "It's a wonder I know anything, really. I suppose you think I'm a complete dummy."

"No, I—" He stopped himself giving her an automatic

reassurance. He took her hand and waited until she looked at him. "I'm sorry about the life you've had, honestly I am. If I ever say anything stupid or hurtful about it, that's just me being thick. I really don't mean to judge you."

Her troubled expression softened into a smile. She leaned toward him and they shared a long, tender kiss.

"So that's 'ow it is, is it?" Harry's voice boomed down at them from the open hatch like the voice of Moses chastening the Israelites.

"Goddammit!" Sandra cursed and glared up at Harry. "Can't you keep your beady eyes off me for five seconds, you scruffy old letch?"

The cabbie's eyes widened in shock and then his face disappeared as he pulled back on the reins, bringing the cab to a halt.

"I guess we're walking from here," Jay said, pulling open the curtains and unfolding the doors.

They climbed down to the pavement and put their backpacks on in time to be joined by Harry, puffing his cheeks and looking like thunder. "Well, I suppose I was 'ad," he began. Jay noticed he had brought a nasty-looking cudgel down with him. "Right royally 'ad, as you might say. I should 'ave known it to look at yer. Circus act! Brother an' sister! My Aunt Fanny!"

He stepped toward Jay with his fist clenched around the cudgel. "Well, I'd like to know what your game is, mate."

Jay and Sandra backed away.

"We're sorry," Jay said. "But we really, really needed a ride."

"Where do you fink you're going? You're gorna pay your fare, mate. And you're gorna give me the truth abaht this little charade you an' yer little strumpet 'ave been playin' at my expense."

Jay just wanted the man to calm down. "Look, we don't have any money. We thought you might look on it as a favour."

"A favour? A bleedin' favour? Will you stand still, you great beanpole, and give me my money?" He raised the cudgel, brandishing it menacingly.

"Jay," Sandra said, looking around anxiously at the people staring at them. "Do something."

Jay gritted his teeth in frustration. "Ah, bugger," he said, and delivered a swift straight-arm punch to Harry's solar plexus. The cabbie stopped dead in his tracks, mouth open, eyes wide with surprise, and sat down slowly on the pavement, unable to breathe. "I'm sorry," Jay told him, and looked it.

They turned away and jogged off up the road.

"Nice punch, beanpole," Sandra said, grinning.

"Thanks, strumpet," he replied, not looking at her.

# Chapter 25

## The British Museum

The boxy little electric railway engine pulled into the Central Line tube station with its liveried carriages behind it. There was an air of newness about the rolling stock that brightened up the dimly lit station. Sniper and T-800 found a part of the train that was less crowded and climbed aboard, trying to avoid contact with any of the other travellers. They sat down and kept their eyes on the seat in front of them.

This tactic worked until they reached Holborn, three stops into their journey with just one more stop to go. The stop when three young men in short jackets and flat caps boarded the train and took seats near the two bricks. The men weren't dirty or particularly untidy but they were obviously of a rougher sort than most of the people Sniper and T-800 had encountered so far. They talked loudly, in strong Cockney accents, and gave the impression they had been drinking since early morning. They hassled the people in the carriage, and some of the passengers changed their seats. Even before the train began to move again, the men had singled out the two bricks for special attention.

"Blimey, what's this 'ere then?" one of them wanted to

know. "Looks like a couple of toffs down on their luck." His friends guffawed and he leaned toward Sniper. "You lost yer titfer, mate? Maybe it fell off when you was sweepin' chimleys this morning." That got a good laugh from his companions.

Sniper looked up at him and his lip curled.

"'Ere! Don't you go lookin' at me like that!" the man cried in mock alarm. "Anyone would fink you was one o' them bloody Boers." Again, he scored a hit with his friends.

Sniper's fists clenched and, seeing it, T-800 looked at their tormentors and spoke in a quiet, reasonable tone. "You will have to excuse our appearance. We have just come from Cannon Street station where there has been a terrible accident. Our friend was killed and we almost died ourselves trying to save him."

The man in the flat cap looked at T-800 for the first time. His good humour. was gone and his eyes were hard and mean. "If I wanted to 'ear from you, fuzzy-wuzzy, I'd 'ave given you a banana. You darkies should learn to speak when you're spoken to."

T-800's nostrils flared, but he held himself under rigid control. Sniper didn't. He was on his feet in a moment with his gun drawn and pointed at the man's head. "You fucking racist piece of shit!" he shouted. "I'm going to splash your tiny brain all over this fucking train!"

A woman screamed and another fainted. A general hubbub arose as men protested at Sniper's outrageous language and his violent behaviour. The man in the flat cap gaped at the gun in his face in mounting fear. The carriage walls began to buckle and an older man in a top hat began to vibrate in his seat.

T-800 was on his feet too and grabbed at Sniper's gun, pushing it down. "For Christ's sake, man, chill out! None of this shit matters. Let's just get this damned ride over with and get out. 'Cause I tell you, I'm not going to die down here in this fucking hole in the ground, not for some arsehole who's already been dead a hundred years."

Even as he spoke, they pulled into British Museum station. All the windows down one side of the carriage cracked, and people gasped and cried out in confusion. The man in the flat cap had pulled back as far as he could. Sniper kept on snarling at him. It was obvious that he dearly wanted to hurt the man. And perhaps he would have had T-800 not grabbed him and dragged him off the train. Tiles popped from the arched roof over their heads as the people inside the train were trying to get out. A general panic was setting in. The splash around them was intensifying, fuelling the growing hysteria.

A large piece of the ceiling fell onto the platform with a dull, heavy thud. It snapped Sniper out of his rage, bringing home the danger they were in. Without a word, he turned to the stairs and bounded up them, T-800 close behind.

They had barely reached the surface when the ground shook. A great gust of warm air rushed up the staircase behind them. Clouds of billowing dust enveloped them. They both kept running until they were outside on New Oxford Street, feeling the rumbling through their feet as the tunnel continued its collapse.

"Look!" T-800 pointed east down High Holborn where a section of the road had slumped and cracked. Horses were shying and people were screaming. Everyone was trying to get away, but the real danger was from the panic itself.

"Man! You brought the whole tunnel down." Despite his shock, T-800 looked impressed.

Sniper regarded the chaos with grim satisfaction. "Serves

the bastards right."

The air above the collapsed tunnel began to shimmer. A woman screamed, and her scream, rapidly oscillating back and forth in time, became an eerie, grating warbling. The front of a large stone building began to sag as if it were made of wet clay. A heavy coach with two horses toppled over the edge of the broken road again and again. It fell and righted itself several times as Sniper watched, savouring the moment.

"Come on," Sniper said. "We're only a couple of hundred meters from the reading room—and we've got eight minutes left."

The traffic on New Oxford Street had come to a halt as the splash spread through the ranks of carriages and automobiles. People who had important dates were prevented from being where they should be, thus future meetings were being missed, future accidents—good and bad—would fail to happen. Small anomalies all of them, but many people were affected, each sending little ripples out through the timestream, enough to damage causality.

Sniper and T-800 dodged shying horses and shouting drivers. Shallow waves were rolling along the pavements. A flock of pigeons moved above the houses with an impossible jerky motion.

"We've got to get past this shit," Sniper complained, breaking into a run. As they turned into Bloomsbury Street, they could see a traffic jam building there too and, with it, the growing splash.

\* \* \* \*

"That was a department store?" Sandra was amazed. No flashing holos anywhere, no robot assistants, no VR booths for trying clothes on, no beamed-audio ads gabbling away in your head. It had just been a big room with items on shelves and in display cases. With real people standing around to help you. A quiet, peaceful place—until she and Jay had entered.

"I guess they evolved a bit."

Jay looked smart, elegant even, in a three-piece suit with a long morning coat and a high-buttoned waistcoat. The top hat had made Sandra giggle, but Jay quite liked it and wore it at a rakish tilt. Sandra too looked different, in a long skirt that trailed the floor and a white blouse with frills and embroidery. The skirt emphasized her small waist, and the high collar of the blouse flattered her long slender neck. With her hair piled up, a little bolero jacket that matched the skirt, and a huge wide-brimmed hat, she looked the very picture of a well-dressed Edwardian lady. When she emerged from the changing rooms, Jay had fallen in love with her all over again. Unfortunately, stunning the shop staff and chasing the few customers out of the shop had caused a significant splash and they'd had to run out as soon as they were dressed. They ran uphill, not because the street ran uphill but because everything ahead of them had expanded impossibly.

"It's not far," Jay said, after they had come up Charing Cross Road and crossed Oxford Street into Tottenham Court Road. The splash had diminished as they'd gotten clear of the department store.

"We should have caught a tube," Sandra said, spotting the Oxford Street entrance.

"No way would I want to be down there with the chance of a splash happening. Look, we're just a couple of hundred meters away. We need some sort of plan for when we get there."

"How long have we got?"

"Eight minutes. Getting this lot on took forever!"

"He could be there already for all we know."

They had each taken large bags from the department store to replace their anachronistic backpacks; he had a substantial Gladstone and Sandra a large tote bag. She reached into hers now to make sure her pistol was in easy reach.

They slowed to a rapid walk, drawing almost no attention—no more than such a handsome young couple would in any age—and made good speed. The chaos that had broken out in the department store was far behind them.

"There."

They stopped dead. Ahead of them was the magnificent neoclassical façade of the British Museum. The building ran for two or three city blocks, its columns marching away down the street in an endless parade.

"Large, isn't it?"

They turned quickly to find themselves standing next to a soldier. He was a tall man—almost Jay's height—and splendidly dressed in a dark blue tunic with gold braid all over his broad chest. He wore a tall dark furry hat with a white plume. A long sabre in a scabbard hung at his side. He smiled at them politely. Jay and Sandra simply marvelled at him.

"Allow me to introduce myself," he said. "Corporal James Pettigrew of the 19th Hussars, at your service." He gave them an abbreviated bow.

He waited in polite silence until Jay snapped out of his astonishment and said, "Er, Jason Kennedy." He held out his hand. The corporal shook it and then looked pointedly at Sandra. "Oh. And this is my, er, sister, Sandra. We're Canadians." He pulled a face and muttered, "She may want to flirt with you at some point."

Not hearing him, the soldier took the hand Sandra offered

and kissed it lightly. "I'm most pleased to meet you, Miss Kennedy. You'll have to excuse all the flummery." He indicated his dress uniform. "Bit of a do on in Whitehall at lunchtime. Regimental thing. Can't get out of it. Thought I'd spend the morning browsing the new Assyrian collection. Is that where you're headed?"

"We came to visit the Round Reading Room," Jay said. "In fact, we're meeting somebody there, and we're running late."

"Then let me walk with you, as we're going the same way." He held out a crooked arm for Sandra to take.

"Really, it's quite all right," Jay began, but Sandra had already taken the proffered arm and set off with the corporal. She glanced over her shoulder and stuck her tongue out at Jay as he hurried to catch up.

"Goodness, you have medals, too!" Sandra was saying.

The Hussar's face darkened a little. "Campaign medals mostly. That one's the Queen's South Africa Medal. The last real action I saw was the relief of Ladysmith." He sighed. "More than two years ago now. Spot of bother with my nerves after that."

"PTSD?" Jay asked, but the corporal had no idea what he was talking about.

They walked across the broad concourse to the gigantic entrance and passed through the doors with no challenge. In fact, there were no guards, no metal detectors, no body searches, no ID checks. It was not at all like Jay's previous visits to the museum.

They passed through the vast entrance hall and out the back into the courtyard. In the centre was the domed cylinder of the Round Reading Room. Jay looked up and saw open sky. Back in 2049 there would have been a glass ceiling over the whole of this huge courtyard. Given the likelihood of a splash happening soon, he was glad not to have that hanging over him.

"Well, I suppose I must take my leave," Corporal Pettigrew said. He turned to Jay. "Will you be in London long, Mr. Kennedy? Perhaps I may be permitted to call on you—and your charming sister? I would be happy to show you some of the attractions, if that would please you."

Jay thought briefly about stunning the man. They didn't have time for this. Instead, he said, "That would be cool, er, delightful. We're staying at the Waldorf. Call any time. Now, we really must be going. So nice to have met you." They shook hands again and the cavalryman gave a small bow to Sandra before turning to re-enter the museum.

"What the hell was that all about?" Jay snapped. He took her elbow and steered her toward the reading room. "We should have ditched him in the street."

"What, and miss my one and only chance ever to be courted by a Hussar?"

"We have just six minutes. Sniper might be in there right now. Or he might walk through those doors at any moment."

"He's not here. If he was, we'd know it."

"We should get out of sight. He'll recognize you when he arrives."

"I don't think so, not dressed like this."

Jay looked into her eyes. "Believe me, any man who's seen you once would know you forever."

Sandra looked at him in amazement, completely thrown by his intensity.

Jay broke the spell. "I just had a thought. He might be dressed up too."

They looked around quickly. There were very few people in the courtyard and none of the men were even close to

Sniper's stature.

"He could have seen us come in here. He might be watching us."

Sandra shook her head. "Not his style. If he thought we were here to spoil his splash, he'd have shot us both without hesitation."

They had reached the door to the library. "All the more reason to get out of sight then."

"Excuse me."

A man of about thirty was standing next to them, waiting to go into the library. He was round-faced with a goatee— hardly a distinguishing feature in 1902—and wore a heavy overcoat. What did stand out was his Russian-style fur hat and heavy Russian accent, obvious even though he had only spoken two words.

They both stood aside to let him pass, watching him in silent awe. Neither spoke until he had closed the door behind him.

"Oh my God. That was him!" Jay could hardly believe it. "He spoke to us!"

Sandra was less impressed. "Five minutes to go and Lenin just walked into the reading room. If Sniper doesn't get here soon, we'll have missed our chance." An idea struck her. She led Jay aside, well away from the door.

"Look, this is the only entrance to the library, right?"

"I think so."

"And Lenin is safe inside, yes?"

"Unless Sniper's inside with him right now!"

"He's not, I tell you. Sniper is … he's like some god of chaos or something. When he arrives, there will be a whirlwind around him. People will be screaming and running. That's who he is."

She seemed strangely excited by the prospect, rather than scared as Jay thought she should be.

"But we can stop him," she went on. "He has to go right past us to get to Lenin and he's got no time to waste. If he turns up at all, we can take him down right there." She pointed to the empty courtyard. "No one inside need ever know Sniper was here."

"Except for the gunshots and the world going haywire, you mean?"

"That's better than letting Sniper get inside."

Jay looked at her and nodded. "Are you all right? Only I thought you'd be … I don't know … scared or something. Yet you seem…"

Sandra frowned. "You're right. I should be at least nervous about this, but I'm not. I'm just keen to get on with it. Get it done, you know?"

Jay looked into her eyes, not at all cheered by her reply. But he didn't have time to worry about it. "We need somewhere to hide."

"No, we don't. We just need to stand out of the way and pretend we're ordinary people."

"Over here then." He began to lead her across to a spot at the side of the library building where they could wait unobtrusively, when a noise came from the museum's main entrance.

Someone inside screamed and there was a bright flash of light at one of the windows.

"He's here," Sandra said.

The excitement was gone from her eyes. Now all Jay could see was fear.

\* \* \* \*

"Whoo! Oh man, this place is crazy!" Sniper shouted as they crashed through the small group of people inside the museum entrance.

Out in the street, the traffic jams were shimmering and chaotic as people and horses bolted in panic. All attempts to keep a low profile had ended a few minutes ago when Sniper and T-800 realized that, whatever they did, a major splash was building up around them. That's when they'd drawn their submachine guns and begun indiscriminately shooting their way through every obstacle. With the bucking road, the panicking crowds, and the falling masonry everywhere, their progress had been slow. They'd reached the museum entrance with just four minutes to go.

Only Sniper's brutality and single-minded determination had kept them moving forward at all.

"Out of the way, bitch!" he yelled, shoving a woman to the floor and running past her. As soon as they entered the building, the causal disturbances began. People jerked and trembled, and massive stone pillars rippled like water. The marble floors heaved and cracked.

"It's that way."

Sniper led them through the treacherous entrance hall to the back of the building where doors opened onto the courtyard and the large round building at its centre.

"At last," he shouted, climbing over the wreckage of the doors. Behind him he saw himself and T-800 come into the hall again. He slapped T-800 on the arm and pointed. "Echoes."

T-800 watched the two of them making their way closer. "Incredible," he said.

The echoes weren't going to make it across the hall. A great rift opened in the floor and they couldn't get across.

They'd seen many echoes of themselves as they'd fought their way across London, little fragments of their recent past, replayed in the tortured timeline they left in their wake.

Sniper grabbed his friend by the shoulder and dragged him onwards. Outside in the courtyard, it was calmer. There was almost nobody there. An elderly man walked about admiring the architecture. An elegant young couple was strolling around the side of the library. T-800 raised his gun to shoot them, just for fun, but Sniper stopped him.

"Don't risk it, man. We've got to get inside. You start a big splash now and we might never get there. We don't have long." To emphasize the point, he pulled his helmet from the carpetbag and put his arm through the strap, tossing the bag aside.

They pushed on. The splash they'd created in the museum hall was spreading into the courtyard, but all Sniper had eyes for was the door of the Round Reading Room. He made his way toward it without seeing the elegant couple turn and point handguns at him.

* * * *

"He's mine!" Sandra said.

Jay glanced quickly her way. She could see he doubted she could make the shot but he said, "Okay. He's yours."

Sandra tried to steady her trembling hands. She watched Sniper over the barrel of her gun, the way she had imagined doing for so long. But something kept her from firing. Sniper looked scruffy and dirty. He'd obviously made some attempt at Edwardian dress but that had long ago been wrecked by the mayhem he'd fought his way through. The light in his pale blue-grey eyes and the vulpine grin on his handsome face told her how much he was enjoying himself. With a jolt, she recognized the man beside him. The same man who had been there at Ommen. The one who had watched silently as Hal was beaten to death.

"Go on then," Jay said. "Take the shot. They'll see us in a minute."

Sandra tightened her finger on the trigger. Just a little more pressure and Sniper would be dead. Gone forever. Her nightmare would be over. She swallowed hard. It seemed impossible that it could actually happen, that she was here, at last, and he was about to die. Surely it couldn't be so easy?

Then Sniper's pale eyes saw them, saw their guns. He looked at her face and stopped in surprise. Not fear, not despair, just surprise. His grin hardened and she could see recognition and cold, cold hatred welling up in him.

Feeling those eyes burning into her, panic hit her like an electric shock. Oh God, he'd seen her. Oh God, he knew she was there, standing exposed, standing where he could see her, where he could get to her. She pulled the trigger. She fired and fired, but Sniper kept looking at her, unharmed, invincible.

T-800 was not so lucky. Sandra's first shot hit him in the chest and he fell dead as her other shots went wild. Sniper looked down at his fallen friend and a flicker of regret crossed his face. Then he was running. He raised his weapon and fired a quick burst toward Sandra. She saw the careless way he did it. All that mattered to him was getting to the library. He didn't care if she lived or died.

The realization hit her like a slap on the face.

Jay dragged her down to the ground, firing back at Sniper from a prone position and managing to clip him on the thigh. The brick stumbled but stayed on his feet. He sprayed bullets in their direction as Jay and Sandra pressed themselves into the ground. Jay was on his feet firing again before Sniper was through the door, but a lucky return shot from Sniper hit him in the right shoulder. He dropped his weapon and fell to one knee as Sandra watched in horror.

"Are you all right?"

Sandra dragged her eyes off Jay to find the soldier they'd met earlier. The daze she had been in cleared instantly as the soldier helped her to her feet.

"I'm fine," she snapped. "We've got to stop him."

"The scruffy fellow who ran into the library?"

"Jay, stay here. You're hurt."

"Well, I'm glad someone noticed."

She grabbed a submachine gun from her bag and rushed to the library with the Hussar corporal in tow. She glanced back at Jay as she reached the door. He had slumped to a sitting position and was watching them with glazed eyes, holding his shoulder. Blood oozed between his fingers.

\* \* \* \*

"Mr. Jacob Richter?" the librarian asked, peering at Lenin above his spectacles. Lenin gave a small nod of confirmation.

The librarian riffled through a tray in which a number of documents were stacked. "Ah, here we are." He handed a ticket over. "It is valid for three months, and must then be renewed if you wish to continue to use the reading room. Now, if I may, there are just one or two rules our new readers need to be aware of."

The man began listing the library's regulations in a polite, slightly pompous tone. But Lenin was barely listening. From where he stood, the magnificent interior of the Round

Reading Room surrounded him in all its glory, from the highly polished reading tables, to the stuffed shelves curving beneath the splendid domed roof. He admired it with the eye of a serious scholar, eager to explore this Aladdin's cave of intellectual riches.

"There. That's all, I think. Welcome to the British Museum Reading Room, Mr. Richter. Good heavens, whatever is that?"

They both turned to face the door. Beyond it they heard what might have been gunshots, interspersed with a loud mechanical roar.

"I must go and invest-invest-invest—" The librarian began an unearthly, jerking motion. Lenin barely noticed. His attention was fully on the door and what might lie behind it. Could the Tsar's secret police have come for him? Would they be so brazen as to assassinate him here, in a foreign capital? And, if it was them, who were they shooting at outside?

The door burst open and a wild young ruffian staggered in. He was dressed like a gentleman, but he was filthy and hatless. His eyes were bright and full of murder and in his hands he carried what could only be a weapon—a short chunky rifle of some sort.

"Lenin!" the young man yelled. Lenin could only think that this must be the end. "I want Vladimir Ilyich Lenin!"

Involuntarily, Lenin stepped back and bumped against the wooden counter. Who had sent such an assassin? His mind ran through the many factions of the many parties he knew. All those thousands of people, all over Russia and throughout Europe, plotting and scheming in their dingy little rooms, just as he had done, each group believing it had the right way to free Mother Russia from oppression, each of them squabbling with the others about whose way was best. Squabbling like children—but children with bombs and guns.

This man looked like a parody of an anarchist, with his hair unkempt and that madness in his eye. And was that a bomb hanging from his arm?

"You!" The young man was looking straight at him. "It's you, isn't it?" He raised the weapon and pointed it at him.

Lenin's thoughts touched briefly on Nadezhda Konstantinovna, his dearest Nadya! He had promised her more than this. He remembered his work—not just Iskra and his pamphlets and reports—but the Great Work of building the glorious Revolution. He felt a hot anger boiling up inside him. He was not going to die here like this. This was not his destiny. This scruffy madman was not to be his executioner!

"Yes!" he said, in a voice already well practised at swaying crowds of workers. He stood tall and puffed out his chest. "I am Vladimir Ilyich Lenin. Who is asking?" His eyes blazed with indignation and power.

But the young man was not at all impressed. "You look bigger in your pictures," he said. Then he grinned like a slavering hound and his grey eyes lit with anticipation. He sighted along the barrel of his strange weapon.

Lenin gritted his teeth and steeled himself for the bullet that would come at any moment. The room around him was shaking and trembling. A wind was blowing inside the library. A strange light glimmered from every surface. The walls behind his young assassin were melting like ice in the sun. It occurred to him that the bullet might already have struck him and that he was experiencing death itself.

A woman and another man charged in through the door. The woman was tall and young and incredibly beautiful. For a moment he thought she might be an angel. She too was carrying one of the short rifles. The man was a British soldier in full dress uniform. They both leapt at the assassin and sent him flying across the floor. The assassin's gun went off with an ear-splitting explosion and the bullets that were meant for Lenin smashed into the counter beside him. The girl—no angel, after all—and the soldier grappled with the assassin on the ground. Lenin watched in shock and fascination.

The fallen man was immensely strong and fast. In an instant, he had turned on his attackers and smashed his gun into the soldier's face. Alarm rose in Lenin for the safety of the girl. He took a step toward her, stumbling on a floor that seemed to move beneath his feet. She had dropped her weapon in the struggle and faced her opponent empty handed. Yet the girl was by no means helpless. She punched the assassin hard in the throat and then again, with amazing speed. Yet, even as he choked, the wild-haired young man grabbed her by the neck of her blouse and slammed his forehead into her face. She cried out and fell back, stunned. They fight like street brawlers, Lenin thought. But not so the cavalryman. He had gained his feet, blood streaming from a cut on his temple. He drew his Webley Mark IV service revolver from the white holster at his side.

"Don't move!" the soldier cried. The gun was pointing at the would-be assassin but the corporal's eyes were flicking around the room. The library had become a heaving, stuttering maelstrom, and the soldier struggled to keep his attention on the man at his feet. When a huge crack exploded through the library wall, scattering books and splintering shelves, he jumped like a nervous cat, and the man on the floor jerked up his weapon and fired at him.

Lenin gasped in amazement as the weapon belched out a constant stream of fire and the soldier was literally torn apart by what must have been dozens of bullets. The fusillade threw the corporal backward, yet he did not fall. Instead, he hung suspended in the air, with blood that had splashed from his chest hanging in a series of high arcs above him.

The assassin didn't spare a moment to admire his magical handiwork, but turned back immediately to aim his weapon at Lenin. The girl, blood oozing from a cut above her nose, was on him again like a tigress. So ferociously did she attack that she managed to knock the weapon from the man's grasp. She rolled away from him across the cracking, erupting tiles, and snatched up her own weapon, pointing it straight at him. He snarled like a savage beast and leapt at her, fingers clawed, as though he would tear her to pieces with them.

She pulled the trigger and fired. Whether it was the diabolical weapon, or some other kind of sorcery, Lenin could not tell, but as soon as the weapon roared into flame, the assassin disappeared.

\* \* \* \*

Sandra yelled in frustration and stood up, throwing the submachine gun to the ground. Sniper had been yanked back. He was gone. There was no way now to kill him. She turned to the man in the Russian fur hat.

"Are you Lenin?"

The man was staring at her open-mouthed, but he seemed unharmed.

"*Da*," he said, forgetting to speak English. "*Mehr zobut Lenin.*"

Sandra didn't understand a word but it sounded Russian and he looked about right and that was good enough for her.

"You should get outside," she told him. "This place isn't safe."

He nodded. "*Da. Spasiba.*"

It sounded as if he understood, as if he had thanked her, but he did not move. She looked at the dome above her and the cracks in the walls and floor. She couldn't drag him out or force him to go. That might bring the whole building down on them.

"Please. You'll be safer outside."

Nodding, he began to shuffle forward.

Taking it as a sign that he'd be all right, Sandra stepped around the still-suspended body of her dashing Hussar and hurried outside.

She had to shake Jay to wake him up.

"I … must have passed out." It took Jay a moment to come to his senses. "Lenin! Is he safe?"

"Yes, I am safe." The Russian stood over them. He looked less stunned now, more in command of himself. Sandra saw that he had picked up the submachine gun.

"Who are you? What are you?" His English was stilted and clumsy. "Why do you come to save me? What…" He looked around at the shimmering buildings and the shifting courtyard.

"What is happening?"

Jay propped himself up on one elbow and immediately fell back onto Sandra's lap. He lay there with his eyes closed for a moment before he looked up at Sandra again.

"Sniper was yanked back," she told him plaintively.

"But you saved him." He looked toward the Russian.

"I want this weapon," Lenin said. "I want lot of weapon. With this…"

"With that," said Jay, "you could overthrow the Tsar. Your revolution would be guaranteed."

He looked at the confused Russian. "That's why you're still able to move around and talk while everyone else is twitching about like it's Saturday night at the disco. You're so focused on your damned revolution that no one and nothing else matters. Even this ... chaos. Nothing could shift you from the path you're on."

Sandra put a hand on his arm. "Jay. Careful."

Jay closed his eyes. Of course, he should mind what he said. Put the wrong idea in this man's head, make him doubt himself, make him make one single decision he wouldn't otherwise make, and the splash could be as bad as if Sniper had killed him outright. He reached out his left hand and grabbed his automatic from the ground beside him. He raised it, shakily, and pointed it at Lenin. "Put that gun down and walk away." The Russian reluctantly obeyed. "Stay outdoors," Jay added. "If you go inside, you could be injured or killed."

"Why do you want me to live? Who are you?"

"Just piss off," Sandra told him, picking up the gun.

Frowning, frustrated, Lenin moved away from them, watching them suspiciously.

"God, I feel sick," Jay moaned.

"You look pretty awful too." Sandra explored his wound, shaking her head. "Our suits are self-sealing if they get punctured. Yours has already sealed over the bullet hole. I can't even see how much you're bleeding."

With a roar, part of the reading room's wall collapsed. Dust billowed out from the hole, then billowed back in again.

"I think we're safe enough here," Sandra said. "And I don't think Lenin's going anywhere. If you can just hang on for fifteen minutes, honey, we'll be on our way back. They'll have medics waiting, I'm sure."

"I'm sorry," Jay said. It was a struggle to stay awake. "I'm sorry you didn't get Sniper. I know what it meant."

Sandra shook her head. "It's okay. It would have been nice

but…" But somehow it wasn't as important as it once was. In fact, it hadn't been for some time, she realized.

Jay nodded as if he understood what she was thinking. "When we get back," he said, "I want to take you to the 'tractives. You know, like a normal couple."

"A date?"

"Yeah. If that's all right. I know I'm not anything special. And you're … you're so…"

"I'd love to. We'll go see a big blockbuster, then have a burger and fries, just like real people."

He smiled. "I've had enough of this running around being shot at for a while. I need a rest."

She stroked his head and smiled at him through a blur of tears. "Fifteen minutes, darling. Then we can both have a rest."

# Chapter 26

## Yankback

The yankback threw Sniper hard against the bars of the cage. The bodies of T-800 and Edna crashed around him. For a moment he was dazed and winded.

But he was alive.

Despite the pain in his leg, he threw back his head and laughed for the sheer unexpected joy of it. He'd beaten them all. He'd been the first to go back so far, farther than any other brick ever had, and he'd come back alive to boast about it. He was the best. No one could ever doubt it. No one would ever dare do again what he had done.

And, as for the splash, the library had looked like it was about to fall on Lenin's stupid, fat head—and on that psycho bitch Patty too. Even if it didn't, he'd left a trail of destruction from Deptford to Bloomsbury. Hundreds of people had been caught in it. Probably dozens had died. When the backwash came, it was going to be a monster!

A small shadow of doubt crept across his moment of triumph. Somehow Patty had gone back to try to stop him. Whoever had sent her could match what he'd done. Well that was all right. It just meant that, next time, he'd have to go back farther, make the whole splash bigger. There would come a point where no one would dare follow him. No one.

Until then, he was alive, and free, and London would soon be in flames. He laughed again. Life was good.

"Having fun?"

He jumped to his feet, pain vying with surprise. A woman was standing there, outside the cage.

"Camilla!"

"Hello, Sniper. Care to share the joke?"

She looked crumpled, her normally immaculate hair and clothing dishevelled. There were bruises on her face. More importantly, she held an Uzi submachine gun in her hands and it was pointing right at him.

Sniper swallowed hard and glanced around the cage. T-800 and Edna were slumped across the only exit and the door ... The fucking door opened inwards! He would need to drag them out of the way before he could get out. He wondered what kind of protection two bodies would provide against a modern automatic weapon at close range. Not much, he supposed. He limped to the back of the cage, adding a meagre two meters of extra distance between him and the gun.

"Good news, Camilla," he said, forcing a smile. "I suppose you're here on behalf of the investors, to see how things worked out. Well, you can tell them it was a huge success. Well, they'll see for themselves in a short while when London turns into a madhouse. Their money was well invested. You must be up for a promotion now, eh? Or at least a big bonus?"

Camilla said nothing. She just continued to watch him with cold, clear eyes. Sniper looked about the room, searching for something that might help. Something to distract her for a few seconds while he dragged those stupid bodies out of the way.

That's when he noticed Klaatu lying face down on the concrete floor beside the control console. The boy wasn't moving. There was blood all around him and ugly holes in his back and legs. It shocked Sniper as much as anything that had happened that day.

Rage boiled up in him. "You fucking deranged bitch! You've killed him. What the fuck was that for? Are you out of your tiny little mind?" He grabbed Edna's body and threw him across the cage. His leg was screaming with pain, but he welcomed it. Pain and rage were all he wanted just then.

He reached for T-800's body and froze as gunfire exploded into the echoing spaces of the warehouse.

"Do you want to die right now," Camilla asked, calmly lowering the gun to point it at him again, "or would you rather have a few more seconds?"

Sniper sat down heavily, his hands still resting on T-800. He tried to look crestfallen and defeated, but inside he was excited and triumphant. Tucked into the back of T-800's harness, out of Camilla's line of sight, was a small handgun. It was just ten centimetres from his right hand.

"Go on and shoot me, bitch," he said. "It's all over now anyway. I did what I wanted to do. The splash was incredible." Imperceptibly, his hand moved toward the gun.

\* \* \* \*

Camilla had had enough. It had been a real pleasure killing the boy and she'd enjoyed watching Sniper squirm, but she needed to get clear before the backwash came. It was time to end it.

"Who gives a toss what you've done, you stupid jerk?" she sneered. "You're just a tool. Something to be used and discarded when the job's done. And that's what I'm here for. To tidy up the loose ends. To finish the job properly. That was always the plan, you know. Get you to do the dirty work, take the risks, and then blow you away. You were never going to live to brag about this. I always had this planned for you. You and your little boyfriend over there."

For an instant, her eyes flicked to where Klaatu lay, and for a fraction of a second, the barrel of the Uzi moved in the same direction. In that moment she realized she had made a fatal mistake.

Sniper rolled behind his dead friend and came up holding a gun, aiming it directly at her chest. Shocked, Camilla couldn't muster her thoughts quickly enough to shoot first. The knowledge that she was going to die right there and then was too much to handle. Sniper, on the other hand, looked cool and relaxed as he squeezed the trigger, clearly savouring the defeat that must have been in her eyes. Click! Click! Click!

They both stared at the empty gun in Sniper's hand. Then Sniper threw the useless weapon across the cage and got to his feet with a roar of frustration and defiance.

With a determination born of fear, Camilla pulled the trigger, emptying the Uzi's clip into Sniper in long seconds of thunder and exploding flesh. The weapon kicked and hammered in her grip. Sniper jerked back across the cage as he was ripped apart by the stream of bullets. Bright sparks dotted the bars of the cage. The screech of ricochets sliced across the roar of the gunfire. Long after her victim had fallen, Camilla kept firing.

When it was over, she had to force her finger to relax on the trigger. She stared at the carnage she had caused, panting as if she'd torn up all that flesh with her bare hands. Slowly, slowly, her heartbeat eased and her breathing steadied. She threw the Uzi aside, never taking her eyes off Sniper's body.

"Now who's the *Arschloch*?" she snarled. She turned and left the building without a backward glance.

# Chapter 27

## Unravelling the Past

The car turned in through the big gates and followed the gravel drive up to the house. It crunched to a halt with a small whine from its electric engine. It was late afternoon and the drive down from London had been hot and uneventful.

The countryside around Bodmin Moor was lush and green. London was one big construction site at the moment as the damage from the backwash was slowly being repaired. A big scar of destruction ran from the British Museum to Cannon Street then along the river, east to Deptford. It was amazing that fewer than two thousand people had died. It could easily have been so much worse.

"Here we are then," Jay said, breaking a long silence. He nodded at the old building beyond the windscreen. "Looks like it should have been condemned years ago."

They peered out at the high red-brick walls of the Porringer Institute of Mental Well-Being. To Sandra, Jay knew, it didn't seem at all unwelcoming. To her it held only the promise of peace and the end of a long journey through darkness.

She smiled back at Jay. "I'm looking forward to it. This

time will be very different."

He took her hand. "I'll come over whenever I can. It's a shame you won't be there for Bauchet's wedding." He had only received the invitation the day before. That the intense, hawk-like superintendent had courted and won the heart of Marie Vermeulen, his cool, elegant PA, was impossible for Jay to believe.

"Isn't it great that he gave you a job?" Sandra's tone was encouraging. He felt a surge of gratitude to her for trying to break his melancholy mood.

"Especially after the way Five treated me. And you. Anyone would think we were the bad guys in all this!" He fell silent for a moment, pondering this injustice. "If only the job wasn't in Brussels. I want to be here. With you."

She squeezed his hand. "I'll be fine. This will take time. Dr. Mason says it might be years before I'm completely okay."

"But not years in there, right? This place is just for a short while, yeah?"

She laughed. "Don't worry. The plan is a few weeks here and then I get out and get a therapist, just like any ordinary nutjob."

"Sandra?"

She shook her head. "I know what you're going to say but you don't have to worry."

He could hardly stand to see the compassion in her eyes, knowing that his own fear and the weakness had aroused it. "Well, I'm going to say it anyway. These past few weeks have been the happiest I've ever had. Even when I was laid up with my shoulder, it was heaven, just because you were there. Now I can't help worrying that—you know—if you tackle all your childhood traumas, and your hang-ups and all that … What if after all that, you're different?"

"I hope I will be."

"No. I mean…"

"You mean, what if I don't want you any more?"

He nodded. "Selfish, isn't it?"

"Perhaps you'd like to pop in with me? Work on your self-esteem problems?"

He sagged in his seat, defeated by the inevitability of what Sandra must do and the terrible risk it carried for him. "I want you to be happy," he told her. "I'll try to be brave."

She continued to hold his gaze. "If I don't work out some of this stuff, I'd be no good for you anyway. Sooner or later my old problems would come back and I'd leave you for some cocky bastard who'd treat me like crap and make me miserable."

He knew all this. It made him love her all the more that she was brave enough to face her demons. He grinned at her sheepishly.

"Strumpet," he said.

"Beanpole."

She pulled him to her and they kissed goodbye.

# Thank You

Thank you for reading *Timesplash*, book 1 of the Timesplash series. I really hope you enjoyed it as much as I enjoyed writing it. If so, I'd be grateful if you'd leave a review on one of the book retail sites, your blog, or pasted to a wall on the nearest underpass. The rest of this series is available from your favourite online book store. To stay informed of when new books of mine are about to appear, please visit my website and sign up for my newsletter.

# About the Author

I am a science fiction writer living in Queensland, Australia. A former research scientist, IT consultant and award-winning software designer. I now live and write in a quiet corner of the Australian bush with my wife, Christine, and a Tonkinese cat called Minsky.

# Other Books By Graham Storrs

*Timesplash*, my début novel, was a Kindle best-seller. The series, *Timesplash* and its sequels, *True Path* and *Foresight*, was originally published by Pan Macmillan Australia. Both *True Path* and *Foresight* were shortlisted for Australia's première science fiction awards, The Aurealis Awards, as Best Science Fiction Novel.

In addition, I have been writing three series of novels set in my Placid Point universe: the Rik Sylver series, the Canta Libre trilogy, and the Deep Fracture trilogy, set eighty, three hundred, and ten thousand years in the future respectively. They are adventure stories, space opera, first contact novels, tales of the first transhumans, and so much more.

I also have a few stand-alone novels out there. *Heaven is a Place on Earth* is a thriller set in a near future dominated by augmented and virtual reality technologies, with all the opportunities for deception they bring. *Cargo Cult* is a sci-fi comedy in which the most ridiculous things that could plausibly happen, keep happening. *Time and Tyde* is a dark comedy set in the present day, about a man stalked by an amoral jerk from the future, or perhaps a man driven insane by a present-day stalker. Either way, it doesn't turn out well. And *Mindrider* – an urban sci-fi thriller about an alien invasion nobody wants and which even the aliens seem unable to prevent.

You can find links to fuller descriptions of all my novels on my website (grahamstorrs.com). Or just type my name into your favourite online book store and they should all appear.

# Acknowledgements

In the past few years, *Timesplash* has had a wild and weird ride. It was initially inspired during a weekend retreat I won as a prize for an unpublished manuscript contest organised by Hachette and The Queensland Writer's Centre (that unpublished manuscript was later to become my novel *Time & Tyde*). I first sold the resulting book to a New York small press called Lyrical Press. They never managed to sell it in quantity but they will always hold a special place in my heart for being my very first novel sale. I reacquired the rights with a view to finding another publisher but I've always been a useless salesperson and my half-hearted attempts were unsuccessful. Besides, I had other books I was engrossed in writing by then.

So I thought I'd have a go at self-publishing it, just so it was "out there." And, to my surprise, it went gangbusters. It rocketed to the top of its categories on Kindle in several countries and reached number 15 on the fiction chart in the US. I was amazed and stunned. I'd never really thought about what being a best-seller meant but I was selling hundreds of copies of the book every single day.

So that was nice. But, after a while the buying frenzy petered out and I realised that, with no sequel, or even any other book ready to be published, the opportunity to build on that huge readership had passed me by.

But it didn't mean nice things had stopped happening. An English writer and voice artist called Emma Newman liked *Timesplash* so much she spent countless hours recording it and we sold the resulting audiobook to a company called Iambik (who later sold the rights to Audible). Emma's interest and support was extremely gratifying – especially back then – because she is herself a great writer of SF and Fantasy.

After the Kindle success, I realised I ought to take selling my books a bit more seriously, so I cast about for an agent and found Ineke Prochazka of Book Harvest in Sydney. She got my work in front of all kinds of people that I couldn't but, most importantly for this story, she sold *Timesplash* to Joel Naoum at Momentum, an imprint of Pan Macmillan Australia. So Ineke deserves a big thank you for lending her talents to this project. And so does Joel, not just for liking my book enough to take it on but for insisting that I write a sequel. Which I did (*True Path*) and which he also bought. And then, when I wrote another sequel (*Foresight*), he surpassed himself by buying that too! It's the kind of support an author can only dream of in a publisher.

I must not forget to mention the rest of the guys at Momentum. Tara Goedjen, my editor, and the team put in many hard yards on this series. I'll never understand how editors put up with authors like me but, somehow, Tara managed to stay the course, contribute considerably to the quality of the work, and steer all three novels into production.

There were many other people who became involved with *Timesplash* in various ways and they've all added to its rich history, but I do need to mention my wife, Christine who read drafts and became my sounding board and guineapig throughout the years of this book's many incarnations. She has been the main victim of my angst and anguish and even provided coffee and food during my 24-hour marathon online marketing events. Even my daughter, Kate, was dragged in to provide artwork for the audiobook, and to offer design critiques for my own sorry attempts at cover design. Both Christine and Kate have been wonderfully supportive throughout the complex history of the Timesplash series and, indeed, my whole writing career.

And now there is a new chapter in that history, a complete repackaging and relaunch of the Timesplash series. For the opportunity to make this happen, I am grateful to the team at Pan Macmillan Australia. For the success of this relaunch, I'd very much like to thank you, the one holding this book, who makes everything worth doing.

# Contact the Author

I am always happy to hear from readers, so don't be shy. And if you enjoyed this book, don't forget to post your review.

Follow me on Twitter: @graywave

or on Facebook:
facebook.com/GrahamStorrsAuthor

For details of all my novels and short stories, visit
grahamstorrs.com